The Man
Who Spoke
Snakish

The Man Who Spoke Snakish

Andrus Kivirähk

Translated by Christopher Moseley

Grove Press UK

First published in the United States of America in 2015
by Grove/Atlantic Inc.

First published in Great Britain in 2016 by Grove Press UK,
an imprint of Grove/Atlantic Inc.

This paperback edition published in 2017

Copyright © Andrus Kivirähk, 2007
Translation copyright © Christopher Moseley, 2015

The moral right of Andrus Kivirähk to be identified as the author of this
work has been asserted by him in accordance with the Copyright,
Designs and Patents Act of 1988.

The moral right of Christopher Moseley to be identified as the translator
of this work has been asserted by him in accordance with the Copyright,
Designs and Patents Act of 1988.

This book has been published with permission of Le Tripode, 16 rue
Charlemagne 75004 Paris, France. The book was first published in Estonia
by Eesti Keele Shihtasutus under the title *Mees, kes teadis ussisõnu*.

All rights reserved. No part of this publication may be reproduced,
stored in a retrieval system, or transmitted in any form or by any
means, electronic, mechanical, photocopying, recording, or otherwise,
without the prior permission of both the copyright owner and the
above publisher of the book.

Every effort has been made to trace or contact all copyright-holders. The
publishers will be pleased to make good any omissions or rectify any
mistakes brought to their attention at the earliest opportunity.

3 5 7 9 8 6 4

A CIP record for this book is available from the British Library.

Paperback ISBN 978 1 61185 527 2

Ebook ISBN 978 1 61185 960 7

Printed and bound by CPI Group (UK) Ltd, Croydon, CR0 4YY

Grove Press, UK
Ormond House
26–27 Boswell Street
London
WC1N 3JZ

www.groveatlantic.com

The Man Who Spoke Snakish

One

he forest has been left empty. These days you hardly meet anyone, apart from the dung beetles, of course. Nothing seems to affect them; they go on humming and buzzing, just as before. They fly to suck blood or bite, or perhaps climb absurdly on your leg if you get in their way, and scurry hither and thither until you wipe them off or flick them away. Their world is just as it was—but it won't stay that way. The bell will toll even for the dung beetles! Of course I won't see that day; no one will. But one day that hour will strike. I know that quite certainly.

I don't go out much anymore, only about once a week do I go above ground. I go to the well; I fetch water. I wash myself and my companion; I scrub his hot body. It uses a lot of water—I have to go to the well several times a day—but it rarely happens that I meet anyone on the path that I might chat to. Not often a human, anyway; a couple of times I've met a buck or a boar. They've become timid. They're even afraid of my scent. If I hiss, they stiffen on the spot, glare at me stupidly, but they never come close. They stare as if at a miracle of nature—a human who knows the language of Snakish. This drives them into even greater terror. They would like to butt me into the bushes, give me a wound in the legs, and run as far as possible from this strange freak—but they daren't. The words forbid it. I hiss at them again, louder this time. With a gruff command I force them to come to me. The beasts low despondently, dragging themselves reluctantly in my direction. I could take pity on them and let them go, but what for? Inside me there is a strange hatred toward the newcomers who don't know the old ways and just gambol through the forest, as if it had been created at the dawn of time just for them to loll about in. So I hiss a third time, and this time my words are as strong as a quagmire from which it's impossible to escape. The crazed animals rush toward me as if shot from a bow, while all their innards burst with unbearable tension. They are torn apart, like the tearing of trousers that are too tight, and their intestines spill out onto the grass. It's disgusting to see, and I get no pleasure from it, but nevertheless I can never let my powers go untested. It's not my fault that these beasts have forgotten the words of snakes that my ancestors used to teach them.

One time it went differently, however. I was just coming back from the well, a heavy skinful of water on my shoulder, when all at once I saw a big deer on my path. I instantly hissed some simple words, already feeling scorn for the deer's plight. But the deer didn't flinch when it heard long-forgotten words of command issuing unexpectedly from the mouth of a man-child. In fact he lowered his head and came up to me, got down on his knees and submissively offered his neck, just as in the old days, when we used to get our food this way—by calling the deer to be killed. How often as a little boy I had seen my mother getting winter provisions for our family in this way! She would select the most suitable cow from the big herd of deer, call her over, and then lightly slit the throat of the submissive animal, hissing snake-words at her. A fully grown deer cow would last us a whole winter. How ridiculous the villagers' foolish hunting seemed compared to our simple way of getting food. They would spend hours chasing one deer, firing many arrows haphazardly into the bushes, and then afterward, often as not, going home empty-handed and disappointed. All you needed to get a deer to submit to you were a few words! Words that I had just used. A big strong deer was lying at my feet, just waiting. I could have killed it with a single movement of my hand. But I didn't.

Instead I took the waterskin off my shoulder and offered the deer a drink. He lapped it meekly. He was an old bull, quite old. He must have been; otherwise he would not have remembered how a deer should behave when called by a human. He would have struggled and grappled, tried to get to the treetops, perhaps using his teeth, even as the ancient force of the words drew him to me; he would have come to me like a fool, whereas now he came to me like a king. No matter that he was coming to be slaughtered. Even that is a skill to be learned. Is there anything humiliating about submitting yourself to age-old laws and customs? Not in my opinion. We never killed a single deer for fun. What fun is there to be had in that? We needed to eat, there was a word that would get food for you, and the deer knew that word and obeyed it. What is humiliating is to forget everything, like those young boars and bucks, who take fright when they hear the words. Or the villagers, who would go out in their dozens just to catch one deer. It is stupidity that is humiliating, not wisdom.

I gave the deer a drink and stroked his head and he rubbed his muzzle against my jacket. So the old world had not completely vanished after all. As long as I'm alive, as long as that old deer is alive, Snakish will still be known and remembered around these parts.

I let the deer go. May he live long. And remember.

What I was actually going to tell a story about was the funeral of Manivald. I was six years old at the time. I had never seen Manivald with my own eyes, because he didn't live in the forest, but by the sea. To this day I don't actually know why Uncle Vootele took me with him to the funeral. There were no other children there. My friend Pärtel wasn't there, nor was Hiie. But Hiie had definitely been born by then; she was only a year younger than me. Why didn't Tambet and Mall take her with them? It was after all for them just a pleasant occasion—not in the sense that they had anything against Manivald or that his death would bring them pleasure. No, far from it. Tambet respected Manivald very much; I clearly remember what he said at the funeral pyre: "Men like that are not born anymore." He was right; they weren't. In fact no men at all were being born anymore, at least not in our district. I was the last; a couple of months before me there was Pärtel; a year later Tambet and Mall had Hiie. She wasn't a man; she was a girl. After Hiie, only weasels and hares were born in the forest.

Of course Tambet didn't know that at the time, nor did he want to. He always believed that the old times would come again, and so on. He couldn't believe otherwise; that's the kind of man he was, strongly loyal to all the ways and customs. Every week he would go to the sacred grove and tie colored strips of cloth to a linden tree, believing he was making a sacrifice to the nature spirits. Ülgas, the Sage of the Grove, was his best friend. Actually, the word "friend" isn't right; Tambet wouldn't have called him his friend. That would have seemed the height of boorishness to the sage. He was great and holy, and had to be respected, not befriended.

Naturally Ülgas was also at Manivald's funeral. How could he not be? He was the one who had to light the funeral pyre and accompany the soul of the departed to the spirit world. He did this at annoying length: he sang, he beat a drum, he burned some mushrooms and straw. That was how the dead had been cremated from age to age; that was what had to be done. That is why I say that that funeral was very much to Tambet's taste. He liked all sorts of rituals. As long as things were done the way his forefathers had done them, Tambet was happy.

Afterward, I felt terribly sad; I remember it clearly. I didn't know Manivald at all, so I couldn't have been grieving; all the same, I was just gazing around me. At first it was exciting to see the dead man's wrinkled face with its long beard—and quite gruesome too, because I'd never seen a dead person before. The sage's incantations and conjurations went on so long that in the end it was no longer either exciting or terrifying. I would just as soon have run away—to the seashore, since I'd never been there before. I was a child of the forest. But Uncle Vootele kept me there, whispering in my ear that soon they'd be lighting the pyre. At first it was impressive, and I did want to see the fire, especially how it burns a man up. What would come out of him? What kind of bones did he have? I stayed on the spot, but Ülgas the Sage carried on with his never-ending observances and in the end I was half dead with boredom. It wouldn't even have interested me if Uncle Vootele had promised to flay the corpse before burning; I just wanted to go home. I yawned audibly, and Tambet glared at me with his goggle-eyes and growled, "Quiet, boy, you're at a funeral! Listen to the sage!"

"Go on, run around!" Uncle Vootele whispered to me. I ran to the seashore and jumped into the waves fully clothed; then I played with the sand, until I looked like a lump of mud. Then I noticed that the bonfire was already burning, and I ran back to the fire at top speed, but there was no sign left of Manivald. The flames were so big they rose up to the stars.

"How filthy you are!" said Uncle Vootele, trying to wipe me clean with his sleeve. Again I met Tambet's fierce gaze, because obviously it wasn't the done thing to behave at funerals as I was, and Tambet was always very particular about observing the rules.

I didn't care about Tambet, because he wasn't my father or uncle, just a neighbor who was fierce but didn't have any power over me. I tugged at Uncle Vootele's beard and demanded, "Who was Manivald? Why did he live by the sea? Why didn't he live in the forest like us?"

"His home was by the sea," replied Uncle Vootele. "Manivald was an old, wise man. The oldest of us all. He had even seen the Frog of the North."

"Who was the Frog of the North?" I asked.

"The Frog of the North is a great snake, the biggest of all, much bigger than the king of the snakes. He is as big as a forest and he can fly. He has enormous wings. When he rises in the air, he covers the sun and the moon. In ancient times he used to rise often in the sky and devour all our enemies who came to that shore in their boats. And after he had devoured them, we took their possessions. So we were rich and powerful. We were feared, because no one got out alive from that coast. They also knew that we were rich, and their greed overcame their fear. More and more boats sailed to our shore to steal our treasures, and the Frog of the North killed them all."

"I want to see the Frog of the North too," I said.

"I'm afraid you can't anymore," sighed Uncle Vootele. "The Frog of the North is asleep and we can't wake him up. There are too few of us."

"One day we will!" said Tambet. "Don't talk like that, Vootele! What kind of defeatist nonsense is that? Mark my words. We will see the day when the Frog of the North rises in the sky and eats up all the paltry iron men and village rats!"

"You're talking nonsense," said Uncle Vootele. "How is that supposed to happen, when you know very well that it would take at least ten thousand men to wake up the Frog of the North? Only when ten thousand men together say the snake-words will the Frog of the North wake up from his secret nest and rise up under the sky. Where are those ten thousand? We can't even get ten together!"

"You must not give in!" hissed Tambet. "Look at Manivald. He was always hopeful and did his duty every day! Every time he noticed a ship on the horizon, he would set a dry stump alight, to announce to everyone: 'It's time for the Frog of the North to wake!' Year after year he did that, even though no one had answered his call for ages, and the alien boats would land and the iron men came ashore with impunity. But he didn't smite with his fist. He just went on pulling up stumps and drying them out, lighting them up and waiting—just waiting! He was waiting for the Frog of the North to come in power to the forest once again, as in the good old days!"

"He will never come again," said Uncle Vootele gloomily.

"I want to see him," I insisted. "I want to see the Frog of the North!"

"You won't," said Uncle Vootele.

"Is he dead?" I asked.

"No, he will never die," my uncle said. "He's asleep. I just don't know where. No one knows."

Disappointed, I fell silent. The story of the Frog of the North was interesting, but it had a bad ending. What was the use of miraculous things one can never see? Tambet and my uncle carried on arguing while I traipsed back to the seashore. I walked along the beach; it was beautiful and sandy, and here and there large uprooted stumps lay around. They must have been the same ones that the departed and now-immolated Manivald had been drying—to light as beacons that no one heeded. Beside one of the stumps there was a man crouching. It was Meeme. I had never seen him walking, only stretched out under some bush, as if he were a leaf of a tree, carried by the wind from place to place. He was always munching on some fly agaric and always offered some to me too, but I never accepted it, because my mother wouldn't let me.

This time too, Meeme was on his side beside the stump and again I hadn't seen when and how he had come. I promised myself that one day I would yet find out what that man looked like standing on two legs and how he moved around at all—upright like a human or on all fours like an animal, or sliding along like a snake. I went closer to Meeme and saw to my surprise that this time he wasn't eating fly agaric, but sipping some sort of drink from a skin.

"Ahh!" He was just wiping his mouth when I crouched down beside him and sniffed the strange odor wafting from the skin. "It's wine. Much better than fly agaric, thanks be to those foreigners and their bit of common sense. The mushroom used to make you drink lots of water, but this here quenches your thirst and makes you drunk at the same time. Great stuff! I'll think I'll stick with it. Want some?"

"No," I said. True, my mother hadn't forbidden me to drink wine, but I could guess that since Meeme offered it, it couldn't be any better than the fly agaric. "Where do you get skins like that?" I'd never seen anything like it in the forest.

"From the monks and the other foreigners," replied Meeme. "You just have to smash their heads in—and the skin is yours." He went on drinking. "Tasty little drink, there's no denying it. That silly Tambet can yell and squeal all he likes, but the foreigners' tipple is better than ours."

"So what was Tambet yelling and squealing about?" I asked.

"Ah, he won't allow us to have anything to do with the foreigners or even try their things," said Meeme dismissively. "I did say that it wasn't I that touched that monk, it was my ax, but he's still twitching. Well, what if I don't want to carry on eating fly agaric? I mean this stuff's much better and goes to your head quicker too . . . A man has to be flexible, not stiff like this stump here. But that's what we're like these days. What use has being stiff been to us? Like the last flies before the winter, we drone our way slowly through the forest, until we slouch into the moss and die."

I didn't understand any more of his talk and I got up to go back to my uncle. "Wait, boy!" Meeme stopped me. "I wanted to give you something."

I started shaking my head vigorously, for I knew that now he would produce some fly agaric or wine or some other disgusting thing.

"Wait, I said!"

"Mother won't let me!"

"Hold your tongue! Your mother doesn't even know what I want to give you. Here, take it! I don't have anything to do with it. Hang it around your neck."

Meeme thrust into my palm a little leather bag, which seemed to have something small yet heavy inside it.

"What's in here?" I asked.

"In there? Well, there's a ring in there."

I untied the mouth of the bag. Indeed there was a ring in it. A silver ring, with a big red stone. I tried it on, but the ring was too big for my tiny fingers.

"Carry it in the bag. And hang the bag around your neck."

I put the ring back in the bag. It was made of a strange kind of leather! As thin as a leaf, and if you let it out of your hand, the wind would carry it straight away. But then, a precious ring should have a fine little nest.

"Thank you!" I said, terribly happy. "It's a really pretty ring!"

Meeme laughed.

"You're welcome, boy," he said. "I don't know if it's beautiful or ugly, but it's useful. Keep it nicely in the bag like I told you."

I ran back to the bonfire. Manivald had been burned up by now, only his ashes still smoldered. I showed the ring to Uncle Vootele, and he examined it long and thoroughly.

"It's a precious thing," he said at length. "Made in a foreign land and probably reached our shores at one time along with the men of iron. I wouldn't be surprised if the first owner of this ring was a victim of the Frog of the North. I don't understand why Meeme chose you to give it to. He could well have sent it to your sister, Salme. What will you do, boy, with an expensive piece of jewelry like that in the forest?"

"I certainly won't give it to Salme!" I cried, offended.

"No, don't. Meeme never does anything for no reason. If he gave you the ring, there must be a need for it. Right now I don't understand his plan, but that doesn't matter. It'll all be clear one day. Let's go home now."

"Yes, let's," I agreed, and realized how sleepy I was. Uncle Vootele lifted me onto a wolf's back and we went home through the nocturnal forest. Behind us lay the embers of the fire and the sea, no longer watched over by anyone.

Two

n fact I was born in the village, not in the forest. It was my father who decided to move to the village. Everybody was moving, well, almost everybody, and my parents were among the last. That was probably on my mother's account, because she didn't like village life; she wasn't interested in farming and she never ate bread.

"It was slops," she used to say to me. "You know, Leemet, I don't believe anybody actually likes it. This bread eating is really just showing off. They want to appear terribly fine and to live like foreigners. But a nice fresh haunch of deer is quite another thing. Now come on and eat, dear child! Who did I roast these joints for?"

My father was obviously of a different opinion. He wanted to be a modern person, and a modern person should live in a village, under the open sky and the sun, not in a murky forest. He should grow rye, work all summer like some filthy ant, so that in autumn he could look important and gobble bread like the foreigners. A modern person was supposed to have a scythe at home, so that in autumn he could stoop down and cut the grain on the ground; he had to have a quern on which to grind the grains, huffing and puffing. Uncle Vootele told me how my father—when he was still living in the forest—would just about explode with irritation and envy when he thought about the interesting life the villagers were leading and the impressive tools they had.

"We must hurry up and move to the village!" he had shouted. "Life is passing us by! These days all normal people live under the open sky, not in the bushes! I want to sow and reap too, as they do everywhere in the developed world! Why should I be any worse? Just look at the iron men and the monks; you can see straight away that they're a hundred years ahead of us! We must make every effort to catch up with them!"

And so he took my mother to live in the village; they built themselves a little cottage and my father learned to sow and reap and got himself a scythe and a quern. He started going to church and learning German, so he could understand the speech of the iron men and learn even better and more fashionable tricks from them. He ate bread and, smacking his lips, praised its goodness, and as he learned to make proper barley gruel, there was no end to his enthusiasm and pride.

"It tasted like vomit," my mother confessed to me, but my father ate barley gruel three times a day, screwing up his face a bit, while claiming that it was a particularly dainty dish, for you had to develop a taste. "Not like our hunks of meat, which any fool can gobble, but a proper European food for people with finer tastes!" he would say. "Not too rich, not too fatty, but sort of lean and light. But nourishing! A food for kings!"

When I was born, my father advised that I should be fed only on barley gruel, because his child "has to have the best." And he got me a sickle, so that as soon as my legs could carry me I would go stooping in the fields with him. "Of course a scythe is a precious thing, and you might think there's no sense in putting it into a tiny tot's hands, but I don't agree with that attitude. Our child ought to get used to modern tools from the start," he said proudly. "In the future we won't get by without a scythe, so let him learn the great art of reaping rye straight away!"

All this was related to me by Uncle Vootele. I don't remember my father. And my mother didn't like talking about him; every time he came up she would become uneasy and change the subject. She must have blamed herself for my father's death, and I suppose she was guilty. My mother was bored in the village; she didn't care for work in the fields, and while my father was striding out to go sowing, my mother was wandering around the old familiar forests, and she got acquainted with a bear. What happened next seems to be quite clear; it's such a familiar story. Few women can resist a bear; they're so big, soft, helpless, and furry. And besides that, bears are born seducers, and terribly attracted to human females, so they wouldn't let slip an opportunity to make their way up to a woman and growl in her ear. In the old days, when most of our people still lived in the forest, there were endless cases of bears becoming women's lovers, trysts that would ultimately end in the man discovering the couple and sending the brown beast packing.

The bear started visiting us, always when my father was toiling in the field. He was a very friendly animal; my sister, Salme, who is five years older than me, remembers him and has told me that the bear always brought her honey. Like all bears at that time, this bear knew how to talk a little, since bears are the cleverest of animals, of course excepting snakes, the brothers of humans.

True, bears couldn't say much, and their conversation wasn't very smart—but how smart do you have to be to talk to your lover? At least they could chat nicely about everyday matters.

Of course, everything's changed now. A couple of times, when carrying water from the spring, I've seen bears and shouted a few words of greeting to them. They've stared at me with stupid faces and taken off with a crackle into the bushes. That whole stratum of culture they possessed down the long centuries in their dealings with men and snakes has been dissipated in such a short time, and bears have become ordinary animals. Like ourselves. Apart from me, who now knows the snake-words? The world has gone downhill, and even the water from the spring tastes bitter.

But never mind that. In those days, in my childhood, bears were still able to exchange ideas with humans. We were never friends; we considered bears too far below us for that. Ultimately we were the ones they pawed with their honey-paws and pulled at, out of primitive stupidity. In their way they were the pupils of humans, for we were their superiors. And of course we knew the lustfulness of bears, and that incomprehensible attraction that our women felt for them. That was why every man looked on them with a slight suspicion: "That fat furry bundle of love won't get my woman . . ." Too often they would find bear fur in their beds.

But things were even worse for my father. He didn't find only bear fur in the bed; he also found a whole bear. In itself that mightn't have been so bad; he should have just given the bear a good hiss and the creature, caught in the act, would have slunk off in shame to the forest. But my father had started to forget Snakish, because he didn't need to speak it in the village, and besides, he didn't think much of the snake-words, believing that a scythe and a quern would serve him a whole lot better. So when he saw the bear in his own bed, he mumbled some words of German, whereupon the bear—confused by the incomprehensible words, and annoyed at being caught *in flagrante*—bit his head off.

Naturally he regretted it straight away, because bears are generally not bloodthirsty animals, unlike for example wolves, who will serve humans, carrying them on their backs and allowing themselves to be milked—though only under the influence of the Snakish words. A wolf really is a fairly dangerous domestic animal, but since there is no tastier milk to be had from anyone in the forest, one reconciles oneself to its sullenness, especially as the Snakish words render it as meek as a titmouse. But a bear is a creature with sense. The bear had killed my father in desperation, and since the murder was committed in the heat of passion, he punished himself on the spot and bit his own tool off.

Then my mother and the castrated bear burned my father's body, and the bear fled deep into the forest, vowing to my mother that they would never meet again. Apparently this was a suitable solution for my mother because, as I said, she felt terribly guilty and her love for the bear ended abruptly. For the rest of her life she couldn't stand bears, would hiss as soon as she saw them, and in this way she retreated from her former life. This hatred of hers later brought much confusion to our family, and strife too, but I will speak of that later, at the right time.

After my father's death, my mother saw no reason to stay in the village; she strapped me on her back, took my sister by the hand, and moved back to the forest. Her brother, my uncle Vootele, was still living there, and he took us into his care, helped us to build a hut, and gave us two young wolves, so we would always have fresh milk. Although she was still shocked by my father's death, she breathed more easily, because she had never wanted to leave the forest. This was where she felt at ease, and she didn't care a bit that she wasn't living like the iron men or that there wasn't a single scythe in the house. In our mother's home we no longer ate bread, but there were always piles of deer and goat meat.

I wasn't even one year old when we moved back to the forest. So I knew nothing of the village or the life there; I grew up in the forest and it was my only home. We had a nice hut deep in the woods, where I lived with my mother and sister, and Uncle Vootele's cave was nearby. In those days the forest was not yet bereft of people. Moving around, you would be bound to meet others—old women milking their wolves in front of their huts, or long-bearded old men, chatting away crudely with the vipers.

There were fewer younger people and their numbers kept decreasing, so that more and more often you would come across an abandoned dwelling. Those huts were vanishing into the undergrowth, ownerless wolves were running around, and the older people said that once you've let it go, it's not really a life for anyone anymore. They were especially distressed that children were not being born anymore, which was quite natural. Who was around to bear them when all the young people were moving to the village? I too went to look at the village, peering from the edge of the forest, not daring to go any closer. Everything there was so different, and a lot smarter too I thought. There was plenty of sunlight and open space, the houses under the open sky seemed a lot nicer to me than our hovel, half-buried in the spruce trees, and in every home I could see big numbers of children scurrying around.

This made me very jealous, for I had few playmates. My sister, Salme, didn't care much for me. She was five years older, and a girl besides; she had her own things to do. Luckily there was Pärtel, and I ran around with him. And then there was Hiie, Tambet's daughter, but again she was too small, tottering around her home on stiff legs and falling over every now and then on her bum. She was no company for me at first, and anyway I didn't like going over to Tambet's place. I may have been young and stupid but I did understand that Tambet couldn't stand me. He would always snort and hiss when he saw me, and once, when Pärtel and I were coming from berry picking and, out of the goodness of my heart, I offered a strawberry to Hiie, who was squatting on the grass, Tambet yelled from inside the house: "Hiie, come away from there! We don't take anything from the village people!"

He could never forgive my family for once leaving the forest, and he stubbornly persisted in regarding me and Salme as villagers. At the sacred grove he always scowled at us with obvious disdain, as if he were offended that stinking village mongrels like us would push our way into such an important place. And I only went to the grove under duress, because I didn't like the way Ülgas the Sage anointed the trees with hare's blood. Hares were such dear creatures; I couldn't understand how anyone could kill them just to sprinkle on the tree roots. I was afraid of Ülgas, although in appearance he wasn't so horrible; he had a kindly, grandfatherly face, and was good to children. Sometimes he would visit us and talk about all sorts of fairies and about how children in particular should show great respect to them, and bring a sacrifice to the water-sprite before washing at the spring, and then another after emptying the water bucket. And when you want to bathe in a river, you should bring a few sacrifices, if you don't want the water-sprite to drown you.

"What sacrifices should they be?" I asked, and Ülgas the Sage explained, laughing affably, that the best thing to take is a frog, cutting it alive from the head lengthwise and throwing it into the spring or river. Then the sprite is satisfied.

"Why are those sprites so cruel?" I asked, frightened, because torturing a frog like that seemed horrible to me. "Why do they want blood all the time?"

"What rubbish you talk! Sprites aren't cruel," said Ülgas, admonishing me. "Fairies are simply the rulers of the waters and the trees, and we should obey their orders and do their bidding; that has always been our custom."

Then he patted me on the cheek, telling me by all means to come back to the grove soon—"because those who don't visit the grove will be torn apart by the dogs"—and left. But I was torn by terror and hesitation, because I just couldn't cut a live frog in half. I bathed very rarely and as close to the shore as possible, so I could scramble out of the water before the bloodthirsty water-sprite, without the propitiation of a frog-corpse, would leap at me on the shore. Even when I did go to the sacred grove, I always felt uncomfortable, looking around everywhere for those horrible dogs that lived there and kept watch, according to Ülgas, but all I met was the withering gaze of Tambet, who no doubt took offense that a "villager" like me was gazing around a sacred place, instead of concentrating on the conjurings of the Sage of the Grove.

Being thought of as a villager didn't really worry me, because, as I said, I liked the village. I was always pressing my mother to know why we moved away from there and asking if we could go back—if not for good, then at least for a while. Of course my mother wouldn't agree, and tried to explain to me how nice it was in the forest, and how tedious and hard the life of the village people was.

"They eat bread and barley gruel there," she would say, clearly wanting to scare me, but I couldn't remember the taste of either of them, and the words didn't provoke any disgust in me. On the contrary, those unknown foods sounded alluring; I would have liked to try them. And I told my mother so.

"I want bread and barley gruel!"

"Ah, you don't know how horrible they are. We've got plenty of roast meat! Come and take some, boy! Believe me, it's a hundred times nicer."

I didn't believe her. Roast meat I ate every day; it was ordinary food, with nothing mysterious about it.

"I want bread and barley gruel!" I insisted.

"Leemet, stop talking nonsense now! You don't even know what you're saying. You don't need any bread. You just think you want it, but actually you'd spit it straight out. Bread is as dry as moss; it gets stuck in your mouth. Look, I've got owls' eggs here!"

Owls' eggs were my favorite, and at the sight of them I stopped whining and set about sucking the eggs empty. Salme came into the room, saw me, and screamed that our mother was spoiling me. She wanted to drink owls' eggs too!

"But of course, Salme," said my mother. "I've put aside eggs for you. You each get just as many."

Then Salme grabbed her own eggs, sat down next to me, and we competed with each other. And I no longer thought of bread or barley gruel.

Three

 uite naturally, however, a few owls' eggs couldn't kill my curiosity for long, and the very next day I was roaming on the edge of the forest, looking greedily toward the village. My friend Pärtel was with me, and it was he who finally said, "Why are we watching from so far away? Let's sneak a bit closer."

The suggestion seemed extremely dangerous; the very thought of it made my heart race. Nor did Pärtel look all that brave; he looked at me with an expression that expected me to shake my head and refuse; his words had indicated his dread. I didn't shake my head; I just said, "Let's go then."

As I said it, I had the feeling that I was expected to jump into some dark forest lake. We went a couple of steps and stopped, hesitating; I looked at Pärtel and saw that my friend's face was as white as a sheet.

"Shall we go on?" he asked.

"I guess so."

So we did. It was horrible. The first house was already quite close, but luckily no one appeared. Pärtel and I hadn't agreed how far we would go. As far as the house? And then—should we take a look in the doorway? We surely wouldn't dare to. Tears overcame me; I would have liked to run headlong back into the forest, but since my friend was walking beside me, it wouldn't do to look so scared. Pärtel must have been thinking the same thing, because I heard him whimpering now and then. And yet, as if bewitched, we kept inching forward, step by step.

Then a girl came out of the house, about our age. We came to a stop. If some adult had appeared before us, we probably would have made off back to the forest with a loud cry, but there was no need to flee because of a girl of our own age. She didn't seem very dangerous, even if she was a village child. Nevertheless we were very cautious, staring at her and not going any closer.

The girl looked back at us. She didn't seem to feel any fear. "Did you come from the forest?" she asked.

We nodded.

"Have you come to live in the village?"

"No," replied Pärtel, and I saw my chance to do a bit of bragging, informing her that I had already lived in the village, but moved away.

"Why did you go back to the forest?" The girl was amazed. "Nobody goes back to the forest; they all come from the forest to the village. They're fools that live in the forest."

"You're a fool yourself," I said.

"No I'm not; you are. Everyone says only fools live in the forest. Look what you're wearing! Skins! Awful! Like an animal."

We compared our own clothing with the village girl's, and we had to admit that the girl was right; our wolf and goat skins really were a lot uglier than hers, and hung off us like bags. The girl, on the other hand, was wearing a long, slim shirt, which was nothing like an animal skin; it was thin, light, and moved in the wind.

"What kind of skin is that?" asked Pärtel.

"It isn't skin; it's cloth," replied the girl. "It's woven."

That word meant nothing to us. The girl burst out laughing.

"You don't know what weaving is?" she shrieked. "Have you even seen a loom? A spinning wheel? Come inside. I'll show you."

This invitation was both frightening and alluring. Pärtel and I looked at each other, and we decided that we ought to take the risk. These things with strange names ought to be seen. And whatever that girl might do to us, there were two of us after all. That is, unless she had allies inside . . .

"Who else is in there?" I asked.

"No one else. I'm alone at home; the others are all making hay."

That too was an incomprehensible thing, but we didn't want to appear too stupid, so we nodded as if we understood what "making hay" meant. Our hearts were in our throats as we went inside.

It was an amazing experience. All the strange contraptions that filled the room were a feast for the eyes. We stood as if thunderstruck, and didn't dare sit down or move. The girl, on the other hand, felt right at home and was delighted to show off in front of us.

"Well, there's a spinning wheel for you!" she said, patting one of the queerest objects I've ever seen in my life. "You spin yarn on it. I can already do it. Want me to show you?"

We mumbled something. The girl sat down at the spinning wheel and immediately a strange gadget started turning and whirring. Pärtel sighed with excitement.

"Mighty!" he muttered.

"You like it?" the girl inquired proudly. "Okay, I can't do any more spinning just now." She got up. "What else can I show you? Look, this is a bread shovel."

The bread shovel, too, made a deep impression on us.

"But what's that?" I asked, pointing to a cross shape hanging on the wall, to which was attached a human figure.

"That is Jesus Christ, our God," someone answered. It wasn't the girl; it was a man's voice. Pärtel and I were as startled as mice and wanted to rush out the door, but our way was barred.

"Don't run away!" said the voice. "No need to tremble like that. You're from the forest, aren't you? Calm down, now, boys. Nobody means you any harm."

"This is my father," said the girl. "What's wrong with you? Why are you afraid?"

Timidly we eyed the man who had stepped into the room. He was tall, and looked very grand with his golden hair and beard. To our eyes he was also enviably well dressed, wearing the same sort of light-colored shirt as his daughter, the same furry breeches, and around his neck the same figure on a cross that I had seen on the wall.

"Tell me, are there still many people living in the forest?" he asked. "Please do tell your parents to give up their benighted ways! All the sensible people are moving now from the forest to the village. In this day and age it's silly to go on living in some dark thicket, doing without all the benefits of modern science. It's pathetic to think of those poor people who still carry on a miserable existence in caves, while others are living in castles and palaces! Why do our folk have to be the last? We want to enjoy the same pleasures that other folk do! Tell that to your fathers and mothers. If they won't think of themselves, then they ought to show some pity for their children. What will become of you if you don't learn to talk German and serve Jesus?"

We couldn't utter a word in response, but strange words like "castles" and "palaces" made our hearts tremble. They must surely be finer things than spinning wheels and bread shovels. We would have liked to see them! We should really talk our parents into letting us spend at least some time in the village, just to look at all these marvels.

"What are your names?" asked the man.

We mumbled our names. The man patted us on the shoulders.

"Pärtel and Leemet—those are heathen names. When you come to live in the village, you'll be christened, and you'll get names from the Bible. For instance, my name used to be Vambola, but for many years now I've had the name Johannes. And my daughter's name is Magdaleena. Isn't that beautiful? Names from the Bible are all beautiful. The whole world uses them, the fine boys and pretty girls from all the great peoples. Us too—the Estonians. The wise man does as other wise men do, and doesn't just run around berserk like some piglet let out of a pen."

Johannes patted us on the shoulder once more and led us into the yard.

"Now go home and talk to your parents. And come back soon. All Estonians have to come out of the dark forest, into the sun and the open wind, because those winds carry the wisdom of distant lands to us. I'm an elder of this village. I'll be expecting you. And Magdaleena will be expecting you too; it would be nice to play with you and go to church on Sunday to pray to God. Till we meet again, farewell, boys! May God protect you!"

Obviously something was troubling Pärtel; he opened his mouth a few times, but didn't dare utter a sound. Finally, when we really did turn to leave, he couldn't contain his question any longer: "What is that long stick in your hand? And all those spikes in it!"

"It's a rake!" replied Johannes with a smile. "When you come to live in the village, you can have one of these!"

Pärtel's face broke into a smile of joy. We ran into the forest.

For a little while we ran together, then we each scurried off to our own homes. I rushed into the shack, as if someone were chasing me, in the certain knowledge that now I would make it clear to my mother: life in the village was much more interesting than in the forest.

Mother wasn't at home. Nor was Salme. Only Uncle Vootele was sitting in a corner, nibbling on some dried meat.

"What happened to you?" he asked. "Your face is on fire."

"I went to the village," I replied and told him rapidly, gabbling, and sometimes losing my voice with excitement, about everything I had seen in Johannes's house.

Uncle Vootele did not change his expression on hearing all these marvels, even though I drew a rake for him on the wall with a piece of charcoal.

"I've seen a rake, yes," he said. "It's no use to us here."

This seemed to me unbelievably stupid and old-fashioned. How? If something as crazily exciting as a rake has been invented, then it's definitely of use! Magdaleena's father Johannes is using it, after all!

"He might really need it, because you can scrape hay together with a rake," explained Uncle Vootele. But they need to cultivate hay so that their animals won't die of hunger in winter.

We don't have that problem. Our deer and goats can fend for themselves in winter; they look for their own food in the forest. But the villagers' animals don't go out in winter. They're afraid of the cold and anyway they're so stupid that they might get lost in the forest and the villagers would never find them again. They don't know Snakish, so they can't summon living beings to them. That's why they keep their animals all winter penned in and feed them with the hay they've gone to great trouble to collect in the summer. You see that's why the villagers need that ridiculous rake, but we get by very well without it."

"But what about the spinning wheel!" The wheel had left a more powerful impression on me than the rake. All those skeins and wheels and other whirring fiddly bits were to my mind so magnificent that it wasn't possible to describe it in words.

Uncle smiled.

"Children like toys like that," he said. "But we don't need a spinning wheel either, because an animal skin is a hundred times warmer and more comfortable than woven cloth. The villagers simply can't get hold of animal skins, because they don't remember Snakish anymore, and all the lynxes and wolves run off into the bushes away from them, or, otherwise, attack them and eat them up."

"Then they had a cross, and on it was a human figure, and Johannes the village elder said it was a god whose name is Jesus Christ," I said. Uncle had to understand for once just what inspiring things there were in the village!

Uncle Vootele just shrugged.

"One person believes in sprites and visits the sacred grove, and another believes in Jesus and goes to the church. It's just a matter of fashion. There's no use in getting involved with just one god; they're more like brooches or pearls, just for decoration. For hanging around your neck, or for playing with."

I was offended at my uncle, for flinging mud at all my marvels like that, so I didn't start talking about the bread shovel. Uncle would certainly have said something foul about it—something about us not eating bread anyway. I kept quiet, glowering at him.

Uncle smirked.

"Don't get angry. I do understand that when you see for the first time how the villagers live all that flapdoodle turns a kid's head. Not only a kid—a grown-up too. Look how many of them have moved from the forest to the village. Including your own father—he used to talk about how fine and nice it was to live in the village, his eyes glowing like a wildcat's. The village drives you crazy, because they have so many peculiar gadgets there. But you've got to understand that all these things have been dreamed up for only one reason: they've forgotten the Snakish words."

"I don't understand Snakish either," I faltered.

"No, you don't, but you're going to start learning it. You're a big enough boy now. And it's not easy, and that's why many people today can't be bothered with it, and they'd rather invent all sorts of scythes and rakes. That's a lot easier. When your head isn't working, your muscles do. But you're going to start on it. That's what I think. I'll teach you myself."

Four

n the old days, they say, it was quite natural for a child to learn the Snakish words. In those days there must have been more skilled masters, and even some who didn't get all the hidden subtleties of the language—but even they got by in everyday life. All people knew Snakish, which was taught in days of yore to our ancestors by ancient Snakish kings.

By the time I was born, everything had changed. Older people were still using some Snakish, but there were few really wise ones among them—and then the younger generation no longer took the trouble to learn the difficult language at all. Snakish words are not simple; the human ear can hardly catch all those hairline differences that distinguish one hiss from another, giving an entirely different meaning to what you say. Likewise, human language is impossibly clumsy and inflexible, and all the hisses sound quite alike at first. You have to start learning the Snakish words with the kind of practice you take with a language. You have to train the muscles from day to day, to make your tongue as nimble and clever as a snake's. At first it's pretty annoying, and so it's no wonder that many forest people found the effort too much, and preferred to move to the village, where it was much more interesting and you didn't need Snakish.

Moreover, there weren't any real teachers left. The retreat from Snakish had started several generations ago, and even our parents were only able to use the commonest and simplest of all the Snakish words, such as the word that calls a deer or an elk to you so you can slit his throat, or the word to calm a raging wolf, as well as the usual chitchat, about the weather and things like that, that you might have with a passing adder. Stronger words hadn't come in for much use for a long time, because to hiss the strongest words—to get any result out of them—would need several thousand men at once, and there hadn't been that many in the forest for ages. And so many Snakish words had fallen into desuetude, and recently no one had bothered to learn even the simplest ones, because as I say they didn't stick in your mind easily—and why go to the trouble, when you could get behind a plow and work your muscles?

So I was in quite an extraordinary situation, as Uncle Vootele knew all the Snakish words—no doubt the only person in the forest who did. Only from him could I learn all the subtleties of this language. And Uncle Vootele was a merciless teacher. My otherwise so kindly uncle suddenly became very gruff when it came to a lesson in Snakish. "You simply have to learn them!" he declared curtly, and forced me over and over again to repeat the most complex hisses, so that by the evening my tongue ached as if someone had been twisting it all day. When Mother came with a haunch of venison, my head shook in fear. Just the thought that my poor tongue had to chew and swallow, in addition to all the twistings of the day, filled my mouth with a horrible pain. Mother was in despair, and asked Uncle Vootele not to exhaust me so much and to start by teaching me just the simplest hisses, but Uncle Vootele wouldn't agree.

"No, Linda," he told my mother. "I'll teach Leemet the Snakish words so well that he won't know anymore whether he's a human or a snake. Only I speak this language as well as our people have from the dawn of time, and one day, when I die, Leemet will be the one who won't let the Snakish words fade into oblivion. Maybe he'll manage to train up his own successor, like his own son, and so this language won't die out."

"Oh, you're as stubborn and cruel as our father!" sighed Mother, and made a chamomile compress for my injured tongue.

"Was Granddad cruel, then?" I mumbled, with the compress between my teeth.

"Terribly cruel," replied Mother. "Of course, not to us—he loved us. At least I think so—but many years have passed since he died, and I was only a little girl then."

"So why did he die?" I persisted. I had never heard anything about my grandfather before, and only now I came to the surprising conclusion that quite naturally my father and mother couldn't have just fallen out of the sky; they must have had parents. But why had they never talked about them?

"The iron men killed him," said Mother. And Uncle Vootele added, "They drowned him. They chopped his legs off and threw him in the sea."

"What about my other grandfather?" I demanded. "I must have had two grandfathers!"

"The iron men killed him too," said Uncle Vootele. It was in a big battle, which happened long before you were born. Our men went out bravely to fight with the iron men, but they were smashed to smithereens. Their swords were too short and their spears too weak. But of course that shouldn't have mattered, because our people's weapons have never been swords and spears, but the Frog of the North. If we'd managed to wake the Frog of the North, he would have swallowed up the iron men at a stroke. But there were too few of us; many of our people had gone to live in the village and didn't come to our aid when they were asked. And even if they had come, they wouldn't have been of help, because they no longer remembered the Snakish words, and the Frog of the North only rises up when thousands call on him. So there was nothing left for our men but to try to fight against the iron men with their own weapons, but that has always been a hopeless task. Foreign things never bring anyone good fortune. The men were cut down and the women, including your grandmothers, brought up their children and died of melancholy."

"Our father, of course, wasn't killed in battle," Mother corrected him. "No one would dare go near him, because he had poison teeth."

"What do you mean, poison teeth?"

"Like an adder's," explained Uncle Vootele. "Our ancient forefathers all had fangs, but as time passed and they forgot Snakish, their poisonous fangs disappeared. In the last hundred years very few of them have had them, and now I don't know anybody who has them, but our father did, and he bit his enemies without mercy. The iron men were terribly afraid of him and fled for their lives when Father flashed his fangs at them."

"So how was he captured?"

"They brought a stone-throwing machine," sighed Mother. "And started firing rocks at him. Finally they got him and stunned him. Then the iron men tied him up, with whoops of joy, cut off his legs, and threw him into the sea."

"The iron men hated and feared your grandfather terribly," said Uncle. "He had a really wild nature, and our ancestors' fiery blood flowed in him. If we had all stayed like that, the iron men wouldn't have stood a chance of building a nest in our land; they would have had their throats cut and been gnawed to the bone. But unfortunately people and tribes degenerate. They lose their teeth, forget their language, until finally they're bending meekly on the fields and cutting straw with a scythe."

Uncle Vootele spat and glowered at the floor with such a horrible expression that I thought, My heroic grandfather's cruel blood hasn't completely gone from his son.

"Even amid the waves, Father bellowed in such a frightful voice that the iron men fled to their castle and closed all the window holes," Mother said, concluding her woeful tale. "That was more than thirty years ago."

"So isn't that reason enough to learn Snakish?" said Uncle. "In memory of your brave grandfather. I can't plant fangs in your mouth, but I can put a nimble tongue in there. Spit out that pap, and let's get started again."

"Let him rest a little at least," begged Mother.

"It's nothing," I said, trying to put on a brave face. "And my tongue doesn't hurt so much anymore. I can do it."

It would be wrong to claim that studying Snakish immediately killed all my dreams of a spinning wheel and a bread shovel. I still thought sometimes about the marvels I'd seen at the home of the village elder, Johannes, and his daughter, Magdaleena, and

I even secretly tried to fashion a bread shovel myself. I couldn't even contemplate trying a spinning wheel; that seemed like a contraption from another world that an ordinary person could never make with his own hands. Not even the shovel amounted to much; somehow it ended up crooked and splintered. There was nothing I could do with it. I didn't dare to take my handiwork home, so it lay abandoned in the bushes.

With Pärtel, naturally, I reminisced about our visit, and we conferred about whether to visit the exciting house again. Johannes the village elder had invited us back, but the sense of nervousness about the village had not diminished in our hearts, and Mother's and Uncle's stories had, at least for me, only strongly increased how alien it seemed. So I resolved to put off another visit to the village for sometime in the future, and Pärtel didn't want to go alone. I did invite him to join me in learning Snakish with Uncle Vootele, but Pärtel said, screwing up his nose, that his mother was already teaching him, that it was disgustingly difficult, and he certainly wasn't planning to take extra lessons. So I remained as Uncle Vootele's only pupil.

After the first painful weeks, during which my tongue swelled like a mushroom several times, my mouth muscles finally started to get used to the effort, and many of my hisses were beginning to sound sufficiently sibilant. If I had at first studied Snakish words mainly out of obedience and respect for my uncle, whom I loved very much, gradually I actually started to like the hissing. It was exciting to try out new sibilations and, when I succeeded, thrilling to see the eagles circling high in the sky and coming down to me, the owls in the middle of the day sticking their heads out of the tree hollows, and the mother wolves stopping on the spot and stretching out their legs, so as to be milked more easily.

It was only insects that didn't understand the Snakish words, since their brains were too small for that sort of wisdom, no bigger than a speck of dust. So Snakish words were no use against mosquitoes or horseflies, or to treat beestings. Crab lice couldn't grasp the ancient tongue at all; they had their own disgusting whine. Even today I can still hear it when I go to the well for water, for although the Snakish words have now inexorably died away, the whining remains.

But then, young and eager to learn, I didn't pay any attention to insects and I simply swatted them when they attacked me. Crab lice didn't seem to belong to the forest; they were like flying garbage. What entranced me were the changes I noticed in the forest thanks to the Snakish words. Whereas I had once simply scampered around in it, now I could talk to the forest. The fun seemed endless.

Uncle Vootele was pleased with me; he was assured that I had a knack for Snakish, and when our meat ran out, he let me call a new goat to us. I hissed, the goat ran docilely toward me, and Uncle Vootele killed it, while Mother looked on, gratified. I was then nine years old.

The best part of my studies, of course, was that I got to know Ints.

The day I met Ints I was alone. Uncle Vootele had given me a few new hisses to practice and learn by heart and I was resting by the little well, hissing diligently, so that my tongue got tied. Suddenly I heard someone else hissing—loudly and in terror.

It was a young adder being attacked by a hedgehog. I hissed my most forbidding injunction at the hedgehog, and it seemed to come out very well. The word I had hissed would make any animal freeze on the spot, but the hedgehog took no notice of my utterance. Then I understood that that same hiss had been used by the little adder, and that it was extremely silly of me to try to use Snakish words to help a snake. No matter what skill a human could manage with Snakish words, against a real snake it came to nothing. It was snakes who taught us the art, not the other way around.

The little snake was expecting another kind of help from me. You see hedgehogs are the stupidest of all animals, and in the millions of years that their species has been running around, they have never learned Snakish. Therefore both my own and the young adder's hisses were falling on deaf ears. Paying no heed to the hissing, the hedgehog had attacked the snake, and probably would have finished him off if I hadn't given it a good kick into the bushes.

"Thank you," panted the young snake. "Those hedgehogs are endless trouble; they're as stupid as pinecones and tussocks. You can hiss yourself to death and it does no good."

My Snakish was by no means good yet, but with clumsy hisses I managed to ask the young adder why he hadn't stung the hedgehog.

"That does no good either. As I said, they're like pinecones and tussocks, completely dumb. Our poison has no effect on them; they just keep on doing their tricks. Once again, many thanks! By the way, your Snakish is pretty good. I haven't met a human for ages who knows it so well. My father tells me that in the old days he had a lot of talks with humans, but now people don't know any more than how to kill a goat with Snakish words."

I was slightly ashamed, because I had just recently used Snakish words for that very purpose, but I didn't tell that to the little adder. I explained to him as best I could that I was being taught by Uncle Vootele, and I told him my own name.

"I've seen that Vootele," said the adder. "My father knows him well. He speaks our language really fluently. He's visited us too. If you want, Leemet, you can pay us a visit. Why don't we go straight away, and I'll tell Mother and Father how you saved me. My snake-name is dreadfully complicated for your tongue, but you can call me Ints."

I agreed right away to go with the adder, because I had never before seen how snake-kings live. The fact that my new friends belonged to the Snakish royalty was self-evident. Snake-kings were much bigger than ordinary adders, and a tiny golden crown sparkled on the brow of a full-grown snake-king. Ints didn't have one yet, but from his build and his intelligence there was no doubt that he was the son of a snake-king. Snake-kings were like queen ants who were surrounded by millions of tiny workers. I had seen them sometimes, but until now I hadn't had a chance to speak to one. And snake-kings wouldn't pay any attention to little boys; they were too grand and important for that.

So I was very excited when Ints led me to a large hole and told me to squeeze inside. It was a bit creepy, but not as creepy as when stepping into Johannes the village elder's house. The snakes were in their own home; they had nothing to be afraid of—but all the same I was a bit nervous. The passage to the snakes' home was dark and pretty long, but Ints hissed encouragingly beside me and that reassured me.

Finally we reached an open cave. There certainly were a lot of snakes there! Mostly ordinary little adders, but among them were about a dozen snake-kings, all with fine crowns on their heads like golden brier-roses. The biggest of them was evidently

Ints's father. Ints told him about how I had saved him, speaking so rapidly that I didn't understand much of his nimble hissing. The great snake-king eyed me and crawled closer. I bowed and gave the greeting that Uncle Vootele had taught me.

"I worry that you, my dear boy, will be the last human from whose mouth I hear those words," said the snake-king. "Humans no longer care much for our language and seek a prettier life. Your uncle Vootele is a good friend of mine. I'm pleased that he has raised up a successor to himself. You are always welcome in our cave, especially since you rescued my child. Hedgehogs are the greatest nuisance to our kind. Coarse, wooden-headed creatures!"

"A pity that humans are going the same way!" said another snake from a corner. "Soon they'll be just the same."

"And no wonder," added Ints. "Humans admire the iron men, but they seem just like the hedgehogs—with the same prickly covering. Humans have been feeding the iron men; I wouldn't be surprised if they soon started pouring bowls of milk for hedgehogs."

At this they laughed heartily.

"The iron man is not quite the same as a hedgehog," said the same snake who had spoken before. "The hedgehog never takes off his spines, but the iron man does take off his coat. Our venom does nothing to a hedgehog, but I jabbed one iron man just the other day when he had stripped himself bare and stumbled straight toward me after swimming. Venom did affect that man; he started screaming in a dreadful voice and ran off."

I had never before heard of a snake stinging a human, and that story horrified me. Ints's father noticed this and hissed soothingly at me.

"A human who lives in the forest and understands our language is our brother," he said. "But a human who has gone to live in the village and no longer understands Snakish words has only himself to blame. If he comes too close to us, then first we welcome him politely, but if he doesn't respond to us, that means he's no longer one of us. He is like a hedgehog or an insect and we don't pity him."

"Why are you talking to the boy like that?" asked a third snake, who I later found out was Ints's mother. "Why are you frightening him? It doesn't concern him; he saved Ints's life and we're eternally grateful to him. He can come to us whenever he likes, and stay here as long as he likes. From now on he's our son."

"Yes, he is," agreed Ints's father. "Our son. And if my friend Vootele allows, I'll be glad to teach him some Snakish myself. In the olden days humans and snakes used to be close together. At least in our own lifetime we could continue that old custom. Whatever happens in times to come."

Five

nts became a great friend of mine. I introduced him to Pärtel, who was not as adept at Snakish as I was, but could hiss a little. That was enough for him to grasp Ints's more simple conversation, and for the more complicated bits, I interpreted. In the course of time Pärtel's skill also improved, because if you have to deal with snakes all day long, some of it rubs off on even the dullest learner. And it was natural, too, that we spent a lot of time with Ints, since all games are better with three than with two.

Then of course there was Tambet's daughter, Hiie. She was bigger now—no longer falling on her bottom after every step—and we would have been glad to accept her into our gang. But she wasn't allowed. Hiie's father, Tambet, was simply that sort of man. For a start he didn't approve of me, because I was born in the village and Tambet thought it wasn't right for his daughter to play with a boy like that. Second he thought there was no need to play at all; one should do work.

Tambet was the sort of person who stubbornly refused to admit a fact that was evident to everyone—namely that the forest was almost empty and was destined to get ever emptier. He was always rambling on about some Estonian Golden Age, when all the peoples of the world trembled before our Frog of the North, and the woods were full of wild hissing men, who rode on wolves' backs and swilled their nutritious milk. He still kept a hundred wolves in his barn, milked them, and trained them, without grasping that for a long time past there had not been enough people in the forest to ride on such beasts, just as there was nobody who would drink up those huge amounts of wolves' milk. Other people had been reducing their flocks of wolves and letting the animals out into the forest—for why would a lone old woman keep dozens of wolves if she didn't have a single child or grandchild? One animal to milk would be enough for her. But that was not what Tambet did; he did the opposite. He regarded letting wolves go free into the forest as an unprecedented act of treachery, a betrayal of an age-old way of life.

"In our forefathers' day, not a single wolf ran free around the forest," he would say indignantly. "They all stayed in their barns, milked and ready to carry people." Tambet was not interested in the fact that no one went to war any longer; he did not seem to understand that, and sometimes seemed to regard real life as just a thick fog that leads fools astray, one through which only he could clearly see. He was absolutely sure that this fog would soon lift, and then people would start living as they had once done. Therefore he would not reduce his pack of wolves, but on the contrary increased it, catching whole groups of wolves, which he said were not created to trot around the forest with their tails up, but to serve men. Naturally looking after such a herd of wolves took up enormous time and effort, and that was one reason why Hiie did not manage to slip out and play with us. She had to milk the wolves and throw food to them, even though she was only a child. My mother thought this was terribly cruel, and often came home cursing Tambet and his wife for torturing their daughter with such hard work.

"Today I came past Tambet's place and I saw poor little Hiie killing hares," she said. "It's a terrible pity to look at her. A great number of hares had been driven into the corner of the yard, frozen in the spot by Snakish words, and little Hiie was just chopping off their heads with an ax. And you'd think that Tambet would give her a nice little ax, but no. The ax was bigger than the child! Hiie is so tiny; she could scarcely lift the great whopping thing! She chopped and chopped, tears in her eyes from the great strain. When they were all chopped off, she started throwing the hares in front of the wolves. Now why would anyone need to keep so many of those great strapping wolves in the barn? Let them trot around the forest and find their own food! That Tambet is a heartless man, and downright crazy! He tortures his own child. And that Mall is even madder. What kind of mother is she, letting her own daughter do a slave's work! I wouldn't let anyone torment my child like that! If my husband forced you to chop up hares like that, I'd have a good chop at him myself on the . . ."

At this point Mother fell silent, because she recalled her own sinful love with a bear, and how my father was left without his own head, and she grew embarrassed. But it was true that Tambet and Mall took very little care of their daughter. For them the most important thing was to live as their forefathers had. As if the sun had stopped moving in the sky, ceased setting and rising, as if the forest had not been drained of people in the meantime and the whole world had not changed. In the name of leaving that impression, they would sacrifice everything. They would work till the blood ran out of their nails, and force their own daughter to do the same.

Hiie had another problem too, apart from having to feed wolves all day long and chop up hares with a big ax. She didn't drink wolves' milk—and that was extremely bad, in Tambet's opinion. Think of the pack of wolves squatting in the barn, lactating rivers! What was to be done with all that milk? Naturally it had to be drunk, and every family member had to make a contribution. Apart from that purely practical reason, Tambet was deeply convinced that every true Estonian ought to drink wolves' milk; it was wolves' milk that had given our forefathers and foremothers their boundless strength. So refusing wolves' milk was a terrible crime, a betrayal of old customs, and in Tambet's opinion nothing was more heinous.

But what was most unpleasant was that such resistance was taking place in his own family. It had to be overcome! Milk was forced into Hiie's mouth, but when the girl began to vomit, Tambet's face went red and he yelled like a roebuck. He couldn't think of any new punishments for Hiie; he had tried everything, but the girl just cried and asked to be allowed to give up the milk. Tambet would not hear of it, and his wife, Mall, banged the table with her long sturdy finger and demanded: "Do as your father says!"

Finally Tambet went to talk with the sage of the sacred grove, thinking that he should be able to help. Ülgas examined Hiie, smoked a few plants around her, smeared her knees with martens' blood, and commanded the girl to suck on the brain of a live nightingale. When her disgust at that made Hiie vomit all over again, Ülgas declared to Tambet that the sprites had bewitched the girl.

"But don't worry. I have power over the sprites and I'll make her well again!" promised Ülgas. Hiie had to go to the sacred grove every day, and the martens' blood flowed in streams, the stinking smoke of the plants rose to the skies, and Ülgas kept stuffing more and more nightingales' brains under the girl's nose.

None of this helped. Hiie still couldn't drink wolves' milk. Actually she could hardly eat at all anymore, for the nightingales' brains had driven away all her appetite, and the suffocating smell of Ülgas's spells stayed in her nostrils and made every kind of food horrible. Ülgas became angry, because he had promised to subjugate the sprites and tried to feed Hiie in new, even more disgusting ways. He took the girl at night deep into the forest to a lonely spring and left her alone with a tub of milk, assuring the girl that at midnight a sprite would rise up out of the spring and strangle her if she had not drunk up the milk by then. Hiie didn't drink it, but poured it onto the moss, and of course no sprite came up out of the spring.

Finally Ülgas got tired of Hiie's fussing and told Tambet that he had freed the child from the sprites' spell, but the girl would only start drinking milk in ten years' time; that was how long the sprites' curse on her would last. Obviously Ülgas hoped that in ten years' time Hiie would be drinking milk for some reason, or had died anyway by then, or even that Tambet had died by then, and the fulfillment of the sage's promise could not be verified. After all, ten years is a long time, and anything can happen in that interim.

In any case Ülgas the Sage inadvertently saved Hiie's life, because if the torture of the girl had continued, she would have given up the ghost. Now Tambet was reconciled by Ülgas's words and no longer forced poor Hiie to drink milk. But he could not love a child who did not behave as the ancient order had prescribed, so he hardly spoke to Hiie at all, and always looked at her with a vague sense of revulsion, as if there were some fault in her.

My lessons with Uncle Vootele continued. We didn't practice Snakish so much anymore, as I was quite skilled at it, but we wandered in the forest, sometimes the two of us, sometimes with Ints too, draped like a ribbon around my neck, chatting about the land and the weather. Uncle Vootele talked about everything that had once been and was now gone forever. He pointed out overgrown shacks in the bushes, whose residents had either died or moved to the village, and told me what mighty old men and stern old women had once lived out their lives in those structures. Hundreds of years ago nobody could have imagined that one day those hovels would lie empty, their walls crumbling and their roofs caving in. We broke through the undergrowth and toured the ruins of these abandoned shacks, finding lots of traces of the former owners. Often we encountered a whole preserved household—crockery, knives and axes, chests of animal skins, and other chests full of gold and precious stones. In ancient times they had been plundered from the ships that used to sail our coasts, whose crews were destroyed by the Frog of the North. It was strange to touch brooches and precious stones that had once come under the giant shadow of the Frog of the North. It felt as if something of the warm flames that came from his mouth was still preserved in them.

We left everything we found exactly where it was, because we had no desire for the skins, the crockery, or the treasures. We already had everything we needed—the fortune we had amassed through the generations down the centuries. So we climbed back out of the decaying ruins, and the bushes covered them like the thickest cobwebs.

Sometimes in our wanderings we did meet living people, however. They were mainly old people, sitting in front of their little hovels, dozing in the shafts of sunlight that fell through the canopy of the trees. Uncle Vootele would chat with them and the elderly folks were happy to respond. They told us about their lives and everything that had once existed when Uncle Vootele was just a boy. The sight of Ints gave them great pleasure, too, and they hissed Snakish words quite competently with their toothless mouths, asking Ints about some snakes they had known in their time. Ints told them as much as he knew, but mostly he had to admit that all those snakes had died long ago, because adders do not live as long as humans.

"Yes, of course," the old ones agreed. "They must be dead by now. That whole world that we knew is dead now, and we'll die soon too, and that will be that."

I really wanted to find out more about the Frog of the North from these old men and women. I was fascinated by the Frog. I really wanted to see him, but I knew that it was no longer possible to call him up with strong hissing as in the olden days. Surely, though, he must live somewhere; after all, he still existed, and was just sleeping, as Uncle Vootele had told me. But where? Uncle didn't know; even he had never seen the Frog of the North. Yet those old people remembered him; in their childhood they had seen the Frog of the North rising in the sky, and one hoary old gent, with a body like a skeleton, had even seen combat in the shadow of the wings of the Frog on the seashore.

"Oh what a battle it was," he muttered, smiling his creepy, scrawny smile, his skin so very thin that you could see every detail of the jawbone in his skull. "The Frog of the North killed them all, or scorched them half to death, so we only had to chop them to pieces and gather up the booty. Those were the days!"

"Where does the Frog of the North live?" I asked.

"Under the ground. But where exactly, that I don't know. That is known only by the watchmen, those who have the key. Without a key it isn't possible to find him."

"What watchmen?" I asked. "What kind of key?"

"The key leads you to the Frog of the North," the old man explained. "Of course, I haven't seen it; it's a very secret thing. The only thing I know is that there are some watchmen who have access to the cave of the Frog of the North, but who those watchmen are, I don't know. They must have been people like us, but who exactly, that's never been revealed. It's a secret, and no one has stuck their nose into the Frog's business. He was our strength and power; we only knew that he was resting somewhere deep down and would rise when we all called on him together. We didn't need to know any more; that was enough. Those were the days!"

Later, when we had gone and left the old gaffer dozing in front of his cave, I asked Uncle Vootele if he knew anything about the watchmen and the keys.

"I've heard about them," said Uncle Vootele. "But I think it's the same sort of nonsense that the Sage of the Grove spouts. Well, all that business about fairies and sprites. They're the sort of old legends that are made up just to find a simple reason for every complicated thing. No one wants to admit that they're foolish. The Frog of the North appeared in the sky from who knows where, and disappeared again who knows where. But people couldn't be content with that! Humans can't stand things that are outside their reach. So they made up a story about some watchmen who know the Frog's hiding place, and a key that leads to that secret place. A thing like that comforts people. They don't know where the Frog of the North is sleeping, but there are some people who do, and with the help of a mystical key it's possible for them to find that magical cave. Thanks to that kind of legend, the world becomes simpler and clearer."

"No one knows where to find the key," I said.

"Yes, but there's even a legend about that, which the old man didn't tell you. I've heard a story that at the summer solstice, when the sun is farthest in the sky, a fern bursts into flower, and that flower is the key that helps to find the way to the Frog of the North."

"So the fern blooms?"

"No, of course not. A fern never blooms, but it's nice to believe that you only need to wander in the forest and find a fern blossom on solstice eve, and the key you need is there. Of course, even finding the fern blossom is no joke, and the legend does say that finding such a blossom is very rare, but even that faint hope is much better than knowing that the dwelling place of the Frog of the North cannot be found in any way, even by standing on your head or doing a somersault. People always want to leave a little possibility; no one can be satisfied with inevitability."

Uncle Vootele was right, for I was not satisfied with that story either. Of course I respected my uncle greatly and believed everything he told me, but since I so terribly wanted to find the Frog of the North, I convinced myself that this time he was wrong. What if there was some key? It was much more exciting to believe that than my uncle's words. Since the solstice was soon coming, I told Pärtel everything I had heard, and invited him to come with me in search of a blooming fern. Pärtel agreed immediately, but Ints declined.

"It's madness," he said. "A fern never blooms; all adders know that."

"But on solstice eve!" I was convincing myself more than him.

"Not even on solstice eve. It's ridiculous. How can you believe such nonsense? You might as well believe that a wolf can fly on solstice eve, or that adders grow legs at the solstice. Nature remains the same, whatever night it is."

Common sense told me that Ints was right, of course, but the blind desire to find the key to the Frog of the North made me obstinate.

"Well I for one am going to look for that fern flower," I declared. "Maybe you don't even think the Frog of the North exists?"

"The Frog exists," replied Ints. "He existed even before the first adder crawled in the forest, and he lives forever. So my father told me. I don't know where he's sleeping. No adder knows that, and there are no Snakish words to find it out."

"The watchmen and the key exist!" I said, and told him what I had heard from the skeletal old man.

"Maybe," said Ints. "Perhaps some people really have found the Frog of the North. I don't know. Adders have a lot of knowledge that humans don't have, and sometimes humans have discovered things that we don't know. But I assure you that the fern blossom is definitely not that key. There's no such thing as a fern blossom and only a fool could look for it."

"I'm going anyway!" I declared angrily. Laughing, Ints wished me luck and crawled home. Pärtel and I stayed to wait for solstice eve.

I won't give a long description of that journey, which lasted until morning; it's embarrassing to recall it now. The only excuse for our foolishness might be that we were just little boys then. We walked across the great land, turning around at every fern we came upon, assuming that the miraculous bloom might be very small, striking the eye only when looked at closely. But we didn't find anything. Not a single fern was blooming, and the morning found us resting by a fallen tree, our legs terribly tired and our whole bodies worn out and heavy from sleeplessness.

That is where Meeme found us. Or rather we found him. As always, we hadn't noticed Meeme approaching; suddenly he was simply sprawled on the other side of the tree, asking, "Boys, want some wine?"

In other circumstances we might have even tried some of that forbidden village drink, out of curiosity, because it was just the two of us, and it's always better to plunge in and do in a strange place what isn't allowed at home. But this morning we were too tired, so we just shook our heads wearily.

"What are you doing here so early in the morning?" asked Meeme. "I thought your huts were pretty far away."

"We're looking for a fern that blooms," said Pärtel, although I was nudging him with my elbow, because I'd started to believe that Uncle Vootele and Ints were right—that the fern really did bloom only in legends. So it was embarrassing to admit that we'd been wandering so far all night for the wrong reason.

As I feared, Meeme fell to jeering at us, until he was choked by the wine catching in his throat.

"A fern that blooms!" he crowed, spluttering with laughter. "Weren't you looking for a green fox? I hear that such an animal has been seen in these woods."

"We've heard there's a key in the blooming fern," explained Pärtel, taking no notice of my nudging—or maybe not understanding it and thinking that I was simply twitching from tiredness. And he told Meeme everything.

Meeme was no longer laughing, but merely snorting scornfully.

"We simply wanted to try," I said then, apologetically. "Of course it was silly. Obviously there isn't really a key at all."

"That's not what I said," replied Meeme with unexpected abruptness. "The blooming fern doesn't exist."

"But there's a key?" I asked.

"So they say," answered Meeme, in his former drunken tone again. "But there's no sense in looking for it. The key will come into the right person's hands when the time is right."

"How do you know that?" I asked.

"That's what my blind grandmother told me," replied Meeme, starting to laugh and cough again. "She also said that you can walk along a rainbow to the moon, and that if you eat a handful of earth, you change into a cuckoo. My blind half-wit of a grandmother told me all sorts of things. Go and figure out whether they're true or not. Anyway, I haven't eaten soil, because I don't want to become a cuckoo. Cuckoos don't drink wine; they have to lay eggs in other birds' nests, but what I want to do is drink. Your health, boys! I assure you wine tastes a lot better than fly agaric! These foreigners are smart people! Let everyone move to the village; that's where they live a proper life! Long live the villagers! Long may they live!"

We left him raving by the tree trunk and trudged home. The sight of Meeme had moved my thoughts in a new direction.

Six

eeme had talked a lot of piffle, but some of his words had made me think. There was no sense in seeking the key; Meeme had said that the key comes to a person. Naturally! My boyish heart swelled with pride, because I felt that I had understood Meeme's words and grasped their hidden meaning. It wasn't possible to find the mysterious key anywhere in the forest or among the moss; it wasn't a milkcap or a lingonberry, which any berry picker could pop into his own mouth. It had to be some quite well protected and covered object, to be passed on by one adept to another. Hadn't the old man spoken of watchmen? The key must be passing from one watchman to another. They inherited it, as guardians. That seemed most likely, for why would a watchman just give away a precious treasure? I wouldn't do that, for any price. But when someone died—that was a different matter. One watchman passed away and another one took his place.

I was biting my nails with anxiety. I felt great satisfaction with my smartness, but I was even more excited by the knowledge that some years ago I had received a gift. A ring! Of course I had no real reason to believe that that ring, given by Meeme, was the coveted key that would help to find the way to the Frog of the North. At the same time there was no denying that there was something strange about the ring coming to me. Why was I the one that Meeme gave it to? Men and boys didn't wear rings. It would have been much more logical for the ring to go to some woman, even though the women of the forest didn't care much for jewelry either, and besides, every family had baubles to jingle on every finger. The old treasures acquired in the days of the Frog of the North had mostly survived, and were lying around in chests, unused. But this ring was wrapped in a leather pouch; it was separated from its fellows, had been singled out. My ring must be associated with some mystery, and in my childish enthusiasm I was certain that it had to do with the key to the Frog of the North.

The only thing that made me hesitate was the fact that Meeme gave it to me. Why did he? Did he know what kind of fortune was associated with it? If he knew, why didn't he keep it for himself? What sort of person was Meeme really? As I have said, I had always seen him alone, lying around swilling wine and, earlier, eating mushrooms. He looked snotty, covered in resin and mud, his eyes blurred and his brows full of scurf. His appearance was not trustworthy. If that ring had been given to me by Uncle Vootele or Ülgas the Sage or even Tambet (of course he would not have given it to anyone born in the village at any price), I would not have doubted a bit that that treasure was somehow noteworthy. With Meeme, though, it could only be the caprice of a drunk. He'd found some old ring somewhere, wrapped it in a bit of leather, and slipped it to me. And now he was sniggering like a jaybird at me putting the ring on my finger and hoping it would lead me to the Frog of the North.

So for a start I sought out Uncle Vootele and said to him: "Tell me about Meeme."

"Why are you suddenly interested in him?" wondered Uncle Vootele. "Did he offer you wine? You mustn't drink that; it makes your head swim."

"He didn't. Or actually he did, but I didn't take it. I didn't take mushrooms either. Tell me who he is! Why is he always lying on the ground and never walking?"

"Oh, he does walk; he doesn't always loll around in one place," said Uncle Vootele, fingering his beard. "Look, Leemet, Meeme is a strange person. In his day he was a great warrior, brave and strong. He should have led that battle in which your grandfather was killed. But Meeme didn't want to go into that battle. In his opinion it was a terribly stupid idea—to fight the iron men with their own weapons. Even the wolves were left at home, and we walked on foot to the battlefield, where the iron men smashed us to a pulp with ease. Meeme could foresee this, and said that such warfare was madness. But no one listened to him."

"Why?"

"Because many thought the iron men were cleverer than us. They secretly admired their coats of mail and shiny swords, even though they were marching to war against them. They thought that riding on wolves and fighting in the thickets was outmoded and senseless, and that no modern army fights like that. When Meeme explained to them that we ought to stick to our own ancient weapons, many people confirmed that such a tactic was downright suicidal. "We should learn from developed peoples," they said. "And if the iron men fight on an open field and without wolves, then that is more correct and efficient. They must know what's good! After all, they sailed here from faraway lands! We should learn from them, not go into battle like some primates. We shouldn't bring the name of Estonians to shame like that! Let the iron men see that we too know how to fight like humans! We aren't one iota worse than any other nation! And so they went to war on foot, without wolves, and took with them the weapons they had seized from the iron men. And naturally they were defeated. Apart from my father, no one came off that field alive, and he was saved only by his fangs, the most ancient weapon, one that has now totally disappeared from human mouths."

Uncle Vootele picked a fiber of meat from between his teeth, swallowed it, and carried on talking.

"Then Meeme started battling the iron men single-handed, and he didn't use a sword or a spear, but good old Snakish words, which drove all the animals crazy. They went on an enraged attack against the iron men, when Meeme simply gave the command. He conducted his own battles at the edge of the wood, ambushing iron men who had strayed there. Wolves leapt on the iron men from among the trees and dragged these foreigners into the thickets, where Meeme chopped them to bits with a good old ax. It certainly wasn't the sort of war that the iron men like to wage, and it was far from modern, but very effective. The iron men feared the forest like fire, for they knew that death lay in wait there. And they couldn't avoid the forest—they had to ride past or through it—and many of them didn't come out the other side. You can only imagine what we could have achieved if all men had acted like Meeme and slaughtered the foreigners in the forest with the aid of Snakish words and wolves, instead of riding onto the open battlefield. Meeme alone did the work of ten men, but even that didn't break him.

"But even though Meeme fought like a madman and chopped at the iron men like lightning, that did nothing to stop more and more people moving to live in the village. Meeme cleared the forest of foreigners, but there was no point in that anymore. The forest became ever emptier, and Meeme, who had made it his goal to save his people and kill the iron men, saw that his people were thronging to take up the beliefs of these same iron men, to buy themselves a little plot of land, turn their bums toward the sun, and cut grain from the ground on all fours with a sickle. Why should Meeme carry on fighting? He saw that people didn't need his help. Then Meeme would only kill iron men when they got in his way; the rest of the time he ate mushrooms and slept."

"Now he drinks wine," I said.

"Makes no difference. There's no order for him anymore; he's given up on everything, and now he wants to rest alone."

I thanked Uncle Vootele and set off. Uncle's story had been very interesting, but the main thing was that it confirmed my belief in the ring. Meeme, the former bold warrior, could be the man to give me the key. He didn't keep it for himself because nothing interested him anymore, not even the Frog of the North. This was hard for me to imagine. How could he give up even on the Frog of the North? How could he be so tired?

But that was not my concern. I hurried home and looked for my ring. I took it out of the pouch and stuck it on the end of my finger.

I had secretly hoped that some mysterious power would lead me by the fingers toward the cave of the Frog of the North if I simply ran fast enough while wearing the ring, but no such thing happened. The ring sat on the end of my finger as a ring always does, and I understood that the search for the Frog of the North would not be simple.

At any fate I was ready to make the effort. But I didn't want to search alone. I couldn't find Pärtel—he wasn't at home—but I met with Ints and invited him along with me.

The adder agreed readily. Unlike the blooming fern, whose existence he vehemently denied, Ints thought it quite possible that the ring might lead us to the Frog of the North.

"I don't know anything about rings and other man-made things," he said. "If you think that's the key, then let's try and find out. How does it work?"

"I don't know that," I said. "We should simply keep walking, and the ring will lead us itself to the right place."

We set off. We tried to move completely randomly, not choosing the paths we usually wandered. I even tried shutting my eyes, so as to walk blind, but that proved too complicated in the forest, for I kept stumbling into thickets and scratching my face.

"Open your eyes," said Ints. "If the ring is really capable of anything, then you don't need all this trickery and your skin will survive."

To snakes, skin is very important. Every snake is proud of his skin. Even the smallest scratch they experience as painful, and if anything does happen, they wait patiently for the time when they can slough off the old skin and wear a new undamaged coat. After moulting they are very sensitive about their appearance, and they may fly into a rage if you happen, say, to drip roasting fat onto them, or touch them with fingers stained violet from eating berries. Toward their old moulted skin, torn in several places, they feel only disgust or even horror. In the long winter months, when snakes don't leave their lairs, mother adders tell their offspring countless horror stories about moulted skins that move of their own accord in a mysterious way, chasing their former owners and wrapping themselves around them. The little adders shiver, and when Mother finishes the story they beg her: "Tell it again! Tell us about the skin again!"

So much for that. For a while Ints wore a still quite fresh and moist glossy skin; he crawled carefully among the tussocks and tried to avoid decaying leaves, which might smudge him. We kept moving forward, chatting with each other, till we came unexpectedly to the edge of the forest, where the trees ended and an open plain began, in the middle of which a narrow path meandered. And on that path a monk was walking.

When I was very small I thought that monks were the wives of the iron men, since they wore the same kinds of wide dresses that women do. True, they weren't very good-looking, and I did wonder why the iron men had such ugly spouses. The iron men didn't look nice either, and as a little boy I was sure that their faces were made of iron and that they had no noses or mouths. Only later did I see iron men taking their helmets off, and I understood that they were also human. Likewise, I also once happened to see a monk pissing, and I ran to Uncle Vootele, breathless with anxiety, my eyes burning in my head: "Uncle, Uncle! The monk has a willy!"

"Of course, all men have them," answered Uncle Vootele.

"Is the monk a man then? I thought she was an iron man's wife."

Uncle Vootele laughed and assured me that wasn't so. At first I couldn't believe him and put forward some counterclaims.

"But they have tits. I've seen them bouncing under their dresses. And they're pregnant too. Surely a man can't be pregnant?"

"They're not pregnant, and they don't have tits either. They're simply very fat, the fat runs around them like resin on a spruce."

The monk who was now striding along the path was also fat. He noticed me and slowed his pace, but then obviously thought I was alone and didn't present any danger. He didn't see Ints, because he was hidden in the grass. But the monk did immediately see the ring on my finger. He stared at it and said something in his own language.

"I don't understand," I replied, and hissed the same in Snakish, but the monk didn't understand either language. He came up to me, squinting at my ring, looked around quickly, and seeing that the coast was clear, grabbed me with one hand by the scruff of the neck, while his other hand pulled the ring off my finger.

I hissed the strongest Snakish words into his face, but since the monk didn't understand them, they had no effect on him. He was like the hedgehog who could calmly attack an adder, since his stupid head defended him from all the Snakish words. The monk gave me a smack on the back of the head and pushed me away, at the same time putting the ring in his mouth—apparently to hide and defend a precious thing from others.

I was hissing frantically and wanted to bite the monk, but Ints got in ahead of me. The monk screamed with pain and collapsed, with two bleeding spots on his shin.

Now he was much lower, and Ints managed to bite him on the throat. The adder jumped; the monk screamed and grabbed with his hand, but that didn't help. Two little fang marks reddened on his neck, right on a vein.

"Thanks, Ints. But I want my ring back!" I said.

"Let's wait until he dies, then we'll take it from his mouth," suggested Ints. We went back into the forest, for the monk's painful yells and moans were disturbing us, and we stretched out happily in the cool of the trees, until everything went quiet. Then we came out of the forest. The monk was dead, but when I prized his jaws open, to my great disappointment the creature's mouth was empty.

"He's swallowed it," said Ints.

"What shall we do now?" I cried. "He's dead now, which means that he won't shit anymore. Are we supposed to wait until he rots away?"

"Cut him to pieces," suggested Ints.

"I don't have such a big knife," I said. "Just a little sheath knife, I'd be sawing all day with that. And I can't drag him home; he's terribly fat and heavy. And I can't leave him here and go home for a knife, because meanwhile someone might come by and take him away or eat him up—and then I'll be without my ring. But, say, Ints, couldn't you squeeze inside him? He's so big that there'd be easily room for you to crawl in. Then maybe you could bring the ring out in your mouth."

"I don't want to go in there," replied Ints. "He's bound to be terribly filthy inside. I'll get covered in smudges, and my skin is so new and beautiful."

"Please, Ints! You're my friend, after all. Afterward you can go and wash yourself in the lake."

"No, I'm not going inside all that mush. But I know what to do. We'll invite a slowworm."

Slowworms were not actually snakes, but simply legless lizards. Adders paid them no attention, since they thought that slowworms were trying to compare themselves with snakes, while being nothing like as clever, and therefore not deserving the name of snake. But they used slowworms to carry out irksome tasks, such as this one. Ints hissed, and pretty soon a long slowworm came slithering closer through the grass and lay submissively before the adder.

"Go inside that monk and look for a ring," Ints commanded.

The slowworm nodded and wriggled nimbly into the monk's mouth. Soon we saw the neck of the corpse bulging and then falling back; the slowworm had crawled through it.

For a while nothing happened. Finally Ints tilted his head and announced, "I think I hear the slowworm's voice. Can you hear it?"

I had to admit I couldn't hear anything, and no wonder. Adders have far sharper hearing. Ints crawled over to the monk's stomach and listened intently.

"Yes, he says he's found the ring, but can't manage to bring it out. It won't fit in his mouth. I think you'd better make a little hole into the monk with your sheath knife, then the slowworm will push the ring out through it."

"Where exactly am I supposed to make the hole?" I asked, taking out the knife. Ints showed me the place. I started cutting. It was quite difficult, because apart from the skin of the stomach I had to also cut a thick layer of fat that covered the monk's belly. The knife had almost vanished among the creases when finally Ints cried, "The slowworm says he can see your knife! Now make the hole wider."

Now even I could hear the slowworm's hissing. I twisted the knife in my hand, and in this way I prepared a hole through which the ring would fit.

"Now push!" Ints commanded the slowworm.

Movement could be seen under the hole, and after a while the luster of gold began to appear from inside the monk. The ring emerged into the daylight. I caught it by the fingers and in a moment the ring was in my hand. It was slimy and bloody, but I rubbed it clean against the grass and popped it onto my finger.

"Come out now!" said Ints to the slowworm. "Everything's all right."

After a little while the slowworm became visible, but he didn't come out of the monk's mouth but out of the fringe of his dress.

"I didn't turn back," he hissed.

"Thank you so much," I said. "Come by our place another time—my mother will give you a haunch of venison."

"With great pleasure!" promised the slowworm, and disappeared into the forest.

"Did you notice how he looked?" Ints asked in a whisper. "Horrible! I couldn't imagine crawling through all that. What would be left of my skin? No fountain could ever wash off that filth."

"The slowworm is the color of shit anyway, so it doesn't look too bad on him," I said.

We considered continuing the search for the Frog of the North, but evening had fallen by now, and we both had empty stomachs. We decided to go home and eat, and look for the Frog of the North some other time.

"Anyway I don't believe this is the right ring anymore," said Ints when we had set off homeward. "A real ring would never have ended up in a monk's stomach. The Frog of the North doesn't live in anyone's intestines!"

"That was just unlucky!" I said, but Ints shook his head doubtfully.

Seven

e went in search of our fortune with the ring a few more times, but it was no use. The Frog of the North could not be found. Each time our journey ended with us at some point not wanting to go on any farther, and just stopping to eat blueberries.

Finally I came to the conclusion that the ring I received as a gift was not the right ring, or if it was, its use required a lot of effort and the sort of knowledge I didn't have. I lost interest in the ring, stuffed it back in its leather pouch, and got on with other things.

In my search for the Frog of the North I had often come upon the Primates' hut. Naturally I already knew them, because quite a few of us humans had remained in the forest. And Pirre and Rääk were actually human, though hairier than any of us. That was plain to see, since they didn't wear animal skins, but walked around stark naked. They claimed that that was their ancient custom, and that the decline of our people hadn't started with moving to the village or eating bread, but with putting on alien creatures' skins and adopting iron tools stolen from ships. There wasn't a speck of metal in their home, just hand axes made of stone. These were clumsy and almost shapeless, but Pirre and Rääk assured us they sat comfortably in the hand and were healthy to use.

"It's our own stone, not some foreign iron," they said. "When you take a stone like this in your hand, it gives you strength, massages your palms, and calms your nerves. In the olden days, with these stone axes you did all the work; you were in a good mood and nobody got upset."

Unlike Tambet, who also held sacred the ways of his ancestors and tried steadfastly to walk their well-worn paths, Pirre and Rääk were very mild. They didn't demand anything of anyone. They didn't want other people to bare their bottoms, and they never quarreled when they saw someone with a knife in their belt or a brooch on their jacket. If anyone had visited Tambet carrying a piece of bread, he might have set his wolves on that person as punishment for their impertinence, or at least cursed such a village lickspittle in the strongest terms. Pirre and Rääk, on the other hand, never spoke ill of anybody. They were friendly and hospitable, and were not offended even when a visitor declined to eat the half-cooked hunk of meat they offered them. "Well, you're not used to it," they would say kindly and laugh, their yellow fangs glistening. "You eat burned food. Doesn't matter. How about we char this bit of meat till it's black for you, if you like it better that way. But it isn't healthy for you. The olden people all ate half-cooked meat; it's good for the digestion. You don't want any grubs? What a waste; they used to be our people's favorite delicacy! Look, you take a grub, squeeze it empty onto your tongue. Mm! Delicious!"

They screwed up their eyes with pleasure and licked the grub mash off their lips, and yet their display of ecstatic enjoyment didn't ever convince me to taste this delicacy. Pirre and Rääk didn't impose their preferences on me, though. They roasted my piece of meat blackish brown and wished me a good appetite, laughing sunnily. Then they let me eat in peace, while they combed through each other's hairs and picked out spruce needles, ants, and spiders.

Even as a little boy I had visited Pirre and Rääk now and then, at first with Uncle Vootele, later alone or with Pärtel. But while searching for the Frog of the North I got to know the Primates better. A couple of times I even stayed the night with them, when an all-day hike through the forest had worn me out, and I didn't have the strength to go home in the evening. My mother knew that nothing could happen to me in the forest, because I already knew the Snakish words well, and thanks to them I had nothing to fear. So she didn't worry if I didn't turn up at home for the night. Sometimes I slept at Ints's snake nest, sometimes at Uncle Vootele's place. But lately I had liked being at the Primates' home, because there were lice there.

Pirre and Rääk were breeding them.

Lice were their pets. The Primates had no children, so they directed all their tenderness and care to lice. The lice lived in specially built cages; there were plenty of them and a whole range of sizes and shapes. There were quite ordinary gray lice, but also frog-sized ones, creatures that were specially bred and fed, which Pirre and Rääk would sometimes take in their laps and stroke with their hairy hands. Most interesting of all, all these lice obeyed their masters. As I have said, insects don't generally understand Snakish words. You can talk to an ant as much as you like; you will make no headway. A grasshopper disturbing your sleep with its chirping will crackle into song regardless of your having repeatedly yelled words of Snakish at it that would have immediately struck any other creature dumb. It isn't possible to make a spider or a ladybird understand Snakish; they are born idiots. Lice are also actually extremely obtuse creatures that would normally never obey your will. All the more remarkable, then, that Pirre and Rääk had trained them up like clever fighting wolves.

The lice did exactly what their master and mistress commanded. They would approach closer, lie down, get into line, climb on each other's backs, roll along the ground like fox cubs. If you stretched out a hand to them, they would politely offer you a paw.

All of these tricks they would do only at Pirre's and Rääk's command. If I tried to force them to do anything, they wouldn't move a muscle. I was very disappointed, because I knew I spoke Snakish very well, no worse than the Primates did. When I asked Pirre and Rääk why they didn't comprehend my Snakish words, the Primates laughed heartily.

"Ordinary Snakish words aren't enough," they said. "Listen carefully to the way we speak to them; we pronounce Snakish in the old Primate way. Long ago, when our ancestors were still living in caves and didn't know fire, they had power over insects. How else would they have survived the attacks of the gadflies and mosquitoes that could freely get at them, without campfire smoke to scare them away? Nowadays their ancient pronunciation has been forgotten. Even we can't speak it as they did tens of thousands of years ago. Of all the insects, we can only communicate with lice, which have lived in the fur of animals for a long time and learned a few things from them. But it's beyond our powers even to scare away blackflies. It's sad that the old skills die out."

It was a pity for me too, because I myself would have liked to keep mosquitoes and gadflies away from me using Snakish. They were disgusting creatures and they bit painfully. Now I was trying to at least learn how to talk to the lice, but it was too hard a nut to crack. No matter how much I practiced, I just couldn't pronounce the Snakish words like Pirre and Rääk. The difference was minute, but whether I liked it or not, my tongue slipped back into the old furrow.

Pirre and Rääk said I shouldn't bother myself, since it wasn't possible to learn Primate pronunciation.

"It must be inborn, just as your forefathers had inborn fangs," they told me. "You can sharpen your teeth as much as you like, and rinse your mouth with any sort of infusion, but your teeth won't ever become poisonous. That's how it is with our language. You are not a Primate. Our families are related, yes, but our ways parted long, long ago. You don't have a tail, either."

Indeed I did not have a tail, unlike Pirre and Rääk, who had a soft little bulge growing out of their behinds. So I no longer tried talking to the lice, and only wanted to know whether they were able to command only their own trained lice, or whether they could manage with an unfamiliar louse as well.

"We think we could," replied Pirre and Rääk. Incidentally, they always spoke together, one saying one word, the other the next, so it wasn't possible to understand with which Primate you were talking. In fact it wasn't possible to imagine them apart; they were always together, moving around side by side, and sitting clinging to each other. I don't know whether this was from their great love, or whether hanging on to each other is simply a Primate habit. Apart from Pirre and Rääk I didn't know any other Primates. There probably weren't any. They were the last of their kind.

In any case, I sought out a bear in the forest, and asked him to give me a louse. The bear agreed happily. At the time he was skulking around the home of a friend of my sister's, and I had a sneaking suspicion they had an assignation, because bears simply can't keep away from girls. This bear must have had some affair going on with my sister's friend, but that wasn't my business. As long as he didn't trouble my sister. I took some lice from the bear and left him sitting under a bush.

A bear like that, on the prowl for a woman, may sit patiently in one place for several days, without eating or drinking, his head cocked, his paws meekly on his belly, and a silly lovesick expression on his face. It makes a huge impression on a girl. "Oh, what a sweet teddy!" they sigh tenderly, and the bear, having managed to create the desired impression, gets to his feet and shambles awkwardly over to his beloved, a globeflower picked from a meadow in his teeth. And when he has continued to show his skill by weaving a dandelion wreath and putting it on his own half-cocked head, then not a single woman can resist such an idyllic scene.

I took the lice I'd received from the bear to Pirre and Rääk, and after the Primates had tenderly stroked them and let them scurry over their hairy fingers for a while, they commanded the lice to lie on their backs—and the creatures did so, waving their legs in the air.

"You see, they obey!" said Pirre and Rääk joyfully. "Smart creatures! We'll let them in with the others; we've got enough room." They could never have enough lice; they picked up every one they came across.

At this time Pirre and Rääk had another exciting task in hand. They had already bred frog-sized lice, but only a few, and wanted to breed lice that were the size of goats. The sturdier lice were separated from the smaller ones, they were allowed to multiply, and from these the very hugest were selected. This did not take long, however, as the lice bred quickly and had plenty of offspring. A few months later a goat-sized louse was born. I have to say that it was an impossibly hideous creature. With a little louse, the ugliness wasn't visible, as it was simply a little speck, but a big louse was the most unpleasant animal you can imagine. Pirre and Rääk didn't think so. They were very pleased with their monster.

"In the olden days, all animals were much bigger than today," they said. "There were incredibly bulky creatures living in the world, which have died out by now, or gone into hiding to sleep forever in darkness. A big animal has a big sleep! They may never wake again, and nobody will see these magnificent giants again. So it's so nice to see this louse, which will do very well bustling about on the fur of some terribly huge and ancient creature. Leemet, look at it carefully! Before you, you see a fragment of a world of hundreds of thousands of years ago!"

I looked at that fragment and I didn't like it at all. I was very pleased to be living now, not hundreds of thousands of years before. I wasn't about to say that to Pirre and Rääk, but for form's sake I praised their louse, and I even agreed to take the animal for a walk, because the Primates thought it needed exercise. Pirre and Rääk themselves strayed away from their cave extremely rarely, since a little piece of primeval thicket remained just around their home, consisting of strange plants that had died out long ago elsewhere that Pirre and Rääk ate, and from which they harvested their grubs. Away from this little ancient ground they didn't feel at home.

I invited Ints and Pärtel along, attached the leash to the louse, and took it walking in the woods. The insect was indeed the size of a goat, but extremely stupid. Apparently it couldn't understand that it was no longer the size of a seed and tried to fit through the narrowest slits, expressing an insane eagerness as it did so. It didn't care about our injunctions, but tried obstinately to press into some little holes that were a tenth its size. As a result the louse often got trapped, flailing its legs helplessly until we heaved it out with great effort. It was a terrible nuisance, and we decided to take it for a walk in some clearer place where it couldn't climb anywhere.

We went to the lakeshore, but the louse was even stupider than we had thought. It didn't perceive at all that the surface of the water was not the same as the grass, rushed headlong straight to the lake, and naturally fell in.

"Can this bastard swim?" squealed Pärtel, and I couldn't really answer him, because I was no expert on lice. But after a few moments it became clear that it could swim after all, since it rose to the surface and floundered in the water, but again so stupidly that it steered away from us instead to keeping to the shore.

"It won't be able to swim across the lake," said Ints. "It will get tired out and sink to the bottom. And as far as I'm concerned it can stay there; such an animal is no use to anyone."

"I'm afraid I'll still have to go in the water and try and save it," I said. "Pirre and Rääk would be angry if we didn't bring it back. It was entrusted to me and I'm responsible for it."

I stripped naked and was ready to jump into the water when somebody sternly stopped me.

It was Ülgas the Sage.

"Where's your sense, boy!" he asked angrily. "Don't you know this lake is sacred? This is the home of the lake-sprite to whom I always sacrifice two squirrels when the moon is young, so that he will stay in the lake and not let our homes drown in its currents. You must not swim here. It would anger the sprite terribly! First he would pull you down under the water, and then he would flood the whole forest. Get dressed immediately and get out of here, your friend too. The lake-sprite loves silence. He must not be disturbed."

"I'm sorry for that, but I want to catch that beast!" I said. Ülgas scowled at the louse splashing in the lake, and his face became pale.

"But that's the lake-sprite himself!" he muttered, falling to his knees, as if at that moment his shinbone had broken in half. "The sacred lake-sprite is showing himself to us. What could it mean?"

He stared at the louse bobbing in the water, his eyes big with wonder.

"Boys, you've offended him in some way!" he thundered, raising his arms heavenward. "He came for you, and I must not let you go. The sprite has the right to a sacrifice."

"That is a louse, not a sprite," said Ints scornfully. Adders didn't believe in sprites, just as they didn't believe in blooming ferns. They knew the forest inside out, and they knew what lives there and what does not. They did not stop people from going to the sacred grove and bringing sacrifices, although in their eyes it was completely senseless. Adders never interfered in other beings' affairs, as long as it didn't affect them directly. In their view, everyone has the right to live their lives just as foolishly as they like.

Clearly, then, the sight of a snake did not exactly please the Sage of the Grove. He eyed Ints disdainfully and then looked again at the louse swimming in the water.

"What are you talking about? What louse?" he said. "Lice are small. That is the lake-sprite. I ought to know such things. Don't make him even angrier!"

"It really is a louse," I assured him, and I told Ülgas about Pirre and Rääk's experiments. The mention of Primates didn't make the sage any happier, because, just like the adders, the Primates didn't believe in sprites, and never visited the grove. "In ancient times there weren't any groves, and these sprites were only invented later," they would explain. "In those days long ago, when the woods were still full of Primates, people would bow in homage to other beings than those, but sadly, we no longer remember who they were and how they were worshipped."

At any rate Ülgas still didn't want to believe that it was an ordinary, if oversized, louse swimming in the water, and not the lake-sprite. Unfortunately at that moment the bug managed to flounder closer to the shore, so that its legs reached the bottom and it clambered onto dry land. It was wet and drooping, shivering a little, and tried instantly to scuttle down into a pine root.

"Now you see that it isn't a sprite," I said. "Apparently it just looks like a sprite. I didn't know that sprites look like big lice."

Ülgas the Sage glowered angrily at the louse.

"Boy," he said then, having turned his back decisively on the creature and putting his heavy hand on my shoulder. "I want to tell you that you have dishonored the lake-sprite by throwing that horrible animal into the water. The sprite's domain is polluted and I will have to bring him many sacrifices to quell his rage. And you must help me, since you are most to blame for angering the sprite. Come back here at midnight tonight and bring with you all the wolves from your barn. This time, squirrels' blood won't be enough! I must do everything in my power to stop the sprite from avenging this indignity."

"Mother won't let me have the wolves killed! They give us milk."

"Your mother will have to get used to it, because her son has done evil!"

There was no trace left of the kindly old granddad; with his burning eyes and whiskers trembling with rage, the sage more resembled a rat standing on his hind legs. "A mother is responsible for her son. And she is guilty too, because if she went to the grove every week as she should, and took you with her, she would know that one has to be very respectful to sprites, and you would know that too. In the olden days people went to the grove every day, to show respect to the powerful forces of nature and to earn their goodwill and friendship. Then it wouldn't have occurred to any brat that he could throw a filthy louse into a sacred lake. Leemet, terrible things will happen to you if you don't respect the sprites! Even I can't placate the nature spirits if you anger them with this shameless behavior. You really would be better off listening to me, instead of befriending Primates and snakes too much. They may be our brothers, of course, but they're quite a different breed."

Ülgas's talk had scared me. Did I really have to bring all our wolves to the lakeshore, so that the sage could slit their throats and buy the friendship of the lake-sprite with their blood? What would Mother say? We needed the wolves. Of course we could get new animals—there were many abandoned wolves whose masters had moved to the village trotting round the woods—but that kind of much-traveled wolf didn't give much milk. It would take a long time for them to get used to a new pack. And anyway, replacing the wolves would be inconvenient and I had a very bad feeling in my heart. In the end I wasn't to blame that the louse rushed into the water. I tried to explain that to Ülgas, but he said that it didn't matter, since the lake-sprite was angry anyway, and that awful things would happen if he wasn't given wolves' blood. He commanded me to be at the grove with the wolves at exactly midnight, adding that in the olden days wolves alone would not have sufficed. In olden days the guilty party— meaning myself—would have had to be cut into pieces and thrown into the lake. But he, Ülgas, was such a skillful sage and such a great friend of the lake-sprite that he was able to placate the sprite with wolf flesh alone. Or at least he would try.

This kind of talk terrified me even more. What if his attempt failed and Ülgas decided to sacrifice me to the sprite after all? We sneaked away from the lakeshore, leaving Ülgas muttering some spells.

I had a very bad feeling, as any child would who has done something naughty and now has to go home to tell his mother. At the same time I knew that the sooner I got this horrible business off my shoulders the better. I wanted to pass the decision on to my mother. Let her tell me what to do: whether to go at midnight to the lakeshore with the wolves or not.

I asked Ints and Pärtel to take the louse back to Pirre and Rääk, while I ran home.

Eight

t home, Mother was waiting for me, her face beaming with pleasure.

"Leemet, guess what I've brought you today!" she asked conspiratorially, and immediately announced, "Owls' eggs! Two for you and two for Salme."

I felt even lousier. Owls' eggs were my favorite food, and it was by no means easy for Mother to get them, because at that time she was getting fat, and climbing up a tree to an owl's nest with a frame like hers was quite a feat. To tell the truth, it was always frightening to watch Mother climb, because you felt that at any moment the branch might break under her weight and she would fall and break her bones. Uncle Vootele had told Mother that she shouldn't climb to the treetops like that, that I should go in her place, but Mother replied that she knew how to choose eggs, and anyway she liked being up in the trees.

"A bit of movement and exercise can only do me good," she said, and I often heard her calls as I roamed around the forest and saw her gesturing from some terribly high top of a spruce, a broad grin on her face. Mother was astonishingly nimble when it came to searching for delicate morsels for her children, and food generally.

All those dangers that Mother had to overcome in fetching owls' eggs made the delicacy especially precious, and I was dreadfully ashamed that in return for the eggs I had nothing to offer except the news that her wolves would that night have to be taken to the lakeside and bled to death. I mumbled that I was terribly glad about the eggs, though I didn't start eating them, but slipped quietly behind the table and waited for the opportunity to talk about the louse and Ülgas.

At the same time, sister Salme was enjoying the taste of the owls' eggs, slurping greedily and licking her lips. I felt envious watching her, seeing that her brow with its white hair was not furrowed by trouble, unlike mine. Mother noticed my strange expression and asked if I was sore anywhere.

"No," I said. "But . . . Look, I want to tell you something."

"Eat up your eggs first," Mother suggested. "And then I'll bring you a cold flank of venison to the table; you can't have eaten anything today. Where do you run around all day? Were you with the snakes?"

"Mother, I don't want to eat now. I was at Pirre and Rääk's today . . ."

"Why do you go there?" Salme interrupted me. "I think they look horrible. Why do they go around naked all the time? It's obscene! I get sick in the tummy when I see that lot. That Rääk's breasts hanging down to her navel, dangling like two great hairy oak leaves. And Pirre has such a big tool that when he sits he takes it in his lap; otherwise his willy lies on the ground like a tail and the ants get inside."

"Salme, what are you saying?" gasped Mother. "Why do you stare at such things anyway?"

"How could I not stare, when he shows it off to everyone? That's just why I'm saying it. I think it's horrible! I get a pain in the tummy when I see those two. And then there's their bottoms! They don't even have hairs growing there! Completely bare and purple, like two big berries in a bunch!"

"Then close your eyes," said Mother.

"Why should I close my eyes? Let those apes put something on their arses! My eyes don't bother anyone, but their thingumy-bobs are completely gross! Other girls say it too. Just thinking about Pirre's dick and Rääk's tits makes you lose your appetite."

"Well, don't think about them then!" exclaimed Mother. "I don't think about them at all. I never see them; they don't move around the forest much."

"Luckily!" snorted Salme. "But I wouldn't be surprised if Leemet invited them around here one day. He hangs around those apes all the time. Leemet, I'm telling you: if you bring those purple-arsed Pirre and Rääk around here, I won't be sleeping or eating in this house anymore!"

"Oh no, Leemet won't be inviting them," Mother assured Salme. "And they wouldn't come either. But what were you doing there, Leemet? What's so interesting there?"

"They bred a louse the size of a goat," I said. "And Ints and Pärtel and I took it for a walk."

I took a deep breath, because now I wanted to get the whole horrible story off my chest, but Mother and Salme wouldn't let me. For a while they debated why anyone would need to breed a louse the size of a goat, and whether such a louse would be dangerous to humans, and whether Salme dared to go out in the forest at all.

"What can it do to you?" wondered Mother. "You can shout at it, or hit it with a pinecone. That'll send it running."

"You don't know anything," snorted Salme. "An animal like that wouldn't be afraid of anything. Only an ape could invent such a stupid thing. But just you wait—I'll tell Mõmmi about this louse, and Mõmmi will break it to pieces."

"Who's Mõmmi?" asked Mother, her voice now becoming icy and wary, because it wasn't hard to guess what sort of animal was hidden by that very ursine name. "It's a bear," replied Salme reluctantly. She realized that she'd said too much, but now it was too late to bite her lip.

"How do you know him?" demanded Mother, and to my dismay I understood that now the conversation was taking a whole different direction, and it would be very difficult for me to come out with my own worries. Bears were a sore point with Mother, and if she feared one thing in this world, it was that her daughter would follow her bad example.

"I saw him one day in the forest," said Salme. "We don't really know each other; we've just seen each other a couple of times. Mother, don't go on about it! I know you don't like any bear, but Mõmmi's very friendly, and actually I'm not going out with him. We just say hello when we meet."

"Salme, you're too young to be carrying on with bears!" said Mother, and sat with a frightened look on her face, as if lightning had just struck the roof of her shack and set fire to the whole place.

"I'm not carrying on! Did you hear what I said, Mother? We just say hello!"

"You don't need to say hello either."

"Well, how else— It's polite! You have to say hello to those you know."

"You don't need to know anyone like that."

"Mother!"

"Salme, bears think about only one thing!"

"Interesting. What thing?"

"You know perfectly well! Salme, I don't want you to meet that Mõmmi anymore. Bears are very handsome and strong, but they bring trouble."

Salme snuffled crossly.

"Maybe they bring trouble to you, but not to me! Mõmmi brings me strawberries and lingonberries!"

"Strawberries and lingonberries!" shrieked Mother, and burst into tears. "That's just it. Strawberries and lingonberries were what they brought me too! That's how it starts. They're great ones for bringing strawberries and lingonberries! No, I knew it! If you've got a daughter in the house, there's no getting away from bears. They swarm around like lizards in the sunshine! So what am I supposed to do? Where should I hide you? A bear will get in anywhere, climb up a tree or scratch a hole in the ground. Oh, those dreadful animals!"

Mother's face flushed and Salme was likewise as red as a rowanberry. They scowled at each other, Salme's expression full of defiance, Mother's marked by desperate anguish. She must have felt that she was seeing her daughter for the last time—that soon a big bear would come and take Salme away to his lair. From her own experiences with bears, she knew that once you get to know one, he will pounce on you. For a while they fell silent, and I felt that now was my last chance to talk about what happened by the lake.

Mother listened unmoved at first, still eyeing Salme and thinking about the bear, but by the time I got to the end of my tale,
she looked at me in dismay and said, "Now wait, Leemet! Tell
me one more time! That's horrible!"

I told her again. Mother looked by turns at me and at Salme,
as if having to decide which child's tale was more appalling.
In any case mine was more urgent, as midnight was fast approaching, whereas nothing could be done at the moment about
Mõmmi the bear. But in the state she was in, Mother could not
do anything about my situation. Two pieces of bad news following each other had the effect on her of sitting dumbstruck,
her arms folded, looking despairingly at me.

Salme, on the other hand, became furious on hearing my
story.

"You're absolutely impossible!" she screamed. "Poor wolves,
what are they guilty of? They gave good milk. You'll ruin us!
Have you no shame?"

"What should I do then, Mother?" I asked unhappily, ignoring
Salme. Naturally I felt ashamed, so terrible that my guts ached. I
would very gladly have curled up in a ball in a corner, but that
wasn't possible. Waiting by the lake was the angry sage, and I
wanted my mother to take all the decisions; I didn't want to un-
dertake anything more myself. "Should I go to the lake or not?"

"I don't know," sighed Mother, utterly helpless. She was completely deflated. "All our wolves . . . "

"Why do you need to mess around with that disgusting
louse?" yelled Salme. "Who's going to give us milk now, you
idiot?"

"And what about the cuddly bears?" I muttered, whereupon
Salme almost exploded and hit me with a hunk of venison.

"Children, stop it!" begged Mother and started to cry. "All this news . . . all at once . . . I really don't know what to do."

"It will soon be midnight," I insisted. "Should I go to the lakeside? Tell me!"

I tugged frantically at Mother's sleeve.

"I don't know," repeated Mother. "It's so horrible."

She wept quietly, wiping her eyes with her sleeve.

I started to cry too.

Salme had been crying a long time already, from her deep insult and anger.

Then Uncle Vootele arrived.

He always had the habit of stopping by in the evenings and listening to how the day had gone. This time he of course saw immediately that something was very wrong. He stood perplexed for a moment on the threshold, but I leapt up to meet him, pulled him inside, and started—prattling and sobbing—to relate the terrible misfortune that befell me by the lakeside. Uncle Vootele was my last hope, because Mother certainly couldn't help me now. But Uncle was wise and clever. I told him everything— about the Primates, the louse, the sage, and the lake-sprite—and Salme studded my tale with some venomous interjections to show that she was much older and smarter, and would never have brought such a calamity on her own family. But I didn't care about Salme; the important thing for me was the chance to speak. And when I finished, I looked appealingly at Uncle Vootele, with one single entreaty: please do something and save me from my responsibility!

"That's a completely silly story!" said Uncle Vootele.

"I told you Leemet is completely silly!" Salme chimed in. "How can he let some disgusting thing swim in the lake?"

"The lake is a lake," replied Uncle Vootele. "Anyone can swim there. I don't understand why any wolves have to die for a lake. Ülgas has gone mad."

"He's a Sage of the Grove, though," Mother interjected, wiping her tears, although it was evident that Uncle Vootele's arrival had improved her mood. She blew her nose, got up, and started cutting meat for Uncle. "Might he be satisfied with just one wolf? I think that should be enough to satisfy the lake-sprite. There's a lot of blood in one wolf."

"What lake-sprite?" Uncle Vootele asked. "Have you ever seen a sprite in your life?"

"Well, it's a sort of custom, you know, an old habit. Sacrifices are always being brought to the sprites. Otherwise why would there be a sage?"

"I've never really understood that exactly," said Uncle Vootele. "But all right, there are habits and customs, which bring people together, and sometimes it's pleasant to stand in the grove and watch Ülgas burning his stalks and singing something. But to kill a whole pack of wolves just like that, that's plain stupidity. The blood will pollute the lake much more than one unfortunate louse. I'll come with you myself, Leemet, and I'll talk to Ülgas."

"You could take one wolf with you, just in case," suggested Mother.

"Not a single one," said Uncle. "Let them rest in the barn. And let's have something to eat now, and stop fretting. I see you even have owls' eggs!"

"You can have them," I said, looking at Uncle, positively enraptured. Suddenly my heart was as light as if a great stone had been cut out of me, and I felt ravenously hungry, as the hollow that had grown had to be filled. But I was happy to give my owls' eggs to Uncle, because he was my hero. Uncle thanked me with a smile.

"I'll eat one; you have the other," he said. "Nice to see you getting your human faces back. When I stepped in, I thought something really awful had happened."

"I was really terribly shocked when I heard I had to sacrifice all my wolves," said Mother. She was calm again, as always, and kept bringing more hunks of venison from the larder, although Uncle Vootele had long ago held up a restraining hand. "Now everything's all right. Off you go and talk to Ülgas."

"Yes, I'll talk to him," promised Uncle. I sucked happily on my owl's egg and Salme seemed likewise pretty satisfied, since the latest events had chased Mõmmi out of Mother's mind at least for a while.

A little before midnight Uncle Vootele and I set out on our way. I felt completely secure with him, and no longer feared Ülgas at all. What could he do to me, with Uncle Vootele defending me? Let him sacrifice his own long nose to the sprite, if he wanted to spill some blood!

It was dark by the lake and the water glistened dimly. Even now in the middle of summer, the lake seemed to be covered with a strange black ice, and you could easily believe that underneath lived a bloodthirsty sprite. I felt a little uneasy and would have liked to hold Uncle Vootele by the hand, but I was too ashamed, because I saw myself as a big boy now. So I just stood close enough to Uncle to smell the consolation of his scent.

"Ülgas!" cried Uncle. "Are you here?"

"Yes, I am here," the sage's voice resounded. "Very good that you came with the boy, Vootele. You will help me with the sacrifice and keep the wolves' legs bound. You must have heard what a terrible desecration your nephew committed."

"I did indeed," said Uncle. "But I'm afraid I won't manage to keep anyone's legs bound if I have to keep scratching my own; there are so many mosquitoes here! We haven't brought the wolves with us. You must understand, Ülgas, that killing them is not the wisest idea. What use will you get from it?"

"You haven't brought the wolves with you?" repeated the sage, as I saw him emerge from the bushes, a long knife in his hand. "What is that supposed to mean? I need to sacrifice the wolves to placate the lake-sprite, for otherwise he will flood the whole forest."

"How will he do that? How can this little lake bury a whole forest under itself?"

"How do you know how big the lake is?" shouted Ülgas. "What you see with your own foolish eyes is only the roof of the lake-sprite's castle! The depths of the earth are full of water, of which he is the master! If we don't allay his wrath, he will raise all that water to the surface, and then even the highest spruce trees will be drowned!"

"Do you actually believe what you're saying? Ülgas, I understand that there are old customs and habits and that our people have always liked to believe that lakes and rivers are not merely large pools and streams but the same kinds of living beings as we are. And that in order to appreciate and imagine it better, all these sprites have been invented, which are supposed to live in the depths of the water. It's a beautiful legend."

"Invented!" thundered Ülgas. "Legend! What on earth are you talking about?"

"I'm talking about what is reality," replied Uncle. "Yes, it might be more exciting and pleasant to walk through the forest if you imagine that living inside each tree is a little tree-spirit, and that the Forest-Mother takes care of the whole forest. And yes, that stops children from simply breaking branches and damaging trees out of mischief. But we mustn't be silly about these old stories and start cutting up wolves with a knife just because some animal swam in some forest lake. What is the lake for, if not for swimming and drinking? Goats and deer lap at this water every day!"

"Goats and deer are under the potection of the Forest-Mother, and the Forest-Mother has an agreement with the lake-sprite."

"That's just another beautiful legend to be told to children in the evenings. Have you, Ülgas, changed back into a child, to be telling me these things with a straight face?"

"I am the Sage of the Grove!" shouted Ülgas. "You're a child yourself, Vootele, just as much a child as your nephew, who arrogantly disturbs the peace of the sacred lake and knows nothing of the old customs. I have heard that you are teaching him Snakish, but you should also teach him how to respect the sprites and the sacred grove. Obviously you don't have enough knowledge yourself for that—and no wonder, because I see you very rarely bringing sacrifices to the grove! You think that Snakish words are the only source of wisdom, but you forget that Snakish has no effect on sprites!"

"That is true," agreed Uncle. "For otherwise I would certainly have been able to converse with them."

"Don't mock me! You are just showing your own ignorance. Only a sage may talk to the sprites—one who knows the most secret arts. I am the mediator between men and sprites, and when I say that all your wolves must be sacrificed to placate the lake-sprite, it is your business to obey. So go and bring the wolves here!"

"Be reasonable, Ülgas! You know that I'm not that stupid."

"Bring the wolves here!" yelled the sage. I began to fear for my uncle. Ülgas had a long knife in his hand, and he looked crazed enough to try it out on Uncle. It was very possible that his lust for sacrifice had so boiled his blood that he simply had to leap at somebody's throat. But Uncle Vootele didn't seem afraid of the sage.

"Ülgas, there are very few of us left in this forest. We are the last, and very possibly even some of us will move to the village. Sooner or later our time will end, and all of your sprites will be forgotten. So is there any sense in poisoning these few years we have left to us with silly madness? Ülgas, I'm afraid that you are the last Sage of the Grove, and after your death no one will remember that there lives in this lake a sprite, and if the villagers come around here picking berries, they will swim contentedly here, and their brats will piss in your sacred water."

"How dare you!" roared Ülgas. "It's just because of people like you that our life in the forest has become so miserable! A hundred years ago the grove wasn't large enough to accommodate all of the people who came to pay their respects, and the sacrificial stones were flowing with warm blood, shed for the honor of the sprites and the Forest-Mother. In those days nobody would have dared to speak to a sage in the way you do, railing against him and making a mockery of his commands. Now I know why your nephew holds nothing sacred and associates with the Primates. He learned it all from you! Why don't you just move to the village, to be with the misfits, your own kind? That's where you belong!"

"I don't want to go to the village," replied Uncle calmly. "I like the forest; it's my home. I just don't like you, Ülgas, but luckily the forest is big and we don't often meet."

"But if you're a true Estonian, you must visit the sacred grove!" jeered Ülgas. "There you'll meet me whether you like me or not!"

"That's why I don't go there anymore," said Uncle. There's nothing of interest there. And if you want to regard me as a false Estonian in that case, then I don't care. It's all the same to me."

"The sprites will punish you," warned Ülgas.

"Don't talk nonsense, Ülgas!" laughed Uncle. "You know yourself that that's rubbish. Or if you don't, you must really be feebleminded. Good night!"

He turned to go.

"Are you going to bring the wolves?" shouted Ülgas.

"I can't be bothered debating with you anymore. I'm going home. If you have to kill some wolves tonight, why not hunt some in the forest? There are enough untamed animals wandering about there. Good hunting!"

"They are no use! I need that boy's wolves, because he insulted the sprite. You must bring them!"

"I won't. Go home, Ülgas, and drink some tea to calm yourself down."

"Then I'll take your blood!" growled the sage in a terrible voice, flinging himself upon Uncle. But Uncle was quicker, and dodged him. The next moment Ülgas screeched piercingly and dropped the knife, for Uncle had sunk his teeth into his arm and spat a little piece of bloody flesh onto the grass.

"You got what you wanted," he hissed, and at that moment I didn't recognize my calm and gentle uncle, for a wild red fire burned in his eyes, and the lines of his face were contorted with a terrible rage. "A pity that I haven't inherited my father's fangs, for then you would not see tomorrow. Keep away from me, Ülgas, and leave the boy alone too, if you don't want me to tear you into little pieces!"

Ülgas did not reply; he had sunk to the grass, wailing as he stroked his arm and staring at Uncle Vootele in terror.

Some time passed in silence. The fire in Uncle's eyes was slowly extinguished. He went to the lakeshore and washed his mouth clean of the sage's blood.

"Go and rest for a couple of days in your own grove, then come back here, and you'll see that the lake is still lapping in the same spot, and everything is nice and peaceful," he said soothingly. "This lake has never risen above its shores. Don't panic about the sprites! They won't even make your feet wet, unless you go for a dip yourself."

Ülgas did not respond in any way. We left him moping by the lake and set off for home. Uncle Vootele didn't say a word, seemingly a bit embarrassed in front of me. I had really never seen him lose his self-control like that before. It was as if a wolf had awoken within him. But I felt proud of him. What an uncle he was! The Sage of the Grove had collapsed before his rage like a rotten tree stump.

I took my uncle by the hand. He squeezed my palm tenderly. Striding homeward through the nocturnal forest, I felt safe.

Nine

he next day we heard many interesting things. My friend Pärtel came and told me that Ülgas had explained at great length to his parents how my uncle Vootele had, because of his stubbornness and pride, almost drowned the whole forest. The lake-sprite had been enraged when he was deprived of the wolves' blood he required. He had emerged from the lake in the shape of a black bull, raising the waters of the lake at his heels, rumbling and threatening like some gigantic subterranean cloud crawling out of its lair. But then Ülgas had demonstrated his true heroism and astounding wisdom. Thanks to some miraculous tricks, he had managed to pacify the sprite after all by throwing a thousand weasels into the lake, in place of the wolves' blood. Thus the sprite was appeased and, at least for the moment, the forest spared from terrible danger.

I told Uncle Vootele the story I'd heard from Pärtel, and my uncle said that now Ülgas had proved that he was a complete liar and a phony.

"Up to now you could still think that he is just a simple-minded man who really does believe in fairies and is afraid of offending them, but this story of the black bull and the thousand weasels is obviously nonsense. Where would he find a thousand weasels at night? Not even with the strongest Snakish words could you summon up so many. He made up this story to explain away why the lake is still in place. Now he can brag that he saved the forest. I tell you I won't be going to the grove anymore. And there's nothing for you there either."

I agreed completely with my uncle, not least because after what happened on the lakeshore that night I feared Ülgas like fire. I still had a fixed image of him roaring at my uncle on the shore. I wouldn't just avoid the grove; I would keep out of Ülgas's way completely from now on. And since I spent most of my time with Ints, who, like all adders, kept his distance from humans and could even tell exactly who it was approaching, it wasn't hard for me to avoid the Sage of the Grove.

One day the three of us—Ints, Pärtel, and I—were together in the forest, when the adder suddenly stopped and listened, saying, "Someone's coming."

"Ülgas?" I asked, getting quickly to my feet to walk away.

"No, Tambet."

That didn't change things. Tambet was just as unwelcome as the sage. He had never liked me, but after the incident with the louse Tambet actually hated me. Ülgas must have told him the whole story, and quite naturally he did not have a good word to say about either me or Uncle Vootele. I had met Tambet once since then, and it was horrible. I was with my mother, and when Tambet saw me, his whole body trembled; he gesticulated and screamed, "You wretched brat! I knew it—everyone born in the village is rotten inside!"

"Don't scream at my son!" bawled Mother. She was not at all afraid of Tambet and liked to tell the story about how Tambet had once made a pass at her many years ago. The young Tambet had wanted to make an impression on my young mother, so had climbed up a spruce tree and brought down several combs of wild bees' honey. Then he called on my mother, but was ashamed to be carrying the honey in front of everyone, so he popped the combs inside his jacket, against his stomach. Having reached my mother's place he wanted to proudly hand over the delicacy, but oh dear—the honey had become warm and started to melt, it had stuck to the hairs of the young man's stomach and dripped down, so it wasn't possible to take it out from under his coat. Young Tambet's face went red and he tried to sit in such a way that no one would notice how uncomfortable he was, but my fanged grandfather noticed him squirming and bawled out: "What have you got there? Show me!" And when Tambet stammered something in response, Grandfather grabbed him by the collar and ripped the jacket open, revealing Tambet's tummy and his willy all covered in honey. It was hilarious, said Mother, when Tambet tried to clean off the honey clinging to his lower body, puffing and panting, driven mad with shame. Finally they invited a bear in to lick Tambet clean, but when he saw what part of his body he actually had to lick, he refused, saying that he was a male. At this point in the story she usually stopped, laughing so much that she fell to the floor, and when I asked her later what became of Tambet and his honey-flavored willy, Mother just waved her hand and replied, "Well, he must have got it off himself somehow; he can't still have honey on it. But then, I haven't had the opportunity to look."

Obviously, with memories like that, Mother didn't regard Tambet with any reverence. She got angry when anyone shouted at her son, and she responded just as loudly: "Go and kill your own wolves if you want to! You have too many of them anyway. Do you swim in their milk, or what? Go and donate them to Ülgas. Then you both can chop them up, if you like. And by the way, you're wearing your daughter out, having to look after your beasts like some little slave! You should be ashamed. Look at how small and weak she is!"

"Leave my daughter alone!" shouted Tambet.

"And you leave my son alone! You're always chastising him for being born in the village! Is that his fault? A person can't choose where he comes from. And as far as where you're born is concerned, look, you were born in the forest, and look how you turned out!"

"How did I turn out then?"

"You're a half-wit."

"Shut your face, you old bear's whore!" roared Tambet. This was the worst insult that could be leveled at my mother, and even I, hearing it, had a feeling that I'd fallen headfirst into a fire. Those words were scorching.

At first my mother caught her breath; then she started a strange sputtering, as if something had got up her nose. She gripped my hand.

"Let's go, Leemet," she said. "I like living in the forest very much, but maybe we ought to really move to the village like the others. Only the stupidest filthy sort is left in the forest."

She spat at Tambet, who stood, his back erect, his head covered with long gray hair down to his neck, obviously convinced that he had worthily defended the forest and its ancient ways, and sent the disgusting traitors packing. And that time we really did flee, my mother and I, and I intended to leave anytime Tambet turned up somewhere on the horizon. That man aroused the same horror in me as Ülgas the Sage did.

So Pärtel and I slipped into the bushes, with Ints at our heels. Crouching in the shrubbery we saw Tambet passing, and we were ready to come out when Ints said, "Someone else is coming."

It was Tambet's daughter, Hiie. Evidently she was going somewhere with her father, but of course Tambet didn't care if his daughter could keep up with him. He marched proudly ahead while Hiie scampered along far behind. We weren't afraid of Hiie, so we came out of the bushes and greeted her.

Hiie was pleased to see us; she seldom had a chance to play with other children. She looked hesitantly in the direction where Tambet had vanished, but he was no longer visible. Of course she should have rushed after her father, but the temptation to stay awhile with us was too great.

We sat down in a clearing and chatted. Pärtel and Ints talked away while Hiie listened and watched, her face happy and lively, as if she were a just-hatched butterfly, emerging from its cocoon and looking excitedly at the colorful world. Though of course no one can see a butterfly's face; it's too tiny. Hiie was also small, very thin, and with a somehow pitiful bearing, and there was nothing we could really talk about with her. We had our own jokes that we laughed at, and our own plans that we discussed, but Hiie didn't mind that there was a lot she didn't understand. She was like a starving person who is offered unfamiliar food and gobbles it up gratefully. Hiie was simply delighted to hear someone else's voice apart from her father and mother, and the wolves, whose howling she must have been really weary of.

Finally there was a pause in our chatting, and it occurred to me that we could after all ask Hiie something, if only to keep the talk going.

"Well, what's new with you?" I ventured.

Hiie took my question very seriously. She even started frowning as she tried to recall what was actually new. The girl was obviously in trouble. So far it had been we who spoke; now it was her turn, and she didn't want to be any worse than us, but simply nothing came into her head. Undoubtedly Hiie's life was dreadfully monotonous. Her face turned white with the strain, and she must have been swallowing back tears, as children do when faced with shame at their own incompetence in front of others, but finally something did come to mind and she cried in a small voice: "Mummy and I are going twig-whisking in the moonlight tonight!"

This was an unexpectedly interesting piece of news. I hadn't hoped for anything of the kind. Hiie smiled happily, because in her own estimation she had just learned the fine art of conversation.

Twig-whisking by moonlight was an old custom. Once a year all the women and older girls—toddlers were not included—went late at night into the forest, climbed as high up a tree as they could, and whisked themselves with oak-leaf switches by the light of the moon. The moon had to be full, and the whisking continued until the moon went down. It was believed that this whisking gave the women vigor, and in a sense that was right, because those old women who could no longer climb trees, and thereby missed the whisking, did not live on much longer.

Men did not go whisking, and didn't even know when the night of the full moon would be. The women never told them;

they slipped secretly out of their huts while the men were asleep. By the morning, when the men woke up, the women would already be at home, imbued with a kind of golden glow. How the women all knew exactly when it was the right night was something that not a single man knew.

Like any boys, Pärtel and I had dreamed of some day coming upon women whisking in the moonlight and seeing exactly how it was done. But we never managed to. I kept a watchful eye on Mother but it was no use. What is more, whisking by moonlight could take place in winter or summer, autumn or spring. In the evenings there was nothing to suggest that Mother had anything in mind, yet in the morning her face would be aglow as she roasted the haunch of venison, rejoicing at how fresh her body felt after a good sauna. In recent years Salme had joined Mother for the whisking, and yet I'd never woken at the right moment to follow them and see it for myself.

So it was clear why the news we heard from Hiie excited Pärtel and me. Tonight we had a chance to realize a long-held dream.

"Are you sure about it?" I asked Hiie.

"Yes!" replied the girl. "Mummy told me this morning."

"Have you been twig-whisking before?" asked Pärtel.

"No," answered Hiie, terribly excited that our conversation was going on so long.

She would have liked to answer dozens more questions and reveal all her secrets to us, if she had any. She was glad to sit with us and keep us company until winter if she could. But then her father's voice resounded through the forest.

"Hiie!" shouted Tambet. "Where are you?"

"Daddy's calling!" piped Hiie, and leapt up, a look of fear on her face. I felt so sorry for her at that moment! Life must always have been terrifying with the stern Tambet. I promised myself that I would call in on the girl more often. Looking at Hiie somehow called to mind a little insect caught in a spider's web, struggling helplessly. I would have liked to save her, but sadly Hiie was not caught in a web but in her own home. You cannot save a child from her father, however terrifying he is. We waved to Hiie, who likewise timidly gestured to us, and we ran back into the bushes. Tambet was approaching with long strides.

"Where did you get to?" he demanded.

"You were walking so fast I couldn't keep up," stammered Hiie. "Then you disappeared out of sight and I didn't know where to go."

"Don't you know the forest paths then? Oh, these children today! In the old days no one got lost in the forest, no one at all!"

He grabbed Hiie by the hand.

"Come on now!"

And he marched off at such a pace that Hiie had to practically run along beside him.

Quite naturally Pärtel and I planned to go that night to look at the women whisking. We invited Ints along, but to our surprise the adder said that he'd seen women whisking themselves several times already and he wasn't interested.

"Why didn't you mention that before?" we retorted.

"I didn't think it would interest you," said the adder. "There's nothing special about it—just naked women sitting on treetops hitting themselves with oak switches. I was crawling past under the trees and I didn't really bother to look up."

"You could have invited us, or warned us when the day was coming around again!"

"I didn't even know you then. And even I can't be sure exactly what day the women will climb the tree to whisk themselves. I saw them quite by accident. Adders see everything that goes on in the forest, but we don't keep account of it. I don't understand. Is this whisking really so thrilling?"

"Oh, it's totally thrilling!" Pärtel and I assured him. We were excited by the opportunity of uncovering this jealously guarded secret. Might we be the first men to see women whisking on treetops? We knew of no one who could boast that. But aside from that it was a thrill to think about coming upon a big group of naked women. We were old enough to feel an interest in such things. For example, there was Salme with her friends. And Hiie—poor little thing—it obviously hadn't occurred to her, in betraying the great secret to us, that she was giving us a chance to look at her naked. But maybe she wouldn't have cared; she was just excited to be able to say something interesting to us.

Pärtel and I agreed to meet under the whisking-trees, which we would find by following our mothers and sisters.

It wasn't difficult. Evidently it didn't occur to Mother that I might suspect something, and I played my part well. I ate my fill properly in the evening as always, and scrambled to my sleeping place. Salme did the same, and a little while later Mother also got under her big deerskin, where all three of us had snuggled down in my childhood.

For a while it was silent and dark; although at first I'd been afraid that I wouldn't hold out and would sleep through it, I was no longer afraid of that. I was as excited and alert as a swallow, and my only concern was to stay in one position, when actually I wanted to toss and scratch all over all the time. It's terrible how the urge to scratch takes over your mind. But I forced myself to stay still, until at last I heard Mother getting up from her position and tugging at Salme.

"Let's go now!" she whispered.

They sneaked quietly out the door. I lay a few moments more in the same position, in case they might have forgotten something and come back. But they didn't, so I leapt out of bed and followed them.

I saw them walking in front of me and I crawled on the damp grass like my friend Ints, trying to make as little noise as possible. Mother and Salme didn't notice anything. After a little while they met one of Salme's friends, who was also on her way with her mother to the moonlit sauna, and the four of them continued on their way. I stayed at their heels.

Finally we arrived at a small clearing. This was undoubtedly their destination, because there I saw other women who were already taking off their clothes and starting to climb the trees, an oak switch between their teeth. There was a rustling in the bushes somewhere and Pärtel crawled up beside me.

"Mine is already up the tree!" he whispered and pointed with a finger toward a tall spruce tree, at the top of which sat his naked mother, her white body shining in the moonlight, slowly and with visible pleasure whisking herself.

It was undoubtedly a beautiful, magical scene, but I was much more interested in Salme's friends than in Pärtel's mother. I let my gaze rove around, and saw the women climbing ever higher up the tree trunks against the night sky, until they found a suitable branch and settled on it, bathed in the bright moonlight, stroking their naked bodies with an oak switch, as if the moon's golden glow were spread all over them. It was an exciting scene, and Pärtel and I stared at the naked girls in fascination. We also

saw Hiie, sitting beside her mother and swishing the little branch
on her bony legs, but she was obviously not our favorite; she was
scrawny, with the body of a child. One of Salme's friends, on the
other hand, had breasts like wasp's nests! We both gulped when
we saw her starting to beat herself as her tits bounced merrily
up and down.

You can only imagine what a scene would have been offered
by the women whisking in the moonlight centuries ago, when
the forest was still full of people. The branches must have sagged
under the weight of all the women. Now there were only a few
whiskers, scarcely a score, including a few old women who offered no pleasure to the eyes. But they were all whisking heartily,
and from the rhythm of the fall of the switches emerged a fine
moonlight dust, which glowed like a living fire.

"Beautiful!" sighed Pärtel, ogling one woman who had put
down her whisk for a moment and stretched out with great
pleasure, thus heaving her powerful bosom farther out.

We heard an enthusiastic sigh come from someone nearby,
and we flinched in fear. Who else could be lurking here? We
turned rapidly around and quite near us saw a large bear, who
was watching the whiskers, his head cocked, gnawing his long
claws with great pleasure.

"What are you doing here?" I asked angrily, because the man
within me was awakening, and no man will tolerate bears looking at women.

"I'm watching," replied the bear. "Oh, they're so sweet!"

"Don't she-bears go switch-whisking?" I asked. "Why don't
you peep at them?"

"No, they don't," sighed the bear, who of course didn't understand that I was making fun of him. Bears never understand

that; they are terribly simpleminded and gullible. "She-bears are not so pretty anyway. They wear a thick coat, and you can't take it off. But these ones here are all so beautiful and sweet! As if they'd been flayed!"

"Go flay yourself!" I snorted angrily. "Go on, scram! Or go flay some goat; then it will be beautiful and sweet too!"

"I've tried that, and it's not the same," sighed the bear, who, like all bears, was not capable of taking offense. But he did toddle off a little way, raising his snout toward the treetops.

We must have been whispering too loudly with the bear, and my sister, Salme, came down from the treetop. I suddenly heard my mother's voice ask, "Where are you going?" and I turned around. To my astonishment I saw Salme standing naked under the tree, not far away from us.

"I heard some noise," said Salme, with a suspicious expression. "I think there's someone here."

She peered between the trees, and Pärtel and I pressed ourselves as deep into the moss as we could. We couldn't crawl out anymore; Salme would have spotted us immediately. But staying put was not without dangers either. Thanks to the full moon, it was very light in the forest. Salme would only have to go forward a few steps and she would discover us straight away, and right now she was about to take those steps.

I felt a cold sweat in the back of my neck, for I couldn't even guess what punishment might await little boys who invade a secret whisking party. The women would certainly be horribly angry that we had spied on them. My mother would of course hardly be likely to do me much harm, but I would feel so ashamed.

We wanted to dig into the ground like moles, but humans have sadly not been given that gift, and not even Snakish would help here.

Salme stepped forward two paces, and would certainly have found us the next moment, when suddenly a delicate little voice called, "Salme!"

It would have been reasonable for Salme to scream now, and even run for help. But she did nothing of the sort. Instead she muttered with a kind of shameful satisfaction: "It's you, Mõmmi! What are you doing here—you're not supposed to be here."

Our ursine acquaintance came out of the bushes.

"Salme, you're so pretty!" he sighed. "I was sitting here and I didn't get a look from you. There are many beautiful women up there in the trees, but you're the nicest."

"Mõmmi, it's not decent to watch in secret like that!" said Salme, shielding her naked body with her hands. She wasn't angry in the slightest. I imagined how differently she would have spoken to me and Pärtel. It was actually insulting: she would have berated her own brother mercilessly for peeping at her and her peers, but with this bear she spoke in a tender and kind voice, as if he were her dearest friend. The bear came right up to Salme and licked her bare feet.

"Don't do that; Mother is up there," whispered Salme. "I have to climb back up too. See you some other time."

"I'll stay here under the tree until morning," murmured the bear. "Let me admire your beauty!"

"You silly thing!" said Salme sweetly and stroked the bear's head. Then she slipped back to her own tree and climbed up.

"Who was there?" asked Mother.

"Nobody," my sister answered. She took the switch and set about swishing again, but in quite a different way than before. She was no longer bathing in the moon rays; she was performing for Mömmi, watching down in the thicket, showing off all her charms.

"Let's go home," I said, angry with both my sister and the bear.

Ten

 was really disappointed in Salme, and I had a good mind to tell Mother that my sister was flirting with a bear. I couldn't do it, however, because straight away she would have wanted to know where I'd seen Salme consorting with a bear, and then I would have had to tell her that I'd been spying on the women whisking in the moonlight. So now I knew my sister's secret, but had to keep it to myself. Even I couldn't lash out at Salme, lest she guess that I had been in the forest that night and had seen everything. It was unpleasant.

What made the whole thing especially embarrassing was that Pärtel had also seen my sister with the bear, and kept asking me: "Are they a couple?" He didn't do it to tease me, but it still irritated me. The fact that Salme was carrying on with a bear was shameful enough—but did the whole world have to know about it? The relations between the bear and Salme were a private family matter! I ordered Pärtel not to tell anyone what we had seen in the moonlit forest, but wasn't at all sure that he would keep his promise.

I knew for myself how difficult that was. The secret turned in my stomach and pressed itself on my tongue—for what is the point of nosing out a secret if you can't boast about what you know! It wasn't just a question of Salme and the bear; we had seen a lot of other things that night that weren't intended for our eyes. Later, when I met a friend of Salme's, my head was spinning with the joy of victory; there she sat and regarded me as just an annoying boy, when I had seen her bosoms and bottom! If only she knew! But I kept quiet about my secret reconnaissance and only smiled strangely when Salme's friends turned to me.

"What are you laughing at?" they would ask, but I wouldn't answer. Instead I quickly twisted my mouth straight and ran away, so as not to betray my secret knowledge of bosoms and bottoms.

The only one to whom I dared honestly talk about it was Ints. But my news aroused neither interest nor amazement in him. For an adder, a bear and a human were quite similar creatures, and he saw no reason why they would not be attracted to each other. Nor did Ints have any opinion on the hidden beauty of Salme's friends. Of course it's quite natural that a snake, a creature that resembles a long smooth rope, would never see the purpose of breasts and buttocks. So Ints listened to my story quite indifferently and said that yes, he had seen all that and there was nothing special about it whatsoever.

I had promised myself that I'd visit Hiie more often, and I did. The girl was chopping up hares again when we crept out of the shrubbery, encouraged by Ints saying that neither Tambet nor his wife were at home at the moment. Hiie looked terribly tired, but when she saw us she suddenly grew downright joyful.

Though she was ashamed of her spattered apron and bare toes, which were red with hares' blood. She hid her toes behind the large ax, and would have liked to chat with us, but the wolves in the barn kept on baying hungrily, demanding food.

"I suppose I'd better carry on working," whispered Hiie unhappily. "Otherwise they'll start making so much noise that Mummy and Daddy will hear."

"And then they'll be angry?" I asked.

"No, no!" replied Hiie, but it was evident from her face that they would.

"Let's go and look at those wolves," suggested Ints, and we stepped into the barn. I had never before seen so many wolves gathered together. It was simply horrible—there were hundreds of them, each in its own little stall. As we looked inside the shed, they all turned their muzzles in our direction and smacked their tongues, obviously hoping that we were bringing the hare meat they hungered for. When the wolves saw that we came empty-handed, they started again with their piercing wail, and some of them threw themselves down on the ground and rolled, to show that they were frantic with hunger.

"They haven't eaten since this morning," explained Hiie.

"And a wolf shouldn't eat so much anyway," added Ints. "They have some fat on them; some are even quite plump. Just look at that beast by the door! It's as big and fat as a bear. Don't feed them so much!"

"But they howl if they don't get food," complained Hiie.

"Let's make them stay quiet," I said, and hissed loudly. Naturally my voice couldn't compete with the ululations coming from the wolves' throats, but a properly uttered Snakish word always reaches its mark; it burns itself through the loudest noise, and it's impossible not to hear it. This Snakish word was intended to lull animals to sleep. The wolves ceased their clamor, yawned—showing their fangs—then snapped their jaws together and spread themselves out languidly. For a little while they eyed us sleepily, then put their heads on their paws and fell into slumber.

"Haven't you been taught Snakish?" I asked.

"I have, but not those words," replied Hiie, watching the sleeping wolves with fascination. "How long will they sleep?"

"Till the evening, or until we wake them. I'll teach you the Snakish words I just used, so you can feed them in the morning and then put them to sleep, so they won't make a noise. Would you like that?"

Hiie nodded excitedly. I repeated the relevant words of Snakish until they stayed in her mind and she could pronounce them. Then we did a test: I woke up the wolves. They got drowsily to their feet and at first were quite peaceful, but then their habit of continuous devouring came back to their minds. Noticing that they had no food, they let their throats resonate. Then Hiie faultlessly hissed the Snakish words she had learned by heart, and the wolves obediently lay down, covering their snouts with their tails, and in a moment were asleep again.

"Well, you see how simple it is!" I said. "Strange that your father and mother haven't taught you that trick before."

"They probably want Hiie to fatten the wolves all the time," said Ints. "My mother always says that Tambet loves wolves more than people."

Hiie blushed on hearing this, because we were talking about her father. She knew that we didn't like her parents, and she felt guilty for being friendly to us. She must have also been afraid that our dislike for Tambet might grow so great that we wouldn't like his daughter anymore either. She could hardly have loved her father much anyway. In fact Tambet was so terribly cruel to her that she could have replied to Ints: "Yes, it's true. He really is a spiteful person." But Hiie was too ashamed and meek to utter such words. I never heard her say anything bad about her parents, even though she was the one who suffered most because of them. She simply felt a constant embarrassment about them, as if she were ashamed of some ugly scar that could not be hidden from the gaze of others.

Naturally we didn't think Hiie was to blame for having a stupid father. On the contrary, we liked visiting her all the more for it. It gave us a chance to turn the screws on Tambet. He wanted his precious wolves to be feeding all the time, but we put them to sleep and in that way were snatching Hiie from the cage her parents had built for her—the big ax and constantly replenishing piles of hares for her to chop up. We visited her every day, and Tambet and Mall couldn't work out why the wolves had become so sleepy and no longer ate in the daytime. They even stayed at home to keep watch, but hissing Snakish words doesn't take much time, and Hiie always found an opportunity to utter them, thus proving to her parents that the wolves went to sleep even when the couple were at home.

Finally Tambet invited Ülgas to come—who else! The sage came and examined the wolves, who were alert in the mornings and bayed as if frenzied, but while Ülgas and Tambet went into the bushes behind the shack to find out whether the Forest-Mother or the tree-sprites had anything to do with the wolves' sleepiness, Hiie hissed the Snakish words, and when the men came back into the barn, all the wolves were sleeping the sleep of the just.

"It's the work of the sprites," said Ülgas. "No doubt about it. I can guess what the trouble is. Tambet, old friend, the baying of your wolves is apparently disturbing the tree-sprites' sleep. You know that the sprites sleep in the daytime, and they are disturbed by the noise from those benighted animals. So they put the wolves to sleep. You'll have to get used to it; the sprites mustn't be annoyed!"

Tambet was satisfied, for when it came to the sprites he was meek as a kid. It would not even occur to him to go against ancient customs or the word of the sage. What did amaze me, though, was that neither Ülgas nor Tambet had thought that Snakish might be behind the wolves' behavior. To tell the truth, I had been sure that they would soon work out our trick, wake up the wolves, and forbid Hiie from putting them to sleep again. Ülgas and Tambet knew Snakish, and although the hiss needed for putting animals to sleep was not one of the easiest, it was not such a rare and unfamiliar hiss, unlike those taught to me by Ints's father, the king of the snakes. Ülgas and Tambet should certainly have known that hiss. But for some reason the possibility that the wolves had been put to sleep with the aid of Snakish words didn't enter their heads. That was odd.

Only later did I understand that although Ülgas and Tambet hated all those who had settled in the village, they themselves no longer really lived in the forest. They were disappointed and angry to see the good old sylvan life gradually dying out, and to overcome that they clung to the especially ancient and secret ways. They cherished spells, sought a way out in the invented world of the sprites, and no longer cared for ordinary Snakish words. To them they seemed too weak; they had not been able to keep people in the forest, so must be of no use. Ülgas and Tambet thought that only sorcery was worthy of attention, but since the snakes knew that there is no such thing as sorcery, Ülgas and Tambet wanted nothing more to do with them. Not even the Frog of the North would have satisfied them. They believed they had found something altogether stronger, and they kept on about their sprites and Forest-Mothers, imagining that they preserved ancient values. They had gone just as far astray as the people in the village. But they never appreciated that.

In any case, more peaceful days came for Hiie, since Tambet and Mall reconciled themselves to the wolves having to sleep in the daytime. It was what the sprites wished. In the mornings they got restless if the wolves were awake too long making a noise, since they feared that the sprites would be annoyed and that they would have to bring sacrifices to restore peace. A few times, at our request, Hiie delayed putting the wolves to sleep, and we hid in the bushes, stifling laughter while we watched Tambet and Mall running anxiously around the barn and trying to somehow calm down the terrible baying so that the revered sprites of the forest could sleep peacefully.

Finally Hiie would hiss the necessary word to the wolves. "Thank goodness!" said Tambet and Mall happily, not noticing what their daughter had done, and went about their own business. They did not try to find another job for Hiie instead of feeding the wolves—or more correctly, they forgot to. Nor did they pay much attention to their daughter. This didn't bother Hiie much. She could go and play with us, and often spent the whole day in our company—something that would have been completely impossible before. We wandered everywhere with her, home to my place and to the snakes' home, and visited Pirre and Rääk to look at the lice. I believe that Hiie had never had such fun before as that summer.

Since the time when Pärtel and I went to the village and were almost stunned by the miraculous things we'd seen in the home of Johannes the village elder, we had not visited any village people. More than five years had passed since then. Although at first I had been burning with enthusiasm for the bread shovel and the spinning wheel, this passion had cooled with the years. I had experienced other interesting things, had learned Snakish with the help of Uncle Vootele, and had grown to like life in the forest more and more. For a long time I had been able to think of the spinning wheel and the shovel without any desire. I had grown up and become more sensible, and understood that there was no need for such tools in the forest. The village no longer interested me much at all, it was something alien and distant, a place that I could conceivably visit again, but was in no hurry to.

For a long time, Pärtel and I had not talked about the village or recalled our old adventures, because plenty of other things had happened in our lives. Ints knew nothing about the village, apart that the villagers didn't know Snakish. Adders regarded such creatures with supreme contempt—unless they were hedgehogs, which they also disdained, but feared as well. They had no reason to fear the villagers, because those people could not withstand snake poison, so that adders always felt themselves their superiors.

Now, when we had Hiie with us, Pärtel and I got the idea of going back to the village. We had taken Hiie around the forest with us and shown her everything we knew and Hiie had never seen. We enjoyed the girl's enthusiasm hugely and wanted to keep surprising her, but we had almost exhausted all the exciting things in the forest. So we began to think about the village, Johannes the village elder, and his daughter, Magdaleena.

"Let's go and see them," I suggested, and Pärtel agreed immediately, all the more so because Hiie resisted and looked really frightened. Tambet must have told her dreadful things about the village at home. Hiie knew, of course, that her father spoke badly about many things, including me and my family, but she did really fear the village. Of course that increased our keenness to take her there—for what could offer a boy more enjoyment than to drag a trembling and reluctant girl in the direction of apparent mortal danger! One can show off one's courage, but when it finally turns out that the danger is not real danger, you can laugh happily and say, "I said there's nothing terrible here; you'll even like it here. Haven't we shown you interesting things?" And so we weren't worried about Hiie's timid objections. We took her with us, and Ints came as well, because he had not visited the village, and thought that one adder should get to know everything there is to be found in and around the forest.

We got to the hillock where you could see the whole village, including Johannes the village elder's cabin, which was closest to the forest. Hiie said nothing; she just panted, and when I took her hand I felt that the girl's palm was covered in sweat. Evidently she was really afraid. She had never gone out of the forest before. The sun was behind the clouds, but still she was astounded by the light and space, a kind she had never encountered in the forest. She looked imploringly at me. Obviously she would have liked to scuttle back among the trees, but I was merciless. So Hiie submitted to me, just as she had always submitted to her mother and father.

We walked quickly down the hillside. No point denying it: my heart was beating quite fast, and Pärtel's probably was too. We had been here once before, but that was years ago, and I felt like a person preparing to jump into a lake from a high treetop. He knows that there is nothing bad lurking in the water, but it's still a little creepy to stare down into the depths from the top, and there is a hollow feeling in his stomach as he falls.

Everything happened exactly as on our first visit. Out of the door stepped Magdaleena, who in the meantime had grown considerably, and Pärtel and I were astonished to see her. She was so beautiful. Magdaleena was also taken aback—that was clear to see—and obviously not at our beauty. Rather the opposite; she must have been shocked to see two boys dressed in animal skins, leading between them a slight girl also wearing skins. The previous time she had greeted us with childish candor; since then, however, she had obviously heard many an unpleasant thing about the forest dwellers, so she screamed, "Father!"

"What's going on?" a voice from indoors asked, and out stepped Johannes the village elder. He was not too startled to see us, and asked, smiling, "Is it you, boys? The same ones who came here once before? Well, you've grown a lot! What took you so long to come? I told you to move with your parents to the village. Poor children, you look so wild. Are you hungry? Want some bread?"

Before we had time to reply, he disappeared inside and came back a moment later with half a loaf of bread.

"There you are," he said kindly. "Fresh rye bread."

He handed the bread to me. For the first time I was holding in my hand an object so despised in the forest: the bread had a knobbly crust, but was soft. Hiie looked at me, her eyes full of terror; she wanted to say something but didn't dare. Evidently she was afraid that even just holding one single piece of bread could somehow do me harm; this must have had something to do with one of her father's many stories. I wasn't afraid of the bread, for I knew that Mother had eaten it at one time and nothing bad had happened to her. Bread wasn't dangerous; it was just supposed to have a disgusting taste. Nevertheless I resolved to try the bread later, even though now would be a chance to show off my courage to Hiie. But for the moment I wanted to show Hiie some other miraculous things.

"Do you still have the spinning wheel?" I asked knowingly. "And that bread shovel? I'd like to look at them."

Johannes laughed.

"We still have the spinning wheel, and the bread shovel too," he said. "Step inside and admire them!"

We were already stepping indoors and Hiie was shaking like a leaf. I felt sorry for her; I nudged her and whispered in her ear: "It's nothing. We'll take a little look and go back home."

But then suddenly something happened. Magdaleena screamed.

"A snake!" she shrieked, her eyes full of blind fear, as she pointed at Ints. "Daddy, a snake!"

"Don't worry, I'll strike him dead!" shouted Johannes. "Out of the way, I'll hit him!"

I was so taken aback that I did step aside, and I saw Johannes grabbing a stick and trying to kill Ints. The adder deftly wriggled aside and hissed viciously. I knew he would bite the first chance he had and I leapt to intervene.

"Why are you beating him?" I stammered. "He hasn't done anything!"

"The snake is the worst enemy of mankind!" cried Johannes. "The snake is the right hand of Satan, and it is the duty of the people of the cross to beat down these abominable creatures! Now where did he get to?"

"He's my friend!" I shouted, terrified, as if I were the one being threatened with death by thrashing. I was even starting to cry. "You mustn't beat him!"

"A snake can't be a human's friend!" declared Johannes. "You've gone astray, poor child, and you're saying terrible things. You mustn't go back to the forest. You must stay here, or otherwise your soul will be lost. You should all stay here. You should be quickly christened and saved! Come in here now, but that snake, that damned snake, I'm going to—"

He squeezed the pole in his palm and looked around with a mad stare, seeking Ints.

I felt horrible. I had once seen a deer between whose ribs the village people had driven a strange wooden stake. The villagers didn't know Snakish, and therefore couldn't summon the deer to them, so they hunted it across the country and fired little sticks into the air. This stick caused the deer outrageous pain, but didn't kill it, and so the poor animal rushed with bloodshot eyes through the forest, shrieking and thumping everything in its path, until Uncle Vootele calmed it with Snakish words and cut the animal's throat, to release it from its suffering. Johannes was now reminding me of that maddened deer; he too was screaming confused words, and wanted to strike the completely innocent Ints dead. Perhaps he too had been struck by some stake? He looked completely crazed, and in my terror I just stood there helplessly, and I would even have let Johannes haul me into the room if Hiie hadn't tugged at my elbow.

"Let's run out of here!" she whispered. "Quick! Let's just run away!"

I heeded her words straight away, grabbed Hiie by the hand, and we ran off toward the forest without looking back. I saw Pärtel, white in the face, running beside me, with Ints crawling a little way ahead, and although I could hear Johannes's shouting behind me, I realized that we'd all escaped alive.

Eleven

n reaching the forest, we sank down in the moss, panting for a while, not saying a word. Ints was the only one who didn't seem shocked; he sought a sunny place and coiled up.

"What came over him?" asked Pärtel at length.

"Whatever did come over him, that's how people are in the village. Father tells me that whenever they see a snake, they go on the attack. Like hedgehogs."

"Do they eat you?" asked Pärtel.

"Just let them try," hissed Ints. "I would have stuck my fangs into that creature if Leemet hadn't jumped in front of me."

"Before you had time to bite him he would have broken your back," I said. For the first time I understood how dangerous a human can be to an adder.

Living in the forest, this had never occurred to me; humans and snakes lived like brothers, and never had a human raised a hand against an adder. To talk of whether a human could do harm to a snake seemed just as senseless as discussing whether an oak could attack a birch. There was eternal peace between adders and humans. But now I saw that nothing is eternal, and a human can kill an adder with one whack of a stick. I couldn't help looking at Ints now with quite different eyes. How fragile he really was! You only needed to keep away from his poison fangs, for he couldn't defend himself in any way against a creature who doesn't understand Snakish and uses a long stick. I felt sick; in my mind's eye I could already see Ints's back broken in two. I looked away.

Only then did I notice that I was still clutching the hunk of bread. My first thought was to bury this gift from Johannes in the swamp, and I let the bread fall with a sense of revulsion.

"What's this?" asked Pärtel. "You took the bread with you?"

"It simply stayed in my hand," I explained.

Pärtel shifted closer, and with his finger cautiously stroked the knobbly brown crust of the piece of bread.

"Shall we have a taste?" he suggested.

"No!" shrieked Hiie. "Let's not taste it! You mustn't eat bread! Daddy won't allow it! Mummy said it's poisonous!"

"It's certainly not poisonous, because my father ate it before he died," I said, and immediately realized how ambiguous that sounded. "I mean, he didn't die from the bread," I hastened to add. "My mother has tasted bread too. She told me. It tastes disgusting, but it doesn't kill you. And those village people eat it all the time."

"But look at what they're like," remarked Ints. "Maybe it's bread that drives them crazy."

"We won't eat much," argued Pärtel. "We'll just try a crumb. We have to find out what sort of marvelous thing it is!"

"Please, boys, don't eat it!" implored Hiie, her eyes wide with terror. "I'm afraid for you! It's dangerous!"

Hiie's terror decided the matter. We had to show her that we weren't afraid of any bread.

"We'll try a little bit," I said. My hand trembled a little as I broke the bread, and it really was a little horrifying to taste this forbidden food. Perhaps it would burn the tongue like nettles? Might it make you vomit? But Pärtel had already broken off his bit; we both held the bread between our fingers and looked at each other. Then we took a deep breath, put the crumbs in our mouths, and quickly started chewing.

At any rate, the bread didn't burn the mouth or make us vomit. But it had no taste either. It was sort of dry and disgusting like tree bark, which you could gnaw at forever but would be troublesome to swallow.

Hiie and Ints followed us intently, Hiie with terror and Ints with disdain.

"Well, how is it?" piped Hiie.

"All right," I said heroically. "It's not doing anything to us."

"Yes," agreed Pärtel. "It's edible."

"Don't have any more!" begged Hiie.

And actually we wouldn't have wanted any more, but it seemed somehow embarrassing to confine ourselves to one tiny morsel of bread. So, despite Hiie's entreaty, we broke off new pieces and started slowly chewing them.

It was actually a rather proud feeling, to eat bread. This secret and forbidden thing, which didn't even taste good—gnawing it felt like a manly act of heroism. A child wouldn't have done it; he would have spat out the tasteless mush. But we didn't mind it, and finally we boldly swallowed the piece of bread. We now felt truly grown up—not boys, but full-grown men.

Egged on by each other's strength, and wanting to test ourselves with more acts of bravery, we now started devouring big bites of the bread.

"You take some too," Pärtel urged Hiie. "Just put a piece in your cheek."

"I don't want to," protested Hiie.

"Take it, go on," I joined in. "You're not a little child any longer; you can try it. What will one little bit do? Daddy and Mummy won't have to know. After we eat, we'll rinse out our mouths with springwater, so there won't be any smell afterward."

"No, I don't dare to," squeaked Hiie. But she did have enough courage to touch the bread with a finger—at first delicately, then pressing more firmly. The bread was very soft. Hiie's finger sank through the crust and stuck inside the bread. Hiie screeched, pulled her finger out, and hid her hand behind her back.

We laughed.

"So what are you fussing about?" I asked. "You're afraid, as if the bread were alive. Come on, take a bite! You're not a little kid!"

Hiie shook her head.

"Don't be silly," urged Pärtel. "It won't do anything to you."

I broke a piece off the side of the loaf and passed it to Hiie. "Now eat!"

"Why are you forcing her?" said Ints. "Why not just eat your own shit? See how repulsive that bread looks, as brown as deer droppings. Maybe it's even made of shit? You humans are always having to try things. You're better off eating lingonberries."

"It's not made of shit," I said. "Mother told me that bread is made from some straws. It must have been a terrible effort. These straws have to be threshed and milled and I don't know what else. Then finally it's thrown into an oven, and there's your bread."

"What's the difference—shit or straws," replied Ints. "I didn't know that you humans eat plants, just like goats do."

"That's interesting," said Pärtel. "New things have to be tried. How do you know otherwise if something's good if you don't try it?"

"So it's good then?"

"No, but—"

"But still you eat it. You've tried it already, now continue."

"We want Hiie to try it too," I said. "Take it, Hiie! It won't do anything. It won't stay in your tummy; it will come out later as poo."

"Are you sure?" asked Hiie.

"Of course. Try! A little piece."

Hiie gave me a troubled look, squeezed her eyes shut, and popped the piece of bread in her mouth. For a while she gnawed it, holding her breath, her face puckered with disgust.

"Well!" we said. "It wasn't so bad after all! Went down, didn't it?"

"Yes," said Hiie. "It did."

"Have some more!"

"No, no!" Hiie shook her head vigorously. "That's enough! I won't eat anymore. I've already got a funny feeling in my tummy. Haven't you?"

We were silent for a moment as we tried to work out what feelings we had in our tummies. Yes, it was somehow strange. We imagined the bits of bread there in the middle of our bellies, lying like uninvited guests. It was unpleasant. In the end, what did we know about bread? That it didn't make our mouths scream, our gums burn—but that didn't mean that it behaved properly in the stomach. Might we get sick after all? Perhaps there was some trick to bread eating that we didn't know. What if we were eating it the wrong way? "I think I'm going to be sick!" said Hiie suddenly and ran behind a tree, where retching could be heard.

This made the rest of us worried. Bread couldn't be right for us if it made us puke. It was never like that with venison. Now we almost envied Hiie, for no doubt the girl was now getting rid of the dubious bit of bread, while we had to carry our burden with us, unable to guess what it would ultimately do to our bodies. Hiie stuck her sweaty, unhappy little head out from behind the tree.

"I'm going home now," she said, and vanished.

"I'm going too," said Pärtel and I in unison, and we each stumbled off to our own shack, clutching our stomachs, sensing the notorious bread, which our foolish heads had gobbled up, starting to rumble inside us.

In the end, nothing terrible happened. The bread kept quiet. And yet I wasn't able to quite calm myself. I had a feeling that a stranger was sitting in my stomach. I got home, snuggled in a corner, and felt my belly. It seemed to me I could feel disgusting lumps of bread under my fingers. Would they stay there forever?

Meanwhile, Mother was in an inexpressibly good mood.

"I got busy today and cooked a whole goat," she said. "It came out nicely, so crunchy that you'll want to swallow your tongue. Come and eat, son. Salme has eaten already and liked it. Didn't you, Salme?"

Salme cast a weary look at me from behind the table.

"Mother is fattening me up," she said plaintively. "She keeps piling it up. Just look at that pile of meat! I told her long ago I can't eat any more of that. Take the meat away, but she won't."

"Why would I take it away? You'll eat it later," explained Mother gaily. "Rest a little and then . . . It's good meat, I spent the day roasting it."

"It isn't possible to stuff yourself that much," moaned Salme. "I'm going to burst!"

"Oh, you're joking. Nobody would burst after a little bit of meat like that," Mother said with an airy gesture. "And I'm telling you, you don't have to eat it all at once. Later!"

"Tomorrow!"

"Why tomorrow? Tomorrow I'll be making a new lunch. Why not today, just in a little while?"

"In a little while I'm going to sleep."

"Well, you'll eat before you go to sleep. Leemet, you come here too now! I'll get some up for you."

Mother piled into my bowl such an amount of meat that I got the impression there was a whole goat lying there, like a large bird on its nest hatching eggs. I got up cautiously, so as not to jolt the piece of bread lurking in my belly out of place, and went to the table. It was quite clear that I wasn't capable of eating anything; my stomach felt tender, as if someone were scratching with their nails from inside.

"Mother, I don't want to eat," I said gloomily.

"What's this about?" exclaimed Mother.

"Eat, just eat," said Salme venomously. "Why should I get fat on my own?"

"You won't get fat," said Mother, and started to shove the bowl of meat closer to me. "Take it now. Take all this goat and gnaw it clean! Just look at that nice clean brawn!"

"Mother, I'm not able to eat," I said, suddenly feeling terribly sorry for her. The nasty bread was squatting in my stomach and hurting me, and I hadn't the faintest idea when it intended to leave me. The meat cooked by Mother smelled delicious. I would have liked to taste it; I wanted to so much, but I simply didn't dare to. I was on the point of crying from self-pity. I felt like a dying man.

"Mother, I ate some bread," I moaned.

Mother glared at me, as if she'd been struck on the head.

"What did you eat?"

"You ate bread!" shrieked Salme and screwed up her nose. "How disgusting! Like some villager!"

"Mother, that bread is now in my stomach!" I said, looking pleadingly at her. Could she save me, help me?

Mother didn't seem to be pitying me, but rather herself.

"You ate bread!" she said in an injured tone. "I see! I cook a goat for you all day. I want to make a tasty dinner for my son, so good that it will take your tongue away, but instead you eat bread somewhere. Don't you like my meals? I try so hard! I want to offer you the very best. But you eat bread! You like that more than a goat I've roasted for you with care and love!"

Mother sat at the table and started to cry.

"Mother," I mumbled in fright. "Mother, what's this! I don't like bread at all! It's disgusting!"

"So why did you eat it? Why do you do this to me?"

"Mother, I only tasted it! I simply wanted to try it! Pärtel ate some too! And Hiie!"

I tried to share the blame, but Mother didn't take account of that.

"I don't care what Pärtel and Hiie do," she said. "But why did you have to put that disgusting bread in your mouth? Didn't you know your mother was waiting for you at home and lovingly cooking a roast for you?"

"Bread is repulsive!" said Salme. "Completely tasteless."

"How do you know?" asked Mother, looking sternly at Salme. "Have you been secretly eating bread?"

"Once, with my girlfriends," sputtered Salme. "I simply put it in my mouth and spat it out again."

"I see," said Mother, humiliated. "You don't like my food either."

"Mother, what do you mean?" said Salme. "I eat your roasts all the time!"

"But you don't like them; you like bread!" persisted Mother, and wept again.

"Don't like them! I simply wanted to try out what sort of thing it is. I'm not a child anymore. I can try bread for once in my life. Leemet is still a little boy. Of course, he shouldn't have eaten it; that was very bad of him, but I—"

"No," said Mother. "You can't either! Your father ate bread, but I don't want you to follow in your father's footsteps. That bread brought him no happiness, and that's why I don't want my children to even taste it."

She sat wiping her eyes and looked at us in a sort of terror.

"You're still so young and sweet, but now you're already trying bread! Don't do it, please. I beg you!"

"Mother, you've eaten bread too," argued Salme.

"I have," sighed Mother. "But very little, not even a taste. And you mustn't go trying out all these nasty things that your mother did when she was young. You are smarter!"

"Mother, I won't ever eat bread again," I promised, quite sincerely. "It was very bad. Your roast is much, much better, honestly!"

"Mother, don't be angry," Salme begged as well. "Look how much goat I ate today. You can cook it so very well."

"I'm glad you like it," smiled Mother through her tears. "Take no notice of me. I'm just afraid that you'll start liking bread. You start eating it, you end up moving to the village. You see your friend Linda moved there yesterday with her family. I went past their hut today. The door was wide open and two wolves were lying on the threshold, their snouts between their paws. Poor abandoned animals."

"I never would have believed that Linda would move away," said Salme. "She promised she wouldn't."

"That's what they all say, but in the end they leave. So many of them have gone! Even we left once, but I came back. I didn't like that village life. Children, just remember this: I'm never leaving the forest. I'm going to die here."

"No, Mother, you won't have to go anywhere!" cried Salme. "We're staying here with you."

"If you suddenly get a taste for bread . . . " began Mother, but Salme cried to her not to start that again.

At that moment I felt inside me a tingle of excitement, a signal that it was time to run behind the hut and relieve myself. It was a wonderful feeling; I wanted to hug and kiss my own stomach. Finally, after all, my digestion was getting rid of that foul bread!

I leapt up, ran behind the house, and—word of honor!—I have never felt such pleasure in shitting. In one moment I was free of the bread!

Somebody coughed and groaned in my vicinity. I leapt up, covering my bottom, and saw Meeme, lying facedown, looking at me from the bushes. He was even shaggier than before, one ear covered in cobwebs, and had in his hand his inseparable wineskin.

"Want some wine, boy?" he croaked.

"No thanks!" I replied, and I couldn't resist showing off. "I ate some bread today. I don't want any more of that village food."

"Bread is hogwash," said Meeme. "But wine is different. It makes you nicely sleepy, so you don't know anymore whether you're alive or dead. You simply lie like a corpse."

I didn't see anything nice in that sort of existence, but the sight of Meeme reminded me of Manivald's ring.

"Meeme, do you remember that ring you gave me once? What am I supposed to do with it?"

"You're supposed to put it on your finger and prance around the forest. What is any ring good for? Well, if you really press it, it might fit on the end of your toe too. If you think it's prettier that way."

"Can't you do anything else with it?"

"Well, what else would you want to do with a ring? Eat it? It's even nastier than bread, and as hard as stone."

"Why did you give me that ring anyway?"

Meeme gurgled with laughter.

"I didn't want anything else to do with it," he grinned. "What would I have a ring for? It would rot away with me and that would be a shame. Pretty little thing, anyway!"

He took another drink, but a bit unsteadily, and the red wine ran all down Meeme's face, as if blood were coming out of his mouth.

I turned my back on Meeme and went indoors, where Salme had started eating again, to please Mother.

"I want some meat too," I announced, flopping down at the table. "My tummy's completely empty!"

I felt healthy and strong. The bread was gone from my stomach like an ugly pimple from my face, and I planned to eat as much goat as would fit into my belly.

Twelve

 saw Hiie and Pärtel the next day. Hiie was still
somehow blotchy faced, and complained that she'd
been vomiting all night.

"You ate only a fingertip-sized bit. What was
there to vomit?" I asked.

"Nothing, but I had such a horrible feeling in the tummy,"
complained Hiie. "And I was horribly afraid too. I was afraid
there might still be a little crumb of bread inside me, and when
I thought about it, I'd run off to the bushes again. My throat is
still sore from all that puking."

On the other hand Pärtel assured me grandly that the bread
had done nothing to him.

"I didn't even understand that it would be any different," he
told me. "I could eat even more of that bread. I could scoff three
loaves of it and it wouldn't do a thing. You want to go back to
the village, grab some bread, and eat some more?"

"Ah, no," I said, not enthused at all by Pärtel's idea. "Why eat
so much of it? It doesn't taste good at all."

I was ashamed to tell others what trouble that piece of bread had caused in my stomach. I made out that eating bread was nothing special for me, though I knew that I wouldn't put that weird muck in my mouth again for any price.

I looked enviously at Pärtel, whose thick frame had digested the dangerous bread without any problems. In the past year Pärtel had grown a head taller than me, and considerably broader as well, so that beside him I looked like a snake with joints. I was lanky and skinny, with a pale face, while Pärtel's hair was red brown and his complexion was ruddy.

I was quite angry with Pärtel at that moment, for he was tactlessly bragging about his bread-gobbling skills, as if it were a matter of honor. He laughed at Hiie, who was still hiccupping now and then from yesterday's piece of bread, and asked me several times with a sly expression: "Listen, you must have been feeling bad afterward too? I didn't at all!"

I put up with this for a while, then lost my temper and said that a fly eats shit again and again, but I don't. Should I make a big deal out of a fly and give it great respect? Now Pärtel got angry, saying that he was going home if I was going to be so disgusting, comparing him to a fly. Bread is not shit. Very many people eat it, and all foreigners do. He stormed off, and I stared after him. Pärtel and I had had our tempers flaring up before, and played happily the next day together despite it all, so I didn't make a big issue out of his anger.

Hiie and I stayed together at first, but after a little while Ints crawled up, and we decided to go and take a look at Pirre and Rääk. They still had the big louse, and every day there were titanic struggles with the birds. Despite its gigantic size, they recognized it as an ordinary insect, and tried to grab it in their beaks and drag it to their nests, but naturally nothing came of this. The louse was so big that even an eagle could scarcely lift it, but eagles do not hunt lice or beetles. Little blackbirds, swallows, and flycatchers pried away with no success at all at the flanks of the huge louse, and twittered in annoyance while the great insect flailed its legs, knocking out some of the birds with its movements.

In the interval the louse had become a lot cleverer. Pirre and Rääk had trained it carefully, so that it no longer tried to scuttle off into crevices, but slouched along calmly on the end of a leash and, when a signal was given, stopped and got down on its belly. It had also learned to appreciate the presence of humans, but not as an ordinary louse does, trying to crawl into your hair and lay its eggs there. The big louse did not go for your head, but simply pressed itself against your leg and snuffled.

For some reason it particularly liked Hiie. The girl only needed to appear, and the louse would immediately scurry up to her. Hiie was small and the louse reached her shoulders. It rubbed itself against her so violently that she fell over, and Pirre and Rääk gave the insect a fierce tongue-lashing. Then it drooped down and sprawled unhappily on the ground, until Hiie started stroking it and telling it that it was a fine and nice animal.

According to the Primates, the louse shouldn't have understood any of Hiie's words, for in talking to the louse Hiie didn't use Snakish words, let alone the ones with the ancient Primate pronunciation. But the louse became ever more cheerful when Hiie praised it, and scurried happily around the girl in a circle. It even let Hiie ride on its back, stepping slowly and solemnly, cautiously stretching out its legs, as if afraid to jolt its cargo too much. It was a weird sight—a thin little girl riding bareback astride a big strange insect—but the Primates told us that in the old days, when there were only very large animals and insects living in the world, such things happened often. In any case, pale little Hiie on the louse's back, with the two Primates sitting beyond her in front of their cave, and around them bushes and trees of species that had long since died out in other parts of the forest, looked like a secret visitor from some distant age. That was just how I had imagined those mysterious sprites of which Ülgas talked so much. If they existed at all, they would have to be like Hiie, riding on louseback.

Hiie herself looked after the louse, and always stroked and scratched it with care. I thought the louse was horrible, and I didn't like to touch it; a couple of friendly pats was the most I could force myself to. Hiie, on the other hand, said it was very sweet.

"He's such a friendly animal," she told me. "And I'm terribly sorry for him, because I don't understand at all where his eyes are, or his ears or his nose. He does have them, right? Just think, if you had to live without eyes, ears, or nose. Whenever I look at him, I get such a tender feeling coming over me. I want to fondle and stroke the poor creature . . . Ah, the poor little thing!"

"I think he has eyes and ears and everything else, but we can't find them," I said. "Insects have that stuff in other places than we and the animals have, but that louse must know very well where anything is."

Hiie shook her head doubtfully and stroked the louse still in the same way, for in her eyes this giant insect was a wondrously dear little creature, and a poor beggar besides.

This time too the louse trotted gladly toward us, rubbed itself against me out of habit, leapt out of the way of Ints, who it feared, and ended up with Hiie, who it knocked over at first, out of sheer enthusiasm. Then it got down to a crouching position, so that the girl could climb on its back. Hiie caressed and fondled the louse, and rode proudly up to Pirre and Rääk's cave. The Primates were sitting in their yard and grinding some plant down on a big stone.

"What are you doing?" I asked, sitting down beside them.

"Take a look," said Pirre, mixing the juice that flowed out of the crushed plants with some liquid slime, which colored it red.

"We want to draw the louse on the wall," explained Rääk. "As a memorial. One day, when he's no longer around, we can look at the picture and remember him."

We went into the cave, and walked quite deep into it, where generations of the Primates' ancestors had painted pictures from their lives. From floor to ceiling the walls of the cave were covered in thousands of tiny drawings, showing Primates and all kinds of long-extinct animals.

"This is our history," said Pirre and Rääk proudly, and in one vacant spot Pirre set about drawing the louse. "Everything that has ever happened is nicely shown here. You see right up there is a picture of the arrival of the first humans. At first they were quite like us; they didn't wear clothes or anything. But here"— and Pirre pointed to another picture—"they've hung skins on their backs."

"Is the Frog of the North here too?" I asked.

"Oh yes, in quite a few places," Pirre assured me, and showed me pictures of a big lizard-like creature, flying around the heads of tiny humans, with other humans' legs dangling out between its jaws.

"These pictures are really, really old," said Hiie respectfully. "The Frog of the North hasn't been seen for ages."

"Oh, dear child!" laughed Pirre and Rääk. "The time since the last time the Frog of the North flew can't even be measured yet. It was so recently! These pictures tell us about times long before that. And actually these pictures aren't all that old. The really old pictures are behind this wall." The Primates pointed to a rock far at the back of the cave. "In olden times this cave was much bigger, but a few hundred thousand years ago the earth quaked here and the end of the cave was buried under rocks. All the old drawings remained there; there was a huge number of them, dating from the very earliest times. No one can see them anymore, and so you can't know exactly what happened in those olden times. If there are no pictures, you can't remember anything. But at least this big louse is now nicely drawn, and all future generations can admire him. He will endure."

Pirre looked proudly at his handiwork, a great red insect painted on the wall, which might be a louse, or just as well a spider or a fly. The Primates were not the best of artists, and lice are quite difficult to draw.

"Look, this is you!" said Hiie tenderly to her pet. The louse shivered with pleasure, as Hiie stroked it. It was not interested in the picture and maybe didn't even see it, since we weren't sure if it had eyes.

We spent the whole evening with Pirre and Rääk, sitting by the fire and listening to the Primates singing their strange songs, which were not at all like the tunes that humans sing. Primates' songs consisted more of vocalizations than of words, together with squeals, growls, and murmurs, but as a whole it sounded very beautiful. We tried to sing along, but couldn't manage at all well. Nowadays, when I have nothing better to do, I sometimes call to mind those ancient tunes, which no one else remembers apart from me, and I hum to myself. I like those old songs much better than these fashionable "regi" songs that the village women crow nowadays, which always give me a headache. They last so interminably long; you think the women will never shut up. The Primates' songs were never long. They either ended with a deafening shriek or subsided into a low hum, and they had a strange power. Even today they make my heart glad and they conjure up before my eyes those happy evenings when Pirre and Rääk still lived in their cave and used to sing to us.

That cave has now collapsed shut. No one will ever see Pirre's drawing of the louse. No one will ever know that such a creature lived here in the forest.

Oh, there are so many things that no one will ever get to know about.

We said good-bye to the Primates and went home. Ints crawled into his nest. Hiie set off for her hut. She had never gone home so late, and she would surely have got a beating from her mother and father, but luckily they weren't there. Lately they had been going more and more to the sacred grove to listen to Ülgas's incantations, and that evening too they were out at some special nocturnal gathering where they sacrificed foxes by moonlight, trying to find out what was on the sprites' minds.

I was plodding toward my shack when suddenly someone called me. It was Pärtel. I was quite astonished that he was still roaming around so late, but I thought he might be doing something exciting, and I was ready for adventure right away. I didn't give a thought to that morning's quarrel.

As soon as I saw Pärtel closer up, I understood that he wasn't out in the forest to play any pranks. He looked very troubled, even frightened, grabbed me by the shoulder, and demanded, "Where were you? I was looking for you!"

"What is it?" I asked. "Something wrong?"

"I don't know," said Pärtel. "It's just that . . . I wanted to tell you . . . Father said today . . . We're moving to the village."

Nothing could have shocked me more. I sat right down among the ferns, completely stunned by my friend's news, and Pärtel sat down beside me, looking at me pleadingly, as if he had fallen into a bog pool and was now waiting for me to heave him out from it and help him back onto dry land. But there was no way I could help him out from the pool into which he had now fallen.

"Why?" was the only thing I could say.

"Father said there's no point in staying here; everyone's leaving," replied Pärtel. "He doesn't want to go, but there's nothing that can be done. There's no sense in swimming against the tide. If the rest of the people have decided to move to the village, you have to get used to it and follow the crowd."

For a while we were silent again.

Finally I asked him, "Do you want to go?"

Pärtel shrugged.

"Not really," he said. "But what can I do? If Father and Mother are going, I have to go with them. I can't stay here alone."

He shifted closer to me.

"Might you come too?" he asked. "Not tomorrow, but some time. In a while. It'd be nice, we'd be together again and . . ."

"I was born in the village," I said. "Mother moved away from there to the forest and said she'd never go back. And I don't want to either. You saw what they wanted to do to Ints. They're all mad there."

"Well, yes, that business with Ints was awful," agreed Pärtel. "And I wouldn't . . . You know me. I like it here! But there's nothing I can do. I have to go!"

"I know," I said quietly.

Pärtel was sitting beside me like a heap of misery. I felt terribly sorry for him.

"Never mind," I said. "The village isn't far away, right here on the edge of the forest. I can visit you sometimes and you can always slip into the forest when you want to play with me. We'll keep seeing each other."

"Yes, of course," Pärtel agreed. "I'll be sure to come looking for you in the forest!"

"And I'll come to your place, and I'll bring Hiie and Ints with me. You won't start hitting Ints with a stick."

"No, I'm not that mad! I'll . . . I'll carry on living as I did in the forest."

"But you'll start eating bread. It won't do you any harm, though. You managed eating it very well."

"Yes, I can eat bread. It won't do anything to me, but I don't like it either. Well, I guess you can always get meat in the village too."

"You see it's not so bad after all," I said. But actually I was thinking it is bad, very bad. It couldn't be worse! My best friend is moving away! How could it happen like this? Surely he won't go after all! Maybe he'll stay in the forest and everything will be as it was.

"Yes, it's not so bad," muttered Pärtel, but it was quite clear that he was thinking the same as I was.

We sat morosely a while longer, until Pärtel finally got up.

"Well, it's nothing," he said somehow soundlessly, as if he'd caught a cold and lost his voice. "I'll go home now. Tomorrow morning we'll get going; before that I have to get ready."

"Have you let your wolves out?" I asked.

"We will tomorrow," replied Pärtel. He stood there snuffling.

"See you then," he fumbled. "You might come tomorrow and see how we're . . ."

"Guess I'll come then," I said.

"Till tomorrow," said my friend and set off on the way through the forest to his shack, to sleep there for the last time. It was terrible and incredible. I traipsed home and curled up in my place, but I couldn't sleep all night; I finally got to sleep toward morning, and slept like a log. Mother didn't wake me; she liked me to sleep in, just as she liked me to eat a lot. When I finally opened my eyes it was already noon. Pärtel has gone, I thought straight away, and actually I was pleased that I hadn't gone to see him off. I lay on my back awhile, staring at the ceiling.

Then I heard hissing at the door. Ints had come looking for me.

"What's wrong? Are you sick?" he asked.

"No, quite well," I replied, getting up and walking into the yard with Ints. Everything there was just as it had been yesterday, except that I had a feeling that the forest was completely empty, and the tussocks echoed under my footfalls.

Thirteen

ärtel and his parents were not the only ones to leave. It was just like the spring thaw, when the first broken pieces of ice are soon followed by others. Apparently quite a few had been weighing up whether to move to the village or not, and Pärtel's parents' decision ended their hesitation. The very next day, one of Salme's friends left with her mother, and after them, more and more and more. Even beforehand there had not been many of us left in the forest, but after a week or two, the only ones who remained were our family, Hiie and her mother and father, Ülgas, Meeme, the Primates Pirre and Rääk, as well as a couple of decrepit old gaffers, for whom the sight of every new morning was a quite unexpected surprise.

In those days I walked around the forest frightened and bewildered and had a feeling that it was crumbling away before my eyes. All at once, trees felled in a storm appeared before me, branches blown down by the wind, and withered bushes, which I wouldn't have noticed earlier, and it seemed to me that their collapse was somehow connected to the people leaving for the village. I can't deny that I asked myself the question at that time: wouldn't it be wiser for us to follow the others' example, because the mass migration of people made the forest altogether less welcoming for me. Some peril seemed to be lurking there, something that had made others flee, and when a strong wind arose and tousled the treetops with a murmur, I flinched with fear: was this the beginning? I didn't know what I was supposed to fear, but the people's departure had somehow bored a hole in the forest, and from that hole there seeped something alien and nasty into the cozy old woods.

Uncle Vootele, who roamed around with me very often in those days, consoled me and told me he had seen many such departures. They had always come in waves: for a few years everyone stays put, but then suddenly dozens of families make a move. Then again many peaceful years pass, when it never even occurs to anyone to leave the forest, but it usually happens that one family decides to go for some reason, and others follow soon after. Those who move to the village are like flocks of birds, heading south in the autumn; some set off as soon as the weather gets cooler, but others only when the first snow covers the ground.

"Those who are going now waited for the snow," said Uncle Vootele. "You can't blame them; they stayed a long time."

"What about us?" I asked.

"We're like the crows and owls," said Uncle, laughing. "We stay for the winter. At least as far as your mother and I are concerned. You and Salme are basically still children, and of course you'll stay with your mother, but when you grow up, you'll be deciding for yourselves whether to go or stay. And if you go, that will be it. Then there will be just the animals and snakes left in the forest."

"I'm not going," I assured him firmly.

"Who knows what the future will bring," said Uncle Vootele. "Of course I would like life in the forest not to die out completely. But just think, Leemet—what kind of a life is it for you here, all alone? One day your mother and I will die, then there will be just you and Salme. Won't that be terribly lonely?"

"There will still be Hiie, and Ints and the other adders."

"Hiie, of course. And the adders won't be going anywhere. So, we'll wait and see. Just don't ever think that your mother or I are commanding you to stay on in the forest at any price. We won't condemn you if you decide to move to the village. Life is like that; all things come to an end. There are some trees where owls have nested for hundreds of years, and yet at some point they leave it empty, don't return there. That's simply how it is. At least you know the Snakish words, and I know that they will live on within you when I'm dead. That's the most important thing. And who knows—maybe you will manage to pass them on to someone else."

Uncle's talk made me unhappy; my future looked miserable and dark. Moving to the village seemed extremely unpleasant, but if I tried to imagine myself as an adult in the middle of a forest abandoned by everybody, I got a lump in my throat. Uncle seemed to understand that, and he patted me on the back, saying with a laugh, "Don't think about those far-off things now! Right now you only know we're going to your place, and your dear mother and my precious sister will offer us a meal of goat that will take your breath away. Everything's fine with us today, and it will be tomorrow too, and so on for years and years to come. What is to come after that, no one knows. Unpleasant things are like rain: sometimes they visit us, but there's no point in worrying about them while the sun shines. And anyway, you can take shelter from the rain, and many things that seem nasty from far away are not so terrible at all seen close up. Let's go and eat!"

And that is what we did. Mother was glad that Uncle came visiting us nearly every day, as he always came on an empty stomach and Mother was able to feed him on haunches and legs of goat.

"You're a fine man, Vootele," Mother said appreciatively to her brother. "You eat so well! If only Leemet were like you! I keep offering him one thing and another, but he only picks at it!"

"Mother, today I ate half a haunch of venison!" I argued.

"Well, what is half a haunch of venison to a growing boy like you? Only half a haunch! Eat the whole haunch! Who are you saving it for? I've got my own. Eat one; you get another."

"Mother, it's impossible to eat a whole deer!"

"Why is it impossible, if your stomach is empty? Look at how Uncle Vootele eats!"

"Mm!" mumbled Uncle. "Very good. I'll take another leg."

"Take it, do! Take two! You too, Leemet, take one! Take it and at least taste it!"

I sighed and picked up a roasted goat leg for myself. I wasn't especially hungry, but sitting in the home kitchen, gnawing on goat legs, helped to give the impression that everything in the forest was as before and that the dewy grass of the next morning would not be full of the footprints of people leaving it.

I hadn't seen Pärtel for several weeks, although he'd promised to come and see me soon. I was waiting impatiently for him, wondering why my friend wasn't keeping his word. What was he up to in the village? It would be natural for him to escape from that loathsome place at the first opportunity, to breathe the forest air again and complain to his old buddy about all the terrible things he was experiencing there. If I were he I would have shown up long ago. He knew where to find me, and also that I couldn't visit him. A couple of times I had in fact walked to the edge of the forest and nervously stared toward the village, hoping to see Pärtel somewhere there, but I couldn't. I did see other villagers, including the familiar Magdaleena and a few of my sister's friends, who had only recently left the forest. They were already wearing villagers' clothes, and once I saw one of them with a rake. It didn't make me envious; actually it made me feel strange, sort of sick. I imagined my sister Salme walking with a rake over the shoulder, and it disgusted me even more than the thought of her kissing with a bear.

At that time my only playmate was Ints, for Hiie was no longer allowed out at all. Tambet had shut himself and his family indoors in their shack, as if afraid that those going to the village had caught some dangerous disease that might also infect his own people. So all Hiie's wanderings had to stop. I saw her a couple of times looking sadly out the window; I waved to her and she gestured back to me—carefully, so that no one in the room would notice.

Tambet did venture out sometimes, hunting for unhusbanded wolves who wandered freely just as in ancient days. In this way his wolf pack continued to grow, but thanks to Hiie and the Snakish words even the new wolves soon learned that they ought to sleep in the daytime, not eat. One time, Tambet caught a glimpse of me; he glared at me and shouted, "What are you waiting for? Why don't you move to the village, like the other traitors!"

I didn't answer him and ran quickly into the bushes.

I was saddened that Hiie was not allowed out to play anymore. Pärtel moved away, Hiie was stuck at home—and I felt completely alone. There was only Ints, who tried to console me by saying that all the emigrants to the village were fools, but his jokes didn't improve my mood. Ultimately, adders can't really understand humans, even when they are speaking the same language. They regarded humans rather as younger brothers, whom they have indulgently taught a secret language, honored with a precious gift that the humans have stupidly thrown away, willfully choosing to become like hedgehogs or insects. Snakes were proud creatures, and they didn't tolerate stupidity, nor did they have any sympathy for the humans who were leaving the forest. Evidently they had already given up on the human race, like a piece of food that has fallen into the river and is carried out of reach by the current.

I understood this, and I hadn't suggested to Ints that he make poisonous jokes about those who had moved away, but I couldn't laugh along with him. I couldn't laugh about Pärtel, because I remembered how sad he had been and how he hadn't wanted to leave. The only thing I didn't understand was why he still hadn't come to see me. More and more often I went to the edge of the forest to lurk, and ended up spending whole days there, having decided to wait as long as it took to see Pärtel. If the villagers hadn't killed him, he must turn up in the end! Ints was with me; he wasn't particularly interested in Pärtel, but they were beautiful warm autumn evenings and in the sunshine of the forest edge it did him good to coil up and doze.

Finally one morning my waiting bore fruit. I saw Pärtel. He suddenly appeared from behind the corner of a house, a scythe in his hand. I hissed at him a long and piercing Snakish word, scarcely audible at all. Pärtel flinched, turned around, and saw me.

The worst thing was that he hesitated. He didn't hiss back; he didn't run at full speed toward me or express anything like the great joy I felt when I saw him stepping out from behind the corner. He stopped and considered. Finally he started walking toward me, his arm covered behind his back by the scythe, a forced smile on his face.

"Hi!" he said. "Ah, here you are."

"I came to watch you gad about the village," I said sarcastically. Pärtel's attitude had made me defiant. I had imagined us hugging each other and then chatting at great length about what had happened to us since we had seen each other. But now I was standing, glaring at Pärtel, while he smiled a forced smile at me. Evidently he was embarrassed about his village clothes and the scythe hidden behind his back. But I didn't intend to be merciful.

"What have you got behind your back?" I asked. "Some tree root or something?"

"It's a scythe," replied Pärtel awkwardly. "I was just on my way to the field. That's why I haven't been able to come and see you; there's so much work. Right now it's harvesting time."

"What do you cut that junk for?" I persisted. I was furious and terribly unhappy that the longed-for meeting with my friend had been such a shabby failure. I felt I had to choose whether to burst into tears or keep my composure by insulting Pärtel, and I chose the latter.

"They make bread from the grain," mumbled Pärtel. He was looking down, avoiding my gaze.

"That mush! Don't you have anything else to eat?"

"Bread is actually very useful," said Pärtel. He looked truly embarrassed; he must have wanted to run away from me back to the field, to cut straws along with the other villagers with his new toy. But he just stood there, asking after my mother's and Salme's health. Never before had Pärtel been interested in my mother's and sister's health, and I told him so to his face.

"You've very quickly turned strange in the village," I said. "What have they done to you? Remember how you told me that evening you didn't want to leave the forest? And now you tell me you couldn't come to see me, because you have some sort of crop cutting to do. What does that have to do with you? You're from the forest! You know Snakish!"

"You don't understand anything!" said Pärtel, suddenly very angry. "Why are you attacking me? I didn't want to come away from the forest because I didn't know what kind of life they live in the village, but now I do. There's nothing wrong with it. It's actually very nice here. There are so many people here, other boys and girls. We play together and have fun. And harvesting crops is great too; I'm pretty good at cutting with a scythe. Later they're going to teach me how to thresh grain and how to mill it. It's very interesting here, and I don't have any need for Snakish words, so it doesn't matter whether I know them or not."

"Ha!" scoffed Ints, who up to now had been lying peacefully coiled. "Only insects live without Snakish words. What kind of life is that?"

Pärtel was startled at the sight of Ints and stared at him for a moment somewhat fearfully.

"Do you want to strike him down with a stick?" I asked. "Have those jolly boys and girls already taught you that all adders must be bludgeoned to death?"

"No," said Pärtel. "But just by the way—in the village they really don't like snakes. They are the enemies of God."

"So who is this God then?" I asked.

"That is the most powerful of the sprites," said Pärtel. "He has made us. He has made all the things in the world and can still make them. He can do everything. He helps those who worship him and fulfills their wishes. But those who are his enemies will perish."

"Who told you that?" I asked. "That's just the same sort or drivel that Ülgas drones on about in the forest."

"Johannes, the village elder," said Pärtel. "By the way, my name isn't Pärtel anymore. I was christened and I'm now Peetrus. God doesn't care for people called Pärtel. But he loves a Peetrus and when I ask him for something he gives it."

"That's just stupid!" I protested. "How can you believe a thing like that? There aren't any spirits!"

"There might not be any spirits, but there is a God," contested Pärtel. "Johannes the village elder spent a long time telling me about it. It was very interesting. He was put on a cross and then rose from the dead."

"You can't rise from the dead," said Ints. "That has never happened."

"But Johannes the village elder says it has!" Pärtel-Peetrus eyed Ints with completely evident disgust. "The whole world believes that he rose from the dead, and all the people can't be stupid."

"All the adders in the world know you can't rise from the dead!" I said. "And I believe them!"

"Adders can't read!" Pärtel gave me a stubborn look. "You think that only you and your snakes are smart. But Johannes has told me things that . . . You've only lived in the forest, but he has been beyond the seas, in far foreign lands. There are huge numbers of people living there and they all believe in God and know that he rose from the dead. And they all harvest grain and eat bread and none of them lives in the forest or talks to snakes. Maybe you're the one who's half-witted. Johannes said that in other places in the world they think that people who live in the forest and talk to animals are complete fools."

"You lived in the forest yourself!"

"I don't anymore! Everyone's left the forest. Everyone!"

"Go to hell!" I shouted. I didn't know how to argue with Pärtel; I didn't want to argue with him. I wanted everything to be just as it was before and Pärtel to be Pärtel again, not Peetrus. But he stood there wearing his village clothes and carrying a scythe, talking to me with a serious face about God and grain harvesting, and behind his back the whole world and the myriads of people who didn't live in the forest and hungrily munched on bread all glared at me. I only had the Snakish words. I turned my back on Peetrus and ran back among the trees.

I kept on walking, striding through the forest, pushing branches away and stumbling through thickets. I passed Pirre and Rääk's cave and saw the louse getting hopefully to its feet; it must have been pining for Hiie, but the girl had to stay at home and couldn't come visiting her friend. Pirre and Rääk were looking out of their cave, but I didn't go up to them. These last Primates were just living in their own strange past, bare bottomed, not having even learned to wear animal skins. I was a primate in comparison to Pärtel in his village clothes. I rushed onward, enraged with the whole world.

I kept on walking all day, through the whole forest, getting to places where I'd never been before. I saw many animals: deer, goats, and elk, who stopped still when they saw me and looked at me thoughtfully with big eyes; bears, who tried clumsily to greet me; a few wandering wolves. I met no humans. Finally, toward evening, when I was dead tired, the forest started to thin out. I kept going until I got to the forest's edge. Yonder was an unknown village. I saw humans there too; they were gathered in a great cleared square, making fire and swaying. They were screaming and laughing. There were many of them.

The forest was surrounded on every side by people and their villages.

"So, what now?" someone was asking, and only now did I notice that Ints had been crawling along with me the whole way. He didn't seem tired at all, coiling himself up and looking up at me benignly. "Let them live in clumps, on each other's backs. That's how ants live, because they are just tiny specks of dirt with legs, not even worth noticing. They have to stick together to survive. They have no other option; they don't know Snakish. Don't worry about them!"

I was too tired to reply. I threw myself down on the moss and closed my eyes.

"I can't get back home today," I said. "I'll sleep right here."

"You'll catch cold here," said Ints. "It's autumn already. But there's an adders' burrow just near here. Actually they're everywhere; our kind has burrowed everywhere throughout the forest. Let's go inside; it's warm there. It'll be good for you to sleep there."

"Thanks, Ints," I said. Ints crawled ahead and I tried to stumble after him on my painful legs. That must have been why Ints stayed so lively; he didn't have legs to get tired. He led me below a fallen tree, under which was a narrow passage leading to a snakes' lair.

I climbed inside. Down in the burrow there were other adders, who watched me curiously. Since I was so far from home, there wasn't a single snake I knew among them. I greeted them with a hiss and laid myself out in a corner. The adders made a cozy space for me.

I fell asleep, feeling more snake than human, and that sensation comforted me a little.

Fourteen

I didn't meet with Pärtel after that. I no longer stood waiting at the edge of the forest; if Pärtel had come toward me in the forest, I probably would have jumped into the bushes, as I did when I saw the Sage of the Grove or Tambet. I didn't want to meet Pärtel, because he wasn't Pärtel anymore but Peetrus, and there is nothing worse than seeing an old friend change into someone alien and incomprehensible.

I had often seen Ints eating, gobbling up a whole frog or mouse in one gulp. A little animal would gradually disappear into his throat and in the end the curves of its body would still be visible under Ints's skin, even when completely covered by the snake. It had been swallowed by the adder, just as my old friend Pärtel had been swallowed up by some village boy called Peetrus. Pärtel's nose and ears were still visible inside that Peetrus, but digestion had already begun, and soon enough the last traces of him would disappear. I would have been much happier if Pärtel had died—then I could have mourned him in peace. But now I knew that he was still moving around in some distorted, defiled form; he existed, but not for me. I had the feeling you have when someone takes your good old trousers and shits in them; the trousers still exist, but they can't be worn anymore; they are full of a disgusting alien smell.

Naturally Pärtel didn't come to me in the forest, so I had no need to flee into the bushes. No doubt he felt much the same as I did. He had entered a new world and was now greedily learning its rules, just as I had once tirelessly contorted my own tongue to enunciate all the Snakish words and get the whole forest to communicate with me. Pärtel no doubt wanted to be absorbed into his new life as quickly as possible, and I was part of his old one. The sight of me embarrassed him. He might have felt a bit like a traitor, but above all he was ashamed of me. Pärtel had nothing to talk to me about, while in the village there were plenty of boys and girls who lived his kind of life, ate the same foods, and did the same kinds of tasks. It was quite natural for Pärtel to exchange me for them; it was simpler that way.

Would I have acted differently if my mother and father had moved to the village and Pärtel had stayed in the forest in my place? I can't say. I'd like to say that I wouldn't have betrayed the forest, would have stayed a true friend to the adders and gone to visit Pärtel every day, that I wouldn't have forgotten Snakish, as Pärtel had done, because the next time I met him—it was many years later—he couldn't force out a single hiss. All the Snakish words were, so to speak, purged from his memory, and if he had remembered them, he wouldn't have been able to hiss them, because he'd lost half his teeth from gnawing on bread and his tongue was swollen from drinking bitter beer, which the village people guzzled instead of simple water. It would be easy for me to say that I wouldn't have changed into such an oaf, but

I'm afraid I'd be lying. Even I would have been sucked into the village, swallowed up as if by a gigantic snake, by the alien and hostile Frog of the North, and gradually digested. And I would have had no power to resist, because my own Frog of the North had vanished, and no one knew where it was sleeping.

So I gave up thinking about Pärtel and became reconciled to the fact that somewhere in the village there now lived a boy named Peetrus, who cut rye with a scythe, played on the swing with the other village children, and had nothing at all to do with me. So I played with Ints and sometimes also visited Hiie. Uncle Vootele often took me with him on his trails, and we went to visit those solitary old men who had stayed on in the forest, but as if by some agreement they all died off during that autumn, and the forest was even emptier of people. Ülgas the Sage burned their corpses on a pyre, but Uncle Vootele and I didn't take part in the funerals, because after the business of the sacred lake our family had nothing to do with Ülgas. So he cast spells and invocations alone by the fire, the only mourner being the deeply silent Tambet, who naturally didn't question any rite that had any of the flavor of the ancient way of life.

It was a bleak autumn, perhaps the bleakest in my life, because although I had lived through even sadder times and experienced much more horrible events, back then I hadn't yet grown that thick carapace over my heart that makes all misfortunes more bearable. To put it in Snakish terms, I hadn't yet moulted my skin, as I did several times later in life, changing into a harder covering, until my skin could withstand all but a few sensations. By now, probably nothing can penetrate it. I'm wearing a coat of stone.

With the forest seeming almost extinct I spent a lot of time at home. Nothing had changed there. Mother would spend whole days in front of the fire, roasting monstrous amounts of deer and goat. She was in a good mood because she liked her children to sit at home all day eating meat instead of wandering in the forest and turning up at the table only in the evening. I ate more than ever before, and I got fat, which pleased Mother very much. She was even more overjoyed at how Salme became nicely buxom, not least because it proved that her cooking skill hadn't declined and the roasted haunches of venison were going down well.

Salme was also often at home that autumn. She had been used to going out in the evenings and coming back late at night; she claimed that she'd been watching the sunset. That was an obvious lie, because at that time of the year the sun set early, and you might rather say you were watching the moon rise. But one day she no longer went out, and sat sadly at the table instead, and I guessed immediately what was wrong: the bears had gone into hibernation.

In fact we were also used to snoozing through the winter. Usually in early autumn a giant amount of meat was collected, and with the forest covered in snow we stayed at home, slumbering, stirring ourselves to eat only once a day. That is what all the wiser creatures of the forest do—snakes, humans, and bears, as well as some smaller animals. In winter there was no sense in roaming around and wading through the snow; it was much smarter to conserve your strength and use the dark days for proper rest. The wolves were released into the forest to forage for their own food, and they enjoyed their winter freedom to the full, killing goats and deer, as well as village people who in their alien way didn't sleep in the winter. Since they didn't understand Snakish, they were easy prey for our wolves.

That year, too, we were prepared to hibernate in the usual way, when one evening Ints crawled into our place and said, "Father said to ask you whether you'd like to hibernate with us this winter. He'd be very pleased if you came."

This was an unexpected offer, because the snakes had always hibernated on their own, in large underground caves, and I had never heard of a human spending the winter with them. But apparently there were so few humans left in the forest that the adders thought it was possible to take them in. All the more so because apart from us no one else was going there. Ülgas and Tambet would never have moved in with snakes, because snakes showed no respect for the sprites who were so vital to them. And the adders would not tolerate conjuring or spell casting or any other noise, which Ülgas would insist on.

Uncle Vootele was at our place that evening and he took it on himself to accept.

"We'd be glad to come," he said. "It's a great honor for us."

We moved in with the adders a couple of days later. The first snowflakes were falling from the sky, and it was high time to set up winter quarters. Mother wanted to bring with us a large supply of venison, but the adders sent to escort us said that wasn't necessary.

"We have plenty to eat there," they explained. "Keep that meat for the spring; there's no sense in hauling those hunks of flesh with you."

I was excited. Although I had often visited the adders, I had never seen the caves where they slept in the winter. And it was wonderful to spend a whole winter with Ints, to doze beside him, and occasionally chat to each other in whispers about our dreams, until we got exhausted again and fell back to sleep. It was only Hiie that I felt sorry for, having to stay aboveground and be satisfied with spending the winter only in her mother's and father's company. There was nothing I could do about that; it wasn't possible for me to bring Hiie along to join the adders.

We trudged through the forest behind two rather vulgar snakes—Mother, Salme, Uncle Vootele, and I—and then descended for a while down a gently sloping passage, until we reached a large warm hall, which was completely dark. But it was a pleasant darkness, soft and caressing. Our eyes got accustomed surprisingly quickly and soon I could see a large number of snakes, who were prettily coiled up—and in the middle of the hall stood a gigantic white stone.

Apparently it was because of that stone that I was able to see so well in the dark. The stone didn't actually radiate light directly, but it was so pale that the dimness became transparent around it.

"What is that stone?" I asked Ints, who crawled up to me and swished his tail in greeting.

"That is our food stone," replied Ints. "We lick it in the winter and fill our stomachs. The stone is ancient and never gets smaller. Try it once with your tongue; it's very good!"

I stepped up to the stone and licked it. The stone was as sweet as honey and I carried on licking until I felt my stomach was terribly full. I felt I had eaten a whole deer.

"Now you won't want to eat for several days," said Ints. "That's how we live in the winter here. We lick the stone, then doze for a couple of days, then we lick again. It's quiet and warm here and sleep comes quickly."

We settled down inside and I must admit that I only had to lie down to be overcome with delicious exhaustion. I stretched out like a fox and fell straight to sleep.

I have only the most blissful memories of that winter. Dreams floated around me, and didn't fly away even when I half-consciously stumbled over to the white stone to get some sustenance, my eyes closed and my body weak from the pleasure of sleep. In the cozy darkness hundreds of adders were snuffling quietly in their sleep; somewhere in their midst were my mother, sister, and uncle. Everything was peaceful, everything good. Pärtel and the emigrants to the village seemed to be just shadows, forgotten as fast as the mind happened to stray to them, and I thought only of how good it is to sleep.

I swam in sleep; its waves rolled over me. I could even feel sleep; it was as soft as moss and crumbled between your fingers like sand. Sleep was all around me; it filled every groove and hole. It was at once both warm and refreshing, enfolding me like a caressing and cooling gust of wind. I had never slept so well as that winter in the adders' cave, and never since then have I felt such pleasure in sleep, even though I often came to hibernate with the snakes. Those times were just a repetition of the enjoyment; that winter, though, being completely buried in sleep was new and especially thrilling.

I lost my sense of time and didn't know whether I'd slept a long or a short time, but at one moment I woke up. At first I thought I simply had an empty stomach, and I crawled on all fours over to the stone, licked it, and wanted to fall back to sleep. But unexpectedly I was no longer sleepy. The sweet pleasure had vanished; I no longer sank into dreams headfirst like a stone thrown into a lake. My leg started to itch, then my ear, and finally I felt I could not lie down a moment longer, and I quickly stood up.

The adders around me were curled around each other, slumbering, and a little way away I saw Mother and Salme, also asleep. But Uncle Vootele was awake. He was sitting, scratching the beard that had grown half as long again in the winter and fixed his eyes on me.

"Good morning!" he said. "Time to get up."

"Is it spring already?" I asked incredulously. It seemed to me that we had arrived here in the cave only yesterday.

"Who would know that in this darkness?" answered Uncle. "But let's go and look. I believe it's beautiful weather outside."

"But the others are still asleep," I said.

"Let them sleep," replied Uncle. "We can be the first to see the new spring."

We climbed out of the cave and, for the first moment, were dazzled by the bright light. The sun, which we had not seen for so long, shimmered through the treetops at us. We kept our eyes shut for a while, and only later did we dare to peep out through our eyelashes.

It really was spring. Here and there was still some snow, but you could see the first flowers by the forest and the air smelled of freshly fallen rain. We gulped down the fresh air and rubbed our faces with the last of the snow; it was so good after a long sleep underground. The last of the sleepiness vanished from our bodies and I felt that I didn't want to sleep again for several years; the fresh spring air in my lungs for a long time made me feel so alive.

"Let's go and walk around a bit," said Uncle. "Our legs have withered away after lying around so long."

It was very exciting to see the forest again after the winter months I'd spent in the snakes' cave. Here and there was a tree half-broken under the weight of snow, and in the bushes you could find traces of wolves' meals—the strong bones of deer, the more delicate skeletons of goats. The forest was familiar, but at the same time a little different, and the change was fascinating and arousing, like a girl's new hairstyle. The forest was like an adder that had moulted. The tempering carpet of snow had given it a youthful flush; the first spring rain had washed it clean.

"Shall we go and eat a little?" suggested Uncle. "We've been licking the sugar-stone all winter; now we'd like something a bit more substantial. How would a cold haunch of venison do? I wouldn't say no!"

I agreed enthusiastically. The sugar-stone, which had filled our stomachs so well up to now, suddenly seemed mushy, and my mouth started to water when I imagined a properly dry-cured piece of meat, tough and good tasting between the teeth.

We went to Uncle Vootele's place. Under his shack he had a deep cellar, where he kept his store of food, and there was a decent stack of venison left from the autumn. Uncle Vootele opened the hatch and we climbed down inside.

"If you don't mind, I think we'll eat right here," said Uncle. "Then I don't have to worry about setting the table. We'll eat simply, like men. You take that shank, I'll take this one, and let's get on with it."

I sank my teeth into the shank and with great pleasure tore off tasty pieces of meat, which cleared away the last remnants of the snakes' sugar-stone from my mouth, and with that, the winter was over for me. Everything was again as before: I was awake, eating meat, and had a whole long year ahead of me. At that moment I was extremely pleased with my life. I had everything I needed—Uncle beside me, a hunk of venison in my hand, and the Snakish words in my mouth. I felt strong and vigorous.

It was at that moment that Uncle started coughing.

He had a bone picked half clean in his hand; he picked at it in a frenzy, and his face turned so red that the skin of it seemed to be ripped off, revealing raw flesh. He was choking wildly, his cough turned into a croak and a horrible rattle. He threw the bone from his hand and tried to beat his own back with his fist.

Only now did I realize that something was stuck in his throat, apparently a piece of meat not chewed small enough, or a little bone. I rushed to Uncle's aid, pounded on his shoulder blade, but now he was making even more horrifying sounds, whimpering, wheezing, and finally fell on his belly, his eyes bulging and his mouth agape.

He fell silent. He was dead.

Of course I didn't realize this immediately. I shook my uncle, turned him onto his back, beat on his belly, even put my hand between his jaws and groped around, hoping to find the piece that had lodged in his throat and pull the meat out, to save my uncle, wake him up again, do something to make that horrible expression leave his face, something to make him get up, spit, and start chatting to me again, as he did before, as he had always done.

But I didn't find anything in Uncle's mouth apart from a swollen tongue, and then I decided to drag him out of the cellar, into the fresh air, so that Uncle could recover in the spring wind and not die.

Uncle was big and heavy; I was slender and weak. It was terribly difficult to haul him out of the cellar, but I tried anyway, pulling as hard as I could, snuffling profusely but not crying— which is strange, but evidently I was in such a state that I still hoped to save Uncle and had no time to fall into despair. I had to get him out of the cellar, because outside there was fresh air, there were snakes, there was my mother—yet none of them could help my precious uncle.

Pushing from below and hauling from above, I managed to get Uncle halfway up the ladder, and I whispered to myself under my breath, "Just a little more!" The tip of my tongue was hanging out from my great effort, my hair covered with sweat from the exertion and the terrible fear. I climbed past Uncle, seized him with one arm, clutching the side of the hatch with the other, and tried to pull. The next moment I plunged with Uncle's corpse back into the cellar, the hatch fell onto the hole, the light vanished, and I realized, with a shooting pain that made me yelp, that I had broken my arm.

It was a dreadful pain; I lay for a while in the middle of the pitch-darkness, whimpering and weeping on the ground. Then I started to scream: I yelled for help with all my might until my voice broke and I was barely able to croak, needles prodding my torn throat. Then I wept again, realizing that no one could hear me, for Uncle and I were the first to wake; the snakes were still asleep, so were Mother and Salme, and a long time would pass before they would wake and come looking for me.

I didn't dare move, because my broken arm was burning with pain, and in the end I fell asleep from exhaustion and despair. When I awoke, I no longer knew if it was day or night, since in the darkness of the cellar I couldn't see even my own finger, and I had no idea how long I'd been asleep.

My arm was still hurting, but I understood that it would do me no good to lie motionless like that, and so cautiously got to my knees, supporting the damaged arm delicately with the other. It was an awful pain, but I took no notice of it, and began slowly moving forward on my knees, until I bumped into the wall. Then I turned around and went to the other side, and came across a mass that was lying on the floor.

At first I thought it was Uncle, and I got a fright, because I was now reconciled to the fact that my uncle was dead. Stumbling over a human corpse in a dark space is not the most pleasant experience. It was strange that Uncle, whom I loved so much, had now changed into something frightening; I saw in front of me his face swollen from suffocation, his bulging eyes and wide open mouth, his grinning teeth, and the darkness multiplied the intensity of my memory. Cold shivers ran up my back when I thought that that corpse with its gaping jaws was lying right here and maybe staring through the darkness right at me now with its glassy eyes. I swiftly jumped aside when the mass touched my knees, and whimpered as a shooting pain ran through my arm.

Then I recalled that somewhere on the cellar floor had lain a large dried haunch of venison. I pulled myself together and stretched out my good arm to find out what it was. I was terribly afraid, because I had to stretch it out in the darkness, and my fingers could very easily find themselves between my dead uncle's teeth. But I was lucky: it was a piece of venison. I ate it; there was a great deal of meat, and I knew that at least for now I wasn't threatened with starvation.

For a while I didn't dare to leave the venison, because although it was also dead, that hunk of meat was somehow safe—nourishing and friendly—whereas my dead uncle was metamorphosing in my mind into an ever more horrible and dangerous being, lurking for me in the darkness and deathly silence somewhere. At the same time there was still a place in my thoughts for that other uncle, the smiling, genial Uncle Vootele, and as much as I feared that bug-eyed corpse, I yearned for the living Uncle Vootele, and

I started quietly sobbing when I realized anew that Uncle was dead and we would never meet again. That awareness came in waves and was just as painful as the gnawing ache of my broken arm, bringing me to despair and then receding, only to return a little while later. I squatted by the venison, wept, and ate, mourning Uncle Vootele and fearing his corpse.

Finally I fell asleep again and when I awoke again I tried to call out a little, but my voice was as hoarse and weak as before. Then, since my arm was hurting a little less for the moment, I hit upon the idea of trying to break out of the cellar by my own effort. That meant, of course, that I had to move around again and risk stumbling over the corpse, but after a moment's hesitation I crawled from my spot. I managed to reach the ladder without coming across Uncle Vootele's body, and with a little effort managed to get onto the first rung. But when I reached the closed hatch and tried to push it up with my good arm, I soon realized that it wasn't possible. The hatch was too heavy; it would have been hard for me to get it open even with two hands, but with only one arm, moreover in a position where every movement caused such pain that I whimpered out loud, it was an unworkable task. I went down the ladder, but in the darkness I slipped on one rung, rolled to the floor, did more damage to my injured arm, and in the horrible rush of agony lost consciousness.

I don't know whether the time was short or long, but in the end I recovered. I was stunned and so weak that I couldn't even get to my knees. I crawled slowly to where I thought the venison was, but naturally I now bumped almost immediately into Uncle Vootele.

I was really afflicted by the pain radiating from my arm, and if I had wanted to escape, I simply wouldn't have had enough strength. So I restricted myself to simply turning my face away after coming across the corpse.

Uncle Vootele did not smell good; he gave off an unpleasant stench, but otherwise he remained quiet and gentle as a corpse should. Suddenly I no longer feared him, I put my whole arm out boldly, and touched the body resting beside me. I had bumped against Uncle's shoulder. There was his arm, on the other side his neck and from there I could go up to the face, but I didn't want to touch that. I left Uncle to rest in peace and crawled away. I was hungry and needed venison, not a dead human.

In the following days I hardly left the pile of meat. Uncle had begun to stink and the stench made me feel ill. I no longer feared Uncle's corpse; it had become repulsive to me. Somewhere in the dark he lay slowly rotting, contaminating the air which I, his nephew, had to breathe. At one time he had taught me Snakish; now he was gradually poisoning me.

I cowered in the dark, having lost all sense of time passing, drowsy and almost stupefied with pain, despair, and the stench of death, and strange ideas and visions revolved in my head. In my exhausted brain the fresh leafless forest that I had seen when I climbed out of the snakes' den and my rotting uncle blended together, and I saw apparitions of those same snow-thawed trees, the leafless branches like putrefied forked joints, and from that forest emerged a suffocating corpse stench.

Then in my thoughts Uncle was transformed into the Frog of the North, a gigantic winged snake, but he too was oozing and decaying. I could almost see him; he was lying beside me, and in my ramblings I lifted my arm and patted the darkness around me, consoling the imaginary Frog: "Never mind. You'll get well!" But my arm passed through the giant snake's scales, for it was decayed and brittle, and fetid air escaped from it with a hiss. In that hiss I recognized Snakish words and answered them; I was hissing on my own in the darkness of Uncle Vootele's cellar, and the air grew thicker and heavier. When I chewed the venison, it too stank of death and I was not sure whether I was eating deer or my own deceased uncle. But even that gruesome doubt couldn't shock me anymore, so weak was I.

Yet it was the hissing that saved me, those same Snakish words that this beloved uncle, now decomposing on the ground, had taught me, choked on the venison that he so loved to eat. I drove the image of the dead Frog of the North from my mind and rambled on, pressing from my parched lips the most diverse hisses. And those quiet, barely audible Snakish words penetrated through the ground surface, to where not even the loudest screams produced by the human mouth could penetrate.

The adders, now awoken from their hibernation, heard me, and the king of the snakes, Ints's father, bit through the trapdoor. They brought me out and carried me home to Mother, who had to spend a long time nursing and feeding me before I could walk and talk again.

My left arm remained crooked forever, broken in two places. Likewise the smell of the corpse never left my nostrils. Sometimes it seems to have gone. For many days I can't smell it, but in a moment it again strikes my nose, ranker than ever, and turns my stomach. It was the last gift I received from my beloved uncle, who taught me Snakish and who moldered away beside me.

Fifteen

he forest has changed. Even the trees are not as they were, or I don't recognize them; they have become alien to me. I don't mean that their trunks have become thicker, their crowns broader, and their tops stretch ever higher; that is all natural. There is something apart from the usual growth; the forest has become careless. It grows in any old way; it sheds leaves where previously the paths were clear. It has become tangled and shaggy. It is no longer a home but lives its own life and breathes to its own set rhythm. You might almost think that the forest is itself to blame for the people leaving its midst, because it behaves like a conqueror, spreading out in the footsteps of its former master. It was the people that vacated the place, and just as they let loose their own wolves, so they released the forest from its bonds and it dispersed itself like a pile of mold. Going to the spring, I'm constantly finding it off the footpath, and I stamp back the footpath into the ground, and the forest falls with an insulted rustle back into a coma, only to gain consciousness and spring back the next moment, stretching out its branches and leaves and covering the ancient human paths with needles. One day I will no longer go to the spring, and then the power will finally be in its hands.

Of course there are still the villagers, and they come here sometimes to pick berries, mushrooms, or brushwood, but they are no match for the forest. They are afraid of the forest, much more than needs be, and to increase their terror they have invented all sorts of monsters—werewolves, leprechauns, and ghosts. These poor idiots even believe in sprites; Ülgas the Sage can really rest assured that he has good disciples and plenty of them. Strange that Snakish has been forgotten while belief in fairies remains. Stupidity is stronger than wisdom. Ignorance is as tough as a tree root that bores into the ground where people once walked. The forest is proliferating; the village people are on the increase—but I am the last man who knows Snakish.

The last man . . . Mother also said that, one evening when I came home and sat in my usual place to taste Mother's roasted deer withers. Seven years had now passed since Uncle Vootele's death; I had grown tall, but remained as lean as before, and my beard was red, though my hair was brown. Mother put before me a decent slice of carefully and thoroughly roasted meat, sat on the other side of the table, and sighed sadly.

"What's the matter now?" I asked, knowing that Mother was sighing to force that question out of me. She sighed once more.

"You're the last man in our family," she began. That beginning was familiar to me; she often spoke like that. Actually I knew what Mother wanted to say, because we had had many talks like this. Nothing much new happened in the forest; everything was peacefully curled around its own tail, and our days looked like the wolves' flea searches: first they nibble at their thighs, then the stomach, then the withers, then the tail, and so on over and over again, always in the same order, without involving any part of the body that might present a surprise.

"You're the last man in our family," said Mother. "You'll have to talk to Mõmmi. Salme's very upset because of him."

Mõmmi was my brother-in-law, a big fat bear, with whom Salme had been living for more than five years. I remembered well how she left home—for Mother it was a matter of terrible shame and unhappiness, because since her own youthful experience she could not stand to look at bears. The fact that a bear was hanging around Salme was long known to us, and though Mother did all she could to keep Salme away from the bruin, there was not much she could do. Salme moved freely around the forest and the bear was likewise shuffling around at will, so it was no surprise that their paths kept crossing somewhere under a bush. It's hard for a young girl to resist a bear, something so big, soft, and cuddly, whose lips taste of honey. Mother combated it as best she could, but when she got home in the evenings Salme's clothes were always full of bear hairs.

"You've been meeting the bear again!" wept Mother. "I told you it's not right! A bear will not bring you happiness! They're evil animals!"

"Mõmmi's not evil at all!" contested Salme. "Quite the opposite, he's terribly kindhearted. I don't know, Mother. Maybe your bear was evil, but you can't tar all bears with the same brush!"

Mother didn't like reminders about "her bear"; her face always turned red and she changed the subject. But in this case it wasn't possible; she wanted to make it clear to Salme that going out with a bear was disastrous. So she grew a little embarrassed and said that all bears are deceitful, and their evil sometimes only appears years later.

"Years later!" sputtered Salme. "You might as well say there's no point in me getting married at all. Mother, I love Mõmmi!"

"Dear child, don't do this to me!" pleaded Mother. "Don't talk like that! It's terrible to hear. All your life I've been keeping you away from bears and protecting you, and now you go and undo all my good work!"

"But mother, who am I going to marry if not the bear?" asked Salme. "There are no young men in the forest apart from Leemet. Or should I go to old Ülgas? Would that filthy old man please you more than a lovely fat hairy bear?"

Mother had nothing to say to that; she just wept uncontrollably, and Salme's meetings with the bear continued. And one day she announced that she was moving in with Mõmmi and would become his lawful wife.

"Mõmmi doesn't like me having to always go home for the night," said Salme. "He says it breaks his heart and he can't sleep at night; he just sighs at the moon and moans."

"If you move in with him, you'll break my heart!" wailed Mother. "That bear is stealing my precious daughter!"

"Why?" complained Salme. "We'll live here in the same forest. I'll come and visit you. And besides, Mother, you can visit me too. Mõmmi's offended that you've been avoiding him like this. Many times he's been wanting to meet you."

"I'll never come to a bear's den!" shouted Mother, shocked, brandishing her hand as if a horrid bear were flying over her head in the form of a fly. "Never!"

"Well, that's a great shame!" declared Salme defiantly, and left home.

Mother resisted for precisely one day; then she roasted two large haunches of venison as a housewarming present, hauled them, groaning, onto her shoulder, and we trudged to Mõmmi's lair. The bear came to meet us, his head cocked in his simple-minded way, and humbly licked Mother's feet.

"And you're Salme's mother," he said in a deep voice. "I've seen you sometimes in the forest, but I've never dared to come up to you, as you're such a charming and lovely lady."

Mother's old love of bears, which she had dammed up like a beaver, now burst into full flood; she burst into tears, hugged Mõmmi, and kissed him behind the ears. She presented the bear with both of the haunches and watched tenderly as he hungrily gnawed on them, polished the last bone but one clean with his tongue, and when he got on his hind legs and bowed to the ground before Mother as a mark of gratitude, my dear mother was completely won over. All the way back she was telling me that she'd never seen such a polite bear, and that she was pleased for Salme.

"That bear knows how to respect her and care for her," Mother declared. "Actually bears are very pleasant animals. The bear that I knew . . ."

At this point Mother stopped, because she realized that it isn't quite polite to praise in my hearing the bear who ate my father's head off. But Mother was wrong. I didn't hold any grudge against that unknown bear. I didn't remember my father, and if I tried to imagine him, the face of Johannes the village elder appeared before me, and I remembered how he tried to club Ints to death.

Mother started visiting Salme and Mõmmi every day, taking them meat and decorating their cave, while Mõmmi picked wildflowers and brought honeycombs down from the trees in return. Salme was happy in her dear bear's embrace, and often rode around the forest on Mõmmi's back, clinging to his furry throat like a little frog, her cheek against Mõmmi's nape.

Of course this did not please Tambet; the marriage of Salme and Mõmmi gave him yet another reason to despise our family. In his opinion a bear was a creature far below a human. Bears never visited the sacred grove, they lived a wild and loose life, and they were gluttonous and lecherous. It was a matter of shame for a human to live openly with a bear. In secret it had of course occurred before—in fact very often; according to my departed Uncle Vootele, in ancient times it often happened that while all the men were rushing off to battle under the protective cover of the Frog of the North, the women left at home had bears waiting for them in the yard who were happy to console them while the men at the front were cutting down foreigners. Tambet would of course never have agreed to admit that anything so crude could have happened in those noble ancient times. For him the olden times were a single uninterrupted ray of sunshine; all the ugly stains that darkened its luster were due to the present day, and our immoral family in particular.

Still, there is no point in denying that Tambet was right in his opinion of bears as lecherous. That was the reason why Mother often sighed in the evenings and called me the last man in the family. Mõmmi, who had been living happily with Salme for years, had started looking for new girls. Only Hiie was available in the forest, and Mõmmi tried to court her, put a wreath on his head and hung around the girl shaking his head sadly, but

Hiie did not take the bait. She could hardly fail to have heard stories at home about the lustfulness of bears. One might think that I was in very bad odor at Tambet's and Mall's home, but this didn't stop my good relations with Hiie.

She was now seventeen years old, still pale and thin, not beautiful, with downcast eyes and bony shoulders. But Mõmmi was trying to snare her all the same, for bears are not attracted to women's appearance particularly; what excites them is their scent, but Hiie would run away every time she saw Mõmmi approaching. The bear got tired of it, and since there were no more young women in the forest, he moved to a new hunting ground—the village.

He didn't have any luck there either. The village girls were desperately afraid of Mõmmi, and every time he appeared at the edge of the forest, they all threw down their rakes and sickles and rushed with piercing screams to their houses, slammed the doors shut, and peered out of the tiny windows to see whether the ghastly wild animal was still lurking in the bushes. Mõmmi was very upset by the girls' behavior, because he had no bad intentions. Quite the contrary, he would gladly have loved all the young maidens. There were so many of them. They smelled so sweet. And that drove the bear to distraction. Day after day he went to the edge of the forest to prowl, but it did no good. The girls only feared him all the more, while the bear went more and more in heat.

Actually Mõmmi's adventures need not have concerned Salme at all, because it was clear that not a single village girl would let a bear into her arms; she would rather die. But Salme was still stricken with jealousy. She didn't like Mõmmi sitting on the edge of the forest, his tongue hanging out hungrily, watching the screaming village maidens. And so I as the "only man" had to be the one to call Mõmmi to order, to go to this wicked bear at the forest edge and take him home.

That is what Mother was now asking me to do.

"He's been prowling round there all day and Salme is quite beside herself," she complained. "I told her the bear can't help his nature; he simply adores all women terribly. Let him look at them. He won't do anything with them!"

In Salme's quarrels with Mõmmi, Mother often took the bear's side; at any rate she loved to emphasize that she "understands bears" and wanted Salme likewise to "learn to appreciate them." At this Salme always got very angry and shouted, "Whose mother are you, mine or Mõmmi's?"

"Yours, of course, dear child!" replied Mother.

"Why do you defend Mõmmi?"

"Because I understand bears," Mother began again, and so it continued for hours.

I didn't bother to scream at Mõmmi, but as the only man I was already used to restraining my mother, my sister, and her bear, and I also knew that Mother wouldn't leave me in peace before I did it. I could already guess her objections that would immediately follow if I were to say I was tired and wanted to go to sleep: "But she's your sister," "she looked after you so well when you were little," "we're one family; we have to help each other," "we mustn't stand aside." So I ate my fill quietly and said, "All right, I'll go. But first of all I'll eat."

For Mother, eating was sacred, and she was not about to hurry me up. I chewed deliberately slowly. I had told Mother a hundred times that Salme could call her bear home herself; it wasn't difficult. Mõmmi never put up any resistance; at the first call he would get to his feet obediently and slouch to his den, sighing sadly to himself. But Mother had an answer to that: "You're the head of the family," followed by talk of the "only man." I finished my roast, drank some springwater, and got up.

"So, I'll go then," I said.

"Do that, darling!" replied Mother. "Do your sister that favor. Don't be angry with Mõmmi. Just tell him simply that what he's doing is not right."

"I never get angry with him," I said, and went out. It was already evening and the forest was getting dark, but I could find the way with my eyes closed. Mõmmi was in exactly the same place where I'd found him more than ten times before, sitting, looking toward the village and sighing longingly. He understood immediately why I'd come, and started getting up, but I didn't say anything to him—just sat down next to him and joined him, staring at the village.

They were making fire. A great bonfire was blazing at the edge of the village, and around it skipped young people—boys and girls. Pärtel must have been among them there; I hadn't seen him since the time we got into a quarrel. I didn't recognize him; all those village boys looked the same, broad shouldered with fat red faces. I didn't like them at all; they seemed dull witted. But the girls were beautiful, much more beautiful than Hiie and more beautiful than my sister. So no wonder that Mõmmi went spying on them every day.

"So many girls!" said Mõmmi dreamily. Then he looked at me and winked, man to man. "You like them too, don't you?"

"I do," I admitted, somehow against my will.

I had tried to keep as far away from the village as possible; I didn't want to have anything to do with it. But the girls really were beautiful. I couldn't deny it.

We sat for a while looking at the villagers.

The boys led the girls to dance. The girls didn't refuse; they took the boys by the waist and whirled around the fire with them. I suddenly felt very bad, got up, and said to the bear: "That's enough, come home! Salme will be worrying. What's the meaning of coming here every evening?"

"I can't help it," replied Mõmmi. "I'm driven here. Salme's a nice woman, but sometimes I want someone fresh so badly."

"And what is Salme then? I think she's still fresh."

"Salme's like last year's honey," said the bear somewhat bitterly. "It's good too, but . . ." He didn't finish the sentence.

"You're shameless you are. How can you talk about my sister that way! You're like honey yourself, sticking to everything. Now go home and try and stay there. It's really annoying having to come and fetch you every evening."

"But you can look at beautiful girls yourself then, can't you?" asked Mõmmi, suddenly mischievous, nudging me with his cold black nose in the groin. This was so unexpected that I blushed and couldn't reply. Mõmmi sniffed the scent of the girls wafting toward him from the village for the last time and lumbered into the bushes. I didn't get up to accompany him. Why should I get involved in other creatures' family quarrels?

Sixteen

can't say that I hadn't thought about girls from time to time. There just weren't any of them in the forest, apart from Hiie. Mother was dead certain that one day I would take Hiie as my wife. I wasn't so sure. In fact if I hadn't seen a single other girl I might have thought that all women are like Hiie and been resigned to my fate. But I had a sister, who might not have been a first-class beauty, but was still luscious and fluffy in every way. I remembered her girlfriends too, whom Pärtel and I used to go and peep at when they were whisking themselves stark naked in the trees. There were some real beauties among them. Now they had all moved away to the village, but the village wasn't exactly seven seas away; in fact it was quite close to us, and there was nothing to stop me from roaming to the edge of the forest every once in a while.

Yes, I was no better than Mõmmi; I too went spying on the village girls. I'd seen them gathering hay and cutting grain with a scythe and—why hide it—even bathing in the lake. I knew very well what a girl should look like, and Hiie was nothing compared to the village maidens. She was sweet and nice, and we met and chatted often, but on no occasion did I feel a wish to caress her. She was a different sort. There are certain species of flower that seem to demand to be picked, with every color of their blossom radiating at you in a meadow, and you notice them even among the tallest grass. As a child I was very fond of picking flowers and presenting them to Mother. In the early spring when the first yellow coltsfoot appeared, I would pick them and take them home. Yet the coltsfoot is not really a flower; it withers indoors almost right away, but with its golden florets it stands out from the dead spring grass, asking to be picked. That's to say nothing of the later globeflowers, chamomiles, bellflowers, and poppies. As a child I just couldn't walk peacefully past them; even when I was in a hurry somewhere, my foot would falter when I saw their many-colored blooms and I felt a terrible desire to go and pick flowers.

But there are also a large number of plants that don't excite you at all. There are all sorts of stalks and grasses that fill the forest. You never pick them. It would seem downright ridiculous to go home with a handful of ordinary grass. Why bring that hay indoors? Of course it's nice that there are such plants, because the forest floor can't be carpeted with flowers alone, but they don't arrest your gaze. And unfortunately Hiie was that sort of plant. I had nothing against meeting her sometimes in the forest, but I didn't want to take her home. I was interested in the flowers that grew in the village, especially when they swam naked in the lake like water lilies.

So it was quite annoying for me to listen at home to Mother's discussions about where she would put me and Hiie to sleep when we started living together. Mother wanted to enlarge our shack, to move herself to an outhouse and leave the whole old hovel to us. I always tried delicately to contest this, reminding Mother that we weren't married yet, but she just shrugged her shoulders: "You ought to think about the future! You'll be taking a wife one day, won't you, and who else but Hiie? There aren't any other girls here in the forest."

Fortunately Mother never pushed me into taking a wife, for in her opinion I was still a child—even if at the same time the only man—and my main task was to eat properly what Mother made for me, and to be a good boy. But even though it was still some time in the future, Mother was starting to yearn for Hiie to enjoy her roasts too.

"It would be so nice if Hiie came to eat with us sometimes," she said, smiling and blowing at the fire. Mother was for some reason of the firm opinion that Hiie and I were already a couple, and thought that I was just too shy to invite my young lady to visit. She tried to embolden me, explaining that even though we weren't living together, I was still allowed to invite Hiie to lunch, because the sooner she got to know her future daughter-in-law, the better.

"Don't be afraid. I'll begin to love her like my own daughter!" she assured me, looking at me as if she could already see me and Hiie in her mind's eye sitting side by side at the table, tucking into a haunch of venison. When she talked like this I always lost my appetite, but I didn't say anything. In the end I consoled myself with the fact that Hiie's father wouldn't allow his daughter to be the wife of a village-born bastard anyway.

Tambet really would never have allowed it. His grudge against our family was as great as ever. I no longer fled into the bushes like a little boy when I caught sight of him—that would have been ridiculous, for I was now even taller than Tambet—but we never greeted each other.

It was in fact a pretty extraordinary situation that prevailed in the forest then; there were very few people left, but we had nothing to do with each other. Tambet and Mall would whizz past our family as proud hawks fly over nettles, without even turning their heads.

Ülgas the Sage was still alive too, and although very old and terribly shriveled, he did acknowledge us and even spoke to us, but only to make invocations and shout threats. Hanging around the empty sacred grove had obviously driven him crazy; he saw sprites everywhere, and could most often be found crouching at the foot of some tree bringing offerings to the spirit living in its trunk. He became a real nuisance to small animals, and his paths were steeped in a trail of blood. With the aid of Snakish words he forced squirrels, hares, and weasels to submit to him, and he would kill them by twisting their necks twice. Then he would crawl on his knees around some oak or linden tree and mark its roots with fresh blood. Finally he would lumber away, but would soon thereafter think he'd seen some new wood-sprite, which he absolutely had to placate, and the whole gruesome massacre would begin again. Foxes and polecats would follow behind him and gobble up the carcasses of the animals brought for sacrifice; that was kind of them, because otherwise the stink would have made it impossible to walk around in the forest.

Ülgas was always shouting curses at our family, and screamed that if we didn't come to the sacred grove immediately, the dogs of the grove would come and kill us. I had lived in the forest all my life, but I had never seen such animals as the dogs of the grove, so I didn't take Ülgas's threats seriously. But he did have an annoying and repulsive way about him, and to tell the truth, I was impatiently anticipating the old man's death. He looked ready to keel over at any moment: he had become as thin as a skeleton, his shaggy beard hung down to his navel, and his tangled hair bristled in every direction. He hardly ate anything, and only stayed on his feet thanks to his lunacy. But that was a strong stick to lean on. He was not dying anytime soon.

Apart from Tambet and Mall, who treated us with silent contempt, and Ülgas, who shouted his rage in our faces, the only one left alive was Meeme, who was sinking more and more under the sod. Moss grew on his clothes, dead insects, fallen leaves, and all sorts of mold were stuck on the beard that covered his whole face. From within that mess shone only the two eyes, whose lashes were tangled with cobwebs, and a mouth with fat red lips. To those lips Meeme raised his wineskin every little while. It was completely incomprehensible how he still managed to get himself anything to drink; from his appearance you would think that roots were growing out of his heels, which held him fixed to the ground. But evidently this human sod was still capable of getting up and killing, because apart from robbing the monks or the men of iron it wasn't possible to get wine.

Meeme had little to do with other people. Sometimes when he saw me with Hiie he yelled a few obscenities and we went elsewhere. Once I happened to see how Ülgas evidently mistook Meeme for some Forest-Mother or moss-sprite, and tried to bring him a sacrifice—then Meeme spat into Ülgas's eye with deadly accuracy and Ülgas fled, just as if his nose had been bitten.

Likewise the Primates Pirre and Rääk were still in the forest, though they no longer lived in their old cave, but had moved to a tree. That is, in their love of antiquity they had gone so far that even living in a cave seemed senselessly modern to them. In their opinion the villagers had already sunk over their heads into the bog; I was wading in it up to my chest—but sure ground was a tree branch under bare ground.

They claimed that now they felt a lot healthier, and that peace and happiness were only to be found in the way of life they inherited from their ancestors. I thought that climbing in the trees was an unnecessary discomfort, and felt bad watching Pirre crawling slowly and uncertainly along some spruce tree, his face wincing as the needles prodded his naked willy. Pirre and Rääk were Primates after all, not primeval apes, whose example they were following, and for them life in the trees was unfamiliar and difficult. Besides, they were no longer young; their fur was gray and it was very troublesome for them to keep their balance on the branches. In the name of their principles, however, they were prepared to undergo any trial.

I visited them quite often, for there was no one else to visit; besides, Pirre and Rääk were nice, despite their odd ideas. Their louse was still living too, perhaps by growing in size it had also increased its life span as well. It was certainly the oldest louse in the world. It had moved to the trees along with Pirre and Rääk, and squatted on a branch like a big white owl. Only when Hiie approached did it scrabble its way down the trunk and go and rub itself against her legs.

By now Hiie was too big to ride on the louse's back, but the insect never seemed to understand that, and slouched invitingly every time. Hiie would stroke and pat it and held the louse by one leg like a child, and the insect hopped on its remaining legs happily beside her.

On that day, too, I was with Pirre and Rääk, who were telling me yet again about how right their forefathers were living their whole lives in the trees, and how great the view was from the top of a spruce. I had seen Pirre and Rääk swinging around up there, and was always afraid that they would come crashing down and kill themselves, seeing the tip of the spruce bending ominously under their weight. One time Rääk did start to fall, but luckily her tits stuck to the resinous trunk, and that saved her life. After this, of course, the Primates talked about how wise their ancestors were in setting up home in resinous trees, and how they couldn't cease to wonder at the wisdom of the ancient apes.

Pirre and Rääk hardly ever came down from their tree anymore—they spent their whole adulthood there—and if the Primates wanted to get anything off the ground, such as strawberries or lingonberries, the lice went to pick them.

At that moment I was sitting under the tree listening to Pirre and Rääk talking, when suddenly I felt someone crawling over my toes. It was Ints. He was now a fully grown snake, a big strong snake-king, with a golden crown on his brow. He put his head on my shoulder and whispered that he wanted to tell me something.

I said good-bye to the Primates and went with Ints to a big stump where he liked to sun himself. Ints had somehow got fat. I assumed he had just eaten something and was now digesting his prey. Ints coiled himself around the stump, looked at me bashfully, and said, "Look, Leemet, I've got news for you. I'm having children."

This really was news. I couldn't have guessed that Ints had a wife. Of course I'd seen him crawling around with other snakes from time to time, but in the first place it's terribly difficult to tell whether a snake is male or female, and in the second, I'd never noticed Ints fondling another snake. I was quite shocked and a little annoyed that Ints hadn't ever introduced me to his wife, and I said, "So, congratulations! This is pretty unexpected. Why haven't you ever shown me your wife?"

"Wife?" repeated Ints, amazed. "What wife?"

"Well, the one who's making you a father," I said.

"No, I'm not going to be a father!" replied Ints. "I'm going to be a mother. I'm having children. Leemet, did you think I'm male? I'm an adderess."

I stared at her, as if she had said she wasn't a snake but a lynx. Ints looked back at me, just as dismayed.

"I thought you knew!" she said. "Leemet, we've been friends for so long. How is it possible that you thought I was male all this time? Leemet, look me in the eye. You can see immediately that I'm female!"

I looked, but all I understood was that I was talking to an adder. I didn't have the foggiest idea whether it was male or female.

"I understood immediately that you're a boy!" said Ints, offended.

"With me, you can see that immediately. For example, I'm growing a beard. Women never have that. Ints, I really couldn't have guessed! Anyway you said yourself I could call you Ints."

"So?"

"Ints is a boy's name."

"I didn't know that. I thought it was just a beautiful word that fitted with my adder name. I'm really deeply shocked by your ignorance."

"I'm shocked too," I replied. "I'm shocked by your sex."

We were silent for a while.

"Well, anyway it doesn't change anything," said Ints eventually. "Now you know I'm female. And I'm having children. Soon I should be giving birth. I wanted to tell you, because you're my friend, even if you're too dumb to know the difference between male and female snakes."

"Forgive me," I said. "But as you said, it really doesn't change anything. We'll still be friends and I'm very glad that you're going to be a mother. Who's the father then?"

"Oh, one of the adders. We got together one night, we were both in heat, and so it happened. We haven't met again, and we don't want to. He's a fairly stupid snake; let him crawl around by himself."

"How do you mean?" I asked, taken aback. "Isn't the father going to bring up his own children? Aren't you going to get married?"

"Oh, you're so formal!" chuckled Ints. "That's not the way with us."

"Your father and mother are still living together today," I said.

"Well yes, but that's an exception. They were friends even before they had children. Mostly it's just a matter of mating. You're in heat, a suitable adder comes along, and that's it," explained Ints. "And if you don't manage to get pregnant, you look for the next one and try it with him, until you finally succeed. So how is it with humans?"

"I don't know," I admitted, blushing. "But surely it begins with falling in love . . ."

"Really?" exclaimed Ints. "Well yes, that's why there are so few of you. Our aim is to multiply."

I shrugged. To tell the truth I didn't know exactly how humans arranged these things. I met with Hiie often in the forest, but obviously we weren't "in heat," to use Ints's expression, and nothing happened. But how was it done in the village? There were plenty of people, the village boys and girls went around together everywhere, and often I would see the boys fondling the girls; a couple of times I'd seen them kissing too. Were they in heat? I fell into daydreams and imagined myself meeting somewhere on the edge of the forest some beautiful village girl who was looking for someone to mate with and had decided to try her luck with me. I didn't know if I was in heat at that moment, but somehow I felt that I was.

"What are you thinking of?" asked Ints. "You're not listening at all to what I'm saying. I said that I have to go to the nest now and we can't meet for a while. I'm already very fat and it's hard for me to crawl around. But come in about a week to see me; by then the kids should have been born. I feel it won't be long now."

She crawled off slowly and I went home. I told Mother that Ints was actually female and expecting babies. Mother got very agitated at this.

"How nice!" she enthused. "I'll definitely come with you when you go to see Ints. Little adders, they can be cute, just like tiny maggots. Oh, I so want to have a grandchild! Leemet, don't wait too long now. You're still young. But look, Ints is your old playmate and she's becoming a mother already. You'd better bring Hiie home soon; it'd be so lovely if you had a little boy!"

"Mother, please!" I sighed, but Mother didn't stop, and talked all evening about how cute little children are. She seemed to entirely forget that it was not I who was expecting children but Ints, and when I reminded her, she said, "Yes, of course I know it's Ints! But you mustn't fall behind her. You must soon be expecting a little family of your own!"

"Mother, unlike Ints I am a male, and I can't have a family!" I objected, but Mother just waved her hand. "Of course *you* can't, but Hiie! I'm talking about Hiie!"

This was followed by the usual speech about where she was going to have us all sleep when Hiie moved in.

I rapidly came to regret that I'd told Mother at all about Ints and her pregnancy, because she would not calm down. It was almost as if she were already preparing for a wedding and the birth of grandchildren. She started sewing little goatskin shirts and dragging furniture from one place to another. I tried to make it clear to her that no child was going to be born in our shack, and there was no point in making little shirts for Ints's young, because they wouldn't have arms to poke into the sleeves. Mother paid no heed to me.

"Do you think I'm stupid?" she asked angrily. "I'm not sewing shirts for baby adders, but for your children!"

"I don't have any children!" I shouted.

At this Mother conjured up a cunning expression, as if to say, "I know you, you rascal. You'll soon have babies around you!" And she carried on sewing shirts, a happy smile on her face.

After a week we went to visit the adders. Ints's father, the old king of the snakes, welcomed us at the entrance to the cave, nodding with satisfaction.

"Welcome!" he said. "We've been expecting you. We have a little family."

Mother burst into tears. We squeezed into the burrow, and there lay Ints, surrounded by three baby adders, as tiny as tiger moths.

"Oh, how sweet!" squealed Mother and hissed tenderly at the young snakes, who crawled into her lap and wriggled around in it.

I stroked Ints and congratulated her, and Ints licked me with her forked tongue, supporting her head on my knees, as was always her habit.

"This is Uncle Leemet!" she said to her young. "Say hello to him!"

"Hello!" hissed the little snakes.

"How cuddly they are!" exclaimed Mother. "Ah, you can be happy, Ints! And you know Leemet will be having a child soon! I know. We're making preparations at home already."

"Really?" said Ints in surprise, looking me in the eye. "Is that true?"

"No," I hissed quietly. "Mother's telling fibs."

"But you really could," said Ints. "Aren't you in heat yet? Or in love, as you call it?"

"No, I'm not!" I said, getting up. Mother was chatting to Ints's father about where she would put me and Hiie and where she would move herself and the several goatskin shirts she had already sewn. It was depressing to listen to. I left the burrow, saying I wanted some water, but actually I just sat down on a tussock and stared out in front of me.

"Leemet!" shouted someone to me. It was Hiie, of course. Just at that moment I didn't want to see her at all. I can't have been in heat.

"Go away!" I said, troubled.

"Has something happened?" asked Hiie. She came and sat beside me. "I came to look at Ints's children."

On top of everything else! I didn't want Hiie to go into the snake burrow for any price. I imagined how Mother would whoop at the sight of her and inform Ints's father: "That's my daughter-in-law! She'll be having children soon!"

"Right now you shouldn't go to see Ints," I said, getting up. "She's not at her best. She hasn't recovered from giving birth."

"Really!" exclaimed Hiie, wanting to rush into the burrow. I grasped her by the waist.

"You mustn't go in there just now!" I repeated. "Please!"

Hiie stared at me, wide-eyed. The situation was odd: I'd never held her in my arms before. She was right up against me, uncomfortably close in fact. I would have liked to let go of her, but wasn't sure whether Hiie would run off to see Ints. So I kept hold of her. We were both silent and at least I felt inexpressibly strange. I didn't know what to do.

Finally I released my arms and pulled away. Hiie stayed put. She had lowered her gaze and didn't say a word.

"Don't go, all right?" I said.

"All right," whispered Hiie.

We remained standing. I bit my lip and looked away to one side. Hiie didn't move.

"Will you go home now?" I asked awkwardly.

"Yes, of course!" Hiie replied quickly, a feeling of relief in her voice. "See you!"

"See you!"

Then she left, quickly, almost at a run, as if fleeing from someone.

I stood in front of Ints's burrow, feeling somehow very foolish.

Seventeen

understood very well that things were going slightly wrong with Hiie. What she might read into our hug was not hard to guess. Even though she was alarmed by my harsh words and my command to go home immediately, she had evidently felt pleasure in being held awkwardly in my arms. She became somehow relaxed and soft, despite being as bony as a hungry fox. I couldn't sleep for half the night, feeling ill at ease. I decided to seek out Hiie the next morning and pretend nothing had happened in front of the snakes' lair. I wanted her to forget both that unexpected embrace and my rude words. I wanted Hiie to be my friend, but I didn't want her to start imagining things that didn't exist, like my mother, who had been steamed up even more at the sight of Ints's offspring.

So the next day I went to look for Hiie. She wasn't at home; luckily there was no one there at all. Then I circled around the forest, visited the Primates, to find out whether Hiie had been to visit her dear louse, but Pirre and Rääk hadn't seen Hiie that morning. I walked on and finally reached the edge of the forest and heard somebody shrieking.

It was a girl's voice, and at once I thought I had found Hiie. Then I saw who was screaming, and it was a village girl. On closer inspection it turned out to be my old acquaintance Magdaleena, whom I'd visited twice with Pärtel.

I stayed behind a tree and peeped at the girl. I didn't understand why she was crying like that, and at first I didn't intend to go up to her, but since she didn't stop her wailing I came hesitantly out of the forest and started walking toward her.

Magdaleena saw me but didn't recognize me, and started screaming even more wildly, calling for help.

"Don't yell like that," I said. "What's wrong?"

"Who are you?" cried Magdaleena, picking up a woven wicker basket to defend herself from me.

"Leemet," I said. "Don't you remember, I visited you a long time ago. You showed me a spinning wheel and your father wanted to beat my friend the snake to death."

Now Magdaleena recognized me, but didn't calm down at all, and flung her basket at me, sending the strawberries that she'd picked flying everywhere.

"And he should have killed that dirty beast!" she screamed. "I hate snakes! Look at what they do! One bit me! Look at my leg! I'm going to die!"

Her right leg really was as thick as a block of wood—red and swollen. Magdaleena tried to move her leg, but evidently it was very painful, as she fell to howling again.

"I'm dying, I'm dying! I can feel the poison affecting me already! That snake killed me! Disgusting, repulsive creature! Help! Father! Help!"

"Don't bawl like that," I said. I was in fact quite dumbfounded that one person could be so helpless and miserable like a little

chick, and let herself be bitten by an adder. Naturally I had
seen with my own eyes how Ints had killed a monk, but in my
opinion the monk and the iron men didn't belong to humankind
at all, because they didn't understand the language of humans
or of snakes, but babbled something completely incomprehensible. They were like insects, and you could kill and bite them
as much as you liked. Magdaleena was human, though, and an
adder had indeed bitten her. That seemed so humiliating that I
was actually ashamed for Magdaleena. After all, why didn't she
understand Snakish? One simple hiss would have made it clear
to the adder that this was his sister standing here, not a mouse or
a frog to fasten on. But instead of learning Snakish as she should
have, this girl was now writhing on the ground here, two red
tooth marks on her calf. She had voluntarily lowered herself to
the level of the animals, instead of rising to the level of adders,
which is the rightful place for a human.

"Help, I'm dying!" Magdaleena kept on moaning. "Father,
save me!"

"Does your father know Snakish?" I asked, somewhat scornfully, because I could guess the answer.

"Of course not!" said Magdaleena, irritated. "There is no such
thing! Only the devil understands that!"

I didn't know who the "devil" was, but I guessed from the
girl's tone that it wasn't likely to be someone from the village. I
sat down next to Magdaleena.

"Then your father will be no help to you now," I said. "To get
the poison out of your blood you have to invite the same adder
that bit you. He'll suck his poison out of your leg and you'll be
all right. It's a small thing; I'll hiss him up right away."

Magdaleena looked at me incredulously, but I uttered a very simple hiss, taught to me as a small boy by Uncle Vootele, and after a little while a snake of a smaller kind crawled up to me. It wasn't an adder belonging to the tribe of the king of snakes, but a common viper, though this viper was known to me; we had hibernated together in Ints's burrow.

Magdaleena was startled at the sight of the snake and tried to crawl away in panic, as if afraid that the little snake was now going to swallow her whole. I held her fast and told her there was no need to flee and the snake wouldn't bite her, because I wouldn't allow it. Magdaleena stayed put and just stared at the little snake, which had coiled itself, waiting for me to say what I wanted of it. I greeted the snake politely and asked it to suck the poison out of Magdaleena's leg.

"Why did you sting her at all?" I asked. "You can see she's a human."

"But she doesn't know Snakish!" replied the viper. "And besides, she wanted to hit me with her basket. I asked her what was wrong with her that she leapt at me that way, but she didn't answer me. Well, then I pecked at her. Don't let her try it a second time!"

I sighed.

"You see, these humans are simply stupid," I said apologetically. "Forgive them. Their minds aren't quite right; that's why they can't learn Snakish words. But there's no point in biting them, so next time just keep away."

"I don't want to bite them either, but this girl started it," explained the viper. "All right, I don't hate her. Make her stretch out her leg; then it's better for me to suck."

"You have to stretch your leg out," I told Magdaleena, who of course understood nothing of our hissing. "And don't beat snakes with your basket again. They haven't done anything to you."

"But they're disgusting!" sobbed Magdaleena, but she did stretch out her leg as requested, and screwed her eyes tightly shut. The viper pressed itself against the wound and began sucking. The reduction in the swelling was visible: the thick red stump became a pretty slender leg. The viper raised its head and licked his mouth.

"This sucking tickles my tongue," he said. "Finished! Not a drop of venom left in there."

I thanked him and the little snake undulated away into the grass. Magdaleena got up and supported her healed leg, a doubtful expression on her face. But everything was all right. The poison had been sucked out.

Then she suddenly fell upon me and kissed me on the cheek.

"Thank you!" she cried, hugging me tightly. "You saved my life! You're a wizard! You're a sorcerer! You do good magic! Come with me; we'll go to my father! I want to tell him what you did."

In any other circumstances I would have certainly refused such a suggestion. I had no desire to meet Johannes. But in Magdaleena's arms, my cheek a little damp from the passionate kiss, I didn't see a way of declining. The previous day I had held Hiie in my embrace. Now Magdaleena was caressing me—but how different those hugs were! With Hiie I'd felt uncomfortable, but standing in Magdaleena's grasp was very good. Now that she was no longer crying or complaining, but quite the opposite, glowing with happiness, I saw how beautiful she was. I can't even begin to describe her appearance. Suffice to say that I thought she was perfect, much more beautiful than Hiie, more beautiful than my sister, even more beautiful than her prettiest and bustiest girlfriend. To use Ints's expression, just at that moment I felt that I was in heat.

So how could I refuse when Magdaleena invited me to her home? I went.

Johannes the village elder, who had turned gray in the intervening years, did not express any surprise at seeing me.

"Things are ordained in threes!" he said, and made a strange movement in front of his face. Later I found out that this was a peculiar spell that was called the sign of the cross, but I never observed that this incantation was of any use. Johannes squeezed my hand and added, "I'm sure that you won't be running back to the forest a third time. A man of the cross does not belong where beasts of prey walk about and Satan rules. Come, step inside, my boy. We'll have breakfast."

"Father, you can't imagine what happened to me today!" said Magdaleena, interrupting. She couldn't wait to get inside, but told right there on the threshold how a snake had stung her, how her leg had swollen, and how she thought her last hour had come. And how I had then invited the snake back and healed her leg.

"Father, isn't that a miracle?" she cried excitedly, and it was somehow embarrassing for me that these people got so excited about such a trifling thing. But at the same time Magdaleena's enthusiasm gave me pleasure, because it was beautiful to see her eyes glistening with great rapture.

Johannes didn't reply; he only crossed his hands on his breast and lowered his head.

"Father, say something!" begged Magdaleena. "I think it was miraculous. Or . . . do you think the devil is at work here?" Magdaleena paled and threw me an uneasy look. "Do you think it was some sort of witchcraft? That I shouldn't have let the snake suck my leg? But Father, I would have died then! You don't know how bad I was! Father, say something, please! Why are you silent?"

"I was praying," replied Johannes the elder quietly, now looking straight at Magdaleena. "Don't be afraid, my child. You haven't strayed against God. Of course a snake is a foul creature, Satan's own handiwork, but the power of God overcomes the power of the devil. He can use even the most abominable creature to a holy purpose. Satan moved the evil snake to sting you, but God in his infinite mercy led this boy to you who saved you. God forced the snake to suck its own poison and choke on it. May the heavenly ruler be praised!"

"Never in the world would the snake choke on its own poison!" I said. "It was simply a mistake that he stung Magdaleena, and I asked him to clean the wound. There's no miracle about it; you only have to know Snakish words."

"Nobody knows those!" claimed Magdaleena. "That's just the miracle, that you understand them!"

"Any human can learn Snakish words," I said quietly. "It's not such a difficult art. In the olden days everyone knew them, and back then no snake would bite a human."

I suddenly felt very sad, and noticed a faint smell of death, a scent that came back to me at these moments. I could not get free of that smell, as if, after the burning of Uncle's body, the stink had been released to the skies and mixed with the blue above, and now, at any moment, the wind could carry it back to me. That stench came like a rain cloud, and I never noticed its approach until the first drops assaulted my nose. It mostly came when I was sad, as I was now, because here they were admiring me for knowing Snakish words, which to me were as ordinary and natural for a human as being able to speak at all, or having legs to walk, and hands to do work. Suddenly I felt terribly alone, in the midst of alien people, with whom I had not the least thing in common. I had felt just as alone and abandoned that time in the cellar, where my only companion was the corpse of Uncle Vootele. I turned my head away to seek fresher air, but the stench would not leave me alone and the whole world seemed full of decay. Johannes the village elder invited me indoors. I went, but even there it stank.

Magdaleena got busy laying the table, but Johannes sat down next to me and laid his hand on my shoulder.

"Don't think that you would have been able to learn Snakish words unless God had marked you out for that," he said. "God doesn't want an innocent child like my daughter to perish, and for that reason he opened your mind to the language of snakes, so that you could appear out of the woods and save Magdaleena's life."

"I don't know anything about God, and I don't want to," I said. "I was taught those words by my uncle. Every human knows them, if he hasn't forgotten them all by moving to the village."

"Even if we have forgotten something, that is God's will," said Johannes, explaining further. "God doesn't want us to talk to the snakes, for a snake is his enemy. And what have we to say to the enemies of God? Nowhere on earth do they talk to snakes. Believe me. I have wandered around and I know what I'm talking about. Why should we be the last miserable people to be on the side of the snakes? I think we should listen to those who are wiser than us. The foreigners, who know how to build fortresses and monasteries of stone, whose ships are big and fast, and whose bodies are covered by armor that no arrow can penetrate. Have the snakes taught them all that wisdom? No, they uncovered these secrets thanks to God! He has enlightened them and made them strong, and he will help us too, if we listen to him."

"If you don't know Snakish words, then neither stone nor iron are of any use," I said. "I've seen my friend an adder biting a monk in the throat. The monk perished on the spot."

"Lord have mercy!" yelled Johannes. "What a heinous crime! Cursed be that snake. Now you see that they are the servants of Satan, when they attack even holy fathers. Fortunately there's no doubt that that monk is now in Paradise, in eternal bliss."

"Actually, I think that foxes and wandering wolves ate his body," I said. "If you don't understand Snakish, you're more wretched than a frog. Why should we be like those fools who don't understand a single hiss of it? They're not humans; they're vermin!"

I immediately regretted what I'd said, because I recalled that Johannes himself was such a verminous creature, for whom Snakish words were a dark land. But Johannes didn't get angry. He even laughed!

"Boy, you really have lived too long in the forest," he said, with an unpleasant arrogance. "How can you think that you are clever, and that these strong foreign people who rule the whole world in the name of God are a stupid bunch? In that case the Holy Father, the Pope, would also be stupid, because he doesn't know Snakish either! Is that what you mean? Better not to say so, it would be a terrible sin. It was actually a sin even for me to ask you that. I will certainly have to confess that."

"Who is this Pope then?" I asked.

"The Pope is God's deputy on the earth," said Johannes in a quiet voice, and his face became as sweet as if he were licking honey. "He lives in the holy city of Rome and keeps his hand over us all like a loving father. I have visited him and kissed his feet, back when I was still a little boy. The iron men took me with them, so that I, a little forest lad as I was then, could see the might of the world, how wise and strong the Christians are. I was taken to Rome and led in front of the Pope, and the glory and splendor I saw there took my breath away. Gold, silver, and precious stones were glittering everywhere; the churches were made of stone and with such high towers that not a single spruce tree here in the forest could reach them. Then I understood that the God that is served by the foreigners is the most powerful, and if we want to achieve anything in life, then it is wise to turn to him and to forget all the silly superstitious customs that make us ridiculous before the whole world. I came back home and was ashamed that we still live like children, while other nations have grown into adults. We should hurry after them; we should learn all the necessary knowledge that has been an everyday thing elsewhere in the world. Fortunately more and more knights and pious brothers were coming to our land. They helped us in every way and showed us how to be like civilized people. Believe me one day we will be no worse than them."

"That's why we still shouldn't forget the Snakish words," I said. Johannes leaned in very close to me.

"Dear boy, keep in mind what I tell you," he whispered. "Actually there are no Snakish words."

This was such a surprising claim that I didn't even burst out laughing; I simply looked the village elder in the eye to see what other odd things he would say or do.

"Yes, they don't exist!" he repeated. "How else could it be that the church knows nothing of them? Do you think that if God has made the Pope his deputy on the earth, he hasn't made him all-powerful? The Pope is omnipotent. Every word he says is true, and with the help of God he can even make the rivers flow backward. If Snakish words did exist, the Pope would understand them too, and so would other holy men, but they don't, for God hasn't given snakes the power of speech. They shouldn't be spoken to. They should be killed, or else be kept away by the power of prayer, and every holy man is able, with the help of the Word of God, to drive all the snakes back to Hell. So it is! The fact that you saved my child from a snake today is not your doing, but God's! He looked down from Heaven and made the snake lick Magdaleena's wound clean."

"What's this you're saying now?" I asked. "I do happen to know that I spoke with him, exactly as I'm speaking with you now."

"That isn't possible!" declared Johannes, and his expression now turned severe. "Snakes don't speak! It only seemed that way to you! You must leave the forest. The devil rules there, and he is leading you astray and making you hear and see things that don't exist. Come to the village, be baptized, start going to church, and you'll soon understand that Snakish words are a delusion!"

"That will never happen!" I said, getting up. "I would have to be completely mad! I do know those words! Listen!"

I gave a long hiss, spoke to Johannes in my best Snakish, but he only stared at me and said, "That's just a hiss, which doesn't mean anything! Forget this stupidity! That is what I meant when I said that our nation is still living like a child. It's time to grow up! It's time to live like the others! Snakish doesn't exist!"

"It does exist, and if everyone understood it as they used to, there would be no foreigners living among us!" I said. "The Frog of the North would have gobbled them all up, and not even their bones would be lying by the seaside!"

"Childishness again!" said Johannes. "What Frog of the North? No one survives against the shining knights and their swords!"

I was furious. Johannes was talking complete nonsense, but it wasn't possible for me to convince him. I had no way to produce the Frog of the North to swallow those knights with their swords. The Frog was sleeping somewhere in his secret burrow and I didn't have the key to find him; and anyway I couldn't wake him up. And I had no way of proving even the power of Snakish words, because I couldn't invite an adder into Johannes's home. Even if I were to chat with some snake, Johannes would only hear what to him was incomprehensible hissing. We lived in different worlds, like two snails who cannot look into each other's shells. I could claim to him that Snakish and the Frog of the North are in my shell, and he wouldn't believe it anyway, because in his shell he saw God and the Pope of Rome.

I wanted to go off home, for my mood was black and my nose smelt the stench of putrescence more and more, but then Magdaleena came up to me, touched me on the shoulder, and invited me to eat. I guessed what they would be eating. Just as I had stepped at Magdaleena's invitation into her father's cottage, now I went to their table too.

Eighteen

y suspicions didn't let me down. On the table was a big loaf of bread, and around it bowls and dishes of different sizes, full of strange, sticky glistening substances. I felt sick at the very sight of them, but Magdaleena sat next to me, and I sensed the scent of her hair penetrating the carrion stench, conquering my nostrils completely and flowing into my throat, so that I thought I could taste Magdaleena in my mouth. At once I didn't care anymore about the disgusting things on the table and was prepared to sacrifice my digestion for the sake of Magdaleena.

Johannes settled himself at the end of the table, crossed his hands, lowered his eyes, and mumbled something. Magdaleena followed her father's example. I guessed that this too was some useless spell, much the same as the incantations of Ülgas the Sage before he started to chop up animal sacrifices. Johannes and Magdaleena did not mumble for long; soon Johannes lifted his head, took the loaf of bread in one hand, a knife in the other, and cut a coarse slice.

"This is for you, visitor from afar!" he said, handing me the slice. "Bread is the main food of the people of the cross. Bread is sacred. Bread is older than we are."

I accepted the piece of bread with barely disguised disgust, drew a breath, and bit a piece off the side. It tasted just as bad as I remembered; it turned in my mouth and stuck to my teeth.

"Spread some butter on it too!" said Magdaleena, passing me a little dish, in which some strange putrid yellow grease stared back at me. Only under the threat of death might I have been prepared to eat it.

"Go on, take it. It's good!" said Magdaleena, herself spreading the yellow grease on a piece of bread with the edge of a knife, biting it, and making such a sweet face that she might have been eating a strawberry.

I summoned up my courage, insinuated a fragment of the butter onto my own piece of bread, and tried to eat it. It wasn't as horrible as I feared, but loathsome all the same.

"Don't you eat meat at all?" I asked.

"We do on holy days," replied Johannes, devouring his bread with great gusto. "Then we always have pig or lamb on the table."

"Why only on holy days? Why not every day?"

"We're not so rich. Our people are still poor," explained Johannes. "Only the gentlemen knights in their fortress can afford meat every day. If we started squandering like that, we'd soon be eating our way to ruin."

"There are plenty of animals in the forest," I asserted. "Deer, goats, hares . . . Why don't you eat those?"

Johannes snorted.

"Who can get hold of them? The knights, of course, they go hunting; they have fast horses and sharp foreign-made spears. But for an old man like me it's downright impossible to catch a goat. Now hares—you can put cords out for them, but they're cunning too; they don't go into the trap."

Again I felt depressed. Here sat a man who had abandoned Snakish and even violently denied its existence. And he was proud of his decision, believed he was going the right way, and wanted to lead me on it too. But in fact he was like a person who has bitten his own hands off and now lies on the ground, as helpless as a bundle of rags. My mother was no younger than Johannes, moreover she was a woman and quite fat, yet she would have no trouble slaughtering one big stag every day. Of course we wouldn't be able to eat a whole stag every day, far from it, but in principle it was possible. This man here, who boasted that he had seen someone called the Pope, wasn't even capable of killing a hare. He fooled around with ridiculous cords and complained that a stupid hare was more cunning than him! He was deadly certain that to kill a goat you need a horse and a spear, and this was accompanied by a hunt lasting hours! Why didn't he believe in Snakish words, with whose help you can force a goat to submit within one minute? I felt once more that I had come from a completely different world.

"Try some porridge too," said Magdaleena, handing me a wooden spoon. In the middle of the table stood a large bowl of gunk that I'd never seen before, which both Johannes and Magdaleena were eating hungrily.

"What's this?" I asked, digging suspiciously in the contents of the bowl.

"Flour porridge," replied Johannes. "Good solid food. Get your fill of that and you've got the strength to work."

"Where does this food come from?" I asked with disgust. I couldn't imagine my mother offering guests such slops. She would fling slime like this out; she would take it into the forest and bury it in the ground so it wouldn't pollute nature. "Does the Pope of Rome eat this?"

Johannes shook his head.

"What does this have to do with the Pope of Rome?" he asked reproachfully. "He is God's deputy on earth; we can't compare ourselves with him. Of course his table of fare is richer: his servants bring him the choicest kinds of meat from game birds and animals; rare fruits are sent to him from distant lands to feed his guests. It would be silly for us to try to live the same way. A person has to know his place: we are a small and poor nation!"

"I eat meat every day," I declared.

"Forgive me, but you, my boy, are only a forest lad," said Johannes sternly. "A wolf devours meat too—but should we follow his example? We aspire toward the light and we serve God, and in return he gives us our daily bread and other things besides."

"I see no sense in this," I said, flinging away my piece of bread. I couldn't finish it, because the sight of the porridge had finally made me feel nauseous. "I'd rather be a wolf, then, and at least be able to eat properly, than to live in the village here and chew on droppings cooked from some sort of straw."

Johannes and Magdaleena remained silent and looked at me oddly.

"Don't talk like that," said Johannes slowly and cautiously at length. "Boy, tell me honestly, haven't you committed the most terrible sin that a person can take upon his soul? Haven't you become a werewolf?"

"What is a werewolf?" I wanted to know.

"It is a person who takes on the shape of a wolf by means of bad magic," replied Johannes. "Pious monks have told me that such a thing is possible; in their home country there are vile people who practice this art. Tell me, really, haven't you done that yourself? It is a terrible crime!"

"Such a thing isn't possible," I said with indifference. "A human is a human and a wolf is a wolf. A wolf is for milking and riding. No human would want to change into a wolf, because nobody wants to be milked or to have someone climb on its back. Those monks are fools."

"They are learned and wise men," contested Johannes. "But I believe you when you say you're not involved with such witchcraft. You have an honest face, and one day you'll become a good Christian."

"Hardly," I muttered, getting up from the table. Johannes nodded to Magdaleena.

"Go now and show the boy the village. I hope he won't be going back to the forest anymore."

"We could go to the monastery," said Magdaleena. "The monks sing there. All the young villagers go to listen to them. It's wonderfully beautiful!"

"Yes, go there," agreed Johannes. "The sacred church singing refreshes the soul. Go on, go on. I still have work to do. A human being is like an ant; it is his lot to earn his bread by the sweat of his brow."

This comparison was quite apt, considering that neither an ant nor Johannes could speak Snakish, and therefore, from the forest folks' point of view, were among the most miserable kinds of creatures. I was not about to say this to the village elder, because I was pleased to be able to go somewhere now with Magdaleena, and I didn't want to stoke up an argument. We walked side by side, and every time my shoulder or fingertip brushed against Magdaleena, something was startled within me. I wanted to wave my hand in such a way that it bounced against Magdaleena over and over again, but I was afraid the girl would take it as an intrusion and so I did the opposite, shrinking from contact like a stick, and tried to brush against her as little as possible. How stupidly bashful that seems to me now, years later! No wonder that shy people like me are dying out. We were still only shadows, lengthening for a while before the sun goes down, to finally vanish afterward. I too have vanished. Nobody knows that I am still alive.

Magdaleena and I walked along, as I vacillated between a wish to touch her on the one hand and a fear of disturbing her on the other, but Magdaleena was thinking of different things entirely. Suddenly she stopped, pulled me behind a tree, and asked in an excited whisper: "Were you lying to Father when you said you don't turn into a werewolf? Actually you do know how to do that, don't you?"

"I don't," I said. "That sort of thing isn't possible. One creature can't change into another. An adder sheds its skin, but that doesn't change it into a grass snake or a slowworm. No human has ever changed into a wolf. It's completely stupid to believe such a thing."

"I believe it!" said Magdaleena, and I was immediately terribly embarrassed that I hadn't chosen my words better. "The monks talk about it too. Leemet, I understand that you don't want to tell me about it. Father said it's a terrible sin, and now you think I believe the same. But I don't; I think it's awfully exciting. I'd love to be able to change into a wolf!"

To this I could do nothing other than shrug my shoulders.

"Tell me, how is it done?" insisted Magdaleena.

"I really don't know!" I replied. I would have liked to help Magdaleena; she was so beautiful that I would have done anything for her, but I couldn't change her into a wolf, because that was impossible. But then I had a good idea.

"You want me to teach you Snakish words?" I offered.

"Can you change into a wolf with their help?" Magdaleena asked.

"No, you can't. But with their help you can talk to all the animals. Of course I mean those that can speak themselves. Many of them can't. But even they understand Snakish words and obey them. For example, without much trouble you can get food for yourself; you simply call a deer to you and kill it. You want me to teach you? It's simple!"

"How does it go then?" asked Magdaleena. She didn't seem to be particularly enthusiastic; Snakish words weren't a good enough compensation against changing into a wolf.

I hissed to her one of the simplest sibilations and Magdaleena tried to repeat it after me, but her mouth managed only a sort of fizzling that didn't sound anything like Snakish.

"Not bad," I said. "It's hard to start with; even I used to twist my tongue until it hurt. Try again. Listen carefully to how I do it, and try to repeat after me."

I hissed again, very slowly and carefully, to make it easier for Magdaleena to catch the vibrations of the sound. She tried cautiously, tensely, so her face went red and mucus sprayed between her teeth. But it wasn't Snakish.

"No, that's not it," I sighed.

"I did exactly the same thing as you," said Magdaleena.

"Actually you didn't," I said, trying to offend her as little as possible. I wanted so much for Magdaleena to be my pupil. We could start having lessons in the most beautiful places in the forest that I could find, sitting together under a tree and hissing in competition with each other. And perhaps other things might happen under that tree too. I didn't want to give up this wonderful future for any price, so I took up a new hiss and asked Magdaleena to try it.

"It's just the same as the previous one," said Magdaleena, when she had listened through my hiss.

"How do you mean? Didn't you hear the difference? Those hisses are not alike at all. Listen again!"

I hissed the first word to her, and then the second.

"To me it's all the same fizzle," said Magdaleena, now a little peevishly. "And I said it the same way too." She hissed again, but this hiss didn't mean anything; if an adder had heard it, he would have said that the hisser had a dead rat in his mouth and he should swallow it first if he wanted to say anything.

I didn't say that to Magdaleena, of course, and there was no rat in her mouth. The fault was in her tongue. Her pretty little pink tongue, which she was poking out of her mouth at my request so I could find out what was wrong with it, was surprisingly clumsy. Magdaleena's tongue didn't move; it was meant only for chewing bread and swallowing pap. I recalled the sad look that Pirre and Rääk always gave to my bottom when I went swimming in their presence; there was no trace of a tail. It had vanished, just as the muscles that made uttering Snakish words possible had vanished from Magdaleena's tongue. Her tongue sat too deep; it was overgrown and weak. People were devolving before our very eyes: I no longer had my grandfather's fangs; Magdaleena didn't even have a proper tongue. Likewise her hearing was blunted; she really couldn't tell one hiss from another. For her, Snakish was simply one endless sibilation, with no meaning, rather like the lapping of the waves of the sea.

I was forced to give in. It wasn't possible for Magdaleena to learn Snakish; she was destined to live forever in the village, among the rakes and spinning wheels. True, that was how she wanted to live anyway. She had lost a priceless treasure, but she didn't care about it.

"I can't teach you Snakish," I said awkwardly. "You'd never be able to pronounce it freely. Your tongue isn't flexible."

Magdaleena didn't seem particularly concerned.

"It doesn't matter," she said. "I don't want to talk to snakes anyway. I'm afraid of them. Listen, let's talk about something else. Have you seen sprites?"

"What sprites?" I asked reluctantly, because this subject immediately brought the Sage of the Grove to mind.

"Sprites live in the forest!" whispered Magdaleena. "Father believes that too, and he's a very clever man after all, who has been in a foreign land and seen all the wonders of the world. He speaks the foreigners' language and has talked with them. They also say that the forest is full of spirits, fairies, and little leprechauns who live under the ground. They're all in the service of Satan, and that's why it's not good for a human to go into the forest. At least not deep into it, because then the spirits and the sprites lead them off the path and take them to their castle. You must have seen them!"

Wasn't this dreadful? These people denied Snakish; everything worthwhile to be found in the forest was unknown and alien to them—but the sprites, those fairy-tale characters made up by Ülgas the Sage, had spread to the village and settled there! I was desperate. What was I supposed to say? If I assured her that the sprites didn't exist, Magdaleena wouldn't believe me anyway, and would think that I was hiding them from her, like the trick that allowed humans to change into wolves. But it was repulsive to me to spout the same drivel that droned on and on from the mouths of Ülgas and Tambet. I shrugged.

"I haven't met many of them."

"But you have met one or two? What are they like?"

"Ohh . . . Magdaleena, weren't we supposed to be going to listen to some singing?"

"You don't want to tell me about them!" whispered Magdaleena. "I understand. The sprites won't let you reveal their secrets. But at least I know now that you've seen them. I can tell other people that—that I know a boy from the forest who's seen fairies and spirits! Oh, they'll be amazed!"

She grabbed my hand and pulled me quickly along the road, and I felt her warm palm and feared more than anything that my hands might get sweaty from the excitement. We passed several houses and finally arrived at the same place where Ints had killed a monk many years before. Near the place was a monastery. Magdaleena drew me over by a wall and signaled to me to sit down.

"Aren't we going to go in?" I asked.

"Of course not! This is a monastery; no woman is allowed in there. Not you either, since you're not a knight or a monk, but an ordinary peasant boy. The foreigners don't allow peasants into their castles."

"But your father has been in there," I said. "I think—to see the Pope and . . ."

"Father's an exception. That's why everyone respects him; he's the most honored man in our village. He knows how to talk to the foreigners in their own language and he's taught me that too. You know what I long for most of all? For a knight to invite me into his castle! I'd like so much to see how they live. They're so handsome and splendid and dignified! Those suits of mail they have! Their feathered helmets! Sometimes they invite peasant girls into their castles, quite rarely, and not all of them. But I hope I'll be taken in there. I must be taken! I won't stand it if I'm not!"

From behind the walls of the monastery, protracted singing began to be heard. Magdaleena snuggled against a wall and closed her eyes.

"Isn't it divine?" she whispered. "How well they sing! I'm crazy about this music!"

I couldn't form any opinion about the monks' singing. It sounded like someone moaning and groaning with a stomach-ache, and moreover I soon discovered that the monks' singing makes you sleepy. I was overcome with enervation; the singing curled around my ears and wafted into my head like a cap made of moss. With the scent of Magdaleena beside me, I would have liked to rest my head on her shoulder and fall happily asleep. But I didn't dare to do that and forced my eyes open. The singing dragged on and echoed like someone groaning deep in a cave. I yawned, and a fly flew into my mouth. I spat it out again and the sleepiness subsided a bit. I gazed at Magdaleena.

The girl was humming along with the monks, resting her head on her knees, with her long skirt tucked under her legs. She looked so sweet and pretty that for me the monks' singing faded somewhere into the background. I concentrated on Magdaleena and started subtly inching myself toward her. My neck became hot and my heart beat with excitement, but I reached my goal and was finally sitting right beside Magdaleena. I slipped my hand onto the girl's bare leg and lightly touched her ankle. At this the blood rushed to my head with such force that it all went misty before my eyes. I stroked Magdaleena's leg again. But then voices could be heard, and around the corner of the monastery came some village boys. Among them was my old friend Pärtel, who I had not seen for years.

Nineteen

here were three boys: apart from Pärtel two little men who were shorter than him (and me), but with the same astonishingly broad shoulders, so that they looked almost square. Later I got to know that their powerful shoulder muscles came from the dull tilling of the fields and walking behind an ox supporting a plow. Their stunted growth was the consequence of poor diet; of course you don't grow close to the heavens by munching plenty of bread and porridge. Tallness is not desirable for the villagers anyway: to cut grain with a scythe you have to be stooping all the time anyway, and if your backbone is too long, it gets hurt terribly. Life is altogether easier for those who have remained stunted and unnaturally stocky. Those are the bastards who are suitable for village life.

Pärtel towered over these toadstool-shaped men, while being no worse than his companions in the breadth of his shoulders. He had become a real strong man, and there was not much left of the boy I used to know, the boy who had accompanied me to spy on the whisking women, the boy who had been my best friend. And yet I recognized him immediately. And he recognized me. He stared straight at me and said, "It's really you. Have you finally come to live in the village? I thought you wouldn't come."

"I haven't come anywhere," I retorted. "Magdaleena simply invited me here to listen to some music. Hello, Pärtel."

Pärtel screwed up his face.

"I've completely forgotten that name, but you still remember it. I told you that last time we met. My name is now . . ."

"Peetrus, yes, I remember."

"That's it!" said Pärtel-Peetrus. "And these are my friends, Jaakop and Andreas. This is Leemet. He's from the forest."

Jaakop and Andreas gazed at me and stretched out their hands. This was another village habit that I didn't understand. Why did they have to keep on touching each other? I understand it if you want to touch a girl you love; that's a different matter. Sister Salme has told me how nice it is to rumple a bear's soft fur; I've never done it, but I do really think that a bear's thick fur feels warm to the touch and tickles your palm. An adder's skin is silky too, and it's pleasant to stroke it. But the village boys' hands are rough, filthy, and clammy, full of breadcrumbs under the fingernails. After a touch like that you want to soak your hand for a few hours in cold stream water. Yet I didn't show my feelings, but pressed both the young men's hands out of respect for their local custom; they were unpleasantly big and coarse, like the Primates' feet.

"We thought there weren't any people left in the forest," said Andreas. "What was wrong with you that you didn't come earlier? Were you sick, or what?"

I wanted to say that I had been sick only once in my life—after eating the disgusting rye bread—but it isn't my habit to be cheeky and start quarrels with people. I simply shrugged my shoulders and mumbled something.

"Never mind," said Jaakop paternally. "Better late than never. You've already looked around this place, for some land to clear and start your own field?"

"No, I haven't," I said, my honest answer for once not being insulting.

Jaakop started immediately to give recommendations, but fortunately Magdaleena interrupted this useless chitchat.

"Boys, be quiet," she begged. "The monks are singing now! Let's listen!"

Pärtel and his mates sat down and were silent.

After a little while, Pärtel said, "It's wonderful. I don't suppose you've heard them before, Leemet?"

"The monks don't go singing to the forest, do they?" scoffed Andreas. "We were lucky that they decided to build their monastery near our village. You'd have to go overseas otherwise, to listen to a proper hymn."

"What's that?" I asked.

"Hymn," repeated Andreas. "The name of this music is 'hymn.' It's highly respected all over the world these days. You like it too, eh?"

"Yes," I replied cautiously, since agreement seemed safest, while saying no would quite clearly have ended in an argument. "But I don't understand a single word."

"Well, it's Latin you see," said Pärtel. "Hymns are sung in Latin; they do that everywhere. It's the music of the world!"

"Boys, you can't keep quiet at all!" snapped Magdaleena angrily, getting up and walking away from us. Then she sat down again, pressed her ear to the monastery wall, and even closed her eyes, to concentrate better.

"We've been thinking about learning to sing hymns too," said Andreas in a whisper. "The girls go mad for it. The monks have swarms of women, and they always start singing when the ladies give them the eye."

"Yes, we've even been practicing," said Pärtel. "It's gone pretty well, too, but we have the problem that we don't have any castrati in our choir."

"Who's that?" I asked.

"Castrati are the most famous singers," explained Jaakop. "There's one of them here in the monastery; he sings with a high voice like a lark. Because he's had his balls cut off."

"But that would be so painful!" I said. I had never heard anything so obscene.

Andreas snorted contemptuously.

"Easy to see that you're from the forest!" he said. "Painful! Who cares if it's painful! People cut balls off all over the world! Elder Johannes himself told me that in Rome, where the Pope lives, half the men don't have balls and they sing so beautifully it'd knock you flat. It's the fashion there. Johannes told me they actually wanted to cut his balls off too. Some bishop had suggested that. But unfortunately something got in the way and he had to leave, so the plan came to nothing. They don't cut balls off hereabouts. We're out in the sticks here!"

Mentally I was thanking fate that Elder Johannes had kept his balls, for otherwise there would be no Magdaleena, just an old man warbling like a lark. What a ghastly thought; it gives you gooseflesh! But Pärtel and his friends really looked sorrowful.

They sat listening to the monks' singing and scratching their crotches occasionally, and the scratching constantly reminded them of their own imperfection.

"You can sing with balls too," I remarked.

"It's not that," replied Jaakop. "In every proper chorus there has to be a castrato. Of course, somewhere by the river or by the cooking stove any man can drone away, but you don't get famous that way. Proper choirs work in monasteries."

"So go into a monastery and become a monk," I suggested. The boys shook their heads.

"You don't get it," said Pärtel. "They don't take people like us into monasteries. Who would sow the fields and make hay, if everyone was singing in a chorale? There's a division of labor, understand?"

"We've got nothing against sowing and cutting," added Jaakop. "Toiling with a plow is just fine. Have you ever stood behind a plow?"

No was my honest answer.

The other three laughed.

"So you're completely in the dark," said Andreas. "The plow is a mighty thing. With it you can sow . . . It's great. Sowing is good, but I want to do the choir thing to get women. Look how Magdaleena's out of her mind about these chorales. Most of all I'd like it if I sowed in the morning and sung in the evening in the chorale and then got with the dames."

"A monk's haircut would be cool too," added Pärtel dreamily. "The girls like it too, but we're not allowed to cut our heads that way. The monks won't allow it. Peasants aren't allowed to look like monks."

"Why do you listen to them?" I asked.

"How do you mean?" exclaimed Jaakop. "They've come from a foreign country; they know better how things are done in the world. We only came out of the forest recently. What do we have to teach them?"

"Snakish words," I said. The trio stared at me scornfully.

"You know them, do you?" asked Andreas.

"Of course I do," I replied. "And at least Pärtel—I mean Peetrus—used to know them. Didn't you, Peetrus?"

Pärtel screwed up his face.

"I don't remember," he said somewhat reluctantly. "As a child I used to play all sorts of games and you can make up all kinds of nonsense. It was so long ago I can't recall."

"You have to remember," I said excitedly. "You can't claim that Snakish doesn't exist. I've heard you hissing it yourself."

"Well, maybe I did hiss something," agreed Pärtel. "But I no longer remember a single Snakish word. And I'm not interested either. What would I do with those Snakish words? I'm not a snake! I'm a human being, I live in a human village, and I talk human language."

"It would be a different matter if you knew Latin well," said Andreas. "Then you'd sing hymns and you'd get all the women into bed." He didn't seem to be thinking of anything else.

"German is important too," added Jaakop. "That's what the knights speak. If you understand German, some knight might take you as his servant."

"Do you want to be a servant then?" I asked, taken aback.

"Of course," answered Jaakop. "That would be great. You could live in a castle and travel with the gentleman knight into foreign lands. It's very hard to become a servant, because everyone wants to, but the knights take on very few former peasants.

They prefer to bring their own servants from abroad, because our people are still too stupid and might embarrass the knights in fine society."

"Elder Johannes was a servant to a bishop for a while," said Pärtel, adding kindly for my benefit: "A bishop is about the same as a monk, but much richer and more important. It was when Johannes was still young, well, at the same time as when he visited the Pope in Rome. Johannes was allowed to live in the bishop's castle and eat from his table. He even slept with the bishop in the same bed, because it's the custom in foreign lands for important men to sleep with both women and boys."

"What?" I was shocked.

"There you go—straight from the forest, straight from the forest!" sneered Andreas. "Shut your mouth and don't make such a stupid face! Yes, that is the custom in the world! Only a man from the forest would be amazed at that. Johannes has said that in Rome sleeping with boys is a divine everyday thing. I've tried that sort of thing myself, with my own brother, but nothing much came of it. It just made you sweaty and ripped your trousers. Obviously you'd have to get trained by some knight or monk; otherwise you end up in a tangle like some amateur."

"But it happens very rarely that some knight or monk lets peasants into his bed," sighed Jaakop. "They don't think we're really worthy of them."

I told them that even in the forest that custom wasn't unknown; it happens quite often that a male fox in heat gets on the back of another male fox. This annoyed all of them.

"So you think I'm like some male fox?" asked Andreas angrily. "Who's interested in what some animals do in your stupid forest?

I'm talking about what goes on in the world. You don't know anything about it. You don't know any languages!"

"Only Snakish," added Jaakop, grinning. "I guess snakes don't get the latest news from Rome?"

"Don't boast, Leemet," said Pärtel, admonishing me. "You've only just come to the village; it would be best if you kept your eyes and ears open and tried to learn as much as possible about living as humans live, not like the animals in the forest. Where are you going to live anyway? You have to build a house, clear some land, get yourself all the tools you need. I can lend you a quern. I've got two."

I wanted to tell him that he could shove his quern up his arse, but this was when the monks' singing ended. Magdaleena slid her hand over her eyes, as if releasing herself from a spell, and came over to us.

"You boys are strange," she said. "Why do you come to listen to hymns at all if you chatter among yourselves all the time? Today that castrato sounded so wonderful that my heart went to my throat. I worship that voice!"

"Didn't I tell you that women melt before those monks?" droned Andreas. "I can sing too. Haven't you heard me at haymaking time? I even sang a song in Latin."

"Ah, Andreas, you do understand that you're not a monk," said Magdaleena. "I've got nothing against peasants singing by the bonfire, but that isn't real music. Real music is only in the monastery."

"Well now," sighed Jaakop. "What do you want from us? We've just come out of the forest; our voices still have a bit of the wild animal's growl about them. I do believe that one day great choir singers and castrati will come up out of our people and be famous all over the world. But for that to happen, our country will have to get so far ahead that they start cutting off balls here as well. It's shameful; we're like some backwoods! Your father mixes with those knights and other important men. Hasn't he heard anything about when we're going to start cutting balls off here?"

"No, Father hasn't talked about it," replied Magdaleena. "I have to go home now. I've got a lot to do there."

"Well, so have we," agreed the trio. "We grabbed some time to listen to music, but now we have to get back to work. You have to earn your bread. God doesn't just give you anything."

I wasn't in any hurry, on the other hand. I knew there was a whopping hunk of venison waiting for me at home, but I wasn't hungry yet. And I didn't have the heart to leave Magdaleena; this sudden rush of love was like a leaf attaching me to her skirt tails, and I couldn't and wouldn't tear myself away. "I'll come with you," I said to Magdaleena.

Pärtel chimed in enthusiastically, "Right, the village elder can give you the best advice about how to start a new life." The five of us traipsed toward the village.

When we got to Magdaleena's house, Johannes was just coming out of the cottage, a sheath knife in his hand.

"What are you doing, Father?" cried Magdaleena.

"Miira is worse," replied Johannes anxiously. "She won't take to her feet anymore."

"Is there something wrong with the cow?" asked Pärtel.

"Yes, she's been sickly for a week or so," said Magdaleena. "She won't eat or anything, just lows quietly and sadly. Poor creature. Father's been treating her, but nothing helps."

"Never mind. I haven't tried the best arts of doing it yet," said Johannes. "I was taught those by one of the knights' stable hands—a genuine German. This was the way he treated his master's horses, so it's a tried and tested trick. Not homespun wisdom, but knowledge figured out in foreign lands."

"Can I look on?" asked Jaakop. Johannes was happy to agree.

"Of course, come with me, young men! This wisdom might be of use to you. As long as you live you learn."

We all went into the barn. Miira the cow was lying on the straw and looked really pathetic and starved. It was immediately clear to me that this beast's days were numbered. She was simply too old. Not even a human lives forever, let alone an animal. Johannes had talked about treating the cow but I hoped that he would just cut the animal's throat and end the creature's suffering. Johannes evidently didn't think so. He had such faith in the German stableboy's teaching that he apparently thought he could wake the dead. He went up to the cow, took the knife, and made a deep incision in the animal's tail. The cow lowed in pain.

"Ahhaa!" said Johannes triumphantly and then split the cow's ears with the knife.

"What are you doing?" asked Andreas respectfully.

"I'm making slits in her body, to let the disease out," explained Johannes, and jabbed a little hole in the cow's udder. Blood started to trickle and the poor cow cried out.

"Keep in mind, boys, you have to make holes in the udder, under the tail, and in the ears!" instructed Johannes, and Pärtel, Jaakop, and Andreas repeated those words in a murmur, so that it would all sink into their minds. It was horrible for me to watch this animal torture, but I didn't intervene. What business was it of mine what the villagers did to their own animals? What I knew for certain was that in the forest no human would have cut into his wolves like that. But that wasn't everything. The German stableboy had taught Johannes many tricks.

Johannes fetched out a tub, in which a strange substance was glistening.

"This is seal blubber," he said. "The cow must eat it."

Naturally the cow declined this confection. Even though dying, she was still strong enough to press her jaws firmly together and turn her head away when she was offered the blubber. Johannes sighed.

"Stupid creature, you don't know what's good for you," he said, a gentle rebuke in his voice. "The seal blubber will drive the disease out through the wounds in your skin. Boys, come and help! Pull her jaws open with the knife, so I can put the blubber in."

After a moment the four of them had forced the cow around; only Magdaleena didn't take part in torturing the animal. True, Magdaleena scarcely regarded it as torture; she was keeping away so as not to disturb the men's important work. In my heart I hoped, though, that the cow would die and once and for all escape all this mauling. You could see that her life was only hanging by a thread.

Nevertheless it wasn't easy for the men to force her to eat the seal blubber. With great effort they had managed to get the knife between her teeth; now Pärtel was holding the animal's jaws open with it, while Jaakop and Andreas sat astride the sick cow's neck, so that she wouldn't flinch. Elder Johannes had dipped a piece of seal blubber inside, and was now forcing it into the cow's throat, with the other hand tugging the long dark tongue out of the way. The cow made a terrible noise, as if starting to choke, and this was no wonder, because it's hard to breathe when a stick is poked down your throat. Johannes twisted the stick back and forth, until he was convinced that the seal blubber had passed down the cow's throat. Then he pulled the rod out; the cow choked and her eyes turned inside out. But she still wasn't able to die and that was her misfortune, for the German stableboy really had taught Johannes many frightful things.

"The blubber pushes the disease out, but there needs to be some force from the outside too," explained Johannes. "One medicine pushes, the other pulls! For the pulling we use steam. Magdaleena, go to the inglenook and fetch the little pot that I put on to boil there. Quickly! I can see that the blubber has started to do its work and is scaring away the disease with full force."

Johannes pointed with satisfaction to the cow's wounds, which had started to bleed profusely from the great mauling. Andreas and Jaakop, who were still mounted on the cow's back, were spattered in blood. They looked at their blood-flecked clothes suspiciously.

"The disease won't go over to us, will it?" asked Andreas.

"Don't worry, it won't! It has lost all its power and strength. Soon we'll put hot steam on the wounds and then the cow will be perfectly well."

I was perfectly sure that the cow would not survive this torture. Magdaleena had come with a steaming pot, and Johannes set about throwing some straws in it.

"Take notice, boys, which plants I put into the hot water!" Johannes instructed. "This is a great art, and not a single herb may be left out. Everything has to go in the right proportion. Look, I'm putting in thyme and finally swallowwort too. That is what you have to put in last, so the stableboy taught me. It's a sure cure; the whole world uses it. Now try to raise the cow's arse a little. I want to put this pot under her tail."

Pärtel and Jaakop started levering the poor cow's arse up from the ground with two poles. The animal was already unconscious, breathing heavily. Nevertheless, when Johannes shoved the hot pot under her tail, she managed a last bellow. Then she died.

I was the only one who noticed it; Johannes carried on treating the cow.

"The disease is almost conquered!" he remarked with satisfaction, eagerly attending to the expired cow. "Now we'll let some smoke into the cut in the udder; that's where the disease is flowing out fastest. That must have been the biggest seat of the disease."

He scorched the carcass all over, muttered some words, patted the corpse, and only a while later did he start to realize that something was wrong.

"Miira!" he cried, and with his thumb opened the cow's inverted eye. "Miira, what's wrong?"

"She's dead," I said.

"What are you saying?" Johannes shouted, only now letting go of his pot. At first he looked quite disappointed, but he soon conjured up a humble expression and piously turned his eyeballs heavenward. "Indeed, you're right. Well now, what's to be done? Evidently God had other plans."

"She was such a good cow," sighed Magdaleena. "How sad!"

"Nothing to be done about it," said Johannes. "Man proposes; God disposes. We did all in our power, but God always makes the final decision."

This talk reminded me very much of Ülgas and his sprites, onto whom misfortunes could always be shifted, so I felt quite strange. Always the same story, there's always some invented bugaboo to take the blame. I asked Johannes whether that German stableboy was ever able to make a horse better with his horrible remedies.

"Of course!" said Johannes, surprised. "Why do you even ask? He didn't invent these arts. He'd learned them from the Franks, and they in turn got them straight from Rome!"

The involvement of Rome reminded me of a certain bishop and his bedfellow, and I won't deny that I stared at Johannes for a little while with quite an odd expression. He didn't notice it; he was suddenly in a great hurry. He discussed some tasks with Pärtel, Andreas, and Jaakop, things that were incomprehensible to me, and since I noticed that Magdaleena had left the barn, I went to look for her.

I found her at the gate. Away on the ridge a solitary iron man was riding, and Magdaleena couldn't take her eyes off him. "Isn't he grand?" she whispered to me. "What a suit of armor! What a helmet! What a splendid horse and what a fine saddlecloth!"

I couldn't share Magdaleena's enthusiasm, since to my eyes both the coat of mail and the helmet were quite useless things; I had no reason to envy their owner. Instead I became a little bitter, for Magdaleena was paying no attention at all to me, but ran out of the gate to admire the iron man as long as possible, and when he finally vanished from view and Magdaleena came back to the house, I told her I was going home.

"Home?" she exclaimed. "So where then? To the forest?"

"Yes, of course," I replied. "That's where I live."

I thought Magdaleena would try to persuade me, as her father or Pärtel would certainly have done, but Magdaleena just nodded and whispered in my ear, "Off you go! I like knowing boys who can change into werewolves and have met the sprites. It's so mysterious! Come and see me again and teach me some witchcraft. I know it's a sin, but it's exciting. Will you, Leemet?"

"I only know Snakish," I muttered.

"No, you know a lot more!" answered Magdaleena. "You just don't want to tell me everything. I know that. On your way, off you go now! I'll expect you back soon. Apart from everything, you're my lifesaver. Thank you again, my dear werewolf!"

She kissed me on the cheek and slipped indoors, while I started to trudge homeward through the darkening woods.

Twenty

 had hardly got among the trees when I stepped in the darkness on something soft. This soft thing belched and then swore obscenely, and I realized my foot had hit upon Meeme's stomach as he lay on the ground.

"I'm sorry!" I said. "It's so dark here."

"Dark!" sneered Meeme. "Yes, of course, eyes that come from the village can't make things out. Everything gets blunted there, starting with your common sense. I'd just been having a drink when you stepped on my belly, you damn idiot." He wiped some spilled wine off his face and licked his hand.

"I apologize," I said. "But there's no need to be in the middle of the road; you could at least go and sleep under the bushes."

"Where is there a road in this forest, then?" asked Meeme. "There are no longer any roads here. Animals walk in the bushes, but humans don't live here anymore. The forest is empty; only you and a couple of other fools roam around and disturb the peaceful sleepers. Why did you come here? You went to the village, could've stayed there. What are you looking for here? Is there no one in the village with a belly to trample on?"

"No, there's no one lying on the ground, and no one like leaf mold as you are," I replied angrily. Meeme laughed.

"I'm not only like leaf mold; it's what I actually am. Can you smell the stink of decay?"

"I can," I replied. That stench had indeed returned to my nostrils, and although a very small whiff of the sweet Magdaleena still clung to my clothes, it soon evaporated in the forest. "I'm not surprised. Look at you!"

Meeme laughed again.

"Yes, I'm decaying," he said. "Not just me. You are too. You can smell your own scent, you unhappy lop-ear! We're all crumbling to dust, starting with your uncle, then me, and finally you. We're like last year's leaves, which melt away under the snow in spring, brown and rotten. We belong to last year and our fate is to quietly change into ashes, because new life has already sprouted on the tips of the trees and new fresh green buds are bursting forth. You can march around the forest and imagine to yourself that you're young and that you have something important to do, but actually you're old and moldy, like me. You stink! Sniff yourself! Sniff carefully! That decay is inside you!"

He started coughing and I quickly took to my heels, my back wet with fearful sweat. Meeme had uttered what I myself had long feared—that the torturous stink of decay that clung around came from me. I had caught it from Uncle Vootele like an infection. When I smelt decay in Elder Johannes's house, I was smelling myself!

Of course it wasn't a visible, open wound that spread this stench; nor was it an internal focus of disease, a swelling hiding in the abdominal cavity or the chest, and you could quite surely claim that apart from me no one else was aware of the smell. Only I could smell myself, just as only oneself can read and understand one's own secret thoughts.

It was the Snakish words in my mouth that stank: in the new world the knowledge that was quietly and insipidly decaying was proving to be useless and unnecessary. Suddenly I saw my own future with terrible clarity—a solitary life in the midst of the forest, my only companions a couple of adders, while outside the woods were the galloping iron men, the singing monks, and thousands of villagers going to cut grain with scythes. Could I change anything? Go to the village and till the soil and eat bread with the other villagers? I didn't like life there; I felt immeasurably better and wiser than the villagers. And I was. I loved the forest, I loved Snakish, I loved that world under whose roof slept the Frog of the North. So what if I had no hope of ever seeing him with my own eyes? But at the same time there was nothing for me to do here. I sensed that especially strongly now. I had spent a whole day in the village, and although I didn't enjoy the monks' whining song or approve of the idiotic torture of the cow, I did at once realize that this outside world was interesting. I had had dealings with many people. I'd conversed, been silent, experienced a lot that was new. In the forest my days passed quite monotonously. Yes, as a child it had been nice to play here; what could I do in the gigantic woods, so empty of people, as an adult? How could I pass my whole life here?

Those few people who lived in the forest apart from me had filled their days with their own invented diversions: Tambet and Mall were raising armies of wolves that nobody actually needed; Ülgas was bustling around the grove and bringing sacrifices to the invented sprites. The Primates were breeding lice and trying to force themselves back into the most primeval past. My mother's days passed in roasting, Salme in watching over her Mõmmi. Hiie? She was wandering around the forest like me, feeling ever lonelier.

Of course there was Ints and the other adders, but they were snakes; they had their own life, especially now, when Ints had become a mother. Suddenly the forest seemed terribly unconsoling to me. In the village they lived like fools, but they lived to the full. In the village lived Magdaleena, whom I adored. I should have gone there, to get rid of the stench of decay in my nose, and yet I didn't want to do that; the very thought was repulsive to me. I didn't have anything to do in the forest. I lacked any kind of a future here—but it was my home. I couldn't become a green leaf; I was one of last year's crop.

This knowledge drove me to despair. I wanted to live in the forest, I wanted to be with Magdaleena, I wanted other people around me, I wanted them not to be fools, I wanted them to know Snakish, I wanted some meaning in my life, I didn't want to decay. But all these wishes were incompatible and in opposition, and I knew that most of them weren't destined to be fulfilled. Everything might have been different if my mother hadn't ever moved out of the village, if she hadn't started to be attracted to a bear, and if that bear hadn't bitten my father's head off. Then I would have grown up among the villagers, my tongue would have been thick from eating bread, and I wouldn't have understood a single Snakish word. I would now be an ordinary villager and my life would be simple and clear. I was wandering in time, and entered a door to the past just before it closed over. It was no longer possible for me to leave. I was bound by the Snakish words.

In an inconsolable mood I trudged home and found my whole family there—Mother, Salme, and Mõmmi, plus a tableful of roast venison through which Mõmmi had managed to gnaw a wide swathe. At first I thought that the topic would again be the bear's bad deeds, which I, as the only man in the family, would have to take a stand against. That I did not want to do. I was so tired and in the grip of such despondency that I couldn't be bothered to start a fuss with a silly bear. But it emerged that this was not the current chapter in Salme's and Mõmmi's love story. The reality was much worse.

Mother was white in the face, and as soon as I stepped inside, she leapt upon me and yelled, "You have to do something! Hiie is your bride, after all!"

Especially on this evening, after my meeting with Magdaleena and the kiss I received from her, I didn't care at all for a conversation on the subject of my relations with Hiie. But Mother was so upset that I understood: this was no tiny domestic issue. Something really bad must have happened.

"What's this about Hiie?" I asked.

"They want to sacrifice her!" said Salme, with tearful eyes. "Where have you been all day, anyway? We've been looking for you everywhere. Mõmmi even climbed up a spruce tree to look, but you couldn't be found anywhere, and he couldn't see you. Where were you?"

"That's not important now," I said. "Rather you tell me what you mean. Who's sacrificing her and to whom?"

"For heaven's sake, Ülgas of course, that evil man!" replied Mother. "Who else? He's taken it into his head that our life here in the forest won't get better until the sprites get the sacrifice of a young virgin. The mad old man! What's wrong with our life? There's meat on the table, full stomachs. What more does a person want? But look, he has little to choose from, and since Hiie is the only young virgin here in the forest, she was picked out. Lucky for you, Salme, that you have a husband! Very good that you found dear little Mõmmi for yourself!"

"Thanks, Mummy," said Mõmmi piously, without stopping from gnawing on a bone.

"What do Tambet and Mall say about it?" I asked, astonished. "Hiie is their daughter after all."

"They don't have a sound thought in their heads," wept Mother. "Ülgas has driven them insane. He's a half-wit himself and makes others like himself. I saw him this morning; the old man was collecting dried twigs and singing in a shrill voice. I asked him what was making him so happy, and he replied that tonight the forest will be saved, because young blood will wash away all the filth, and out of the sacrificial smoke the ancient world will arise before us again. He showed me those twigs he'd collected, and announced that on that sacred wood we would burn a young virgin. I got frightened—I'm the mother of a daughter too—and I asked, 'What mad scheme are you planning, who are you going to burn?' 'Hiie.' He said he would first let out the girl's blood to please the sprites, and then burn the corpse on a pyre. The sprites are supposed to have told him that only the blood of a young virgin would make the world as it was. I felt sick, because I saw that Ülgas was serious. He's completely mad. His eyes were shining, as if he were rabid! I lifted up my skirts and ran to Tambet and Mall's place. Me, a fat old woman, my heart wanted to jump out of my mouth I was rushing so! Tambet and Mall were in front of their shack and I shouted even from far away: 'Help, help, Ülgas has gone crazy. He wants to burn your daughter!' And can you imagine: Tambet said that he knew. His face was completely gray as ash and he was hunched and stiff. Mall looked the same; her face was no longer human, and most horrible of all were their eyes: they didn't seem to see anything; they stared out like dead fishes' eyes. I screamed, 'For pity's sake, if you know it already, why don't you do anything? Go and strike down that mad Ülgas or tie him up.' But Tambet raised his hand and said that it had to be so. That they were ready to bring the biggest sacrifice of all, to save the ancient world and bring life back to the forest. I tell you it wasn't a human voice that came out of his mouth; it was like a corpse talking. I don't know what Ülgas had done to him. I screamed, 'This is your own dear little daughter! Are you really going to let her have her throat cut like a hare?' Then Mall bit her lips, so she wouldn't burst into tears, but she didn't say anything, and Tambet was quiet too, only staring into the distance.

"Then I screamed that Hiie is my son's bride, but that drove Tambet into a rage; he came up to the fence and yelled at me that it was much better for Hiie to be sacrificed to the sprites and in that way save the old way of life than to start living with a traitor born in the village. 'What life would she expect here?' he screamed in my face. 'I'd rather kill her with my own hands than give her to your son! Better for her a noble death, in the name of a better future for her people, than your son making her his own and moving to the village with that scoundrel, spitting on the bones of our forefathers!' I saw that there was no talking to this man. He's completely mad. I started crying and came home. Then we started looking for you, but you'd disappeared, and now it's already evening and we have so little time. They'll kill Hiie! They'll kill your bride, Leemet! Tell me, what are you going to do?"

I really didn't know what I should do. I only knew that I had to try to save Hiie. Of course she wasn't my bride, but she was a sweet and dear girl and didn't deserve such a gruesome end. Two mad old men wanted to bring her as a sacrifice for their own sick ramblings. It mustn't be allowed to happen! No one could bring the olden times back to the forest, least of all the imaginary sprites. And even if these sprites really did exist, the death of one innocent girl was too high a price to pay for any miracle.

Hiie was my friend; we had grown up together. I had always felt sorry for her, because there is no greater misfortune than having a mother and father who don't love you. They had always mauled and bullied her, but I would still never have believed they would want to kill her. Tambet and Ülgas were for me so evil that I felt an unexpected rush of rage; at that moment I could have torn their hearts out of their chests with my nails, beat their heads against a tree, ripped them to pieces. This terrible wave of hatred frightened me more than before, because usually I was such a bashful boy, the kind who would rather flee from his enemy into the bushes than seek a battle with him. But now I wanted war. I recalled how Uncle Vootele had, that time by the lake, gone on the attack against Ülgas, like an adder driven to rage. I yearned for my old grandfather's fangs. I would have wanted to sink them into Ülgas's and Tambet's throats. I wanted to kill those bastards. Evidently the others also noticed that something strange was going on within me, for Mõmmi's hackles were raised on his neck when he looked straight at me, and Mother and Salme shrieked in unison.

"What's wrong? Are you feeling sick?" asked Mother. "Your face is so . . . strange!"

"Nothing wrong," I replied, breathing in deeply. "I'm going to Tambet's now and I'll bring Hiie out."

Mother and Salme shouted something to me, probably warning me to be careful, but I didn't hear what they said. A rage was throbbing inside me. It seemed to have welled up from the depths of my body, and I had the feeling that I had discovered some secret cave within myself. Moss that had long lain dry was suddenly struck by a thunderbolt and was crackling ablaze. Into the dark evening sky I hissed a long sibilation that the adders use just before they strike their teeth into the body of their victim with lightning speed. Then I ran to Tambet's hut.

It was dark and silent there. For a moment I listened at the door, then I leapt in. The shack was empty. There was no Tambet, Mall, or Hiie. So they must have already left. I would have to run like a wolf if I still wanted to save the girl.

I rushed into Tambet's barn. The wolves were lying there side by side, but at the sight of me they leapt to their feet and started baying. I hissed the necessary Snakish words to them, the wolves fell silent, lowered their heads obediently, and I jumped onto the back of one of them and together we sped toward the sacred grove at breakneck pace.

Yes, they were already there. The flames were blazing. Ülgas was standing in the light of the fire, his arms raised heavenward, and Hiie crouched there like a little crumpled ball, Tambet and Mall like two stone statues a little way off.

On the wolf's back I charged into the middle of the grove, which was actually a terrible desecration, since animals had no right to enter the sacred grove. Before they could comprehend it, I pulled Hiie to myself on the wolf's back and hissed Snakish words meaning "run now as fast as you can!"

The wolf rushed away and behind my back I heard Tambet cursing me and Ülgas screaming in an unnatural, bloodcurdling voice. After a little while the noise abated. Along the forest path we raced at full gallop. It started to rain, and soon we were wet through. Hiie was unconscious; she hung limply over the wolf's neck and was starting to slip downward. I hissed to the wolf to slacken his pace a little. Actually he would have done that anyway; two people were too much of a burden to him. Just at that moment we heard the baying of other wolves behind us.

These were Tambet's wolves, and he sat on the back of the first of them; behind him galloped Ülgas, and they were gaining ground on us, as my wolf was tired and had to carry two people, while the wolf pack behind us was running without a load. It was clear that they were almost upon us, and I turned my face to my pursuers and hissed to the wolves through the ever-increasing rain a sibilation that would put them to sleep.

But the wolves did not fall asleep, their baying approached ever nearer, and I heard Ülgas screaming, "Hiss, oh hiss, pupil of the adders! These wolves won't obey you! Their ears are stopped up with wax. You have no power over them!"

Pouring wax into the ears of animals was a disgusting and also dangerous trick, because it would not be possible to gouge out the wax, and in the future these wolves could never be guided in any way by Snakish words; from now on they would be their own masters and would do whatever they pleased. But in his blind hatred of me and his insatiable desire to cut Hiie's throat, Ülgas was prepared to take this step. My wolf was now starting to stumble and I knew that soon the game would be up.

At that moment there galloped out of the thicket another wolf, which jumped alongside my steed and I saw, sitting on the wolf's back, Mall.

"Turn left," she said without looking at me, looking only at the unconscious Hiie, whom I was holding in my arms. "There is the sea. On the shore you'll see some rocks; hidden behind the biggest one is a boat. Take it and go; then you'll be saved."

The next moment she led her own wolf into the bushes and was gone. There was no time to thank her for her good advice, and in the end Mall had only done a mother's duty. She had never treated Hiie tenderly, but the sacrifice of her daughter was too much even for her.

I directed my wolf to the left and in a moment we were by the seashore.

For me it was a familiar place; just here, years ago, old Manivald the coast guard had been burned for his funeral. I saw the big rocks, and behind me I heard the wolves' breathing and Ülgas's fearful yelping. If Mall was wrong or lying, and there was no boat, they would catch me I knew. Summoning the last of its strength the wolf sped across the beach sand, straight toward the rocks.

There was a boat. I threw Hiie into it and pushed with all my might. The boat was sunk deep in the sand and didn't want to leave the spot. I yelled in desperation, bit my lips hard, gathered all my strength—and got it to move. A moment later we were on the water. I found the oars in the bottom of the boat, and when the wolf pack, with Tambet and Ülgas, reached the shore, we were sloshing away at a safe distance.

Of course the wolves could have jumped into the water and tried to swim after us, but since their ears were stopped up with

wax, they couldn't be given the order, and naturally they didn't
want to voluntarily make themselves wet. But Ülgas and Tambet
waded into the water, although the decrepit sage almost immediately stepped on a rock on the sea bottom and went sprawling.
Tambet kept on wading until the water reached his chin, then
started swimming furiously and far, but it was all in vain. The
boat was much faster than the old man, and his bobbing head
became ever smaller, until it merged with the darkness. However,
we heard Tambet's voice long afterward. "I'm coming after you!"
he screamed. "I'll find you, wherever you escape to! I'll bring
you back! I'll catch you!"

Twenty-One

iie was sleeping in the bottom of the boat, curled up like a little snake. In the meantime I had started to worry for her and feared that she had been hurt in the escape, but when I looked more closely I saw a faint smile on her face and heard her breathing deeply and peacefully. She was all right.

We were drifting slowly on a completely smooth sea, not a single wave in sight. The rain shower had stopped long ago. At first I had rowed, but then I stopped bothering, since I wasn't able anyway to choose where to go. I was waiting for sunrise so as to find out exactly where we were.

The strange and wild fury and the hitherto unprecedented brutality that had taken over me the previous night had long since dispersed. I was again the ordinary cautious and pious Leemet, and I was quite frightened to think about the peril I had been in. Had I really hissed Snakish words into the night sky like an ancient warrior going into battle? Where did I take that unexpected strength and rage from? By now it had completely dissipated and I thought with dismay that Mother would surely be worrying and expecting me, and I regretted that I had got involved in this mess.

Dawn finally came. The first rays of the sun were spreading wide over the sea, as if someone had dripped liquid wax into a mirror of water, and at that moment Hiie also woke up. She opened her eyes and looked at me, at the sea surrounding us, and her look contained no hint of surprise or dread. And yet she had been unconscious since the time when I pulled her onto the wolf's back from under Ülgas's knife. The last thing she could remember was being in the grove at night and hearing the strange tones of the sage, his arms stretched heavenward. Now she was in a boat with me. But Hiie seemed not to find this odd at all. She smiled at me, sat up, and stretched herself.

"So you saved me," she said. "I knew it."

"How could you know it?" I asked. "I got there at the last moment and the escape wasn't easy at all. They almost caught us."

I told Hiie quickly about the events of the past night—how we had ridden on wolfback and how Ülgas had poured wax into the ears of the other wolves. Hiie giggled, as if I were telling her something terribly funny. Only when I mentioned the part played by her mother in our plan of escape did she grow serious for once.

"Poor Mum!" she said, but then burst out laughing again. "And poor Dad!" she giggled. "He must he furious with us. He had arranged everything so nicely and spectacularly; just a little more and the forest would have been saved. But now we broke it all up and the ancient life won't ever come back again. Oh, how disappointed he must be!"

Laughter fairly burst from her mouth. I had never seen Hiie like this before. Her eyes blazed, mischievous dimples had appeared on her cheeks, and when she tried to suppress her laughter even a little, and pressed her little white front teeth on her lips, she looked like a tiny mouse. That night she had changed beyond recognition; on the open sea, in the bright light of the first rays of the sun, she was strangely beautiful. By leaving the forest she seemed to have pulled herself free from some invisible threads that had oppressed and bound her until then. She seemed to have emerged from a cocoon. I must have been gazing at her in such amazement that Hiie started laughing again, stretched out her arm, and splashed me with water.

"Why are you staring at me like that?" she asked. "You saved me, you sent the forest to destruction, and you struck down the ancient way of life—what next? What else can you do?"

She laughed, rested her head on her knees, and gave me a sly look. At that moment I was madly fond of her. She was so sweet and glowing, and in her eyes was a naughty glint that charmed me. Suddenly I felt that maybe Mother was right and that it might really pay me to take Hiie . . .

This is what I was thinking at that moment, though only the previous day I'd fallen in love with Magdaleena. That love had not faded away, but Magdaleena and Hiie were simply such different girls that I could calmly admire them both. Magdaleena was primevally female, luxuriant, with long blond hair—a real beauty. But Hiie—at least at this moment in the boat—was still slender and boyish. Her hair was dark and not long at all, but she gazed at me with a special, fresh, newly budded charm.

You could almost claim that during her long sleep Hiie had been reborn. This thought terrified me: I was afraid that the new and radiant Hiie might vanish just as suddenly and change back into the pallid and timid girl who used to melt into the bushes. That fear alone would have held me back from returning homeward, because I didn't want the miracle that happened at sea to fade away when Hiie got back to her old familiar surroundings. In any case, it wasn't possible to return home. No doubt there was waiting for us on the shore a whole pack of deafened wolves, which Ülgas and Tambet would set upon us to leap on our necks. We had to choose some other route.

"We could go there," said Hiie, pointing to a distant dimly blackish strip of land, which must have been some island. "It must be quite far away. Can you manage to row there?"

"If I get tired, I can have a rest. We're not in a hurry," I answered. "But what will we do there on the island?"

"What will we do here either?" asked Hiie. "Or do you want to spend the rest of your life in a boat?"

She chuckled again.

"It's quite nice here, in a way," she said. "It's easy to wash and you don't have to go far for a swim. As for eating, that's a more difficult matter, and if the weather gets cooler, we're going to get cold, won't we?"

"Yes," I admitted. "It would be awful to spend the winter here. So by the time snow arrives, we have to get to that island. It's so important, because in winter the sea freezes over and I won't be able to row anymore."

"Yes," agreed Hiie. "So don't have too long a rest, a couple of months at most, then you have to start rowing again."

"I'll try to manage that," I promised.

"Let's try to make the best possible use of these few days," said Hiie. "Such a beautiful morning—how about going for a swim?"

"Swim . . ." I only had time to say in reply before Hiie had pulled off her wolfskin jerkin and jumped naked into the water.

I stared at her in amazement. Hiie swam around the boat and cried, "Come on in! The water's so warm!"

I didn't like the idea of stripping off in front of Hiie, but it was impossible to refuse. Shyly I removed my jacket and trousers and lowered myself into the water so that the boat was between us.

For the first moment the sea was still very cold and I swam a few strokes quickly to get warm. Hiie's wet and impish face approached me; we met and swam awhile side by side. The sea covered us, but I knew all the time that right beside me here swam a naked girl, and Hiie suddenly seemed so wonderful to me that I decided to marry her no matter what—and simply visit Magdaleena in the evenings.

I summoned up my courage, swam very close to Hiie, and kissed her nose. She laughed and kissed me back.

This excited me so much that I wanted to take her in my arms right there; I stopped swimming and the next moment sank under the water.

When I rose sputtering back to the surface, Hiie had swum to the boat and was laughing there.

"You're not a fish!" she cried. "Come onto dry land." She hauled herself back into the boat and sat there, naked and wet. Bathing had made her even more beautiful. Hiie had truly changed her skin, just like a snake, and this new Hiie, free from her parents, wolves, and all the problems of childhood, was so sweet, so tempting, so irresistible that I swam at my fastest speed to the boat and climbed up to her.

"Keep in mind that we've only got until the winter!" whispered Hiie when I kissed her. "Then we'll be frozen stuck!"

"I know. Before the winter I'll start rowing again."

In fact I started rowing much earlier, on the afternoon of the same day. We had been sloshing in the middle of the sea all day, kissing, making love, swimming again, and climbing back into the boat, resting in each other's arms and talking. I had never heard Hiie talking so much! Usually she was pretty silent, especially back when she used to play with me and Pärtel; it was always we boys who talked and thought up new games, while Hiie only looked at us with round eyes, enchanted at the mere fact that we had taken her into our gang, agreeing with everything that we had to offer.

She was our silent shadow, our little girl grasshopper, whose greatest wish was to keep on our tails—serious and absorbed, as if playing was an important task, to be done with as much care as possible, and as if she were afraid that if she accidentally made a mistake, she must be excluded from our company and would have to stay at home. But at home there was her father, who demanded silence while he meditated on his nation's illustrious past, and the child's foolish prattle disturbed him. It had been to Hiie's advantage to remain as invisible as possible at home, for otherwise Tambet might be reminded, for example, that his daughter didn't drink wolf's milk—so it was best for Hiie to move on tiptoes. And so that is what she did, everywhere, always, until now, here in the boat, where she burst into bloom under my gaze. She rested in the crook of my arm, happy and naked, and just kept talking. She was like a fox cub who has suddenly got its eyes and is now greedily ogling the world, and crawling out of the den, instead of drowsily and helplessly lying beside her mother as before. Hiie chatted and laughed until I forced her into silence for a while with kisses, and then she would talk again. And I kept on listening and feeling her warm body against mine. It was one of the most beautiful days of my life: we were completely alone, far from all other people and animals, the sun warmed us, and there was not a cloud in the sky.

Toward evening we were reminded that a person must also eat and that by nightfall it would be wise to seek some other dwelling place than a little boat, because you cannot always know the sea, and if a storm should suddenly arise, sleeping in a little boat is no fun at all. I put on my trousers and cape and took up the oars. After a couple of hours we reached the island.

"Interesting—are there people living here?" asked Hiie. "I hope not. Most of all I'd like to live here with just you, the two of us."

"Me too," I replied. I was no longer worried at all that Mother was waiting for me at home, not knowing anything about our fate. In the end it was she who advised me to go and rescue Hiie, my own bride, and I did, although at that moment I didn't yet believe that Hiie was my bride. Mother would have to be happy, because Hiie was indeed rescued and had become my bride, so all her little baby clothes had not been made in vain at all. I had to admit that Mother was in the end wiser than I as I trudged hand in hand with Hiie around the island, looking for a suitable cave, because we didn't care to start building a shack as evening fell. A large hare hopped across our path. I called it with Snakish words, it stopped, and I killed it.

After a little while we found a suitable overnight spot. I lit a fire and Hiie set about cooking the hare, while I lined the cave with skins and tried in every way to make it pleasanter. Sometimes life moves terribly quickly: only that morning had I fallen in love with Hiie; now we already had our own home, and my wife was preparing our first evening meal together. I had become a husband and a homeowner, maybe even the ruler of a whole island, because so far we hadn't encountered a single human. We thought we were alone on the island, just the two of us.

But that wasn't the case. I was just coming with a new load of branches to our brand-new cave when I was grabbed by the leg, so hard that I screamed and fell to my knees. It was already quite dim and I saw to my amazement only two burning eyes, which almost leapt into my face, and I heard a hoarse voice demanding, "Who's your father? Tell me, who's your father?"

"My . . ." I stammered. "He died long ago." I saw a nose, which stuck out from a gray thicket of hair covering the whole face like a mushroom out of moss.

"Was his name Vootele?" demanded the voice. "Tell me, was his name Vootele?"

"No," I said with a groan, for my leg was still in an iron grip. I imagined one might have a feeling like this when a wolf gnaws at your shinbone. "You're hurting me. Vootele was my uncle, but he's dead too."

"Ah, uncle!" cried the hairy creature with the burning eyes. "So you're Linda's child!"

Linda really was my mother's name and I said so. The grip slackened immediately, and instead I felt something very hairy and piercing sinking into my face, as if I were being forced headlong into the spruce branches. I was kissed on the mouth and shaken by the ears.

"That's what I thought; a stink doesn't lie!" said the stranger. "I always recognize the smell of my own blood. What's your name, grandson?"

"Grandson?" I repeated in amazement. "My name is Leemet, but are you then . . ."

"Your grandfather!" announced the hairy old man, hugging me with terrible force. "Your mother, Linda, and your uncle Vootele are my children. Ah, so Vootele has died then! What a shame! My dear son! What happened to him then? Did he die in battle?"

I was too surprised to reply. My grandfather! Apparently then the same one that Uncle Vootele had told me about long ago, the crazy man with fangs, whose legs were chopped off and who was then thrown into the sea to drown. But he hadn't drowned; he was alive. Indeed only his legs were missing; below the knees his trousers were tied up, so that his empty trouser legs wouldn't drag along the ground. The old man followed my gaze and declared, "They chopped off my legs, the bastards. But never mind. I'll still get them in the necks for it. You've come at the right time, nephew. I need help. But we'll talk about that later. Is that girl who's roasting a hare there yours? I didn't try to bite her. I thought I'd bump the man off first, but then suddenly I got a whiff of my own blood. What are you doing here, Leemet? Are you on a crusade?"

I told my grandfather the whole story in brief. The old man listened with interest. His face was covered in a bush of fur, and from inside this bush two very large and very white eyes stared out, glowing in the dark. Grandfather's arms, on which he supported himself, were of huge size and terribly bony, like an eagle's claws. When they pressed into the moss, as he looked at me unblinkingly, he looked like an owl. He didn't like the end of my story and shook his head disapprovingly.

"A man doesn't run away!" he said sternly. "I would have attacked those shitty wolves and crushed them to death like rats. I'd have yanked the guts out of the sage with my teeth, and

Tambet I'd have taken by the dick and ripped it out with his innards up to the chin. Open your mouth, nephew!"

I obediently opened my mouth. Grandfather looked inside and sighed in disappointment. "You don't have fangs," he said. "A shame. I don't know why it is that I wasn't able to pass them on to my descendants. My son didn't have them, nor did my daughter . . . I hoped they might appear in the third generation, but in vain. Yes, so it's of course harder to go into battle with wolves without fangs, but you always have to try. Fleeing is not what a man does! I'm a legless cripple, but do I hide in a burrow for that? No, I attack every stranger by the leg. This is my island and I defend it."

"How did you get here in the first place, Grandfather?" I asked. "Uncle Vootele said you were thrown into the sea."

"The seals brought me," he replied. "They understand Snakish too. They carried me here and I took control of this island. Over the years all sorts of shit has barged in here; a whole shipload of knights came ashore here ten years ago and a little later a troop of monks with their farmhands, who had a plan to start building something here. I bumped them all off. I crawled in the grass like a snake and bit them in the thighs with my fangs, pulled them down and cut their throats. Then I flayed them and boiled them until their bones were clean of flesh, and for amusement I made drinking mugs out of their skulls. There's not much to do here in the evenings, so to scare away the boredom I carved on their skulls."

"Why did you boil them?" I asked, with some abhorrence. "Surely you don't eat human flesh?"

"I don't," replied Grandfather. "I've got plenty of hares and goats here. But I need the bones. You see I'm building wings for myself out of them! Human bones are the best for that. You drill a hole in them, to take out the marrow, so the bone will be lighter, and then you put them together properly. The only thing is you need a lot of those bones. You have to chop up at least a hundred people to get proper wings that will carry a man. I'm not intending to die on this island! I'll give those iron men a bitter battle yet! I'll descend on them from the sky like lightning and I'll bash their brains out. They cut my legs off and threw me in the sea! To hell with it, they won't get rid of me with childish tricks like that! I'll never give in!"

Grandfather opened his mouth and roared hoarsely, to reveal two blackened but still sharp fangs. I looked at them with wonderment. Here before me sat a real ancestral person, wild and full of strength, in his own way a little Frog of the North, whose mad life force radiated out, scorching his enemies to ash. You chopped his legs off, but he will build himself wings and attack from the air! When had he disappeared? Many years before my birth, and all that time he had prowled this island, hatching his plan of revenge, never giving up hope, still warlike and as tough as a tree branch that when it bends down straightens up again and strikes you when you least expect it.

I imagined what confusion and death Grandfather could sow in the forest. He would wriggle through the grass straight to the highway, sting the knights riding past, bite the monks' noses off their faces, and do harm to village elder Johannes and all the other friends and henchmen of the iron men. He might well get struck down himself, but before that such a furious and crazed old man could lay waste to several villages. He was dangerous, he was full of primeval strength, and in his presence I felt rising within me that same boldness that had struck me that night when I rescued Hiie—the blind desire to fight and kill. Grandfather was brimful of that madness, and like a heated stone pressed against my body he radiated his warmth into me.

"Would you like me to show you my chalices made of skulls?" asked Grandfather.

At that moment Hiie called me. She had cooked the hare and invited me to eat.

"Your wife's calling!" said Grandfather dryly. "Let's go and polish off that hare; the skulls can wait. They won't be walking anywhere!"

He laughed, showing his fangs again.

The sun had already set when we got to the fireside. I walked, but Grandfather wriggled on the ground with amazing agility like some hairy adder. It had been a truly strange day, at the beginning of which I found a wife and at the end a grandfather as well.

Twenty-Two

iie was of course amazed when she saw a hairy old man wriggling out of the grass, but I quickly explained things to her. Grandfather crawled up to the fire, grabbed the still-hot hare, and ripped it quickly in half.

"Very good. Crunchy!" he declared, gnawing his own half and spitting out the bones. "At least you know how to roast a hare, whatever else you do here."

Half of the hare disappeared with amazing speed into the old man's belly. He licked his fingers clean and stared at us in wonder.

"What? You haven't even started eating? What are you waiting for? Hare is best eaten hot. If it cools off, you get a taste of clover on the side."

We divided what was left of the hare into two and sank our teeth into the meat. Grandfather watched us with burning eyes.

"Nice to see some living people again," he said. "Otherwise I don't have time to watch them, for when I see movement, I attack straight away and bite. Only when the chap is already dead and it's time to boil up the corpse do I have time to glance at him. But, well, it's a bit late when the flesh is starting to come off the bones and it's all just porridge."

Hiie screwed up her nose, and suddenly it seemed that it would be hard for her to go on eating the hare. Grandfather noticed this and shook an admonitory finger.

"Don't make faces like that, girl!" he said. "The charnel house needs supplies. And anyway, thanks to me this island is still free. Not a single iron man has set up a claim here. Listen, tell me the news from the forest! How is my daughter getting on? Do you have brothers and sisters too?"

I told Grandfather that Mother was doing well and that I had a sister, Salme, who lived with a bear.

"Why does she live with a bear?" asked Grandfather angrily. "Are there no more men in the forest?"

"No, there aren't," I replied. "They've all moved to the village."

"Well, nothing can be done about that then. Better to be with a bear than with some village blockhead. A bear is your own, even if it's stupid. In my day I had many friends among the bears; they were good for leg pulling. Bears believe everything you tell them. I always used to feed them hare droppings. I'd say, 'Look, these are big brown strawberries. Eat!' The bears always ate them too, maybe even a whole basketful; they'd thank you afterward too. Enough to make you laugh out loud! Well, I think your sister has a jolly life! She doesn't need to make meals; she can just take a hare and sit it on a nest like a bird, then offer the bear the droppings and say that they're hare's eggs, just freshly hatched!"

This crude trick amused Grandfather so much that he cackled with pleasure for a while afterward. "It's such a shame that I'm on this island; I'd really like to see your brother-in-law!" he said. "If I could just pull his leg! But never mind. Soon my wings will be ready, I'll fly back to you, and then we'll play out that hare-eggs joke with the bear."

"When will you get those wings ready?" I asked. "How many more bones do you need?"

"Not many more. It'll take two or three men. I'll get those together in a few months. But I've got something much more important missing. You see those wings don't rise into the air on their own. You need wind for that."

"Wind?" I repeated. "The wind blows all the time."

"It does, but that's not enough," explained Grandfather. "It has to blow in the right direction and when I need it. I need a windbag, boy, and you have to bring it to me."

"From where?" I asked.

"From Saaremaa. An old friend of mine lives there—Möigas, the Sage of the Wind. You'll get a windbag from him if you tell him I sent you."

"Are you sure that this Sage of the Wind is still alive?" I cautiously inquired. "When did you last see him?"

"It was long ago, but these island folk don't die off so quickly, especially wind-sages," explained Grandfather. "They reach two hundred years, because now and then they let the wind blow through them. They press the windbag to their mouths and then it whooshes through all their intestines, it cleans all the infection and trash away, and spurts out of your arse with such a bang that big pines bend to the ground and break in half. After an airing like that your insides are so healthy again that unless someone runs an ax into your back you can happily live another fifty years. So don't worry at all about whether old Möigas has died. He'll outlive us all and calmly carry on tending to his winds."

We agreed that we would set off first thing the next morning, because Grandfather was in a hurry to get hold of his windbag.

"You never know. Maybe a whole fleet of iron men will land here tomorrow," he said with enthusiasm. "Then I'll finally have the bones I need. It would be silly to wait around on the island just for the lack of a windbag. You know, boy, I've already been lolling around here so long that I'm downright ashamed. Every night I dream of beating iron men until they foam like liquid shit. I want to get back to war! And you're coming with me, because when those bastards run for cover under the spruce trees, so that I can't catch them from the air, that's when you must kick them into returning to the field, so that I can strike them with a club right on the crown."

Grandfather's enthusiasm had fired me up so much that at that moment the plan seemed like fun. Even to me, who had never cared for struggling or fighting! Somehow the image of me driving out the fleeing iron men from under the trees into the open like goats toward Grandfather as he rampaged in the air appealed to me. The old fanged man sitting by the campfire inspired me with the urge for battle, and my muscles tensed themselves with excitement.

"But first we'll sleep," said Grandfather, suddenly changing from a bloodthirsty bird of prey into a caring old grandpa. "Tomorrow you have a long sea journey ahead; you must rest. Children, I will now crawl into my own lair, otherwise some fox will come and start to gnaw the precious human bones. What a sad end that would be! I've counted every bone. You stretch out here; tomorrow I'll come and get you up. Breakfast is on me. Today you treated me; tomorrow I'll give you a treat. You'll come to Grandfather's to eat!"

He wriggled into the undergrowth like some great lizard, whose enemy has nipped his tail off.

"How old is he really?" asked Hiie.

"About eighty," I answered. "I don't know exactly. Uncle and Mother always spoke of him as someone ancient and long departed."

"He certainly is ancient," said Hiie. "I'm a little afraid of him, but I find him very refreshing. It's quite different to my father and mother's obsession with the past. What they do smells musty, but your grandfather is just like some plant that simply blossoms even though winter has arrived."

We snuggled in each other's arms, but for a long time I got no sleep, thinking of my unexpectedly discovered grandfather. In a way he reminded me of Uncle Vootele, although in a much wilder form. They were made from the same tree, except that Uncle Vootele was the tree's smooth and strong trunk, which a storm might be able to break, while Grandfather was like a coarse and tough root pulled from deep in the ground, which not even a bear would have the strength to twist in half. And I was the crown of the tree, bending with the wind and fragile. I was the top, where the branches become so fine that they couldn't even bear a little warbler. Nothing was higher than I was, only the sky, empty and blue.

But at this moment all that seemed unimportant. Hiie snuffled to sleep on my arm; she had ears that stuck out a little from her head, and she looked like a little rat. I pressed my nose against her cheek and fell promptly to sleep.

Grandfather woke us in the morning with a loud hiss, splitting the ear like a knife and scaring away sleep at once. Hiie and I leapt up. Grandfather was sprawled beside us, in the sunlight even hairier and more wrinkled, and winked his eye.

"Come and eat!" he said. "I've roasted a whole deer for you. Eat as much as you can; the rest you can take to Saaremaa with you."

Grandfather lived in a very peculiar structure, built partly of wood, partly of stones. One can only imagine what effort Grandfather had required to roll the knee-high rocks into place. He couldn't lift them, so had to push the stones in front of him as he crawled like an ant. At the same time one could only wonder at the force that Grandfather had shown in dragging whole tree trunks into place. I couldn't resist asking Grandfather how such a thing was possible, but he only snorted vaguely and said that the house had to be strong, or it would not be able to withstand war.

"I can never know when some ship might sail to this island, so full of iron men and their henchmen that I can't kill them all at once," explained Grandfather. "Then I'll need a fortress to go into, to resist a siege. Here between the stones I have all kinds of narrow passages that I can wriggle through, to attack the iron men by surprise, but they won't find me in the maze of stone and wood."

"But still, how did you manage it?" I persisted. "You don't have legs. You're alone, but these stones and beams weigh . . . I don't know how much."

"Ah!" chuckled Grandfather. "It's not worth talking about. Every true man in the olden days could manage with stones and trees. Come on in. I'll cut the venison for you and show you my bowls."

We went to the fireplace, on which a huge stag was roasting. Nearby stood a stack of hundreds of skulls—all properly scrubbed to a polish and with the excess holes stopped up with precious stones and gold. These were apparently ornaments and treasures carried by those unfortunate iron men whom a cruel fate had led to this island that at first sight seemed so beautiful and safe, but in whose grass lurked a cruel Grandfather, fangs in his mouth.

Grandfather filled three bowls with springwater.

"Water from this spring is especially sweet and pure," he said. "There you are, children! Drink! Your skull, Hiie, belonged to a monk. But yours, Leemet, was the chief of the iron men. Let's drink a toast!"

We knocked together the beakers made of skulls and drank the springwater. I can't say that drinking from such strange vessels didn't induce a certain hesitation. Hiie's hand trembled a little as she raised the cranium to her lips, and I feared that the springwater might have the taste of death. But no, the water was really pure and amazingly delicious. Actually I had to admit that Grandfather was very reasonable. What else was he to do with the crania of the iron men? Now a use had been found for useless objects. It's very pleasant to drink from skulls. I emptied mine and filled it again.

"Isn't it good?" nodded Grandfather. "Making these bowls is my passion. I don't actually need that many of them, just the one would be enough for me, but I simply like carving. Every cranium has its own peculiarities. Some are oblong; others are as round as a lingonberry. Some have a lump on the side. Some are very small. Look at this one! It just makes you laugh. You might think it was a rat's skull! But actually this was on top of this man's neck, and the man himself had a quite ordinary build. He must have been extra stupid, if he had such a small head!"

"Interesting," I said, turning over a small cranium in my hand, in which there was room for only a few sips of water.

"Did you have bowls like these at home?" inquired Grandfather. "No? Well then, I'll give you one when you get back from visiting Möigas. Take as many as you want and take them home. That's my wedding present."

Hiie and I looked at each other and smiled awkwardly.

"We don't even know if we can go back home," said Hiie. "They wanted to sacrifice me and they're probably looking for us even now."

"Hit them on the head with an ax and there's an end to it," suggested Grandfather. "I have never feared anyone. I always went where I wanted, and soon I'll be going again—I mean flying—when you bring me the windbag. Are your stomachs full? You'd better get going then. The sooner you leave, the faster you'll come back, won't you?"

He ordered us to fill the boat with meat, because "you have to eat; food gives you strength." It was clear where my mother had acquired the practice of stuffing all relatives and friends with food. We took with us a couple of skull cups too. Grandfather ordered us to give them to Möigas the Sage. And then we were in the boat, and I tried by rowing to keep to the direction where Saaremaa was, according to Grandfather.

The trip to Saaremaa lasted quite a lot longer than our first sea journey. Maybe we could have got there a little faster, but we didn't rush. Of course Grandfather needed the wind, but one day more or less no longer mattered to a man who has spent decades alone on an island. Time and again I rested the oars and then we bathed and cuddled and ate cold venison. This was our honeymoon, although we didn't know it at that moment. We were simply happy to be together with no one disturbing us, apart from the inquisitive seals who poked their heads out of the water and watched us with great interest. There were also several sorts of small and large fish splashing in the sea whose dark backs could be seen quickly slipping past as you looked into the water. We could have caught them, but we didn't bother. It wasn't possible for us to cook fish in the boat, and there was plenty of venison. I tried to keep our course by the sun and we were more drifting than rowing toward Saaremaa.

By evening we still hadn't got far, and we spent the night in the boat, amid the splashing of the waves, and the gurgling caused by the seals rising to the surface and then sinking to the depths of the sea. In the morning we woke early and I tried to work out where we had got to. On the horizon appeared something dark, which apparently was a shore. I put the oars in the water and started to row, but the boat didn't move from the spot.

"We're stuck on some seaweed," said Hiie.

I looked into the water and saw that the boat was surrounded by a strange gray substance that looked exactly like a furry skin grown onto the sea. I stretched out my hand to try to scrape it off the side of the boat and discovered to my surprise that this peculiar skin consisted of long hairs, each of which was about the thickness of a hay stalk and extended who knows where.

"I've never seen anything like it before," I declared. "And even Uncle Vootele didn't tell me that hairs can grow in the sea. You might almost think we were on the back of some animal."

"We're not on its back; we're in its beard," replied Hiie. "Look behind you. We're on a fish's beard, but it doesn't seem to be a fierce one."

I turned around quickly and saw an unprecedented scene. At a distance of several tens of boat lengths, amid the lapping waves, was the most extravagant creature you could imagine. It was a fish, but as big as a mountain, and evidently terribly old, for the whole sea was full of its long gray whiskers. Its greenish scales had over the years been covered by thousands of shells and other marine detritus, its huge fins dangled limply like the wings of some enormous bat, and its very old and very tired eyes looked at us fiercely, and yet also curiously. We stared back, and then this strange creature opened its mouth and hissed in clear Snakish, though mixed with several other unrecognizable words, apparently so ancient that nothing but a fish would understand them: "Good morning, humans! Where are you going to?"

"To Saaremaa," I replied.

The fish blew away the whiskers that were floating into its mouth.

"It's right in front of you," he said. "You should be there by noon, though I wouldn't dare to say that very certainly, because I've never seen humans in such a small boat before. Last time I came to the surface, three warships passed me, each one with at least forty rowers, and that time it seemed funny to me, for in previous years there were also many more of those ships. And now only one tiny boat and two humans. Well, well, what's to be done. So it must be arranged that way that you are the humans who see me for the last time, and who I see for the last time."

"Why the last time?" asked Hiie.

"Because this is the last time I come from the sea bottom for fresh air. I have come to the surface once every hundred years, but I can't be bothered anymore. I've become old. Even today I thought a long time whether it was worth dragging myself out of my own comfortable lair and swimming here, but then I decided to let this be the last time. My beard has grown so long that it isn't easy to carry it with me; it gets full of water and becomes a heavy burden even for me. But I did it anyway. Yes, the sea has been emptied. Where are all those humans who once used to speed around in ships? Is there some epidemic among you?"

I didn't start explaining to the fish that many of us had moved to the villages, were growing rye, and no longer went in ships to distant lands like our forefathers. Yet still the iron men's ships were moving about, and in ever-greater numbers. I asked the fish whether he had seen them.

"The iron men?" wondered the fish. "No, I haven't encountered them. What a shame, I would have liked to see them, because I won't be coming above the water anymore. Might they be passing by here today? I don't have much time. I have to swim back soon to my cave, but maybe I'll be lucky? What are they like?"

"Rather like humans, but with an iron coating," I said. The fish plashed in astonishment.

"Never heard of it, never seen it," he murmured. "I've been to the surface too rarely and many things have passed me by. Yet it seemed to me that every hundred years it's best to get a little air. Everything was always just like the last time. The sea was full of warships and the Frog of the North was flying in the sky."

"Have you seen the Frog of the North?" I shouted.

"Of course, many times!" replied the fish. "And not only seen, sometimes he's landed on my back, to rest from flying. He was big and strong, but at that time I was even stronger and I could carry him without much effort. By now it would be beyond my powers. That's not important, for I haven't seen the Frog of the North for a long time. Do you know where he went?"

"He's asleep," I said. "And no one knows where."

The fish exhaled approvingly.

"That's right too. Sleep, rest, that's good. I'll soon be going to rest too; I'll dive right down to the bottom, I'll sink into my burrow, and I won't come out again. My beard will cover me and I can doze in peace. A long, long sleep. I can feel how good it will be."

He closed his old eyes and slowly moved his fins.

"I suppose I'll go now," he said then, opening his eyes. "I'll have to go without seeing the iron men, but never mind. In my life I've seen so much: things to think about as I lie on the seafloor. To tell the truth I'm not especially interested in those men of iron. What do I lose if I don't see them? Nothing. If you do meet them, tell them that the great fish Ahteneumion has gone down to the bottom. I won't see them and they won't even see me, and for them it's the bigger loss."

This idea seemed amusing to the old fish; he moved his tail and looked us in the eye.

"Just think, they're always traveling around in their ships, these iron men of yours, but they can't even guess that somewhere on the bottom of the sea I'm sleeping under my beard," he said, bursting out laughing again. "They think there are only little fish and jellyfish and other rubbish like that in the sea, whatever is floating on the surface, but they can never know that I'm there too. Poor fools!"

Again he blew away the whiskers that floated into his mouth.

"Good-bye, I'm going now," he said. "You were the last humans I saw and who met me. You know who Ahteneumion is and what he is doing. Others don't. You are now the wisest people on earth. The last ones to see me. Farewell!"

The next moment the great fish dived. The water started to ripple and the boat almost capsized. The whiskers surged around us and I was afraid that they would drag us with the fish into the depths, where we, together with all our knowledge, would bleach away in Ahteneumion's embrace. But it all turned out well: the beard vanished with its owner into the depths, the sea became calm, and we were alone.

"So now here we sit, the two wisest people on earth," said Hiie. "The last ones to see the great fish."

"It bothers me—to be the last of everything," I replied. "In my family I'm the last man, the last boy in the forest. Now I'm also the last to see the giant fish. How does it happen that I'm always the last?"

"For me you're the first," said Hiie, kissing me, and after a little while, when we'd got dressed again, I rowed onward.

Actually I was of course also the last for her, but I didn't know that then.

Twenty-Three

 was pretty tired when we finally got to Saaremaa, and it immediately occurred to me that Grandfather hadn't given us any clues about where to find Möigas the Sage. As always, here too I had the help of Snakish. I only needed to hiss a couple of times for a nice fat adder, head raised, to come crawling from among the junipers.

"I have to say I'm pretty surprised," he said after the usual greetings and polite expressions. "I did see you landing, but it didn't even occur to me that you might understand Snakish. Nowadays that is sadly very rare. All sorts of people come to the island, but there's no talking to any of them; they might as well all be dumb and just babble incomprehensibly. So, in all honesty, I was quite amazed when I heard you calling. Things may be bad here with us, and yet there are still educated people in other places."

"Things are no better in other places," I replied. "I was actually looking for Möigas the Sage of the Wind. Do you know where he lives?"

"I do indeed," said the adder. "Follow me. I'll lead you to him."

Möigas didn't live far away. His shack was on the seashore and was surrounded by juniper bushes. The adder wished us a good day and wriggled off.

I knocked on the door. It opened, and looking back at me was—a monk! I certainly hadn't expected that. I took a few steps back, as if I'd encountered a wasp's nest.

"Are you Möigas, the Sage of the Wind?" asked Hiie, who was also amazed to see a monk and took me by the hand.

"No, dear girl, I'm only his unworthy son," replied the monk in a thin voice, as if milk were being sucked from his mouth. He was still a young man, but hairless and, stranger still, also without eyebrows, so that his face resembled a bird's egg. Behind the monk's back some grumbling was heard, and out of the shack climbed a stunted old man with a long red beard, braided into hundreds of little plaits. This had to be Möigas.

"Here stands my esteemed father," said the monk, putting his hand on the red-bearded old man's shoulder. "Daddy, these people have come to see you."

"Yes, I can see that myself," muttered Möigas. "What can I do for you?"

"Are you Christians?" asked the monk, before we had time to reply. "Do you like Jesus Christ?"

"Be quiet, Röks!" snapped Möigas. "Don't embarrass me!"

"Daddy, I've told you my name isn't Röks anymore," chirped the monk, making a kindly face, as if the utterance of every word were an extreme pleasure. "It's not a proper name; no one in the Christian world has it. My name is Taaniel. I've told you that a hundred times, dear father. Brother Taaniel, that's what the other reverend brothers in the monastery call me."

I was reminded of Pärtel and I became very sorry for the old Sage of the Wind, because to lose a friend is unpleasant, but to lose a son is far worse. Möigas seemed to have read my thoughts; he looked at me sadly and said, "My son has gone to waste. Forgive me. It must be because he lost his mother early. I wasn't able to bring him up properly. But what am I going to do. He's my own child; I can't abandon him just because he has become—ugh, it's horrible to even say it—a monk."

"Daddy, you've brought me up very well," said the monk. "I'll be grateful to you till my dying day that you sired me and tenderly looked after me."

"What do you know about siring, you wretch?" sighed old Möigas. "You haven't even got balls!"

"Nobody has in our monastery; it's the fashion nowadays," replied Taaniel the monk. "Thanks to that, we can sing the praises of God in a high voice. Daddy, I've invited you to come and listen. Why haven't you? You'd certainly be proud to listen to your son singing with the reverend brothers."

"I don't want to hear it or see it. I'd be ashamed of my own eyes!"

"Oh Daddy, what are you saying! What is there to be ashamed of; they do this all over the world. And our choir has many admirers, women cry when they listen to us, and even men wipe away tears, so light and beautiful are our voices."

"Don't make me sick!" said Möigas, turning toward us. "Forgive me, guests, that you have to see and hear such ugly things. What brings you here? Tell me! And you, Röks, be quiet and don't interrupt!"

I quickly explained what we were seeking and who sent us. Tears came into old Möigas's eyes.

"Ah, old Tolp is still alive!" sighed Möigas. "Well, not to be wondered at, he was always a tough guy. Oh, so now he's taken it into his head to start flying! Why not, why not!"

"A human being can't fly," said the monk. "Only angels fly. And Jesus walked on water."

"I told you, Röks, don't interrupt!" barked Möigas. "And don't talk rubbish! Why do you embarrass me in front of these nice young people? You'd be better off following their example. Look how good they are! They respect their grandfather and don't go around with any iron men or monastic brothers. You see this young man, Leemet? He still has his balls. Haven't you, Leemet?"

"I have," I quickly replied.

"Hear that, Röks! Why do you have to be such a will-o'-the-wisp, flying wherever the wind blows?"

"Dear Daddy, to start with, I'm not Röks," the monk began to slowly chirrup, his eyes half-closed, but old Möigas snapped at him to be silent.

"Why do you tell me all the time you're not Röks! As far as I'm concerned you're still Röks. I'm never going to start calling you Taaniel. Now sit down and shut your mouth: I have to go out and look for that windbag. And you, dear guests, wait a while. Take no notice of what my son says. He's a bit half-witted, a disgrace to the whole family!"

With these words Möigas disappeared into his shed. Taaniel the monk settled down in a sunny spot, nodded amiably to us, and said, "Daddy's very old now; his head can't take in young people's concerns anymore. What can you do; time has passed him by. What do young people think of Jesus in your neighborhood? I'm terribly fond of him. I have his picture over my bed."

"I don't know who Jesus is," I said.

The monk made a noise of amazement that sounded like the shriek of a seagull.

"You don't know who Jesus is?" he repeated and kneaded his hands, gazing at me kindly and sympathetically. "Baptized, are you?"

"No," I replied.

"Really?" intoned the monk. "I thought that all young people these days are baptized. Baptism is cool; they pour water over your head. Without baptism they won't take you into the monastery."

"I don't want to go into a monastery!" I declared, by now quite irritated. The monk reminded me of Magdaleena and of how we'd been to listen to the monks singing, and also that I was up to my ears in love with her. Now, sitting next to Hiie, it was somehow unpleasant to be reminded of it. I felt that the monk might suddenly say, "Ho, I saw you with a pretty girl behind our monastery wall!" What would Hiie do and say? I knew that such a thing wasn't actually possible, that it was an entirely different monastery and other monks singing there, but the bad feeling remained. I was upset by these modern people who boasted all the time about their new customs and strange pets like this Jesus, whom I didn't know anything about and didn't want to either. I wasn't interested in whose picture a monk kept by his bedside, and I said so, though not quite so abruptly.

The monk remained as gentle as before. "It's silly to close your eyes to education," was all he said, raising an instructive finger. "You simply won't get on in today's world if you don't know about Jesus. You'll have nothing to talk about to other people. All right, if music doesn't interest you, then you don't have to enter a monastery, and castration isn't absolutely necessary. But you can't get to be a knight's henchman either, if you aren't baptized and you don't know about Jesus!"

"Why should I have to be anyone's henchman?" I asked. This was another horrible trait that united all these modern people—the desire to be someone's servant.

"Well, but what do you want from life, anyway?" asked the monk. "You want to be a peasant, sowing and reaping? That is of course noble; Adam also sowed and reaped and cultivated the land by the sweat of his brow. Yes, those who have not been given any higher gifts of the spirit must be content to work the fields."

"Who is this Adam?" Hiie now asked.

"Our forefather, the first human, whom God created out of the dust," explained the monk. "Before that the land was empty and bare, but then God made everything in six days, and so it has been untouched until today."

"That's nonsense," I said. "I've seen the Primates' history, which over thousands and thousands of years they have drawn on the walls of their cave. There was no God and no Adam. And what does 'untouched' mean? So many things have disappeared forever. For instance the Frog of the North. For instance the great fish Ahteneumion, who rose to the surface of the water this morning for the last time and then dived to the bottom of the sea forever. Or Snakish words. Do you know those, Röks?"

"Snakish words are from Satan," declared the monk, excited for the first time. "A human cannot know them. Satan created the snakes and gave them the power of speech, so as to tempt Eve, the first woman. They are all servants of Satan."

"Now I can really see how stupid you are," I said. "You yourself serve God and the iron men and some sort of Pope in Rome. But snakes are nobody's servants. Nobody created them; they existed in the most ancient times, back when neither humans nor even Primates lived in the forest. I do know what I'm talking about, because I know them well. I do know Snakish! I think that snakes would laugh out loud if they could hear your nonsense. You've simply been taught in the monastery a modern legend, but there are many legends in the world. Some are forgotten; new ones are invented to take their place."

"Dear boy," said the monk, having regained his former composure. "I don't want to argue with you, because you haven't been to school and you don't know anything. Humankind has become wiser than you realize. I'm simply sorry that you don't want to live like other young people. Even if you do speak Snakish words and they aren't from Satan, well, what will you do with them in the wider world? Who will you speak them to? Nowadays young people are interested in Jesus. They talk about him a lot; he's very successful."

"He doesn't interest me," I said.

"A great pity," replied the monk with a smile.

We were silent for a while. Hiie and I looked at the monk, but he seemed to be dozing in the sunshine. Suddenly he started singing in a high voice, so that Hiie and I were both startled.

Immediately Möigas the Sage rushed out of the shed and cried, "Be quiet! At once! Don't shame me in front of the whole world!"

"Daddy, it's just an innocent hymn, where I extol Jesus's mercy and grace," said the monk lazily. "How can this beautiful music shame you in any way? This hymn is making big waves in the world at the moment; it's being sung at all the feasts."

"But not under my roof! Not here! In the world they might go in for that sort of thing, but in my house we do things the right way!"

He gave Hiie and me a signal to follow him.

"I don't have a single windbag ready at home," he explained. "But never mind, we'll soon pack the right winds together. Then it will be good for your grandfather to fly. Let him fly to visit me too."

"Yes, let him come," said the monk. "I'll be glad to welcome your friend, Daddy, and I'll pray for him."

"No, better he doesn't come," said Möigas. "Tolp is a fierce man; he'll knock you dead in his great rage."

"Good, then I'll die a martyr," declared the monk. "And I'll go straight to Heaven, where I can sit on the right hand of Jesus. To be a martyr is a great honor; books are written about you and your picture is put up in churches. Daddy, just think, your son a martyr!"

"That might very easily happen. If you don't keep your mouth shut for once, I might do you some damage myself. Children, let's go inside quickly! My son is driving me mad!"

We went with the sage into his shed. On its walls hung a huge number of fine, coarse, and even coarser ropes, all tied into large knots. Möigas started rummaging among them and chose about ten bundles of ropes.

"These are wind knots," he explained. "On the side of each rope is one wind. I go in a boat to sea to catch them, like any other man fishing. But a wind is much harder to catch. It's fast and slippery; you have to be enormously skillful to get it to run into your noose. Then quickly you tie it on and you can hang the wind on your wall until you need it. A wind is not a fish; it won't go bad. It can hang on the wall for up to a hundred years, but if you let it open, it howls and pants, as if it had been caught only yesterday and is completely fresh. I have here quite old winds, captured by my father, storms and tempests that you won't find anywhere today. Here we have, still surviving, the first wind that I caught when I was still a little boy. It's quite a weak summer breeze, the kind that brings a little nice coolness on a hot day. Look, the same here. A wind like this is quite easy to catch, but at that time I had a lot of bother with it. A little boy's thing, with ten fingernails I had to keep hold of the other one, stopping the rope from getting tangled, but when I finally hung it up on the wall, it was a great feeling! Just as if I'd captured a whirlwind. In fact I've got a few of those, but I'm not sending them to your grandfather; they're not good for flying. They were used in war: let one of these loose and it'd capsize the enemy's ships or raze their villages to the ground. Worse than fire! Oh, I've got every kind of wind here: winter ones, which bring snow with them, and autumn ones, which blow the rain clouds in. These ones are spring winds: let one of these loose and soon you'll be breathing light and fresh. There are following winds, which help sailors, and headwinds, to help you defend yourself against enemies. All kinds. I won't be catching many more. I'm old already, and I probably can't catch a really big storm, haven't got the strength, and what will I do with these winds anyway? I wanted to make my son a wind-sage, but that good-for-nothing is not interested in my wind collection at all. So I'm happy to send a few winds to your grandfather; at least one person cares about them and knows how to use them. I chose ten winds; that should be enough."

"Do we take them with us like that, on the end of a rope?" I asked.

"No, not like that," replied Mõigas. "A wind is smart and cunning, like a living creature. As long as he's in my hand, he keeps still, because he recognizes that I'm a wind-sage and I'm not going to play tricks with him. But if he understands that some ordinary person is holding the end of the rope, he'll start to struggle and push, and try to tear himself from the rope end. No, I'll put them in a bag, so they won't get out and you can get back nicely to Grandfather's place."

From under a table the sage took out a pouch, sewn together from several skins, the mouth of which was pulled shut with a rope. He took hold of the first wind and carefully undid the knots that held it in a bunch. Suddenly the air in the room started to move, and Hiie's hair started fluttering, as if a sudden gust had tangled it. Then Möigas pushed the wind into the bag. He did the same with all the other bundles of ropes, and by the end the pouch was quite fat. If you pressed your ear to it, you could hear a muffled whooshing and roaring, as if a storm were raging inside.

"Now it's ready," said Möigas. "Now there's nothing more to do than to carefully open the mouth of the bag and let out just enough wind as you need. Your grandfather will know what to do. Yes, he's one fine man, and he raised his children to be sensible. See, I couldn't do that with my son; he went bad, so it's terrible to look at him. Oh, spare me! He's singing again! I told him that if he isn't quiet, I'll box his ears." A wail could indeed be heard from the yard. Mixed with the monk's high-pitched singing someone swearing could be heard. We rushed outdoors and saw the monk arguing with a short but horribly fat old man, who was brandishing a stick furiously and yelling, "Will this whining stop for once? I can't get peace; you're always opening your jaws and howling like a wolf! What's wrong with you, Röks? Are you in pain or something?"

"Dear old neighbor," replied the monk, piously rubbing his hands slowly together, as if washing them with sunshine. "You could be a bit more agreeable. This kind of music is what the young people appreciate these days. You're old; you have your own favorite tunes. But you should understand that times move on, and what you don't like might provide happiness for a new generation, who take their example from Christ."

"It was Christ that taught you to sing like that, was it?" shrieked the stocky neighbor.

"Of course," replied the monk. "He is my idol, and the idol of all young people. These songs are sung by the angels in paradise; they're sung by the cardinals in the holy city of Rome. Why shouldn't we sing them too, as the whole Christian world does?"

"My backyard isn't the Christian world!" interjected Möigas now. "I'm sorry, Hörbu, that you were disturbed. You must have been having your noontide nap."

"Well, of course I was having my noontide nap!" complained Hörbu the neighbor. "And just when the sleep was sweetest, your useless son started whining. Why do you let him come here at all? Let him sit in his monastery if that's what he's chosen."

"He's my own flesh and blood," sighed Möigas.

"So what if he's your son! I told my daughter: 'If you ever become a nun, you slut, don't ever show your face in my house again!' The whore!"

"You didn't have to bless your daughter with such ugly words, dear neighbor," countered the monk. "Johanna is a very exemplary nun. I meet her often. Why should she have stayed in this wild place? There's no better way for a modern girl of today to get into the wide world than by becoming a bride of Christ!"

"She should've got married!" shouted Hörbu. "There are fifty of those brides of Christ there in the nunnery. It's a disgusting obscenity, and it's putting everything upside down!"

"You've misunderstood everything," sighed the monk sympathetically. "Pious nuns live out their days in deep virtue and have nothing to do with men."

"You go there yourself! You said yourself that you meet her often!"

"I'm a monk. Oh, neighbor, you don't understand anything about young people today."

"I don't understand, and I don't want to," declared Möigas. "And don't speak in the name of all young people! Leemet is young too, and he isn't involved in that kind of filth."

"He's from the forest, completely uneducated," replied the monk, with scorn in his voice. "It's a shame, Daddy, that for you there is more value in spiritual darkness and clinging to past times than in ambition and the desire to learn."

"If you're so keen on learning, why didn't you want to learn to catch the winds?" asked Möigas sadly. "This ancient art will now go to the grave with me. You would've had an honorable profession, one which would always keep you fed."

"On the contrary, Daddy, there's no future in that profession. You don't need to catch the winds; it's enough to humbly turn to God in prayer and he will roll the winds toward you where you need it; he quietens the storm and calms the tempest."

"Sadly it's not so simple," sighed Möigas. "But you believe only in what you're told in the monastery, not what your own old father says."

"Forgive me, Daddy, but there in the monastery they read books printed in Latin. When the wise men in foreign lands wrote them, our ancestors were still running around the forest with the foxes," said the monk with a smile, as if feeling pleasure that he had raised up such great wisdom from such harsh circumstances. He shook his head in a saintly way, looked at us all in turn, and rose with a sigh.

"I shall pray for you, poor heathens, and especially for you, dear father," he stated. Then he looked once more at Hiie and me and added, "If you start to take an interest in Jesus Christ, then you know where to find me. Sharp young men are always welcomed with open arms to our monastery."

I didn't reply. The monk nodded again, made the sign of the cross in the air, and left.

Hörbu spat on the ground.

"Forgive me, Möigas, but that son of yours is as mad as a polecat."

"Yes," sighed Möigas bitterly. "In his younger days he was such a sweet little boy. These new winds, they're changing people."

"My daughter was such a strong little grasshopper," said Hörbu. "But then she started hanging around that monastery. I forbade her. I even gave her a hiding, but she kept on going where she wasn't allowed. What was driving her there? Why did she become a nun? Perhaps we really are old and we don't understand a thing about the new world?"

In my nose I smelt again the carrion stench that assaulted me from time to time. I would have liked to open the windbag and let out all Möigas's storms and tempests, to scare away the rotting odor, let myself be cleaned by the airs. But these winds were intended for Grandfather. So we said farewell to Möigas and Hörbu and sat down in the boat.

On the way to Grandfather's island we saw one of the iron men's ships passing on the horizon.

"Ahteneumion rose to the surface a bit too early," said Hiie. "Now he would have seen the iron men, and the iron men would have seen him. But now they're sailing there and they don't even know what's lying on the sea bottom under his own beard. Only we know. Isn't that exciting?"

At that moment it seemed to me that we knew perhaps too much that others didn't know, and on the other hand too little that was known to everyone else, but I said nothing to Hiie.

Twenty-four

fter we got back to Grandfather's island, the first thing we noticed was a strange boat drawn up on the shore, which Hiie thought she recognized. She shrank from the sight of it, clinging to my sleeve and, without saying a word, beckoned me back toward the sea.

"What's wrong?" I asked.

"Let's go away, back to Saaremaa. It doesn't matter where; let's just go," whispered Hiie, looking at me with troubled eyes. "Please, let's go, quickly!"

"Whose boat is that?" I inquired, guessing the answer already.

"Father's, of course," whimpered Hiie in a tiny voice. "Don't you recognize it? He's come after us, he's chasing us, he still wants to kill me, he's mad! Leemet, let's go! Let's row far from here, as far as you possibly can! Please!"

I have to admit that the knowledge that Tambet was somewhere here filled me with dread. This crazed old man couldn't rest with having failed to save the world. An obsession, once taken into the head, grows in it like a horn. I wasn't at all sure how well I could defend Hiie if her father were to suddenly leap out of the bushes and wanted to carry her off. Tambet was a big strong man; compared to him I was like a young rowan beside an oak. I tried to awaken in myself the rage and courage that had sustained me that evening when I stole Hiie from the sacrificial grove, but the flame inherited from my ancestors this time didn't want to catch fire. I was also overtaken by dread when I looked into the forest and on the shoreline and tried to guess whether Tambet was lurking in it now and whether he'd already noticed us. I began to feel that Hiie's plea to get into the boat and row to some safe place wasn't such a bad idea. Hiie was already in the boat, weeping and shouting, "Come on! What are you waiting for? We've got to go before he sees us. You won't get away from him on the sea he rows so fast! I know."

I had just about agreed to do as she wanted. Only Möigas's windbag held me back. I had to take it to Grandfather! There was a chance that if we left now, hid somewhere for a couple of days and quietly rowed here to the island, Tambet might have left, the coast would be clear, and I could calmly hand over the windbag to Grandfather. But it was shameful to run away like this, to admit our own weakness and fear, while my grandfather had fangs in his mouth and was preparing for an air war with the whole world. When I started thinking about Grandfather, one thought occurred to me: with him I could perhaps even overcome Tambet. After all, Grandfather had built himself a real fortress, to withstand a siege. If we could get there without Tambet noticing us, we would be in quite a secure place. And yet—would it not be better to row back to sea in fright, as Hiie had suggested? Or was it wiser to stay on the island and fight Tambet with Grandfather, to tell him that

Hiie was now my bride, and that there could be no talk of a sacrifice? Let him go back to his forest; we would stay here on the island. We wouldn't argue with him; we would just wish him to leave us in peace.

"Why don't you come?" asked Hiie from the boat. She must have wept and cried herself out by now, for now she was sitting very quietly and looking at me with sad eyes. The first wave of terror had passed, Tambet had not appeared yet, and Hiie wearily awaited developments.

"We're not leaving," I said. "We'll look for Grandfather. I have to give him the windbag, and then we'll ask him to talk to your father himself."

"Father won't listen to anyone," said Hiie.

"Well, my grandfather will force him to listen," I said boldly, trying to encourage Hiie. I took the girl by the hand and dragged her up.

"Come on now. The most important thing is to get to Grandfather's house. Once we're there, your father can't do anything more."

Hiie didn't protest, but only sighed, kissed me unexpectedly and very hard, and stood up next to me.

We sneaked through the bushes, and every time a branch cracked or leaves rustled, we had the feeling that Tambet was just behind us, ready to grab us by the elbows and drag us to his boat like a couple of hares. However, that didn't happen. We didn't encounter Hiie's father and perspiring with fear we made it to Grandfather's house.

Grandfather was sprawled in the middle of the grass and was boiling something in a big pot.

"Grandfather!" I cried, rushing up to the fire. "We're back!"

"I know," said Grandfather. "I heard you sneaking through the forest. Did you get the windbag?"

"We did," I replied, handing Möigas's bag to Grandfather. "But—"

"Aha!" interrupted Grandfather with a triumphant roar. "The windbag! At last! Now just a few more bones to collect and a suitable spot to find, then look out, iron men and monkish rubbish! I'll be flying on top of you, as if the moon had fallen from the sky, to flatten you to a pulp!"

"Grandfather, my father is here on the island," said Hiie. "Remember, we said he was chasing us? Now he's come here."

"Yes, he did have that misfortune," replied Grandfather, fishing from the pot a huge skull. "This will make the biggest drinking bowl I've ever had," he added proudly. "I would otherwise give this bowl to you, girl, since it's your father's head, but what would a woman do with such a big beaker? A woman can't drink that much at once."

We were dumbstruck. Tambet, whom we had feared so much and from whom we were almost ready to flee back to Saaremaa, was boiling here in a big pot, chopped to pieces like a goat. His skull really was enormous and thick; no wonder that new ideas had such trouble getting into it, and that every idea that did finally enter that hard shell stayed forever like a bird caught in a trap.

I looked at Hiie, because I wanted to see her expression when shown the skull of her father in the flesh, which was almost ready to be a splendid drinking bowl. She eyed the skull, bit her lip, and finally covered her face between her knees.

"Are you crying?" I asked quietly.

"No," replied Hiie without raising her head. "Why should I? He wanted to kill me; he was mad. I simply feel exhausted.

The fear has worn me out. I was so horribly afraid when I saw Father's boat I thought that, that now I'd be taken back home, and even if I wasn't sacrificed to the sprites, everything would be just as before, so cruel, so sad, so bleak. But now I know that nothing will ever be the same again. He no longer exists; he's been turned into a beaker. I'm now so peaceful that I feel sleepy. You won't be offended if I go off and sleep for a while?"

"Why would we be against that, dear child?" replied Grandfather. "Go and have a doze as much as you like! We'll be getting you up by suppertime."

Hiie got up, smiled at us, and disappeared into Grandfather's cave. Grandfather accompanied her with a friendly look, while stirring her father's remains with a big ladle.

"She's a good girl," he said. "Doesn't make a quarrel about nothing. I really needed a lot of bones; I just couldn't let that thickset bloke walk away. Anyway I recognized him and I knew straight away that he was on your tail, so it made sense to strike him right down. I didn't attack him without warning, though, because after all he was a human being, not some shitty iron man who's worth nothing more than an insect. I hissed at him: "Careful! I'm going to bite you!" so he'd have a chance to defend himself. But he didn't take any notice, as if he hadn't understood; he just kept on wading forward through the hay, with a grim expression on his face. Well, there was nothing to do about it. I crawled on his heels and when there was a suitable moment, I bit him through the left knee. When he fell down screaming, I bit into his throat, and the thing was done. I flayed him, cleaned the meat off the skeleton, and got rid of most of the offal, and now I'm boiling the bones so they'll be white and clattering when you strike them together. By the way, Hiie's father had splendid shinbones; I've been looking for ones like these for ages, but you don't get ones like them from iron men. Their legs are curved, because they sit on horseback all the time."

Grandfather turned Tambet's head bone around in his hand. "But best of all is this skull," he said. "I don't get tired of admiring it. This will be my victory mug; from this I'll start drinking the blood of my slain enemies in war. To ancient freedom!"

Tambet could not have wanted a better fate for his bones, I thought, smirking bitterly. His bones would bring wings to carry my warlike grandfather to the land of the iron men, while his huge skull would be used as a victory chalice. In his blindness Tambet wanted to sacrifice Hiie to the sprites, but it was he that was sacrificed. His strong skeleton could now carry the last army of the Estonians into battle. True, it consisted of only one old man with fangs, but it was still better than nothing.

Tambet had always hoped that one day people would live in the forest in the ancient way again, and now he had happened on an island where undoubtedly the most ancient living Estonian was crawling around. Tambet should have been happy here, but it turned out that he too had become too modern. He had forgotten Snakish! Or he simply didn't care about it, regarding Grandfather's warning as just an annoying hiss, and believing, no doubt under Ülgas's influence, that his fate was directed by the sprites, not the adders. Tambet did not get a foothold in his primeval world; he didn't understand its language: that is why he was killed and boiled and had his skull made into a drinking bowl.

"Come, I'll show you my wings," said Grandfather and wriggled behind the bushes. I followed him and saw two big white lattices, carefully put together out of larger and smaller sets of bones. They were like two bushes in hoarfrost—dense, yet so thin that you could look through them. Building wings like these was undoubtedly complicated work; Grandfather had not been lazy all these years. To me these wings seemed perfect, but Grandfather assured me that some important bones were still missing.

"Here and here and of course here," he declared, pointing with a finger. "Everything has to be precise; otherwise I'll fall from the sky like a dead crow. I don't need many more bones, but a couple of iron men will come in handy, to be on the safe side. Just let them come soon!"

He stroked his handiwork tenderly.

"And once I've risen into the sky," he said, "then I'll make up for all those years I've spent squatting like a badger stuck in its burrow."

His head turned up to the moon, which had risen in the sky, and he cackled from the base of his throat, which sent cold shivers up my spine.

"I'm going to bed," I said to Grandfather, but at that moment he wasn't listening to me.

"There you are," said Hiie, when I crawled into Grandfather's cave.

"You're not asleep?" I asked, throwing myself down beside her.

"No, I've woken up already," replied Hiie. "What are we going to do? Are we going home? Now we can."

I hadn't even thought about that, but when Hiie put it that way, I understood that indeed we could go home now! Grandfather had solved all our problems with a couple of bites. How simple it actually was! How ridiculous our plans now seemed—to convince Tambet to leave us in peace, and agree that we would move somewhere far away and never disturb one another again. How stupid! It was only necessary to get rid of Hiie's father and everything was all right.

Grandfather was aware of this, and that is how he ruled over the whole island and was seething with vitality even in old age. He really was the root in which flowed all the juices that give a tree its strength. We were the crown, only rustling at a whisper while Grandfather roared. Maybe in the final analysis there was no more use in this roaring than in our modest rustling, but at least his roar resounded over the forests and hills, giving gooseflesh to the skin. His roar contained life and rage; it was haughty and heedless of all consequences. Grandfather had the force and fire of the Frog of the North; in us it had extinguished. But perhaps it could be rekindled?

Lying next to Hiie in Grandfather's cave, I started to feel a force bubbling inside me, the force that had filled me the night I saved Hiie from Ülgas's knife. I'd go back to the forest with Hiie, set up home there, and live as I want to, a man who knows Snakish and is capable of chopping someone to pieces, with the wolves, all the iron men, monks, and villagers. For the first time I truly understood this power given to me by the Snakish words in a world where all other humans have forgotten them. I could send the snakes to bite them and could still save them even after death by asking the snakes to suck the poison out. I could do anything I liked, just as my grandfather did what pleased him. True, I didn't have fangs, but I could grow them.

Of course I would love to go back to the forest! I hugged Hiie, laughed in her ear, and whispered, "Let's go home tomorrow and you'll be my wife!"

Hiie pressed her nose against my chin.

"That's wonderful!" she said. "The only thing that worries me is Ülgas. He's still in the forest and he might still want to sacrifice me. Of course now that Father isn't . . ."

"And soon Ülgas won't be a problem either," I declared. "If he dares to show me his face, I'll knock his head off, boil his corpse, and send the bones to Grandfather. Ülgas is very old and rotten, but perhaps there's still a healthy bone left in him that can be used. We won't be making a drinking cup from his head, because it's certainly decayed with stupidity, everything would just drip through."

"Leemet, what's wrong with you?" asked Hiie, taken aback. "You've never talked like that!"

"Today I received my grandfather's inheritance," I said, grabbing Hiie firmly by the waist and rolling with her across the cave floor, sending the animal skins flying.

"What are you doing?" shrieked Hiie. "You've gone mad!"

"I love you," I announced, kissing her navel.

"That's good," replied Hiie. "But still you're somehow crazy. I hope it'll pass."

"I hope it won't," I answered. "I feel that I've only understood today how I should live."

Twenty-Five

he next morning we set off for home. Grandfather accompanied us to the shore, and assured us that he'd follow us soon, when the last bones were in place and the wings ready.

"Greetings to your mother and my daughter!" he said to me. "I haven't seen her for so long and I miss her very much."

"Maybe you could start right away by coming with us, visiting, and coming back to the island afterward," suggested Hiie, but Grandfather shook his head.

"What nonsense! There's no time! The most important thing still is to get the wings ready. Women have to wait when a man's on a crusade."

For our provisions he had roasted a few hares, and we also had to take with us a great number of skull beakers.

"Share them between yourselves," he instructed. "Give your mother and your sister some, and keep some for yourself too. Don't worry. One day when I fly in, I'll bring some more."

When we were already sitting in the boat and rowing away from the shore, Grandfather waved to us and shouted, "Don't go on the attack on your own, boy! Wait for me too! Then you can mash from below and I can hack from above, like two jaws. Ahoy!"

He had almost faded from view. I rowed with swift strokes homeward and the water was again calm, almost without a single wave, as it had been all these days. It really seemed that on our visit to Grandfather we had gone back into the past, to some mysterious waters where time stood still and no wind blew. Or was it all a dream—starting from the evening when we were fleeing from the deaf wolves and jumped into the boat and drifted out to sea? Could it be that I simply dreamed up my fanged grandfather, the giant fish, the roped winds of Möigas, and even how I completely unexpectedly fell in love with Hiie? Maybe this was Dream-Hiie, who was quite different to the quiet and shy girl whom I'd known before I went to sleep?

In that sense, anyway, the dream hadn't come to an end, for Hiie was sitting right here beside me in the boat and her eyes were as radiant as before, so I simply put the oars aside to embrace her.

"You're my dream," I said. "And I plan to sleep forever."

"Horrible sleepyhead," said Hiie and pulled me down, but one skull with a sharp jaw lay beside me, and we sat up straight.

"There are too many skulls here in the boat for lovemaking," I said, and Hiie showed me her hip, into which the two eye sockets of a skull had pressed two rings.

"He's been peeping into you," I said.

"I won't allow that, for some filthy iron man to stare at me like that," declared Hiie, tossing the offending skull into the sea. "Let him look at the fishes for a change."

But there were still an enormous number of skulls in the boat, so it wasn't possible to lie down, and we had no choice but to row on.

The first thing we noticed on the home shore was the louse. It was scampering back and forth on the shoreline and gesturing with its legs excitedly.

"What's wrong with him?" wondered Hiie. "He doesn't usually run away from Pirre and Rääk. But they're always up in their tree. Maybe something has happened?"

It was soon clear to us, though, that it had not left its masters at all, because the Primates were stumbling between the trees. Endlessly sitting in a tall tree had had some effect on their ability to walk; when walking on two legs they wobbled noticeably and from time to time they had to support themselves on their palms to keep their balance. I had not seen them come down from a tree in a long time, and such an unusual sight worried me.

"What has happened?" I cried, trying to row even faster.

"We saw you from the tree," replied Pirre. "And the louse got so restless. We decided to come and meet you. Wonderful that you've come back alive and well."

"We were afraid for you," added Rääk. "From our treetop we can see everything that goes on in the forest. We saw you being chased by the wolves and how you managed to escape in the boat. We sighed with relief. But the very next day Tambet went off in search of you and again we were worried, because even we can't see over the sea from the tree, no matter how high we climb. This morning Pirre spotted your boat and we were so glad that we climbed down and came to welcome you."

"Even though walking on this flat ground isn't easy at all," said Pirre. "The old Primates were so wise to build their houses in the treetops. All illnesses and disasters come from walking on the ground."

He sat down with a sigh and rubbed his tired soles.

By this time we had reached the shore and the louse was prancing around Hiie like mad. I took two skulls from the boat and handed them to the Primates.

"These were made by my grandfather," I added. "I'm giving them to you."

The Primates turned the beakers over in their hands.

"Beautiful work," they declared appreciatively. "Ancient work! These days no one knows how to make these tankards, and all skulls are left to rot. But don't take it wrongly if we don't accept them anyway. You understand we have our principles and these skulls are too modern for us."

"How so? You said yourselves that they're ancient work," I said.

"In the sense of handicraft, they are," replied Pirre with a smile. "But look at the material. Look at this cranium, its curves and angles. This is a human skull of today; obviously the owner of this skull must have been an iron man or a monk. Objects of this kind of material we don't take into our homes on principle. It wouldn't be appropriate."

I wasn't going to argue with the Primates. Moreover, I didn't get the opportunity. At that same moment, Ülgas rushed onto the beach screaming, "Caught you! I knew that Tambet would find you and bring you home by the ears. The sprites never let one of their sacrifices go."

It was obvious that like the louse Ülgas had been impatiently expecting us, except that while the louse's aim had been to rub itself against Hiie's legs with great abandon, the sage wanted to kill us, and as quickly as possible. He looked repulsive: flaky skin clung around his bones, his long gray hair fluttered in the wind, and his eyes sat so deep in their sockets that from a distance they appeared to be empty.

His head is a ready-made chalice, I thought. It only needs to be lopped off the neck. I showed Ülgas the mug I had wanted to give Pirre, and cried, "All that's left of your friend Tambet is a mug! You want it? I can give it to you. But there's probably no point. Soon I'll be making one out of your head."

When I had said that, I leapt at Ülgas and struck him with my knife. Within me foamed up a colossal anger. I wanted to chop off Ülgas's head and was enjoying the anticipation of the moment when a thick cascade of blood would burst forth from the stump of his neck. But I was too inexperienced in this sort of activity and, as it happened, I had missed, and didn't hack off the sage's head but only cut his right ear and cheek. Ülgas's face streamed with blood, and on the sand lay, beside part of the cheek, a single ear, from which a gray wisp bristled.

Ülgas began yelping and fled away, but I was disappointed that I had not managed to bump off the old man, and strove at him with my knife again.

"Criminal!" screamed Ülgas as he ran toward the forest, his head like a flayed hare, giving off bubbles of blood. "You raised your hand against the Sage of the Grove! The sprites won't forgive you! The dogs of the grove will come and bite you to death! They have no mercy! Remember that. The dogs of the grove!"

"I've lived in the forest all my life and I've never yet seen a single dog of the grove!" I called after him. "Those dogs exist only in your skull, Ülgas. I'm sorry I haven't had a chance to cut it in half. Then I might have seen those miraculous creatures at last. Go home, and if you don't bleed to death, try to perish as quickly as possible, because you can count on this: the moment I see you, I'll chop you to pieces. I'm back at home, I'm marrying Hiie, and it would be best for a bastard like you to hang yourself in your own sacred grove!"

Ülgas was howling about the dogs of the grove and the sprites, but I couldn't be bothered listening to this rubbish anymore. I piled the remains of the roast hare into a net bag with the skulls and said to Hiie: "Let's go to my place now, home."

"Yes, darling," replied Hiie. "Tell me, may I take Ülgas's ear for myself? I'll dry it in the sun like a dead frog and then it'll be nice to wear around my neck on the end of a band. Would you like your wife to have an ornament like that?"

"Yes," I said. "It would remind us of this day, and how I must learn to strike better. I would have liked it even more if you carried that bastard's dried heart around your neck, with rowanberries inside it, so it would rattle like a child's toy."

We laughed and kissed each other.

"You weren't away for long," said Pirre in surprise. "Yet it seems as if I hadn't seen you for years. There's a feeling as if all those years had rolled backward. It seems to me that those times of long ago have come back, the days when your forefathers were chopping up foreigners and you could see the Frog of the North flying over the sea, coming to gobble up the latest shipwreck victims."

Hiie and I burst out laughing again, and Hiie said, "By the way, it may happen that the Frog of the North really will come flying in."

"We wouldn't be surprised," replied Pirre and Rääk, nodding thoughtfully. "After all, it's only the recent past, which isn't really gone for good. This is the world our forefathers imagined on that cave wall you've seen. The really ancient pictures have crumbled away, and nothing will bring those days back."

Nor did Hiie and I have any need for those times of long ago; we were satisfied with the present. We motioned to the Primates, who remained on the shore massaging their unaccustomed limbs, and we set off. The louse, tired from hopping around Hiie, lay panting on the sand and licking Ülgas's hacked-off cheek.

Mother opened the door and squealed with joy.

"Heavens, it's you, Leemet! And you too, Hiie, alive and well! How wonderful! How worried I've been! Come straight to the table. I've got a goat on the fire!"

We stepped inside. Salme ran toward me and hugged me firmly, bursting into tears. Mõmmi, lying in a corner, got up and motioned with his paw.

"What's happened to your bear?" I asked. "Why is he resting there under the skins?"

"Mõmmi's been injured," replied Salme. "You don't know what we've all had to live through. You can't imagine it!"

"Salme dearest. I'm sure that Leemet and Hiie have also had to live through many horrible things," said Mother. "Although yes, what they did to our Mõmmi is dreadful. Just imagine:

that same evening when you escaped from the grove, Ülgas and Tambet came here. They wanted to know where you had gone with the boat. I shouted back in their faces and swore all I could, called them murderers and miserable fleas and said they should get out of my shack right away, because I didn't want to see such vile creatures in my house. Forgive me, Hiie, for yelling at your father like that, but once a pig, always a pig."

"Doesn't matter," replied Hiie. "He's dead now anyway."

"Dead?" exclaimed Mother. "How did he die then? Tell me, but wait a little; I'll finish my own story. Anyway I swore at them as much as I could. They were as cold as fish, just standing and staring. Well, I don't know if they'd been eating fly agaric or drinking Meeme's wine, or simply been hit over the head, but they looked very strange. Sort of grim and furious."

"They told Mother: 'Be quiet, you old hag; we'll find her anyway in the end and sacrifice her to the sprites,'" said Salme, interrupting.

"Why do you remember them calling me an old hag now?" railed Mother. "Why are you telling Leemet and Hiie that?"

"Well, that's what they said!"

"They did, the beasts! I'm not an old hag yet! I told them, too, I said, 'You, Ülgas, you look like a corpse walking on two legs; you're a fine one to be calling somebody old! And you, Tambet, you're no longer young either and you don't look too good, your hair all gray!' Ah, but now he's dead? You see, and there he was, calling me an old hag!"

"Mother, that's not important!" interrupted Salme. "Anyway, then they started to leave . . ."

"Wait! Let me tell it!" said Mother. "They didn't start leaving so quickly; they stood around for a while demanding to know:

where did you go, where did you go? Let's tell it as it actually was, Salme! You'd be better off going to see if the goat's ready!"

Salme went to the inglenook, offended, while Mother carried on with her story.

"Well now, where was I? Yes, they stood asking questions. I said how would I know where you went? You didn't say a word to me about a plan to go somewhere with Hiie; I guessed that you'd bring Hiie to us and make her your wife. Of course Tambet went blue in the face when he heard this, but I wasn't afraid of him. I said straight out: 'I see that my son did the right thing. That he's a wise and good man, for if he'd brought Hiie home, he'd have had to fight you, and what kind of a life is it if you have murderers lurking around the house all the time, wanting to strike down your wife.' And I went on: 'Even if I knew where he and Hiie went, I wouldn't say a word to you about it! And now get lost, because my son-in-law will be home soon, and if you upset me any more, he'll bash you up!'"

"And then Mõmmi did come," sighed Salme, who was now carrying the cooked goat to the table.

"He did come, yes, and I said, 'Look, if you please, here's my son-in-law. Now clear off!' And imagine the scene: Tambet pushed Mõmmi, so that Mõmmi fell on his backside into the fireplace and burned his bottom. Mõmmi, show Leemet and Hiie where you got hurt!"

"No problem, I'm getting better," muttered the bear from his bed and turned on his side, so that we could see the singed fur on his lower half.

"Aren't they cruel people!" sighed Mother. "Poor bear! Well, how can a person be so wicked as to push a living animal into the fire? I'd have quite happily stabbed them in the back with a knife, but there was no time. Mõmmi was yelling in the fireplace and I had to help. At that moment those scoundrels took off, and I haven't seen any more of them. Isn't it terrible what we've all had to go through? I tell you there are few people left in the forest, but half of them are crazy."

"Mõmmi, can you manage to come to the table?" Salme asked her husband, stroking the bear's head tenderly.

"I might be able to get to the table," answered the bear. "But I couldn't sit down. Leave it. You eat; I'll just rest."

"I won't hear of it!" said Mother. "You have to eat; otherwise you won't get better. We'll bring the meat to your bed and lift the table over beside you, so you won't feel alone. Leemet and Salme, drag the table over to Mõmmi's bed; today we'll eat there."

It took a while before we got the table into the right position, and then we had to find a suitable piece of meat for the sick Mõmmi and get him into a position where he could eat comfortably. Only then could we sit down at the table, and Mother looked at us in amazement.

"Why don't you say anything? We're waiting! We want to know where you've been all these days and how you got away from the disgusting sage!"

"And how did your father die, Hiie?" added Salme.

"Your grandfather killed him," replied Hiie.

"My grandfather?" Salme repeated. "I don't have a grandfather."

I put one skull beaker on the table and shifted it in front of Mother.

"This is from your father," I said. "He sends his greetings and said he'll come visiting soon."

"My father . . ." whispered Mother, looking at me with hazy eyes. "He's dead. They threw him in the sea."

"Oh no, he's very much alive," said Hiie. "He doesn't have legs, but he's built wings for himself and soon he'll be flying to us with them."

Mother stared at the skull chalice.

"I remember I had one of these as a child," she murmured. "Father made it for me. I drank warm milk from it. It was my favorite cup."

She kissed the beaker, pressed it against her cheek, and began crying quietly.

"Children, you don't know what this means," she whispered through her sobs. "To find your own father, and at my age. I thought he was dead long ago . . . But you say he's coming back home. I feel like a little girl again. I was quite small then . . . Children, this is a miracle. Don't worry that I'm crying like this, but I really . . . I just can't . . ."

She kissed her beaker once more, and her tears dropped into it.

"A shame that Vootele didn't see this day," she said. "He was always very proud of our father. He was older, and remembered him better. Children, this is the most wonderful day of my life."

"Mother, Grandfather hasn't come home yet," I said. "This is only a beaker made by him that you're clutching. Wait until he arrives himself!"

"No, no," sobbed Mother. "This cup is just as dear to me. It reminds me of my childhood. But now tell me everything! How did you meet my father? Where does he live?"

Hiie and I started competing with each other in retelling our adventures. Mother listened and interrupted only to occasionally shout, "Eat up! You're not eating at all! But tell me what happened next?" So we had to gobble a piece of roast without chewing it and carry on talking. Salme sat beside Mõmmi on the bed, stroking her bear and continually passing him more bones, which he gnawed slowly but surely clean. His bottom was indeed singed, but his appetite was unchanged. Gradually the evening was rolling in. All the stories had been told. We had loaded onto the table all the remaining skull cups, and Mother's rapture knew no bounds. She arranged the crania in a row and stroked them delicately.

"Father is quite a master! Perhaps he'll teach you, Leemet, this art of making drinking bowls. That would be nice."

"So what do you plan to do from now on?" asked Salme.

"We're thinking of getting married," I replied, taking Hiie by the waist.

"That's so lovely to hear," smiled Mother. "Let's hope that Grandfather will get to your wedding."

"I think we won't wait for him," I said. Something within me told me that perhaps it would be wiser to hold the wedding before Grandfather's arrival, since Grandfather would naturally say that women can wait, and would take me off to war. Although I had nothing against fighting together with Grandfather, I wanted at least to enjoy a few days of quiet peaceful family life before that.

"We'll get married as quickly as possible," I announced.

Mômmi nodded from his bed.

"If I had such a beautiful bride, I would do exactly the same," he said, eyeing Hiie lovingly.

"How's your bottom?" shouted Salme, annoyed, shoving the bear painfully with her elbow.

"Hurts," sighed the bear, turning his amber-colored eyes obediently toward Salme.

Twenty-Six

e slept in our shack, but the next morning Hiie wanted to visit her mother, and naturally I went with her. It was actually Mall who had saved our lives, and we hadn't properly thanked her for it. We also had to bear her the news of Tambet's death. Mother fed our bellies full to bursting and warned us about wolves wandering in the forest.

"They're the same animals whose ears Tambet and Ülgas stopped up with wax," she explained. "Now they won't obey anybody. They just keep running around, their teeth bared, and they're likely to bite. You can hiss at them as much as you like, but a feral wolf won't notice it, so there's nothing for it but to try and run home for cover. I tell you, this is the stupidest, stupidest trick, pouring wax in wolves' ears. Sooner or later they're going to eat somebody up. Be very careful and if you see any mad wolves, then climb a tree."

Sure enough, Hiie and I had hardly gone any distance in the forest when we saw a wolf. It was prowling on us from the bushes and it wasn't at all possible to read from its green eyes whether it was just watching us or planning to leap on us.

I hissed a few Snakish words, but the wolf's expression didn't change; it started slowly creeping closer to us. It was most definitely one of the animals that had been deafened. Maybe the wolf recognized us and now wanted to execute the last command that had reached its brain before its ears were walled up forever. I pulled out my knife from its sheath and prepared to defend myself.

"Perhaps we'd be better off going up a tree as your mother recommended," suggested Hiie.

"Would my grandfather run away from a wolf up a tree?" I asked.

"Your grandfather definitely wouldn't," said Hiie. "I think the wolf would be the one who'd try to save his skin by climbing a tree if he saw your grandfather. But you're not your grandfather. Do you believe you can start killing wolves?"

"I do," I replied, and I was speaking the truth. I was quite sure, even though I'd never before fought with a wolf. But the trip to Grandfather's island had opened a new door within me, so to speak, from which flowed a feeling of self-assurance and a desire to struggle with someone, to chop up living flesh and drink the blood of my enemies. The wolf flew over me and I cut open its stomach with my knife, starting from the throat and ending at the tail. Its innards tumbled out and I was barely able to roll aside to avoid getting the wolf's intestines in my face.

"Beautiful," cried Hiie, clapping her hands. But then she added worriedly, "But there are two more coming."

Indeed two new wolves had trotted onto the field of battle and were now creeping closer to us, a bloodthirsty expression on their faces. Hiie hissed a few Snakish words, but naturally they fell on deaf, or rather silenced, ears, and the wolves didn't turn their heads. I roared at them, as Grandfather would have done, and prepared myself to take them on.

But I didn't have time to clash with the new wolves. Before I could, I heard a familiar hiss, and the wolves bayed at the air, only to tumble in a cramp to the ground and slowly perish. Two snake-kings appeared from among the long grass and I understood that they had bitten the wolves' throats. I recognized the snakes instantly: they were Ints and her father. Ints was accompanied by a whole nest of little adders.

"Hello, dear Leemet!" said Ints's father. "How nice that you're back!"

"I wanted to be with you that night," said Ints. "I would have stung all those filthy wolves to death and Tambet and Ülgas as well. Who cares if they understand Snakish? They are no longer our brothers. But I wasn't able to get away from my children. Now even they know how to bite. I swear to you today they actually killed a wolf themselves."

"Not quite by themselves, let's be precise," objected the old snake-king. "You're like all mothers, always praising your own children. First of all I bit the wolf in the hip, so it could no longer move, and then the little ones finished it off. But I have to admit they were really good."

The little adders listened to their grandfather and nodded their heads proudly.

"Where are you going?" asked Ints. "Might you come with us? We're crawling through the forest looking for the wolves with the silenced ears, to finish them off. An animal that no longer understands Snakish must die. They're too dangerous and unpredictable. Father and I have already finished off six animals and all the other adders are at work in the forest, but there are still a lot of deaf wolves roaming around. Let's go hunting them! I haven't seen you for so long, Leemet, old friend!"

"Right now I can't, Ints," I said. "Another time. We're on our way to Hiie's mother's place. Ints, you know, I'm getting married."

"It's great," said Ints, "that even you are finally in heat. I'm really looking forward to next spring, when you can mate again. How long does your heat last?"

"Forever," I said, embracing Hiie. "And all year round."

"Oooh!" hummed Ints enviously. "In one way, humans are better than us after all."

"Thinking all day only about reproducing is maybe a bit too much, though," opined the old snake-king. "In any case, I wish you the best of luck! Come past our cave in the evening and tell us where you've been and what you've seen."

We promised to come. The snakes crawled off to hunt the wolves, but we were soon at Hiie's house.

The first thing that struck our eyes was the door of the wolves' barn, which was swinging in the wind. When we stepped closer, we could see that the giant barn that had once harbored hundreds of wolves now stood completely empty. All the wolves had gone.

"Did he really stop up all the wolves' ears with wax?" cried Hiie in amazement. "The adders have a lot of work to do . . ."

"No, not all," said someone. It was Hiie's mother, Mall, standing at the door of her shack, looking at us with damp eyes. "There were about thirty of them whose ears he poured full of wax. The rest I released into the forest. I didn't want to see them anymore. I couldn't live in the same house with the wolves, not after that night when they chased you, dear daughter. You're alive! The sprites kept you safe!"

Mall came over to Hiie and hugged her daughter, with love, but still somehow awkwardly. One might think that she hadn't done it often. Evidently her mother's embrace felt unfamiliar to Hiie too. She did respond to the affection, but seemed confused, and when Mall let go of her, she pulled quickly aside. "Yes," sighed Mall guiltily. "We haven't hugged very often. Your father didn't like it; he was very stern. With himself and with others."

"Mother," said Hiie. "Father is dead."

"I know," replied Mall to our surprise. "Somehow I knew immediately when he rowed off from here that he wouldn't be coming back. Then I let the wolves loose. Do you think I would have dared to do that if I'd thought your father was still coming back? Never! Wolf rearing was special to him," she added with a bitter smile. "You never did learn to drink their milk."

"It repulsed me," said Hiie. "But you forced me; you poured it down my throat."

"Well, yes," muttered Mall hesitantly. "I have been too hard on you I know. That's what your father wanted; he wished you brought up to be a real Estonian."

"He wanted to kill me," said Hiie.

"That was what Ülgas wanted," sighed Mall, who appeared to be collapsing into such a tiny, wretched bundle that I began to feel sorry for her. "For Father it was very hard, but he was used to bringing sacrifices. He knew that the sprites' wishes must be fulfilled; you can't contradict them. They always get their way."

"But we are here!" shouted Hiie. "We're alive! We haven't been sacrificed to the sprites. They haven't got their way."

"I started believing that they don't want you killed," replied Mall. "Ülgas was mistaken. The sprites are good. They protect the forest and its dwellers; they couldn't want a forest child to die. They helped me, gave me strength, so that I could ride after you and lead you to the boat. Children, the sprites saved you!"

She shook her head so excitedly—this tiny, elderly, shriveled woman—that I didn't have the heart to laugh in her face and say that there are no sprites, and that if she did save us, it was thanks to her heart, which Ülgas's legends hadn't managed to taint. Her husband's heart had been turned by these endless tales of the sprites into a lump of mud. Mall had still remained a human being and a mother. She was looking at us with such a simple and yet saintly gaze that I pitied her. Let her believe in her sprites, then, if she can't do anything else. I bowed before her, kissed both her hands in turn, and said, "Mother, I'm taking Hiie to be my wife now."

"I'm pleased," replied Mall, smiling timidly and stroking my head with her fingertips. Quite certainly she couldn't have forgotten all the stories that Tambet had told about me, and she must have felt a certain dread seeing me here in her house. I was a strong opponent of the so-called sprites, ever since the business of the swimming louse. You can't become beloved overnight, but I wasn't so interested in that either. It was Hiie I was marrying, not her mother, and I really didn't care what Mall thought of me.

"Could I perhaps talk with Ülgas . . ." began Hiie's mother, but she felt clumsy, because even she knew that neither I nor Hiie had good relations with Ülgas. "But . . . I suppose you don't want to invite Ülgas to the wedding?"

"No," I replied. "He's hardly likely to come and bring us together. Yesterday I ripped off one of his ears and a cheek, and I promised that if he comes before me again, his head will fly off."

Mall looked at me in amazement, swallowed, and turned her eyes helplessly to Hiie.

"Where will you marry then, if not in the sacred grove?"

"We'll get married anywhere, but not there," replied Hiie. "Mother, the last time I was there Ülgas and Father tried to kill me! I'm never going there again and the only wedding present I request from Leemet is that he razes the whole grove to the ground and burns down the trees."

"Dear child, don't talk like that!" begged Mall. "Our ancestors have visited it for thousands of years bringing sacrifices! A sprite lives in every tree in the grove. Those trees are sacred!"

"No tree is sacred!" said Hiie. "The trees in the grove will do just as well for making a bonfire and cooking meat as any other beam or branch. Yes, we'll celebrate our wedding with a big fire! We'll set light to all those disgusting old trees in the grove; we'll roast a deer and dance around the fire. Leemet, that's the kind of wedding I want, and no other!"

"Very good," I said. "I'll go today and raze the grove and I hope I manage to raze Ülgas to the ground too!"

"Children!" squealed Mall. "Children!"

She looked at us in terror, as if she were afraid for our lives.

"Mother, enough of this silliness," said Hiie. "Father is dead, Ülgas is probably running around now bleeding to death, and we have no more need for these senseless pieces of timber, which don't mean a thing. There are so few of us left here in the forest that we could at least try to live honestly, without tricks and lies. Mother, if you want to believe in the sprites, then believe.

The forest is full of trees to worship and adorn, but I want that disgusting grove, where I was led like a hare to the slaughter, to burn at my wedding and crumble to ash. I hate those trees! Understand, Mother?"

"Child, that talk is horrible!" said Mall. Her whole body shook. "You're inviting misfortune. If the sprites hear you . . . And they certainly will, for they hear everything!"

"They don't," I said. "Mother, calm down! There's no point despairing over some half-rotten tree. The important thing is for us to have a beautiful fire and a nice wedding, that we get to eat nicely roasted brown meat and we have fun!"

"I'm afraid for you," said Mall. "I'm afraid something terrible will happen. The sacred grove . . . Please don't destroy it!"

"I won't live in the same forest as that abomination!" declared Hiie. "If Leemet doesn't chop it down, I'll take an ax myself, the same one that Father forced me as a child to chop hares' heads off with."

"No need," I said. "I'll do it. With pleasure."

One might fear that razing the sacred grove was hard work, but it wasn't. The enormous old linden trees were rotten to the core. They were just decaying corpses, into which you only had to make a cut and each giant would collapse of its own accord. In places the trunks were so soft that the ax got stuck in soggy material as if I were chopping mud. It was a miracle that those trees hadn't collapsed earlier. As they fell down they broke into hundreds of little pieces, collapsed into decayed wood pulp, and all kinds of insects that had laid their white eggs in the trees were now scurrying stupidly around, unable to understand why their soft sludgy home was suddenly split apart.

"Those are the sprites," I said to Hiie, showing her the alarmed centipedes and other insects that were running headlong into the grass in search of new nesting places.

"They've bored out the insides of the trees so empty and gnawed them so soft that we won't be able to get a proper bonfire here. The deer will remain uncooked if we make a fire only from the sacred grove. We'll have to bring more good dry wood. These linden trees will only hiss and fume."

We piled up the rubbish that was left of the grove's trees into one big stack, and looked for dried branches, which burned well and weren't sacred at all. I had hoped that the razing of the grove would bring forth Ülgas too, to try and defend his nest from us, giving me the chance to have at him once more with my knife, properly this time, so that a third attack wouldn't be necessary. The Sage of the Grove didn't show himself, however, but must have been suffering somewhere, nursing his hacked cheek—or hoping that the sprites would make him whole. Maybe he was even stalking us somewhere in the bushes, rustling indignantly in the grass like the other beetles whose home had been the old grove. In any case, no one tried to obstruct us.

By evening all the trees in the grove had been chopped down and the pyre was ready. There was no point in killing a deer before the morning, so now Hiie and I could rest. We had planned to go and visit Ints, as we had promised that morning, but suddenly I saw Meeme. He had appeared just as quietly as always, supporting himself against a tree and sipping on his wineskin. Seeing that we had spotted him, he beckoned to us lazily.

"Tell me, how do you always manage to creep up without anyone hearing?" I challenged him. "You lie around here, you lie around there, and yet I've never seen you coming. What's the trick of it?"

Meeme giggled.

"You have Snakish words in your mouth and you're terribly smart for your age, but you don't know everything, and you can't either," he smirked. "Yes, understand it or not, how does old Meeme move around so quietly from one place to another so that even your sharp ear doesn't hear him?"

"I can't be bothered to work it out," I said. "It doesn't matter to me. By the way, I'm getting married tomorrow. You're invited to the wedding."

"I'm here already," replied Meeme. "The last wedding here in the forest will be a thing to watch. It's as if, just before dying, someone was polishing the stumps of their old teeth to a shine, as if it mattered whether you burn on the funeral pyre with clean or dirty fangs. If there is anyone left to set it alight, that is."

He burst into laughter, coughed, and spat phlegm down his front.

"Again the last!" I chuckled bitterly. "The last wedding in the forest! For me this wedding is the first, the only one, and the most important, and for Hiie too. We don't intend to die or be laid out on a pyre. For you it might be fine to be weak and facing death, if you decide to carry on that endless wheezing. If you got married, it would really be ridiculous; there's really no point in you polishing the stumps of your teeth to a shine."

"Ahhaa, how spiteful!" smirked Meeme into his beard, taking a swig on his wineskin. "Bridegroom! Navel of the world!"

"By the way, I promise you that when you do die, I will build a proper pyre for you and set it alight with my own hands," I added, to bring the subject to a close.

"No, on the contrary!" shrieked Meeme, raising a warning paw, whose nails had grown enormously long and crooked like old pine roots. "You must promise not to build me a funeral pyre. I want to rot away right where I peg out. You can see that I've already made a start on it, and you mustn't interfere with your good heart and your sympathy. Burning is for great warriors and important people; folk like me should quietly rot away like acorns fallen on the ground."

"All right then, be an acorn," I said, quite bored. "I don't care. I'm getting married tomorrow and have more to think about than death and decay; those are your problems. It would be nice if you didn't prattle on all the time about those things tomorrow at the feast. A wedding is supposed to be fun."

"Are you offering wine?" asked Meeme.

"Wine is the iron men's drink," I replied. "It's not the custom in the forest to drink it."

"Don't talk such rubbish, boy!" screamed Meeme. "You come to me talking about customs. Just now you were razing the grove to the ground; even though in a couple of years that shit would have collapsed all on its own. So don't come playing the ancient prophet with me! The end is at hand, and there's no point holding back on the good stuff. So what are you going to offer your guests?"

"We wanted to roast a deer," said Hiie.

"Bah! I'm not talking about food. I'm thirsty, not hungry! Do you want to wash the bit of roast meat down with springwater like the animals? Think about wine, boy. It lifts the spirits! Or are you planning to chew fly agaric? I've tried both things, not just a little either, and believe me wine is better! It's the only good thing you can get from the village. I'm not recommending you bring bread into the forest. Let the hares nibble on that. But wine was their good invention. Listen to me, boy. I know what I'm talking about!"

Hiie and I looked at each other. After all—why not? In the course of a few days everything had been turned inside out. I had razed the sacred grove to the ground and cut half of the sage's face off. Nothing was as it had been. So what if another joist in the old life was sent toppling? Really, why couldn't we drink wine? The forest was empty; we didn't have to reckon with anybody else's opinion. We didn't intend to live like villagers, cutting straws with a scythe in the field and going to the monastery to listen to the singing of castrated monks, but nor did we plan to hang tooth and nail to ancient habits. Hiie and I wanted to live our own way, freely, exactly as we liked, a good way.

"What does that wine taste like?" I asked Meeme.

"Try it!"

I took the skin and had a swig. The wine was surprisingly sweet and tickled the throat pleasantly. It really was delicious, quite different to bread and porridge. What a surprise that those odd foreigners could think up something so good. I took another sip.

"Getting to like it?" smirked Meeme. "What did I tell you? It does the trick."

"Where can you get it?" I asked, handing the wine back.

"Go to the edge of the big road and look for some iron man or monk passing; they always have a wineskin with them," said

Meeme. "Then knock him down and the wine is yours. If you're lucky you can get a whole vat."

A desire to kill was rising in my stomach and getting my mind throbbing. I was already imagining those iron heads rolling in the dust of the highway.

"I'm thinking of wine," I told Hiie. "This will be the first wedding in the forest—remember that, Meeme, the first, not the last—where a drink from over the seas is drunk along with good old venison."

"If that's the word you like, then why not use it. First or last, there's no difference."

Twenty-Seven

e spent the night with the adders, but in the morning we arranged a division of labor. Hiie had to kill a deer, but we entrusted the cooking of it to my mother. It was the only option. Mother would have been fatally offended otherwise. She never let anyone else roast meat, and if Salme or I tried to help her, she only took that to mean mistrust, and sometimes even started crying. "Ah, so the food I make isn't good enough for you?"

So it was natural that Mother would be preparing the wedding roast.

We told her that Hiie would procure the deer; Mother nodded at this and said she would bring two goats and about ten hares in that case.

"No, Mother, we were thinking of roasting only one deer," we explained.

"Are you joking?" exclaimed Mother. "This is a wedding! One deer is not enough. There definitely has to be goat and hare as well."

"Mother, there's no need for such a large feast!" I tried to convince her. "Why so much? Who will eat it?"

"They might not eat it, but the table has to be laid plentifully," maintained Mother. "Of course it's another matter if you don't like the food I make . . ."

Her eyes were growing damp again.

"No, no!" we said. "We like it very much! Go on then. Cook the goats and hares as well as the deer. Do just as you like!"

Mother was satisfied. She rolled up her sleeves and started flaying and chopping.

I set off to get the wine, and Ints came with me.

"I'd like to get some fresh air," she said. "Sitting at home with the children wears me out terribly."

"So where are you leaving your children?" I asked.

"The children are coming with me, of course," replied Ints. "They need some recreation too. They've never seen a single iron man or monk, and they're very excited. Just a couple of days ago I was telling them how we killed that monk, and how the slow-worm retrieved the ring from his stomach; the children found that very funny. Do you remember that story?"

"Why wouldn't I?" I said. "Come on then; maybe I'll be needing your fangs."

We set off for the edge of the highway, where the monks and iron men always rode by, and lay in wait. The little adders chased each other and frolicked among the crowberry plants.

Finally a lone rider wearing chain mail came into view.

"Is that a suitable one?" asked Ints.

"I can't see if he's carrying a wineskin," I said, peering more closely at the iron man with a peculiar kind of pleasure that I had only recently learned to feel. "But let's knock him down anyway."

When the iron man had come right up to us, I gave a long hiss. The horse understood these words immediately and reared on its hind legs, whinnying. The iron man toppled out of his saddle and fell on his back on the road.

The next moment I was upon him, and struck off his head with my knife, giving a loud roar.

"There!" I screamed. "That's what they used to do in the days of the Frog of the North!"

I kicked the iron man I had cut down, and he flew into the bushes with a clatter.

"Splendid!" shouted Ints, and her children hissed with pleasure, coming over to nose around the dead iron man. "Where did you learn that?"

"It came by itself," I said. "A lineage from my grandfather."

I was still panting excitely. If someone had told me at that moment that I had to go to the wedding immediately and give up lurking by the roadside, I would have refused. Now I truly understood Grandfather's words: in a time of war, a woman must wait. At that moment I would not give up my war for any price. I wanted to experience again that feeling that overcame me when an enemy's head bounces and clatters along the road. And in any case, we still didn't have any wine.

I dragged the dead iron man in among the trees and threw myself down right there to await a new victim.

"Coming," said Ints after a little while, having much keener hearing than I had. "And it's a cart, not a rider."

I soon saw that she was right. We were incredibly lucky. Along the road came two bullocks, pulling behind them a cart with two monks and two vats of wine in it.

"That's the wine for my wedding going by," I told Ints. "It couldn't have gone better."

Ints curled up into a ring.

"I think you can begin this yourself," she said. "I'm not going to intervene at all you're so nimble. Children, come out of Uncle's way! Later, you can look at the monks later!"

"But then they won't have their heads on anymore," said one little adder.

"What's the difference? Come out of the way!"

It all went as smoothly as the previous time. On hearing the Snakish words, the bullocks' eyes bulged; they suddenly became overanimated and pulled the cart straight into the forest. With a yell the monks rolled off into the bushes with their vats and I did what I wanted with them.

"That's all," said Ints with a yawn. "Children, let's go home and eat now."

By evening the preparations were made and the wedding feast could begin. The bonfire made of stacked trees was blazing and an enormous amount of meat was cooking on it. The vats of wine were in place, and Meeme was resting between them, one of Grandfather's skull cups in his hand. He was already completely drunk, but still helping himself to more and more of the tipple that trickled from the barrel.

"Try some," I told my mother, offering her some wine.

"I don't dare to drink it! I've never put such stuff in my mouth before. Leemet, don't you drink it either. I'm watching; you're just like your father. He liked those village foods too. I never understood what he saw in them. Now look at you too!"

"Mother, the villagers don't drink wine. They aren't given it; they're taught to be content with porridge and a bit of bread. Wine is drunk by the iron men and the monks."

"That makes it worse!" said Mother, wringing her hands. "No, no, I'm not touching it! Leemet, you'd be better eating some hare. Just look at this beautiful well-cooked shank!"

"Yes, I will," I replied. "But you try some wine. One drop!"

"Why are you tempting me?" sighed Mother, screwing her eyes tight and swallowing one little swig from the cup. She smacked her lips and screwed up her nose.

"Not as bad as porridge, but not good either. They think up all sorts of silly things. What's wrong with springwater and wolf's milk then?"

"Let me have a taste too," begged Mõmmi.

At first Mother and Salme had assured me that the sick bear definitely wouldn't be able to come to the wedding, since his backside was hurting him dreadfully. Salme had even thought that she better stay at home and look after the ailing Mõmmi.

"He can't walk at all; he just lies around," she had said bitterly. "I'm so sorry for him! That beautiful brown fur. It was that fur that I fell in love with about him! Now it's all burned and horrible."

"Only in one place," I consoled her. "And it's sure to grow back."

Hiie and I went to Mõmmi's bed and nodded at him.

"Sorry you can't come," said Hiie. "We're getting a goat for you too."

"Why can't I come?" exclaimed Mõmmi, sitting straight up. "I want to go to the wedding too!"

"You can't, darling, but never mind," said Salme, comforting him. "I'll stay at home with you so you don't get bored."

"No, Salme, that's not a good idea," said Mõmmi decisively, getting out of bed. "How can you stay at home when your brother's getting married? You have to go, and I'm coming too."

"Oh, but you can't! It's painful for you to walk!"

"Of course it's painful," agreed the bear, taking a couple of limping steps. "But if you support me, I think I can do it anyway."

"You really think so?"

"Of course! Now listen, Salme, what's the point in having to bring me food home from the wedding, if I can go there myself and eat right there?"

And so Mõmmi, panting and groaning, lumbered up to the bonfire. Now he sat down contentedly under a tree and wolfed down the meat.

I handed him a beakerful of wine; Mõmmi swallowed it in one gulp, and licked his nose with his long pink tongue.

"I like it!" he declared. "Pass me another one."

When he had drunk a second beakerful, he hiccupped slightly, gave me a sly look, and ran with great agility behind Salme's back.

"Peek-a-boo!" he cried, covering Salme's eyes with his paws. "Who am I?"

Guessing wasn't particularly hard, for the only one at the wedding with bear's paws was Mõmmi.

"Mõmmi!" cried Salme. "Why are you walking around? You'll hurt your wound! I was just about to bring you a new haunch of venison."

"I don't want to eat any more," announced Mõmmi grandly. "And there's no damage to my wound, I've been licking it with my tongue. Don't you know that a bear's tongue contains nine medicines? Wait, sweetie, and I'll show you!"

He drew his tongue far out of his mouth and licked Salme's face.

"Mõmmi, what are you doing?" tittered Salme. "People are looking!"

"You're as sweet as honey," cooed Mõmmi. "Let's dance!"

"But your bottom, Mõmmi! You were hobbling just now!"

"That was this morning, but now it's evening! In the morning I was hobbling; in the evening I turn somersaults. That's the kind of bear I am!" bragged Mõmmi, trying to roll over on his head, but he fell down and lay on the ground on his back, laughing, his four paws in the air.

"Mõmmi!" begged Salme. "What's come over you? What are you raving about?"

"Let's dance, Salme. Let's dance!" said the bear, getting up and starting to lope around heavily, occasionally bowing and twisting his body around. He was mumbling some strange bear song and appeared to be overjoyed.

"Mother, look at what Mõmmi's doing!" whispered Salme. "Shameful!"

"Why shameful?" laughed Mother, who had started clapping to the rhythm of Mõmmi's song. "It's just nice. It's fun! You're supposed to have fun at weddings. Go and dance with your husband!"

"I won't!" declared Salme, scowling at her spouse as he staggered around her.

Hiie's mother was also at the wedding. She kept a little apart from the others, looking timidly at the blazing linden trees and the bear tramping out his dance.

"Mother, come and eat!" called Hiie.

"I don't want to," said Mall, and in her again was the strict woman who had brought her child up so sternly with Tambet. "Meat cooked on wood from the grove would stick in my throat. And that disgusting foreign drink is quite out of place here. Maybe I'm old and I've seen out my days, but I'm sorry, daughter, all this is insulting to me. I have my principles."

"It doesn't matter what wood the meat is cooked on, as long as it gets juicy enough," said Hiie. "And if any drink tastes sweet to us, there's no reason to refuse it. Mother, I grew up in a home that was so full up with principles that I didn't have room to breathe. I hate principles. I only want what's good for me. I want to be happy!"

She grabbed me by the neck, kissed me, and dragged me to where Mõmmi was reeling around.

"Let's dance too!" said Hiie.

She pushed me away from her, stretched out her arms, and writhed in the red glow of the bonfire. Just at that moment a large wolf leapt in between us and sank its teeth into Hiie's neck.

I yelled as if I had been bitten myself. I heard Ints and the other snakes hissing piercingly. I struck the wolf with my knife, but in my panic wasn't able to kill the animal, only cutting a long wound in its neck. The wolf let go of Hiie and turned toward me, enraged with pain. Just then her mother rushed toward Hiie and the wolf sank its jaws into her face, so that blood spurted between its teeth. I lashed out at the wolf with my knife once again, but it didn't fall; a second wound merely appeared on its back, forming a red cross with the first slash. Then a roar was heard from Mõmmi; the bear's paw came down and the wolf's backbone broke with a sickening crack.

All this happened in a mere moment.

I bent over Hiie. She was unconscious, her neck was broken, and blood was bubbling out of it.

"Ints!" I screamed. "Can't you do something? Stop the blood! Isn't there a Snakish word that could do that?"

"There's no such word," said Ints's father, the snake-king, who had crawled up beside me. "Nobody can stop the flow of blood, the same as with a river. We aren't able to save Hiie. Look at the moss; it's thick with blood. Most of her life has already left her, and the little that is left will soon flow out too. I'm terribly sorry, Leemet."

Ints had also wriggled up to me, and was nosing against Hiie's pallid cheek. For the first time in my life I saw a snake crying.

Beside Hiie lay her mother, recognizable only from her clothes; her entire face was torn away by the wolf's teeth. And yet she was still alive, and even spoke: "A fire from the grove wood," she murmured. "I was afraid it would go this way. Misery! The sprites won't ever forgive it!"

"Shut up!" I shouted, completely losing my self-control.

"The sprites! The sprites!" repeated the lump of blood that had once been a human face. "They'll pay you back!"

"Your husband is the one who brings us misery, even in death," I yelled. "He drove the wolves mad! He turned them deaf!" Mall spoke no more. She was dead.

I was so enraged, so desperate, that I kicked her corpse. Then I grasped Hiie by the waist and bellowed. I shook her so that her broken neck lolled to one side and the wound gaped at me to its full depth. I kissed Hiie, grabbed her with such force that if she had still felt anything, she would certainly have screamed with pain. Oh how I wanted her to scream! I squeezed her so hard that I must have broken her ribs, but I didn't care. I was completely crazed, and only when Mõmmi, using all his bear's strength, pulled me aside did I leave Hiie's corpse in peace.

Yes, she was dead.

"How terrible! How terrible!" repeated my mother, who was also spread-eagled on the ground, as if she were a third corpse, weeping uncontrollably.

I felt sick. My nostrils were again invaded by that old familiar stench of decay, nauseating me. Supporting myself on a wine vat, I vomited. Undigested bits of meat mixed with red wine gushed onto the moss.

To this day I remember in detail what I did in those moments after Hiie's death.

After vomiting I walked several times around the still-burning bonfire. I wasn't thinking anything, just concentrating on breathing. I had the feeling that if I didn't, I would forget to inhale and choke. No one spoke to me; no one dared to stop me.

Then I went and cut the legs and the tail off the dead wolf, doing it with a strange numbness as if I were carrying out some tedious but necessary task. When the legs and tail were cut off, I left them there, threw away the knife, and marched into the forest.

I just walked and walked, heedless of the direction. Owls were hooting; some goats and hares ran across my path. I broke a path through the densest thicket, not feeling the scratching of the branches and twigs. I didn't have a single thought in my head. It was as if I were seeing myself from somewhere afar, up in the tree-tops, seeing a tiny human, struggling along alone in a dark forest.

Then suddenly it came to me—Hiie! I turned around immediately, as if I had only just received the news of her death, and rushed back the way I had come.

The fire was still smoldering and all the wedding guests were still there. Hiie had been lifted up alongside her mother, and squatting beside her was the louse.

It was nestling against Hiie's shoulder, and suddenly I had the ghastly thought that the louse was sucking blood from her wound.

"What's it doing?" I screamed, and rushed closer to scare the louse away with a kick.

"He's not doing anything; he's dead," said Ints. I crouched down and touched the great insect. Ints was telling the truth: the louse was completely stiff and its tiny legs were curled up helplessly.

"He came straight after you left," said Ints, crawling up by my feet. "He ran here, pressed himself against Hiie, and died."

"We saw from the tree how the wolf was attacking her," Pirre said now. I hadn't noticed him at first. The Primates were sitting in the shade of a tree; they had been walking on two legs again and were now massaging their cramp-stricken toes. "We came straight here and the louse ran ahead of us. He loved Hiie very much. Let him lie there beside her."

"Let him lie," I repeated, and then I blacked out.

Twenty-Eight

was ill for several months. I simply had no desire to get well; it was so good to remain in feverish unconsciousness, without any thoughts, any memories. Dreams came and went, but if there was anything bad or alarming in them, it didn't remain in my mind and quickly dissolved into new dreams. I liked to keep my eyes closed and the colorful apparitions, without name or clear form, swam around in my head in a kind of luminous haze, as if warning me not to wake. Even when I felt that someone— probably Mother—was spooning broth into my mouth, I didn't want to return to the real world. My pharynx was working, but my brain remained hidden like a child, crouching in the forest in the shade of branches that reach the ground, hearing the call to come home but not coming, not letting itself get caught and pulled indoors. Being there in the forest under the branches was best, I sensed; indoors, only anxiety and oppression awaited me. I hovered in the middle of a nonexistent space, like a bird that has emerged on the other side of the clouds and is now suddenly separated from everything earthly.

This game of hide-and-seek lasted a long time and I would gladly have made my illness permanent. But it couldn't be helped: my body betrayed my hiding place, someone's strong arms pulled me out from under the spruce branches, and although I kept my eyes tightly closed as before, as if hoping that would make me invisible, the world and its sounds and colors gradually began to encroach on me. From time to time I found myself staring at the ceiling; turning my head I saw Mother, tending the fire and boiling something in a pot. Sometimes I also saw Salme and her bear, sitting at the table and gnawing on venison bones with a crunch. I tried to swoon away again, to escape, but the fever had receded; it had slipped away from me like a warm animal skin, and without it I felt naked, cold, and terrible. For days on end I had to listen to Mother's and Salme's conversations, mostly revolving around Mõmmi's activities, occasionally diverging to the state of my health, and floating me on a wave of upsetting sympathy. I tried to seek a way out of sleep, but that was a miserable substitute for the splendid state of unconsciousness that had protected and soothed me for several months. Ordinary sleep now seemed too brief to me; it was merely like a little puddle into which I could at best dip my head, whereas I longed for a deep lake of dark water, into which to dive, and stay.

Morning arrived over and over again; Mother started clattering and preparing food. Soon Salme and Mõmmi would arrive too, and I knew that the moment was not far off when they would all gather by my bed, look at me tenderly with pity in their eyes, and ask, "Well, dear Leemet, how do you feel?" I didn't answer them, not because I couldn't, but because I feared the intoxicating joy that my first words after a long illness would excite in them. I feared that if they started clapping with excitement and congratulating me on my recovery I would resist, leap out of bed, and bite them; yes, I believed I was capable even of that. So I simply closed my eyes whenever they gathered to look at me again, drank the hot broth obediently, and listened to them sadly sighing. I felt Mother stroking my head. It annoyed me; I wanted them to move out of the shack and leave me in peace. At the same time the head stroking made me tearful, which irritated me even more; that was why I yearned to get back to my long sickness, where there were no tears, there was no anger, no pain, only silence and drowsing on the border between life and death.

Finally I understood that I could no longer stand the constant chatter that surrounded me day in, day out. There was only one way out of this: I had to get to my feet. Then I could escape from the shack if I wished, spend a day somewhere in the forest, far from all the botherers, and return home only at night, if at all. I assumed that I was well enough by now; only the fear of the burst of joy that would follow my getting out of bed kept me back a couple more days, but then I took courage.

One morning I pushed the animal skins aside with a rapid movement, sat up in bed, and said to Mother: "Mother, listen to me! I am well, but you mustn't say anything to me, not a single word. I'm getting dressed, eating, and going out. I don't want to hear a single shout; I don't want to see a single tear. I want silence. Do you understand, Mother? Don't say anything."

Mother nodded dumbly and looked at me with round eyes. She had covered her mouth with her hand and her eyes glistened, so that I understood: she could control her voice, but not her tears. This worried me; I wanted to get dressed as quickly as possible and escape from home at once. Getting dressed wasn't easy at all. I was still very weak and clumsy—and driven wild by the knowledge that now Mother certainly was weeping. I didn't look at her, just grabbed a bit of cold roast goat from the table and rushed out of the door.

The sun dazzled me. I shaded my eyes with my hand and stumbled deep into the forest, into the shade of the trees. I was seeking a lonely spot where no one ever went, somewhere I could throw myself down and see out the day until the evening. I was very pleased that I still had the courage to get out of the house. I really couldn't stand the discussions about whether Mõmmi had worms in his stomach or not, and if so how to get rid of them. Of course I did understand that life in the forest goes on, and that worms in the stomach are the most burning issue for some people and animals, but this chatter was driving me mad.

It was not easy to find a lonely spot; everywhere there was some bird hopping or hare jumping, and this confused me. I kept moving forward, until I reached the edge of the forest. There I saw some village girls.

Magdaleena was not among them I soon established. Actually I should have gone away, for the village girls were undoubtedly more befuddling than any titmouse or hare, and they weren't appropriate for a man seeking solitude. But I stayed there, getting down on my stomach among the bushes, watching the girls.

They had brought some sheep with them, and now were intending to let them stay and eat grass in the meadow at the forest's edge.

"But what happens if a wolf comes?" asked one girl.

"There's a medicine against that," answered another. "Don't you remember what Elder Johannes taught us? You have to take that belt that you wear to church and draw a line with it around the pasture. A wolf won't be able to cross that sacred line, because Jesus won't let it."

"Do you have a belt like that?" asked the first.

"Of course, I always think before I leave home," said the other girl, glibly. She undid a long colorful band from around her smock and began tracing an invisible ring through the meadow around the sheep. The first girl followed her friend's action with reverence.

"Next time I'll bring my belt with me," she promised. "Just think how simple it is to fight off wolves! Jesus can do everything."

"Yeah," agreed the second girl, who had completed the protective circle and was now tying her belt back on. "This is the foreigners' wisdom; life is much simpler if you know it."

They set off, carefree in the certain knowledge that the sheep were protected from all danger.

Naturally a wolf was soon on the scene. Strangely, the sight of it did not excite any feelings in me, although it was the first wolf I'd encountered since that evening. I had no desire to kill it or pour out my wrath on it in any way. Actually there was no hatred in me, only indifference. What could this wolf do to me? Attack me? I wasn't even sure that I could be bothered to defend myself.

But the wolf didn't come up to me; it was more interested in the sheep. Naturally it didn't notice that the girl had waved a belt around; that strip of clothing probably hadn't even left a scent. The wolf leapt on the neck of one sheep, brought the animal down, and dragged it off among the trees.

The sheep all bleated anxiously for a little while, then carried on eating the grass; then a second wolf came and carried off the next sheep. I didn't care to look at this massacre any longer; there was no doubt that if the girls didn't come back soon the wolves would polish them off. It might of course also happen that when the girls came back, they would also be eaten up, along with Jesus and the belt.

I suddenly found this idea very unpleasant. I didn't want to see that; I had to prevent it! Let the wolves gobble up the sheep; I didn't care. But the idea of another girl between those creatures' jaws made my head spin with rage. So I stayed on the spot and looked on while the last of the sheep were slaughtered.

Some time passed before the girls came back. They didn't come alone; with them were Elder Johannes and Magdaleena.

I crouched down as low as I could. I had not seen Magdaleena since the time when I walked home that evening in love with her; that seemed to have been in another life. After that had come the escape with Hiie, meeting Grandfather, and everything else—but that world had now vanished, cut from under me like Grandfather's legs.

What had become of Grandfather, who had promised to fly in after us soon? Had something happened? Had he not been able to get the last essential bones?

At the same time I was dreaming of Grandfather on his distant island and thinking of Magdaleena, who was standing right here, so close to me that if I had stood up she would have seen me immediately. She had grown a little plumper, but was still wonderfully beautiful, and I felt to my own amazement that I still loved her.

I tried to ward off that feeling; it seemed obscene to me. I had come to the forest to seek solitude, to mourn in silence then melt into the moss like Meeme, for what could life be without Hiie, whom I had loved so much—but I caught one glimpse of Magdaleena and couldn't take my eyes off her.

All these feelings that had seized me by the monastery as we listened to the monks' singing, the desire to touch her, to sit in her presence, smell her, came roaring back like an unexpected cloudburst.

But—it also occurred to me—Grandfather did not lose his mind after he lost his legs; he started building wings. If things don't go one way, you have to try another.

That train of thought seemed repulsive to me. My only consolation was that I could nonetheless acknowledge it.

And yet I yearned for Magdaleena. I liked her. In fact I was in love with her.

How repellent it all was! How good it would be to smolder in a fever, without a single thought, without a single doubt!

While I was at war with myself in the bushes, the girls and the village elder were dealing with the sheep. Or rather with their absence. The traces in the grass left no doubt that the sheep had fallen victim to wolves.

"But I drew a sacred ring around them with my belt," wept one girl. "It was supposed to help!"

"It does help," Johannes assured her. "But it protects only against ordinary wolves who are subject to God's commands. In the case of a werewolf, a belt is no help; Satan helps it to jump over it."

"Did a werewolf come here then?" screamed the other girl, shrieking with terror.

"There's no other explanation for the sheep disappearing," replied the village elder. "The church belt keeps all ordinary wild animals away; that wisdom has been known for centuries in Germany and in the holy city of Rome. Consequently it must have been a werewolf doing the mischief here."

"Can't Jesus do anything about it?" sobbed the second girl.

"Oh, he can!" said Johannes, consoling her. "But against a werewolf you need more effective weapons than a belt. I'll have to consult with the holy monks and ask what they recommend doing. There must surely be some prayer or relic to ward off that servant of Satan."

"I'm afraid!" said the first girl. "Let's go home!"

"Yes," agreed Johannes. "A shame about the sheep; we don't have any more of them in the village. But God will help us in time!"

They set off, and I stretched out to look at them leave, to see more of Magdaleena before she disappeared from view. But Magdaleena did not go to the village. She said something to her father, turned aside, and started going a different way. Then she slowed down her pace, looked around, as if wanting to make sure that her father and the other girls no longer saw her, and ran back to the edge of the forest. I thought she had lost something, but to my great surprise I heard Magdaleena quietly calling: "Leemet! Are you there? Leemet!"

I got up and stepped out of the bushes.

"Hello," I said. "Did you see me?"

"No, but I knew you must be somewhere nearby," replied Magdaleena, coming up to me and putting her hands on my shoulders. She looked into my eyes and smiled slyly. I felt her scent and it made me weak in the knees. I pulled Magdaleena to my breast and kissed her.

Magdaleena didn't resist; I felt her licking my lips with her tongue.

"You killed the sheep!" she whispered.

I pushed her away in amazement. "What did you say?"

"Your lips don't have the taste of blood, but I know it was you," giggled Magdaleena, as if anticipating a lot of fun. "You know how to change into a werewolf. Who else does?"

"I told you, a human being can't change into a wolf. That's rubbish," I explained. "They were quite ordinary wolves that ate up the sheep. I saw them myself."

It was clear that Magdaleena didn't believe me.

"I understand that you can't tell me all your secrets," she said. "In church, too, there's plenty that I don't understand, because the monks talk in Latin. Powerful spells have to be well hidden away. I don't want you to teach me to change into a werewolf anymore. I don't have time for that. But I want you to teach my child."

"Your child?" I repeated, astonished. "You have a child, Magdaleena?"

"Not yet, but I soon will!" replied the girl. "Listen, I'll tell you. I don't want to keep it secret, and besides, it's not something that can be hidden. It can't be hidden; quite soon it will be clear to everyone how things are with me. I'm so happy! You know it happened that last evening when you and I saw each other. You went off to the forest and I walked back toward the village. Do you remember, just before that we'd seen a knight riding by so grandly on his stallion? Can you imagine? As I was trudging back to the village I met him again! This time he came right up to me. I bowed and greeted him in German. I don't know much German, but enough to greet someone. The knight stopped his horse, looked at me, and asked me my name. I was so excited I could hardly reply. I'd never talked to a knight before. I told him my name and then the knight took me by the chin and looked at my face. He tousled my hair, felt my breasts, and then—can you believe it?—pulled me onto his horse's back and carried me straight to his castle. How splendid everything was there! Pure silver drinking cups, a bed covered with expensive drapes . . . He slept with me! Leemet, you understand a foreign knight slept with me! He made a child inside me!"

I looked at Magdaleena as she glowed with pleasure as if she were demented, but I have to admit that her story aroused me and I would gladly have liked to follow the knight's example. In some way Magdaleena now seemed a lot more worldly. If a foreign iron man had been allowed to fondle her hair and breasts, then why not me too? The only thing that slightly disturbed me was the knowledge of the child hidden inside the girl; it was as if a third person was looking on, keeping a watchful eye on Magdaleena.

"So do you live in the castle now?" I asked. "You're this knight's lover?"

"No, what do you mean?" chuckled Magdaleena. "Of course he took me home the next morning. Why would he keep me at the castle? There are so many village girls that he can make happy. Although I hope he won't. I haven't heard of any other girl from our village getting into a knight's castle. I'm the only one he chose. I'm the only one he gave a child to! You understand, Leemet. I'm giving birth to a jesus!"

"I don't understand, no. Is this jesus of yours something like a sprite? God, or whatever you call him in your village."

"Yes, he's a god, but the knights are God's friends and pupils. To me they're as good as Jesus himself. God has taught them all sorts of wisdom and made them strong and handsome. He can do that to us too, if we all listen to his word, but it takes time. The child I'm carrying in my womb will be like them from birth, because his father is one of the jesuses! His blood is flowing in my child! Jesus's blood! What a privilege that is for me, what an honor! He'll become a knight and I think he'll start speaking German right from childhood like his father. Fortunately he's sure to learn Estonian as well, because I'm his mother. Otherwise I wouldn't be able to talk properly to my own child. That would be sad!"

Magdaleena shook her head and carried on talking.

"My father is terribly glad too," she said. "For him it's enormously important for our family to get ahead as much as possible. He was born in the forest himself, but I'm a village girl, and my child will go out into the wide world and become a famous man. Maybe he'll even go to the holy city of Rome and settle down there. Why not? He won't be a peasant anymore, he'll be a jesus, and jesuses rule the world right now."

"Congratulations from me too, then," I mumbled. I was beginning to feel that I wouldn't get to sleep with Magdaleena after all. What could a forest boy like me do for her, when she already had an actual jesus, a future ruler of the world, living in her tummy? Clearly it was the fashion these days to get your child from a knight, not from some stale Snakish-talking man. Again I felt that my insides stank of decay; the stink was so strong that it was downright incomprehensible that Magdaleena couldn't smell it.

"Thank you, Leemet," said Magdaleena. "But now I want to ask you a favor. I want you to be my husband."

This was so unexpected that I simply stared at Magdaleena.

"Why me?" I finally managed to utter.

Magdaleena took me by the neck and pressed herself close to me. It was pleasant, and yet I couldn't suppress the thought that somewhere right here, snuggled against my stomach, was a little jesus, and this made me slightly uncomfortable. But then Magdaleena slipped her hand under my jacket and I did the same and forgot about all the jesuses in the world. To me they might as well have been mere midges. As long as I could stroke Magdaleena's bare back, I didn't care about them one bit.

"I know that God is strong," whispered Magdaleena in my ear. "But I also know that sometimes he gives way to the devil. Often it happens that holy pictures and crosses can't stop it, and today the belt didn't help either. It didn't stop you; you killed the sheep anyway."

I couldn't be bothered arguing; right now I didn't care what Magdaleena said, as long as I got to caress her bare hot skin.

"Things like this come up quite often in the village," continued Magdaleena. "Father is very wise. He has studied many useful spells in far-off lands, but they're all supported by God's power. He's forgotten the devil; the monks and the other foreigners don't know the devil either. They're only afraid of him, because they know that God won't always avail them against him. But you're not afraid of the devil. You know him; you can talk with him. You've seen the sprites and you understand the language of snakes, but a snake is almost the same as the devil. My son will be a jesus, and he will have the whole of God's world open to him, but I want you to open up the devil's world to him too. I want you to bring him up and teach him like a father in the flesh, to teach him Snakish, and the art of changing into a werewolf, everything you know how to do. Leemet, will you fulfill my wish? If you can't leave your forest, you won't have to live with us, but you should visit every day, because my son must become a man who understands the language of both God and the devil. When you get cold in the forest, there'll always be room for you in my bed."

"I'm cold already," I said.

"Already?" murmured Magdaleena. "I don't have a bed here in the forest to invite you into the warm. This is your world, werewolf, and your bed. This is where I have to ask you if there's room in your bed."

"Always," I replied, and indeed we had plenty of room.

Twenty-Nine

Are you coming with me?" asked Magdaleena afterward, as we were getting dressed.

"Yes, I'm coming," I replied. For why shouldn't I go? I didn't want to stay in the forest. Especially now—after having got out of bed for the first time since Hiie's death, and gone straight off and slept with a beautiful village girl—it seemed completely impossible for me to go back home. I imagined Mother and Salme waiting for me there, their eyes full of pity and sadness, competing with each other to chat about everything that had happened since that fateful wedding. They would tell me about Hiie's cremation; they might even want to show me the remains of the pyre. But I would be coming from another woman, carrying her scent on me, and feeling like a villain. That would be horrible; I couldn't stand the idea of it. If I even just thought of Mother's weeping eyes, her mournful expression that would follow me day in, day out from then on, the drowning sympathy that drove me out of the house, a choking lump came into my throat. I didn't want to be pitied, and there was no danger of that in the village. Nobody sympathized with me there. Not a single person suspected that I was an unhappy man, deprived of his wife on his wedding day. This was an opportunity to escape from my own mourning.

Besides, I wanted Magdaleena as much as before. I appreciated that this was crude and repulsive; I should have remained true to Hiie's memory, but if I had behaved like a bear in heat anyway, I would no longer have anything to lose. So I would move to the village. I would sink myself among those stupid village folk, start gobbling that nauseating bread, and working in the fields like the worst of fools. It was best for me. That was my punishment. I would no longer be Leemet, but somebody else completely, a nameless villager. Leemet died with Hiie; a new slouching little man would be the one to start living in the village, as idiotic as his neighbors.

If I refused now, I would die in the forest full of regret—both that I had betrayed Hiie and that I had given up Magdaleena's alluring beauty, which she herself was offering me so generously. I couldn't live as before anyway; that was impossible.

I was terribly afraid that at the last moment Ints, or my mother, or Mõmmi, or a Primate would appear out of the bushes and say something. I didn't want any human or animal from the forest to ever see me again. I wanted to vanish without trace, and at a stroke draw a veil over my whole past, like a lizard that discards its own tail and staggers off who knows where.

"Let's go," I said to Magdaleena. "I love you. I'll always stay with you. I won't ever go back to the forest."

"You're so sweet," replied Magdaleena with a radiant smile. "I knew you'd agree. You'll start teaching my child, won't you, and look after him as if he was your own."

"I will," I assured her. I really did intend to do that. Magdaleena's stories of gods, devils, and jesuses were of course completely harebrained, and I understood nothing of all this strange twaddle, but I really did want to be the father of her child. I recalled Uncle Vootele's talk about Snakish and how the time would come when I would have to pass it on to my successor. In this case, the Snakish words would live on, and at least I wouldn't be the last man in this world who understood the language of the serpents. I needed a child with whom to share all my wisdom, and where else would I find such a child but in the village? There were no children in the forest, and by now it was abundantly clear that no more would be born there. Hiie was dead; the whole forest was dying. But the Snakish words would live on, as long as I was alive, and I wished them to live on a little longer than myself.

I was not troubled in the least that the father of Magdaleena's child was an iron man; I didn't feel any jealousy toward that rattling creature that had impregnated Magdaleena one night. If my training met its mark, then one fine day Magdaleena's child might, with a single Snakish word, break the stride of his father's horse and the neck of the old iron man. If Magdaleena's hopes came true, and her child really did wander out into the wide world from his home village, then with the help of Snakish he could achieve a great deal. I knew from my own experience how helpless people are when they don't understand Snakish and are attacked in the right way. I wanted to make this child my heir; I wanted to give him that great secret weapon that only he in the whole world could use. That was the only thought I had, the only goal that my life could still have.

I strode along at Magdaleena's heels toward the village and didn't look back once. I no longer wished to ever see my mother or sister again. In the normal course of events, I should have died of the fever; my recovery was absurd and incomprehensible. Everything had changed too much, and it was no longer possible to find one's way in the world. The only possibility was to leap straight into the bushes. That was what I was doing. I saw Johannes's house before me, and I took a deep breath, as if before diving.

Johannes greeted me with his own overweening friendliness.

"Poor boy," he said. "You look so thin and worn out. But your days of misery are now at an end. Come inside. I'll give you some bread. You can eat as much as you want, because, thank God, we still have a crumb of bread."

I forced a smile onto my face, but inside I was thinking, So it begins. You've hardly got your foot over the threshold when they're already rushing to smother you with bread. But I had made my choice. I hadn't come to the village to enjoy life or to gourmandise, apart from on Magdaleena, and I had all the more reason to forgo all other pleasures. The mosslike bread was a suitable foodstuff; it was enough to keep you alive, and I needed no more.

"I'd be glad of a piece of bread," I said to Johannes.

I was handed a fresh slice of bread, I bit into it, and I gobbled up the unchewed bits into my intestines, as if wanting as fast as possible to fill myself with an alien substance and thus change into a new being. Johannes attributed my greed to desperate hunger; he looked at me sympathetically and sighed, "What a terrible life you must have had in the forest. Poor boy! Why didn't you come and stay with us earlier? This time you won't be leaving, and besides, winter is coming. You'd die of cold and hunger in the forest."

Before my eyes appeared the gigantic white stone in the snakes' lair, which was so sweet to lick and brought that pleasant lassitude, a long soft sleep. I knew I wouldn't be going to spend the winter with the adders ever again—the last miserable human among the energetic and fruitfully propagating snakes. I didn't want to be a poor relation. I didn't want to play the part of a unique specimen, miraculously preserved down to our own day. It was all over; our kind had died out.

"Yes, I won't be leaving anymore," I told Johannes. "Now I'll stay here."

"The right decision. We'd better find you a place to stay to get you started, until you set up your own land."

"Father, Leemet is staying with us," said Magdaleena. "He's going to be my husband."

Elder Johannes was slack-jawed.

"My dear child, this is news to me . . . Why him? You've caught the eye of others too, boys in our village that you've known from childhood. You've always been so haughty . . . But this one here is straight out of the forest."

"That's just it, Father!" cried Magdaleena. "Why should I get married to a peasant, who doesn't know how to do anything but what he's picked up from the knights and the monks? I don't want a pupil in my bed. I want a master, and that's what I've got. You know, Father, whose child I'm carrying in my belly and what he will grow up to be!"

"I do know," said Johannes, looking at Magdaleena's midriff with such a reverent gaze that I was reminded of the story of how the elder had shared his bed with some bishop as a young boy. Evidently the poor man was hoping to get pregnant himself, I thought. What a disappointment it would be to him if not even his beloved God could get foreign men to have children. I didn't say anything, because obviously I had to start living under the same roof as Johannes, and it wasn't sensible to get into an argument with him on the first day.

"I understand that very well indeed," said Johannes. "You're like me, daughter: you aim high. It's a great thing that you got to know a real knight; no other girl in our village has that experience and I'm proud of you. But Leemet? Look at him! He's a savage!"

I was surprised that he was not ashamed to talk like that in my hearing, but apparently the old man thought I was so hungry that my attention would be only on the bread.

"Father, I have my own reasons why I chose Leemet," declared Magdaleena. "You might call him a savage, but he's special to me."

"He's special, of course, but being special like that is not worth anything," countered Johannes, eyeing me with evident embarrassment. "I'm not saying he won't become a decent peasant, that he won't learn how to sow and reap—but right now he's a nobody. He's been living like an animal. He isn't even baptized."

"Father, I know what I'm doing," said Magdaleena, rising to her full height. "Don't forget that I'm the mother of a future knight! Father, in your time you've traveled a lot and seen a lot, but now you're old and I understand the new world better. Leemet is the one I need, no one else. He will be the father of my child. He's the one best suited for it."

She looked at me loftily, but then smiled almost apologetically.

"Besides, I love him," she said, and sat down next to me on the bench, taking me by the neck. "Father, don't even try to argue. The matter is settled."

"All right," sighed Johannes. "Let him stay. Well now, I was supposed to go to the monastery anyway today and ask advice of the holy brothers on the question of werewolves. I might as well arrange a time for baptism too. Leemet must become a Christian and be given a Christian name. He must get to know the Word of God and the Lord's commandments."

"No God," I said. Really, I was prepared to swallow bread, cut straws in the fields, turn a quern, and do all the other idiocies that the villagers had learned from the foreigners, but I wanted to keep away from God. I was sick to the back teeth of all these sprites and jesuses and other invented beings. They had aggrieved me in the forest and now even in the village they wouldn't go away. They had changed their names, but they were still just as invisible and senseless. I didn't want to hear about any such stupidity; it reminded me of Ülgas and the fact that I'd only been able to chop half of his head off. I had destroyed the sacred grove so that no one would set foot there ever again, and I didn't intend to now go to church.

"What do you mean—no God?" snapped Johannes. "I cannot allow an unbaptized pagan living on my land. That's impossible! We have a Christian village and we belong to the Christian world. We are a worthy part of it, even though poor and a little backward, but even we are kept in place by our Holy Father. You must have yourself baptized and receive the proper faith; you must go to church and learn God's commandments!"

"I don't intend to do that," I replied. "Now listen! I agree to do all the work, till the fields, and prepare the same bread, which doesn't taste good but fills your stomach—everything that is tangible and edible, and thus real and actual. But I don't need new sprites!"

"I'm not talking about sprites!" shouted Johannes. "Sprites naturally only bring misfortune on people, because they're in the service of the devil. They are really to be feared. I'm talking about God, who protects us!"

"Elder, I have lived in the forest all my life and I tell you there are no sprites! There is no need to fear them; what you should fear is people who believe in sprites. The same goes for your God. It's just a new name for the sprites, given by the monks, like me changing my name if I were christened. I'll still be myself; it doesn't matter what I'm called. I can't be bothered to play this game."

"This is not a game!" shouted Johannes, rising up. "You have to choose: will you become a Christian, like all the people in this village, or will you go back to the forest? I'm not going to allow a pagan to live among us, no way!"

"Father, be quiet!" Magdaleena cried. "Leemet doesn't have to go to church if he doesn't want to. He doesn't have to be christened. I want him just as he is."

"But he's a pagan! All pagans serve the devil!"

"Father, why do you think we don't sometimes have a use for the devil? Do you think God is all-powerful? You saw today that the sacred belt didn't save our village's sheep. Maybe turning to the devil might have been more useful?"

"Child, what you're saying is a terrible sin!" said Johannes, his face turning white. "The devil is unable to protect anyone; he only knows how to bite and attack. You will see; today I'm going to the holy brothers and they will give me a potion to destroy this damned werewolf that brought death to our sheep."

Magdaleena looked fearfully in my direction, evidently worried that the monks' potion might really put an end to me,

the werewolf. I grinned back at her and she seemed calmed.
How stupid they were! Magdaleena was at least beautiful, but
there was nothing to excuse Elder Johannes. Suddenly I was
terribly tired of all this. How different this argument was to
my conversations with Hiie! I felt on the verge of crying. But
there was no way back. Here I sat now, in the middle of modern stupidity, and I had to stay here till the end of my life. I
yearned for Magdaleena to give birth right then, wishing that
the child might be born and grow at supernatural speed to the
age when I could teach him Snakish. But I knew that in that
hope I was as stupid as the village people were with their gods.
Supernatural things don't exist; everything proceeds according
to the natural order, and births and deaths take place at their
appointed time.

"Well?" I asked, annoyed. "How far have you got with your
chattering? Can I stay here or must I go back to the forest? What
do you say, Johannes?"

I looked at the village elder's rage-reddened face, and suddenly
a good idea passed through my head—to kill him and end all
this ridiculous arguing, make a drinking goblet of his skull and
live in peace with Magdaleena without having to put up with
the idiotic old man. But I hadn't come to the village to fight; I
had come to bury myself. I was awaiting an answer and listened
to Johannes panting with exasperation—but it was Magdaleena
who started speaking.

"Of course you'll stay here," she said calmly. "You're my husband and the father of my child, and you don't have to become
a Christian. There are many Christians here in the village; if I'd
wanted to find a husband among them, I could have had one
long ago. But I wanted you. Did you hear, Father? I want Leemet

and my child—who is the child of a knight and in whose veins runs the blood of jesuses, don't forget that!—wants Leemet too."

"So be it," said Johannes, though I thought I heard his teeth grinding. "Let him stay then. But I tell you, Magdaleena, God won't forgive us for giving shelter to a pagan. He'll punish us for it. One cannot serve two masters!"

"I won't serve anyone," I said. "I don't need a master, and even less do I need to invent one."

"So be it, but you know you are the only and the last pagan in our village!" declared Johannes.

I didn't reply. What was there for me to say? I was used to the knowledge that I was the last. Everywhere and always.

Thirty

n the evening Magdaleena invited me to the swing. I no longer wore my old animal-skin jacket. Magdaleena had peeled that off me and instead given me some old rags of her father's. They weren't bad, but no better than my previous clothes—and it was quite clear that a lot of trouble had to be taken to make such clothes, whereas for us in the forest a proper animal skin was no more than the work of a lunchtime.

By the swings I met first of all my former friend Pärtel—now Peetrus—and his mates Jaakop and Andreas, whom I'd met that time by the monastery. There was also a large group of village boys and girls, swinging, sitting around the fire, and joking with each other behind the swings.

It was quite clear that Magdaleena was treated by this group with the greatest respect. If it was usual for the boys to pull the girls' hair and try to pull their skirts over their heads, with Magdaleena no one was permitted any such behavior. The girls tried to stay close to her, hung on her every word with great attention, and from time to time put timid questions to her.

They seemed to be most fearful of being embarrassed or saying anything foolish in front of her. For her part Magdaleena treated them with maternal sternness, and never lost an opportunity to emphasize the fact that she was carrying the child of a knight in her belly. Every time she reminded them of it, a hum of wonderment passed among the girls.

The boys, on the other hand, kept a respectful distance from Magdaleena and only glanced at her from the corners of their eyes, rather as a little weasel looks greedily at a lynx's slaughtered prey, licking its lips, but not daring to go closer. I could feel great satisfaction in the fact that I was the only one who was allowed near such hallowed flesh.

My arrival by the swings was greeted with curious looks and quiet murmurs, but since Magdaleena held me proudly by the hand, all the girls at once reasoned that if the all-wise Magdaleena deemed it good to carry on with a man from the forest, this must be the last word in fashion, and they rushed to get to know me. Magdaleena scared them off with an icy look and a sharp word or two. Her whole being gave to understand that men from the forest were in vogue, but only selected women could possess them—those who had been bedded by a foreigner.

I left the girls and went to greet Pärtel, the sight of whom awakened happy childhood memories and nourished the deceptive dream that people who have vanished from one's life are still around somewhere, even if changed and living by another name. Unfortunately I knew that this applied only to him, and actually even from Pärtel there was no joy to be had.

Pärtel greeted me fairly indifferently, though this wasn't out of any special unfriendliness, but because Andreas had found a dented knight's helmet from somewhere. This bit of junk was being passed around the group; they were trying it on and admiring it with extreme reverence.

"I know this is Spanish steel," said Jaakop, tapping delicately with his fingernails on the helmet and smiling happily. "Ah, what workmanship! They know how to do it there!"

"That's not Spanish steel," objected some fat village man, taking the helmet in his arms and pressing it harshly between his coarse paws. "This is obviously the work of German smiths!"

"Don't twist it like that, Nigul!" snapped Andreas. "It's mine. I found it. You'll break it if you squeeze it."

"Now," laughed fat Nigul. "That's a thing I'd like to see, a peasant like us with his bare hands being able to break the work of German smiths in half. A helmet like this can withstand a heavy blow from a sword if it has to."

"All the same, you don't have to mangle it so hard," said Andreas, taking the helmet in his hands. "It's beautiful, men; there's no denying it. World-class quality. Ah, those knights have fine things."

"No disputing it," they all agreed. "Quite different to our headgear."

"Why are you even comparing such a fine helmet to some old cap of ours?" cried Andreas. "This is gleaming and it's made of metal. Well, in our village no man has anything to put against it. I'll put it on and all the women will line their arses up for me!"

They all laughed, except Pärtel, who asked doubtfully, "Do you dare to go around with that on? What if some knight sees you?"

They all fell silent, and even Andreas became thoughtful. But still he put on a brave face and with a swagger continued,

"Well, why shouldn't I? Obviously not in daylight and on the main road, but in the evening when it gets dark. Who will see me if I put the helmet on and bundle around with it? I'll go behind the cowsheds; no knight will come snooping around that dunghill!"

"You're right they won't," said the others, terribly glad that their friend found a way out of a tricky situation, already anticipating his future conquests. "They won't want to soil their horses' hooves with manure. If you hide behind the cowsheds, they surely won't see you."

There was no jealousy; they obviously all thought it was right that the owner of such a splendid foreign helmet should pounce on all the women in the village.

"Oh, if only I could find one of those!" fat Nigul sighed. "But I know you only get a privilege like that once in a hundred years. Such precious things don't grow everywhere like mushrooms. The knights look after their helmets."

"I think they're easy to get," I said. "You simply have to kill a knight, and the helmet's yours."

My words were followed by a hesitant silence. The village men looked at me as if I'd recommended them to go home and eat their mothers. Finally Jaakop said, "What rubbish you talk. How could we kill a knight?"

"Well, why not?" I questioned. "Do you think they're immortal? Eternal like rocks?"

"No, it's not that; it's that we wouldn't overcome them," said Jaakop. "They sit on horseback and they have armor. They have a sword and a lance. They're much stronger and more powerful than we are. Attacking them would be insane."

"Squatting there in the forest, maybe you simply haven't seen them?" added Andreas scornfully. "Here in the village we meet knights every day, and know very well what they're worth. They are mighty masters. Do you remember, Nigul, just a couple of days ago you didn't dip your cap low enough, and a knight knocked you flat with his sword? Lucky that you jumped into the ditch; otherwise you would have got a good walloping."

"Why do you have to take off your cap?" I asked.

"Well, you really are from the forest! It's a famous old foreign custom! Abroad they always do it: when a knight comes riding along the road, a peasant doffs his cap. It's polite. If you don't take your cap off, you're a boor."

"I'm not a boor," objected fat Nigul. "I always take my cap off when a knight rides by, and I bow down to the ground too. I'm a decent person. I know how to behave among the finer folk. But that time I simply didn't see my lord the knight. The bloody sun was shining in my eyes!"

"Yes, and you got a lesson!"

"That I did. I'll be more careful in the future."

"Now you see how stupid you were," said Jaakop, turning toward me. "Good lord, you want to kill a knight! What for? Because he brings such beautiful helmets to our country? We would otherwise never see the miracles of the outside world if the knights and monks weren't looking after us."

I couldn't be bothered arguing with them. I didn't tell them that I'd killed several knights and thrown their helmets into the woods like useless rubbish. I could even have led those men to the exact spot where those helmets and coats of mail would be rusting away to that day under a rotting corpse, if the wolves and foxes hadn't dragged them to gnaw at elsewhere. But I didn't wish to help them.

I left the men admiring the helmet and walked toward the women. Even from afar I could hear Magdaleena's voice, explaining, "Yes, he knows the devil." She was obviously talking about me. The girls gasped and looked at me with horrified eyes, but when I sat down among them, only a few of them shifted away, probably the timidest ones. Others, on the other hand, gradually slipped closer and glanced at me with greedy curiosity, as if hoping I would suddenly bring about something frightful.

However, I merely sat and chewed on a stalk of grass. I noticed a few girls picking up similar stalks and putting them in their mouths, probably thinking it involved some fairy trick or spell. Finally a little flaxen-haired lass dared to speak to me, clearing her throat a little at first to beg my attention, and piped up: "I have a question! Please tell me, is it true, if you give the devil three drops of blood, you become a witch and you can fly in the sky?"

To a few especially well-mannered girls this very question seemed so horrid that they got up, startled, and went off to swing, preferring that innocent pastime to this dangerous conversation. The bolder ones, however, stayed there and awaited my reply, holding their breath. To my mind they were dreadfully childish. In the forest a three-year-old brat might have thought up something similar. I told the girls that I had never seen anyone flying. I wasn't going to tell them about my own grandfather and the wings he'd made of human bones; it would have given rise to too many more questions.

"I've also heard that if you kill the king of the snakes and eat his crown, a person can learn the language of birds," continued the flaxen-haired one. "That's true. Magdaleena told us you can talk to the animals."

"There is no language of birds," I replied. "I know Snakish. To learn that you don't have to kill anyone, and certainly not the king of the snakes. Eating his crown wouldn't help; you have to learn the Snakish words. It takes a long time, but when you finally master them, then it's really possible to make yourself understood to the animals. And the birds too. But you can't talk with them, because very few animals can answer you back. They understand and obey a word, but they don't talk themselves."

The flaxen lass wasn't satisfied with my answer: "Eating the king snake's crown does give you some power, though. People don't tell such stories for nothing. There must be a grain of truth in it."

"There's none," I said. "Pure silliness. People who've never even seen a snake-king talk a lot of twaddle."

"Have you seen a king of the snakes?" asked Magdaleena, evidently anticipating the answer and wanting to make an impression on her friends.

"I have," I said. Again this was a subject that I didn't want to dwell on too long; all too clearly I envisaged Ints, her father, and all the other adders. They were my best friends, but now I was sitting among humans who wanted to kill them and devour them only in order to learn the nonexistent "language of birds"—what an idiotic idea. What had I got myself into?

"I don't want anyone attacking the king of the snakes!" I said angrily. "Before you reached out your hand for his crown, he would have time to sting you ten times. As I said, there's no need to go after the crown. You could eat a barrelful of them, and the language of birds wouldn't be any clearer to you. Eat bread, not snake-kings, and be content with your own sweet life."

I got up and walked away, disgust and pain in my heart. I had wanted to bury myself here, forget all my previous life—but could that be done? Ignorance was splashed in my face and kept reminding me of the happy times in the forest. How long could I put up with this? I was too different to these villagers; I could never become like them. I had escaped to the village from mourning; now, though, I was very close to leaving the village to escape from stupidity. But where would I go?

Somebody was stroking my head; it was Magdaleena. She had come after me and was now kissing my neck.

"Take no notice of them!" she whispered in my ear. "That's why I didn't want a peasant for a husband. They don't know anything about the forest, the place where they too came from but which they've forgotten, nor about the wide world, where they have never been and never will be. They wouldn't have anything to teach my son. You're a different matter; you know the old world and all its secrets. You will teach my son Snakish, his knightly father has already given him his blood, and I will add mother love and bring him up as a great man. Leemet, forget those idiots! I saw from your face that you'd like to run back to the forest, but you mustn't do that. You and I have to bring up my son together, so he can learn about the old and the new world equally. Then there will be at least one man like that, not only just people who don't know either one properly."

"Why are you so sure that it will be a boy?" I asked.

"What else?" replied Magdaleena, astonished. "His father is a knight. Knights don't have daughters."

I stroked her soft cheek and kissed her earlobe tenderly. But I was thinking, Oh, she's just as stupid as the others. But what of it—I'll stay. Where would I go anyway?

We stayed by the swings, but Magdaleena and I sat apart from the others and it felt good. The villagers swung in a great arc, rocking back and forth between earth and sky, and hooted for all they were worth. In this way they seemed actually quite pleasant, because their faces couldn't be made out in the gathering dusk. By the firelight one could see only a single large bundle of noisy merriment.

And so I stayed in the village. With the other villagers I went to the fields to cut rye. I helped to thresh, winnow, and grind it. I felt an actual awe for the enormous trouble people were prepared to go to in order to imitate foreign ways and munch the bread that to me still tasted like tree bark.

Occasionally, however, I did allow myself proper food, and with the help of Snakish words I caught a hare in the meadow, took it home, and roasted it. I ate the hare with Magdaleena and Johannes, who had still not reconciled himself to having an unchristened heathen in his house, glancing sidelong at me and reminding me in those moments of the late Tambet. But nonetheless he did eat the hare, unable to resist the animal's delicious meat.

As he greedily gnawed on a hare bone, I tried to force the old man to admit that it would actually be wiser to throw away the bread and dine every day on roast meat. But Johannes argued with me, as he wiped the grease off his chin, explaining that bread is a human being's main nourishment, since God has ordained it so. When Johannes proudly declared that eating rye bread is what distinguishes us from the quadrupeds, I told him:

"All right then, next time I bring a hare home, you can suck his toes in a corner or eat bread, but you won't be getting any more meat." At this, Johannes glared at me bitterly and tried to get at the marrow in the bone, as if afraid that I would carry out my threat right away.

The villagers ate meat rarely, because they hunted animals with strange traps, into which only sick or especially stupid animals fell, or with bows and arrows, which mostly missed their mark. My success in hunting hares was much remarked on, but nobody wished to understand that I was helped by ordinary everyday Snakish words, and everything was attributed to some secret spell. Magdaleena felt very proud of me; she went around the village talking of all the things I could achieve, exaggerating terribly and making me out to be some sort of sage who could move the clouds or call down a thunderstorm with magic words. I explained to her that I wasn't a sage, that a sage was just a swindler who does tricks under his sacred linden trees. I added that I had already chopped one such sage almost in half, and if any other figure like that turned up I'd do the same again. Magdaleena smiled; she liked my wildness. As she moved around the village, though, she carried on calling me a sage, since that word, whose real meaning no one in the village understood anymore, aroused vague memories in them of a bygone era, and brought shivers to their spines—or so Magdaleena told me. I was very saddened that instead of all the good and beautiful things that had once been people's memories clung to the image of the Sage of the Grove; why couldn't they remember Snakish and the Frog of the North? To crown it all, one day in the fields fat Nigul asked me was it true that I had once sacrificed young virgins at my own grove to appease the devil. I gave him a smack in the face to make his nose bleed; he had reminded me too painfully of Hiie and those days when I was still happy.

Despite the fact that I had Magdaleena, I didn't feel happy in the village. Our nights were beautiful, but our days were depressing. Although I kept apart from the villagers as much as possible, it wasn't possible to avoid them completely. There was always someone hanging at my heels, making my blood boil with senseless jabbering.

The only thing in the village that interested me apart from Magdaleena was her child. I awaited its birth impatiently. I really had the feeling that I was about to become a father, even though the baby she was carrying was not put there by me. He was going to be my pupil, and that was just as important.

Winter came, and Magdaleena's belly grew so huge that she seemed to have a bear cub under her smock. As she moved around the village she was accompanied by admiring looks: many women came up to her and put their ears against the round belly, as if hoping to hear the German language or the jangling of chain mail in there. The villagers really seemed to think that the son of a knight would come riding on horseback out of his mother's belly, a white feather fluttering on his helmet. There were no limits to the people's superstition; even Magdaleena was deadly certain that she would give birth to a boy, whereas I, on the other hand, expected a daughter, just to taunt her. At the bottom of my heart, though, I was also hoping for a boy, because I felt it would be easier to teach him; before my eyes I saw Uncle Vootele and Magdaleena's son as myself. I was longing for that child, the only person in the village who was still uncorrupted and pure, who knew nothing of the foreigners' mad nonsense or the villagers' idiotic ways. There had to be a person with whom I could converse in Snakish, my pupil, my friend, my child.

In spring he was born—and he was indeed a boy. Magdaleena's foolish faith was confirmed. That didn't bother me. I bent over the suckling and tenderly stroked his face. The child opened his mouth and poked out his miraculous little tongue, and to my great joy I saw that his tongue was flexible and agile, just the kind that is needed for talking Snakish.

I hissed a couple of words at him. The child looked at me with big eyes; his expression was serious and attentive.

Thirty-One

aturally I wasn't able to set about teaching Snak-ish right away. I'd anticipated the child's birth so impatiently that I hadn't actually thought about how much time must pass before the boy was able to start learning. I had to wait a few years! The only thing I could do right away was to explain to Magdaleena that the child's tongue must not be blunted by bread and porridge. To begin with he had to be fed on breast milk of course, but after that I wanted to take care of feeding the boy. Magdaleena agreed with me.

The child didn't have a name yet. Magdaleena wanted to chris-ten him Jesus of course, but Johannes claimed that the monks would not allow that, because there could be only one Jesus in the world. Finally the child was christened Toomas, as that was supposed to be a suitable Christian name for a knight's son. I didn't go with them to the church, but since christening was so important to Magdaleena and her father I didn't say anything. It did the child no harm, and while everyone was out of the house, I was able to take a nice little nap.

When Toomas was brought back home, I tried to whisper his name in Snakish and it sounded quite good. The boy smiled on hearing my voice, and when I stroked his face, he turned his head and started sucking my finger, mistaking it for a nipple.

"He wants to eat," I told Magdaleena.

Magdaleena came and picked up Toomas.

"Toomas the Knight must have everything he wants!" she whispered in the child's ear, putting the boy to her breast. I was often surprised by the way Magdaleena treated the suckling. It wasn't ordinary motherly tenderness, but something much more; in her tone of voice there was humility, even supreme subjection. I was sure that when the boy grew bigger, Magdaleena would never be able to deny him or beat him; for her little Toomas really was a higher being.

The same attitude could be observed among all the villagers. When they came to us to look at the infant, they didn't dare to step farther than the threshold, but squinted at the corner where the little boy was sleeping, and if he suddenly woke up and started nodding, they all drew into a huddle and listened respectfully to the child's babbling. The villagers obviously imagined that the knight's son was talking German to them. I noticed that even Magdaleena listened to her son's utterances with intense interest, and if she thought she caught something German sounding among the babble, she smiled, enraptured.

Most ridiculous, though, to my mind, was Johannes's behavior. He had a habit of occasionally sitting by the child's bed, and when little Toomas started chuckling to himself, he listened to the child's incoherent shrieks with a deadly serious face, nodding and saying "ahhaa!" from time to time. I couldn't understand whether he was simply trying to give us the impression that he, a man who had visited holy Rome and shared his place with a bishop, understood the babblings of the offspring of a knight, or whether the village elder was simply off his rocker. He never explained his actions: if the child fell silent, Johannes always shook his head, as if he'd received supremely important tidings, went to his corner, and sat there for hours, as if he were meditating on something.

This respect and reverence that people expressed to the baby of knightly blood was so stupid that I, on the other hand, behaved as freely as possible with the child; I tickled him under the chin, jiggled him in my arms, and blew on his tummy so that he roared with laughter and flailed his arms and legs joyfully. When I frolicked with him like that, Magdaleena always stood beside me looking concerned, as if she hadn't quite decided whether such behavior with the son of a knight wasn't too wanton, but she never actually forbade me. I noticed that after our romps, she was especially tender and caring to little Toomas, as if trying to exonerate my naughty behavior with an individual of such noble lineage. They really were peculiar, these villagers.

Soon there was not much time left for playing with little Toomas, for spring arrived and I had to start on the exhausting and, to my eyes, completely useless tasks in the fields. But I did what was asked of me without grumbling, because in my life I had lived through much harder things than mere sowing, and if the villagers wished, I could help them cultivate crops. I was tired out by my companions' talk much more than by the sowing.

Their newest favorite subject was horseshit. The men of the village had few horses of their own, only a few old and bony creatures with shaggy manes. They sowed with bullocks. The iron men would gallop around everywhere, even trotting over the fields if they wished. It often happened that in the middle of sowing one of the villagers would discover a horse turd, signaling his find with a shout—and a moment later all the sowers were gathered round the dropping.

They all regarded themselves as great experts on horseshit.

"Now that's a turd from an Arab thoroughbred!" said Jaakop. "I always recognize an Arab's turd; it's sort of curved at the end and a bit crumbly."

"Mm . . ." murmured fat Nigul doubtfully, almost pressing his nose into the shit and sniffing fiercely. "From the smell this should be from a Spanish horse."

"A Spanish horse doesn't make droppings like that!" argued Andreas. "Believe me I know a stable hand who sometimes brings me turds from his gentleman knight's horse. You know I collect them. Come to my place. I'll show you a Spanish horse's shit. Of course there's a slight similarity to the layman's eye, but I could see right away that this horse is actually from England. Notice those varying brownish tones."

Conversations like that took place every week, because there were plenty of iron men and they rode around widely. At first the men's passionate interest in horseshit had seemed a joke to me, but later on it just made me yawn. I was carrying on calmly sowing, when suddenly I saw a village girl scurrying toward me in terrible pain across the field.

"Help, help!" she screamed. "Snakebite! A snake bit Katariina!"

Katariina was the same flaxen-haired girl who had asked me about the snake-king's crown up on the swing hill. I understood well what was expected of me; everyone knew that I had once healed Magdaleena's leg. It wasn't really difficult—I only had to call the snake that had bitten the girl—but I didn't want to do that. I was afraid of meeting some adder who knew and remembered me. What kind of look would it give me, Leemet, who had repeatedly spent the winter with the adders, been one of them, but was now wearing village clothes and smelling of porridge? I watched the girl approaching ever closer and just wanted to run off in the other direction.

But naturally I didn't do that. The bite might be serious, and I couldn't let silly flaxen-haired Katariina die.

"Where is she?" I asked the girl, who had now reached me and was panting terribly. "Lead me to her, quick!"

"Ah, ah!" gasped the girl. "I ran so fast I can't even stand up anymore!"

She fell spread-eagled on the field and fanned herself with her skirt.

"Well!" I said. "You were in a frightful hurry, but now you want to lie down!"

"Ah, ah, I'm right out of breath," panted the girl, and finally was able to pull herself together enough to explain to me where Katariina got bitten.

I left the foolish messenger gasping on the field and rushed off on my own. Katariina wasn't far away; it was quite a wonder that running over such a short distance would tire the silly girl out. But she was of course fat, with short legs.

Katariina was sitting on a rock, white in the face and looking like she was about to faint. Seeing me, she couldn't even speak; she only pointed to her leg, where two large bloody tooth marks were visible, and whimpered like a little animal.

I quickly hissed the appropriate words, and the next moment who should come crawling out but Ints.

"You!" I muttered, taken aback. I had been prepared to meet some familiar adder, but seeing Ints was unexpected. The tooth marks on Katariina's shin suggested a small snake. Ints was of serpentine royalty, and if a king snake stung anyone, it was only in the throat, and after that it wasn't possible to save anyone.

"That's the snake, yes!" Katariina was quick to scream. "The same disgusting creature!"

"Be quiet!" I snapped over my shoulder at the girl, looking awkwardly at Ints. I felt terrible shame because of my village clothes, but Ints didn't seem to pay much heed to that: she curled into a ring as always and said, "Hello, Leemet! Nice to see you again. That's just why I gave this girl a jab, to lure you here; otherwise you wouldn't show yourself. You know I'll start by sucking the venom out of the girl, and then you and I can have a calm chat, without this girl whining."

"Please do," I replied, and Ints crawled up to Katariina and quickly cleaned the wound.

"Doesn't hurt anymore?" I asked the girl.

"No," said Katariina, looking spellbound at Ints's head, which wore a splendid crown. "So that's the king of the snakes!"

"Yes, but you can't have the crown!" I said. "Now go home."

"What about you?" asked Katariina.

"What about me? What I do is none of your business. Get going!"

Katariina departed slowly. We waited for her to disappear behind the trees; then Ints wriggled up to my knees and put her head in my lap.

"We haven't met for a long time," she said. "How have you been, old friend?"

"Not bad," I said, trying to be vague. Life in the village was not a thing I could or wanted to talk to Ints about. "How's my mother doing?"

"She's doing fine; she's living with us now. She came in the winter and stayed. She said she wasn't used to living alone. You could come and see her; she misses you badly."

I nodded, but Ints didn't let me say anything, and carried on. She told me about Salme and Mõmmi, and for his birthday how my sister had sewn him trousers that are put on with so many buckles and hooks that Mõmmi couldn't take them off, and now Salme could be sure that the bear won't be unfaithful when left on his own. Ints told me that during the winter Pirre and Rääk had grown very old and their fur was now gray all over, so that when they crouched in their tree they looked like two big cobwebs, and that her own sons were now big and living their own lives and they had new, very beautiful skin. As she told me all this, I realized suddenly how terribly I longed for the forest and how much I missed my mother. The sight of Ints cleared my head. That whole world that I had regarded as forever lost to me was wriggling and undulating around me in the slender person of Ints, and at once I felt like a fish that had fallen back into water.

Suddenly I was no longer able to understand the reasons that had forced me to leave the forest and move to the village. In whose name had I been sitting here through a whole winter, many long months, among stupid villagers, while in the forest my own mother in the flesh, my sister, my friend Ints were waiting for me? All right, Magdaleena's son, little Toomas, was to be my pupil, but that didn't mean I had to spend the rest of my life in the village, that I couldn't visit my mother and friends. I no longer feared sympathy; for me it would not be terrible even for Ints or Mother to start talking about Hiie. On the contrary, right now I almost even wanted that. For a while now I had been living with swollen eyes, but now suddenly the swelling had abated and I saw everything again just as before.

"Ints, I'm coming today to visit Mother," I said. "It's wonderful that you've been looking for me. Otherwise I might have stayed here moldering who knows how long."

"Yes, I thought too I ought to simply pull you out of here," replied Ints. "Now you can come back to the forest and forget this village."

"No, not quite," I said, and I told Ints about Magdaleena's son, whom I had to teach Snakish, so that there would be at least one person in the world who would understand it after my death. Ints listened and sighed.

"You're always hoping," she said. "Leemet, old boy, don't take this the wrong way, but I think humans are finished. It's sad and it's nasty, but what can you do? You and your family are exceptions, and if you teach that boy, he too will be an exception, but the rest of humanity are like little blue tits that have pecked their own wings off and are now hopping about on the ground like feathery mice."

"All the more reason," I said. "At least one of those tits has to learn to fly too, so that it will be known in the future: a tit is a bird, not a mouse. At least one!"

"Well, but a child of the village . . ." Ints began scornfully, but I interrupted her.

"Ints, I do understand that that child should have been my son with Hiie," I said. "But that child wasn't born, and never will be."

"Yes, I know," said Ints quietly. "I thought you wouldn't want to talk about Hiie."

"It's not important anymore. As you said, you've already pulled me out of that old life. Let's go to the forest now. I'm longing to see my mother."

Mother had grown older, but otherwise was much the same. She fell on my neck when I squirmed into the snakes' cave, squeezed me as much as she could and then let me go, took a look at me amazed, cried "oy!" and ran away.

"Mother, what's wrong?" I called after her. "Where are you going?"

I tried to follow her, but Mother had vanished. She had rushed out of the cave and it wasn't possible to find her among the trees.

I went back into the cave to talk to the adders, to look over Ints's children and praise them for how much they'd grown, and after a while Mother came back.

"Mother, where did you go?" I asked—and then I noticed that Mother's cheek was bloody and her clothes torn in places. "What happened?" I cried in astonishment.

"Nothing, nothing!" Mother protested. "Everything's all right."

"All right, when your cheek's gashed? Did someone attack you?"

"Oh, it's just a little graze," said Mother, trying to wipe the blood off with her sleeve. "Nobody attacked me. Who would do that? This is my home forest! I simply fell over."

"Where did you fall?" I wondered.

"Out of a tree. My foot slipped on a branch you see. I must be getting old," said Mother, almost apologetically. "I used to climb like a squirrel; no tree was too tall for me."

"But Mother, why did you have to climb a tree? I don't understand. I haven't seen you for a long time, and when I come, you climb a tree."

"I wanted to fetch you some owls' eggs," replied Mother, taking two beautiful big eggs from her pocket. "They were your favorite when you were a child, and all the time you were away I was constantly thinking that when my dear boy comes home I'll offer him owls' eggs, as I used to when you were still small. Now you've come, and I didn't have a single owl's egg! I was embarrassed, so I ran to fetch them. There's an owls' nest just near here, but you see I was so excited that I stumbled and tumbled out of the tree. Lucky I didn't have the eggs in my pocket yet, otherwise they would have broken. So I climbed again and got the eggs anyway. There you are, son. These are for you."

I took the owls' eggs from Mother's hand and simply held them for a while, unable even to thank her. Mother was still rubbing her cheek; the wound was deep and the blood kept on oozing.

"Now look, my son comes visiting after a long time, and like a fool I'm bleeding," she muttered, almost angrily. "Oh, I'm useless! I'm sorry, Leemet. I know how horrible it is with my torn cheek . . ."

"Mother, what are you saying!" I cried. "I should be asking your forgiveness that I haven't shown my face for so long. You understand . . ."

"I understand!" interrupted Mother. "Leemet, I understand it all. My poor child . . ."

She sat down beside me, took me by the waist, sobbing, and asked, "But why don't you eat your owls' eggs? Don't you like owls' eggs anymore? Are the village foods better?"

"Mother, what do you mean!" I said. "How can you even ask that? Nothing compares to owls' eggs!"

"So suck them empty then!" Mother pleaded. "They're at their best right now."

I knocked a hole in an egg and sucked the yolk out. Mother looked at me with mournful satisfaction.

"At least I can still offer you owls' eggs, dear child," she said. "When everything else is gone, you can always eat your fill at your mother's house."

She drew her sleeve once more over her bloody cheek and got up decisively.

"Suck the other egg out and come and eat," she said. "Roast venison is waiting for you, darling."

Thirty-Two

 t really is ridiculous how persistently everything in my life has gone awry. It reminds me of a bird that builds itself a nest high in a tree, but at the same time as it sits down to hatch, the tree falls down. The bird flies to another tree, tries again, lays new eggs, broods on them, but the same day that the chicks hatch, a storm comes up and that tree, too, is cloven in two.

If I looked back at my life now and didn't know that all these events actually took place, I would say it wasn't possible. Ordinarily it wouldn't be. But that's just it: I haven't lived an ordinary life. Or rather, I tried to, but the world around me changed. To put it metaphorically: where there was once dry land, the sea now splashed, and I had not had time to grow gills. I was still gulping air with my old lungs, which would not serve me in this watery new world, and therefore was always short of air. I tried to get away from the encroaching water and burrow a hole for myself in the shoreline sand, but every successive wave obliterated my efforts. What could I do about it? Nor is the bird to blame for always failing to hatch when its tree collapses. It acts as all birds have acted for thousands of years, and it chooses to nest in the same oak trees in whose crowns its ancestors have always hatched their young. How is it supposed to know that time has run out for those trees, that they are rotten from within and that even the smallest gust of wind can split these once-mighty giants?

That day in the snakes' cave really showed me that once again I had found a little patch of dry land that was not reached by the flood. Mother was beaming with joy; she kept bringing me delicious venison, a food I had not tasted for so long. Moreover this was not just ordinary roast venison, but Mother's roast venison—and I couldn't wish for anything tastier. Ints and the other adders were with me. We chatted as friends, and for the first time in over half a year I heard myself laughing.

"Mother, will you be staying here to live with Ints?" I asked.

"Oh no, now that you're back, I'm going to our own home of course," replied Mother. "Being there alone was simply so sad, but with you it's a different matter. You will be staying in the forest?"

I thought for a moment. Moving back to the village seemed completely repugnant. Sitting here in the snakes' lair, all of life there looked so foolish and alien. But I didn't intend to give up Magdaleena and little Toomas. Especially Toomas. But also Magdaleena, I was as fond of her as before. I believed that Magdaleena would forgive me if in the future I only visited her—sometimes in the daytime, to engage with little Toomas, sometimes at night, to spend time with Magdaleena. After all, she did believe that I was a werewolf and a sage and whatever else. I had things to do in the forest; she had to understand that. "Yes, Mother, I'll be living at home," I said. "But I'll still visit the village occasionally. I have a few things to do there."

Mother nodded vigorously.

"Yes, yes, yes, of course, of course!" she concurred. "Do exactly as you want. You're the only man in our family and you decide. Don't be afraid. I won't forbid you! If you have to, you can stay a longer time in the village. I won't stand in your way."

"Mother," I said. "To tell you the truth, I've had it up to here with that village."

At that moment Ints nudged me with her nose and said, "Leemet, we have visitors. Your friends seemed to have tracked us down to the cave and are now prodding at the burrow."

"You mean—villagers?" I asked. "Won't they ever leave me in peace?"

"Yes, they will," replied Ints, laughing soundlessly in her adderish way, jaws open and the strong fangs prominently on show. "I don't believe they'll get this far, so if you don't want to see them, you can stay and wait calmly. We'll go and settle this business quickly."

"No, I'm coming with you," I said. "I want to see who it is. They might have Magdaleena with them . . . I don't want anything to happen to her."

"Then come with us, because we don't know your Magdaleena and can't protect her," said Ints. "Let's take a look at our dear guests."

We crawled along the tunnel in the direction of the entrance, I on all fours and the adders slithering in front and alongside. Quite soon I heard voices. Someone said, "I don't know how far we have to crawl."

"Quite horrible in this darkness," said a female voice, which I thought belonged to Katariina.

"It doesn't matter," said a third voice, apparently Andreas. "Whatever these snakes do to us, we are all wearing the holy cross. As soon as we see that king of the snakes, we'll grab his crown off his head and take off."

"He might take off after us," said the voice I'd heard first, which I now attributed to Jaakop.

"He won't," replied Katariina. "The monk told us that if you pull the crown off the king snake's head, he turns into a stone."

I let out a sigh. Poor idiot! To even think up such rubbish!

"How will we divide up that crown?" asked Andreas. "Will each of us get a third?"

"I should get more!" said Katariina. "I was the one who noticed where Leemet went off to with that nasty snake. I was the one who crept after them and saw how they wriggled down this burrow."

"Yeah, but you didn't dare to go after them alone. That's why you asked us along," said Jaakop. "So it should be divided equally into three. To you for finding it and to us for coming along to help you and taking the crown away. You're a girl anyway; you wouldn't dare rip the crown off the king snake's head!"

"I would!" argued Katariina. "Look, I've even got an ax with me. If the crown doesn't come off by itself, I'll chop the snake up and then yank it off."

"That's the same girl that I stung today," whispered Ints into my ear. "Never a good idea to waste good venom on a bare shin. If you're going to bite, go for the throat."

And that is what she did. With lightning speed she rushed out of the darkness and sank her fangs under Katariina's chin. All three crown hunters screamed, but Katariina's scream died away quickly.

"Take out the holy cross and brandish it!" yelled Andreas. "The holy cross . . ."

In the next moment Ints's father attacked. The powerful king of the snakes swung at Andreas like a falling tree and fixed on his face so that his fangs pierced Andreas's eyeballs.

Jaakop, who witnessed this, let out an unnatural scream and fled toward the mouth of the cave.

A couple of young adders wanted to go after him, but Ints's father said there was no need.

"Let him go to his village and tell them what happened," he said. "Then they will know, and they won't come back. Filth! So they want my crown! Are they really so hungry that they have nothing left to eat?"

"They believe that it will give them the power to understand the language of birds," I said dolefully. For some reason I was terribly embarrassed, as if I had been one of the crown thieves. In appearance they were deceptively like me, after all.

"The language of birds?" wondered Ints's father. "What foolishness! But it's no wonder they get these peculiar ideas. They live in their own village. They have no one to talk to, because they don't know Snakish . . . Then they gradually go mad from loneliness. Poor mites."

I was staring at Katariina, whom just that morning I had helped to cure from a snakebite. Now she was stung again, and this time I couldn't have helped her. She was dead, and so was Andreas. I suddenly felt sorry for them. Why did they have to crawl in here? Why couldn't they stay in the village with their rakes, bread shovels, and querns? If they had built a new world for themselves, they should have left the old one alone, forgotten about it. And yet apparently they couldn't do that; they were still enticed by the king snake's crown and the language of birds and all the other secret things that were strangely distorted in their memory and had taken on an entirely different, foolish importance. They had not got quite free of their own past—but when they really did come across something ancient, they didn't know how to treat it. They were like little children admiring a spring, leaning in too far and falling headfirst into the water. So now here they lay, mortally wounded. The snake-kings could have been their brothers, but they became their murderers.

"I have to go," I said to Ints. "I'll go to the village. Tell my mother that I'll be back by tomorrow evening at the latest."

"What's wrong?" asked Ints. "Are you sorry for them? They wanted to chop off my head with an ax. Should we have licked the soles of their feet?"

"No, it's all right," I said. "They got what they wanted. I simply need to do a few things in the village before I move to the forest for a longer time."

"Might I be able to come with you?" asked Ints. "I'd like to see that boy that you want to teach Snakish. It's nighttime now and people should be asleep, so I can perhaps get inside without any fuss."

"Come on then," I said. "Let's not hurry. I'd like to walk in the forest a little. I haven't been here for so long."

We didn't rush, and only got to the village in the middle of the night. We walked slowly up to Johannes's house. I pushed the door open and whispered to Ints: "The child is asleep in the cradle. Have a look, then get away; I don't want old Johannes to wake up and see you."

"I don't either," replied Ints and crawled over to Toomas's cradle. She writhed up the side of it and looked down on the sleeping child.

"Leemet!" she hissed a moment later, so loudly that I was sure everyone would wake up and there would be unpleasant confusion. "Leemet!"

"What's wrong with you?" I hissed back. "You'll wake people up!"

"Leemet, come here!" shouted Ints. "This child is dead!"

I had a feeling as if someone had splashed scorching hot water in my face. I was at Ints's side in an instant. It was so horrifying that I started screaming. The infant's throat had been bitten through. The whole cradle was full of blood.

"Magdaleena!" I screamed at the top of my voice. "Magdaleena, what's happened?"

I rushed to Magdaleena's bed, which for the past half year had been mine as well. But this night Magdaleena was there alone, lying on her back, her hair over her face, and her neck broken.

I don't remember what happened next. For a while I knelt in the middle of the room, and before my eyes Ints's head was wavering; she had raised herself up and was hissing comforting Snakish words at me, the kind that make you sluggish and drowsy. I drew my hand over my face and looked around. The room was completely ransacked, the benches and table split to splinters, and the spinning wheel broken in two.

"What happened?" I asked Ints, yawning, as the Snakish words were having their effect as always.

"You went mad," replied Ints. "You were yelling and roaring and you turned the place upside down like a trapped stag. You rampaged. You smashed everything to bits and overturned it all. You left only the corpses alone."

I cast a glance at Toomas's crib. It didn't reveal its gruesome contents in any way, but I felt my insides turning once again.

"Should I calm you down again?" asked Ints, who could apparently see in my eyes that another wave was coming over me.

"No, no need to," I replied, and felt myself how my lips were curling into a ghastly grin. "There's nothing here left to smash up."

"I'm sorry," said Ints. "I didn't know these people, but I'm truly sorry. What an utter bastard!"

"Who?" I asked. "Who's the bastard? Tell me, Ints. Who put them to death? Some wolf? Again, some damned wolf?"

"Not at all," declared Ints. "You lost your head when you saw these corpses, and you didn't look at the marks properly. No wolf has been here, and actually these are not tooth marks at all. No animal has teeth like this. Go and look for yourself!"

"I won't, Ints," I said. "I don't want to see them anymore. I can't. Tell me who killed them, then I'll go and grab the creature and torture it to death."

"Your old friend Ülgas the Sage," replied Ints.

I burst out laughing at this unexpected turn, and felt my whole body shaking with rage.

"So he's alive then?" I cried.

"Yes, unfortunately he is," replied Ints. "You cut off half his face, but that didn't kill him. I've seen Ülgas a couple of times in the forest. The old man looks loathsome, but he's alive. I think he's become demented. He walks around naked, filthy from sleeping in the mud, and the last time I met him, he'd attached claws made of sharpened twigs to the sides of his fingers. He waved his arms about, snapped his false fingernails, and muttered something confused. Leemet, it's those same wooden claws that have ripped these people's throats!"

"Then let's go and find him," I roared like a fanatic, leaping up and throwing myself against a wall so that the house trembled. Again I was seized by a strong urge to fling things around and smash everything in sight, but Ints's calming hiss made my head a little clearer again.

"So where is old Johannes?" I suddenly thought of asking. "Is he dead too?"

I cast a glance at Johannes's bed, but it was empty.

"He can't have been at home," said Ints. "Interesting—villagers don't usually roam around at night. Anyway it saved his life. Yours too. If you'd been sleeping here, there wouldn't be much of your throat left either."

"That beast did go for my throat!" I said, opening the door with a bang. "The sacred grove! It's the sacred grove that he can't forgive me for, and it's revenge for half of his face. Today he paid me for chopping off his whole face, but I've chopped off only half. I have to hurry and knock the rest of his block off. No job should be left half-done, and what is done today is not a care for tomorrow, as Uncle Vootele used to say. He was rotting beside me, Ints, and since that time there's been a strange stink in my nostrils. I've never told you this before, but now you know; it's a kind of smell as if I were rotting myself. But look. I'm not rotting at all. It's everyone else who's perishing! Everyone else around me! They're dying and rotting, and I have to go on living with the smell. Well, what's left for me, still alive!"

I ran out of the room and stuck my knife into the trunk of a tree growing in front of the house.

"I'm still alive!" I screamed.

"Leemet, come on now," said Ints. "Let's go and look for Ülgas."

"Ülgas!" I growled. "Yes, he must be hunted down and killed, because he's still alive, not dead as he should be, because I'm the last! I'm the last one, not he!"

I bayed at the moon, as my grandfather on his island had done, and marched behind Ints into the forest, hacking with my knife at branches around me, blind with rage.

Thirty-Three

oming among the trees, Ints raised her head and hissed piercingly. She was calling other adders.

After a few moments, snakes started crawling toward us. Ints put just one question to them all: "Where is Ülgas?"

The first snakes that wriggled there were unable to answer. That didn't matter; there were many adders, and nobody could move about in the forest without being seen by snakes.

About the tenth adder nodded at Ints's question and said, "I saw him just a few moments ago. He was huddling under that old linden tree, the one that was split by lightning two years ago, eating wood sorrel."

"Thanks very much," said Ints. She looked at me.

"Well, Leemet?" she asked. "Did you hear that?"

"I did," I said. I had been waiting impatiently, massaging my knife in my palm. I had even cut a wound in my own palm, but hadn't felt the pain as the blood coursed down my fingers. "Ints, remember. I'll kill him myself. Today I don't need your fangs."

"I understand," replied Ints.

Then I ran to the burned linden tree, by the straightest path and as fast as I could, paying no heed to the branches poking my face, and Ints stayed at my heels.

Ülgas was indeed there. If I hadn't been blind with rage, his appearance would have moved me. The sage was naked and his skeletal body was covered by something like bark, formed of mud, with twigs and other rubbish that lay around the forest clinging to it. Half of his face was gone and the former wound was covered by a large scar, strikingly pink next to the brown skin, and somehow moist looking. To his fingers Ülgas had tied short whittled spikes; with these he was pulling wood sorrel from the ground and stuffing it, along with the soil, in his mouth, quietly mumbling to himself. Some of the wood sorrel had got tangled in the sage's beard and hung from his chin like a green mold. This was not a human. This was a monstrous animal or even a plant, a tree from the grove come back to life, gobbling herbs and staring at me with a single crazed eye. He recognized me and screeched, "You! You chopped down the sacred grove! The dogs of the grove won't forgive it. They'll chew you to a pulp!"

He raised his hands threateningly, stretched out his wooden-clawed fingers, and barked.

"You see, the dogs of the grove know your scent!" he squealed. "They'll come and bite you to death!"

I noticed that the wooden claws were brown with caked blood. No doubt this beast had ripped Magdaleena's and little Toomas's throats with these same spikes. I felt the world going hazy before my eyes. Hatred was choking me; I stepped closer and with a single stroke lopped Ülgas's left hand off. The sage squealed shrilly, but didn't retreat; he tried to grab me with his right hand. I jumped out of the way and the wooden claws groped at the air without hitting me. A moment later the other hand fell among the wood sorrel. I stepped on it and screamed, "These aren't dogs, you son of a bitch! They're your own hands, with which you killed two innocent people! You're a beast, a beast!"

"I wanted to kill you!" screeched Ülgas, pressing his blood-dripping stumps against his belly. "I spied on you and lay in wait, but just that night when I came after you with my faithful dogs, you weren't at home. But the dogs wanted to eat. The sprites had promised them blood, and so they quenched their thirst. No one can oppose the sprites; they are all-powerful!"

This tale was so horrifying that I pulled Ülgas upright, and with one stroke split his stomach open. He let out a whine and collapsed to the ground.

"Bastard!" I panted. "Understand once and for all that there are no sprites and no dogs of the grove; there's just your sick brain. Why didn't I kill you before? All this is my fault!"

I put my hand inside Ülgas's wound and pulled out his intestines. The sage roared and howled. I tied the guts to the old linden tree and kicked the old man in the face.

"Now crawl around your own sacred tree, you villain!" I screamed. "Crawl until all your guts are twisted around it! Crawl, you hear me, crawl!"

And he did start to crawl! A bloody and loathsome trail formed behind him, the long slimy entrails hung out from his belly and stretched ever longer. The wood sorrel beneath the tree turned brown from Ülgas's blood. His tongue, now blue, hung from his mouth, as he drew himself slowly forward, wheezing, his single eye bulging and lifeless. Having done two circuits around the linden, he was drained of blood.

"That is obscene," said Ints, turning her head aside in disgust.

"Come and eat and enjoy your feast, honorable sprites and dogs of the grove," I screamed at the top of my voice. "The table is set! Come and have a good taste; this dish should please you! Be sure to come, for today you're being fed for the last time! Tomorrow no one will remember you. From tomorrow you're condemned to oblivion and starvation! Last chance, respected sprites! Dogs, aoouu! Where are you? Come and gobble!"

Only flies flew there at my bidding, a great cloud, and soon Ülgas's corpse was covered in a humming black crust.

"Let's get out of here," said Ints. "This is making me sick."

I spat on the flies and the remains of the sage, turned around, and marched away.

"Where are you going now?" asked Ints, crawling along beside me.

"I don't know."

"Are you going to the village?"

"No."

"Are you coming to our place?"

"I don't know. I don't know."

I would have liked to just keep going and fall off a precipice where the path met a cliff, just like that day when the wolf killed Hiie. Again it was all over, again it was all past, again everything had vanished.

"Come to our place first," suggested Ints. "You should rest. You can lick some of the white stone and go to sleep."

"And then?"

"Then what?"

"When I wake up?"

"I don't know, Leemet. We'll think about that later. Please, come with me."

I didn't argue with Ints. So be it, I would go to the snakes. Actually it didn't really matter where I went or what I did.

We went back to the path that led to the snakes' cave and went along for a while in silence. Then suddenly Ints hissed in alarm.

"I can smell smoke!" she hissed. "Hurry! Something strange is going on!"

I too could smell fire. I started running, and my self-confidence began to return. Smoke and flames blazing between the trees might mean that again I had the opportunity to fight, to bury my own dejection in blind rage for revenge. Who could be making a fire there? Maybe some monks and iron men? I took out my knife and fingered its handle greedily.

"That smoke is coming from our cave!" hissed Ints beside me, horrified.

We rushed onward and in a moment we were there. It was not iron men or monks at all. It was a group of villagers, with Johannes at their head, and Pärtel and fat Nigul and Jaakop and all the other men. They were standing in a circle around a huge fire that had been built right in front of the burrow leading to the snakes' cave, and in the fire one could see several charred adders, which had evidently tried to get into the fresh air from the smoke invading the cave. The only thing they had achieved was to exchange death by choking for death by roasting.

My mother was in the cave too! And Ints's father, the king of the snakes! And her children, whose crowns were only just starting to grow on their heads! They were all there and couldn't get out.

Ints hissed in a horrifying voice and attacked the villagers from behind. One boy screamed and fell to the ground stung by Ints, then an old man roared, covered his face with his hand, and collapsed. Ints struck out to the right and the left, and fear and confusion reigned among the villagers.

"Help! Help!" they screamed. "A snake from hell has got out!"

I didn't intend to let Ints fight alone. I summoned all the power in my lungs and rushed to help her. With my first blow I cut through fat Nigul's throat and the greasy man fell down like a sack. I hit out heedlessly in all directions, and sometimes I had to close my eyes as the blood sprayed in my face and stung my eyes. There were too many people, and if I lunged in among them, I couldn't defend my back. Someone flung a stone at my neck, my skull cracked, and I fell to my knees, spitting blood that came from I knew not where. The world revolved before my eyes, and before I had time to collect myself, I was bound up. Ints was lying beside me. She was still alive and moving slowly, but her backbone was broken.

I saw my old friend Pärtel bending over us, in his hand a heavy club.

"These snakes are actually not all that dangerous," I heard him saying. "You just have to bash them in the middle of the back and they're done for. It's as delicate as a twig: one bash and the backbone is broken."

"Pärtel," I mumbled, spitting blood. "Don't you remember? This is Ints! She used to be your friend!"

"A snake can't be a Christian's friend," said Pärtel. "You're the one who makes friends with snakes, because you're a pagan. That's why you're going to be burned at the stake!"

"You're a monster," I said quietly. Pärtel's words didn't frighten me. They could burn me if they wanted to; everything was finished anyway, and now they had killed my mother and Ints's whole family and all my old friends the adders. There was no one left, only Ints with her broken back; no doubt they were about to make an end of her as well. Very well, let them do it; it was painful for me to watch Ints wriggling helplessly in the dust like some miserable earthworm.

"Hold on, friend!" I hissed to her. Ints looked at me; she understood what I had said, but she was no longer able to answer. Spasmodic convulsions ran through her body. I could see she was in great pain.

"Shall we throw the snake in the fire?" asked Jaakop, stepping closer and shoving Ints with his foot.

"No, better to take it to an ants' nest," answered Pärtel. "Then you can see some fun; the ants will pick the flesh off the bones so clean as if the damn snake was boiled in a pot."

"You wretch, you beast, you turd!" I screeched on the ground, as Pärtel, accompanied by the village men, lifted Ints's twitching body on a forked branch and took her away somewhere. I recalled how scornful Ints used to be about ants' nests, and now she had to fall into such filth. Those same repulsive and stupid tiny insects would eat her flesh, carry her off bit by bit into their tiny passageways and leave only a white skeleton. Those wretched little creatures did not know Snakish—just like the villagers, thanks to whom they now had such an abundant meal to eat. The villagers had grown bold. They had summoned the courage to kill the adders, and now there was nothing left to impede the onslaught of the new world. To their deaf ears Snakish words were of no use; they offered no defense against something so crude as a stick, with which it is so easy to smash the delicate back of an adder.

Pärtel had said I would be burned at the stake, and I had expected to be thrown into the fire there and then. Evidently the village men had other plans. Johannes stepped up to me, looked at me seriously for a while, then bent over me, and said, "Now you see, Leemet, what happened to you because you rejected the sign of the holy cross. If you had let the reverend brothers christen you, the devil would not have got you in his power."

"I am not in anyone's power," I murmured.

"But why did you attack us then?" asked Johannes. "Why did you kill so many honest Christians?"

"Because those Christians killed my friends," I retorted. "Do you know, you stupid old man, that you murdered my mother today?"

"Your mother? We were destroying snakes, Satan's most loyal servants. Yesterday evening those disgusting animals killed two of our village people, young Andreas and dear Katariina. That crime could not go unpunished, so we suffocated the whole damned lot of them in their own cave."

"My mother was in that cave too," I said.

"In the snakes' cave?" cried Johannes, brandishing his cross. "Then she was like a snake herself—or worse still, a witch! In that case she got her rightful fate!"

"Old man," I said. "Today I ripped out the guts of a fairy-worshipping misfit like you. I'd sorely like to plunge a knife into your belly too and yank your liver out, and then bash you in the face with it."

"You talk like a wild animal," said Johannes scornfully. "And that's what you are. Your soul is so strongly in the grip of the devil that you have no hope of partaking of God's mercy and appreciating his grace. You attacked us together with your friend, the diabolical snake, but God protected us and guided the hand of bold Jaakop, who threw a stone at you. Your demonic lord is powerful, but he can't prevail against God. Soon, at dawn, we'll burn you, up on the hill of swings. Magdaleena can pray for you, but I'm letting you perish. For too long I've allowed a henchman of Satan in my own house; I have been weak and sinful myself."

I burst into bitter laughter, although I would rather have wept—but I had no more tears.

"Magdaleena won't be praying for me," I screamed into Johannes's face. "Don't you worry about that! Ah, so that's why you weren't at home when Death came visiting your house! You were in the forest, killing snakes! Indeed your God did keep and preserve you and led you out of great danger. Rejoice now, old man, and thank your merciful God, who loves and protects you so much!"

"What are you talking about?" asked Johannes uneasily. "When did Death visit my house?"

"In the night, of course!" I sneered, sobbing. "Death comes at night and asks, 'Knock-knock, is Elder Johannes at home?' But he isn't. So where is he? The elder is cooking adders in the forest! He has much work to do; his God has chosen him for it! But Death doesn't want to go home with empty hands; he wants to fill his mouth with something! There's no Johannes, no Leemet. But Magdaleena and Toomas are at home! Oh how nice! A beautiful girl, a little boy! How tasty! The sprites and the dogs of the grove also want to eat! God is busy gobbling up the adders that Johannes is cooking for him; well then, the sprites and the dogs can taste human flesh. All these beings are so hungry! They have such big bellies they're never filled!"

The last words I absolutely roared, rolling on the ground as if I were on hot coals. The villagers stood around me in astonishment, not knowing what to do. Johannes was trembling.

"Have you . . ." he stammered. "Have you done harm to my child?"

"Not I!" I bellowed. "It was the dogs of the grove, the sprites and the other gods! They drink blood. Not I! I only know Snakish, nothing else, and I'm the last one who does. The very last. For there aren't even snakes anymore!"

I burst into laughter, and the next moment I tried to bite the leg of the man standing nearest to me. The man leapt aside in alarm.

"Don't be afraid, you bastard! My teeth aren't venomous; you won't die of them!"

"He's gone mad," said Johannes, his face pale. "Let's take him with us and go quickly to the village. I'm very worried about Magdaleena."

"Too late, you old idiot, too late!" I brayed in a truly demented way, smashing my head against the ground. "Too late!"

"Faster!" screamed Johannes, tearing at his beard. "Faster!"

Thirty-Four

hen I now think back to that night, the only feeling that prevails in me is a slight embarrassment at my own wild behavior. So much needless shouting and desperation! After the wolf bit Hiie to death, I should have been used to all those close to me being lost. The people and animals that I cared about were disappearing like fish that had swum too close to the surface; a single flash of the fin and they were no longer visible. One by one they were diving to a place I couldn't follow. That is, of course, I could have followed them, just as it is possible to fling yourself into the sea to try to catch a fish, but you never will. One day I will follow all my dear ones, but although we're heading in the same direction, we will never meet again. So great is the sea and so tiny are we.

Today I can think about it completely calmly. I'm not happy to recall the memory of losing Magdaleena and little Toomas, Ints and the other adders, and my mother all on the same night. But that was how it had to go, for the death of a rotten tree is always rapid: one violent shake and over it goes. Its broad canopy, which for many years rose up in its place in the forest, has suddenly vanished. For a while there is a space in the forest cover, but soon the space is filled by new growth, as if nothing had happened.

I no longer feel bitter that I have no one to whom I can pass on the Snakish words. On the contrary, I feel a gloating pleasure. Let them live without Snakish, those future generations of humans, whom I will never see, nor would I want to! Stupid, poor little insects, I don't envy them. Of course they don't know what they're missing by not knowing Snakish—but I do. I know much more besides, but my foolish successors will never be able to know those things.

Such a thought gives me pleasure. I try to imagine just such a new world as I lie for hours in my cave—a world without Snakish. Sometimes I laugh to myself, because that future seems so ridiculous to me; it's a world in which I have no place. Strange and unpleasant.

I am not bitter about the past. For me it is already too far away. The people whom I knew and loved then have by now become just pictures on the wall of Pirre and Rääk's cave. I look at them but I don't feel anything.

That early morning when I was carried up to the village I was far from such peace of mind. I snarled and shrieked like a wolf cub and cursed everyone I saw, until one scruffy villager gave me such a bludgeon across the chops that some of my teeth flew out. Then I fell quiet and only spat blood, but the rage boiled within me as before, and I felt no pain, in either my smashed mouth or my limbs being cut to ribbons by cords.

My screams, however, were as nothing beside the roaring that broke out when the gang of snake incinerators finally reached Johannes's house and could behold all the work and effort that Ülgas the Sage had that night committed indoors. Elder Johannes ran up to me, shook me, and screamed, "You killed them! You bit them to death! You're a werewolf. I've known it all along!"

I was not surprised or enraged by these accusations; I had been anticipating them. I didn't intend to answer Johannes at all, but since he wouldn't leave me alone and kept on tugging at me, I mumbled through bloody lips: "Leave me alone, you idiot. I didn't kill them. It was a mad old bugger like you, and if it satisfies you, then I've already torn out his entrails. He's paid for his evils and one day you will too."

"You or some other pagan from the forest, what does it matter?" bellowed Johannes. "You're all werewolves! What's wrong with you? What evil spell forces you to do such horrible things?"

"Never mind. Let's toss him into the fire and burn him," said Jaakop.

"We will, but what use is that to Magdaleena and her son, who was a little knight besides?" wailed Johannes. "No revenge will save them."

"You're right there, old man," I said, thinking of Ülgas. I could have killed him a hundred times; it would be of no use to Magdaleena or Toomas. It was in every sense an unequal exchange: the life of a miserable mad sage counted for nothing to anyone; not a single man or beast mourned him. He should have been dead long ago, but instead he went around killing those who should have lived.

People came and wrung their hands, weeping to heaven. They were certainly wondering how all those gods and jesuses, on whose help they counted and for whose protective support they had moved out of the forest, could now suddenly allow such a dreadful crime to happen. Especially on the same night when they had been so abundantly burning snakes in accordance with their God's commands. I knew it wasn't hard at all to find answers to their troubled questions. I had after all lived for years in the forest with Ülgas and remembered well the ease with which he explained everything to Tambet, using for that purpose the invented sprites and his own wily understanding. The villagers didn't trouble themselves for long about it; thanks to Johannes they had an explanation.

Naturally I turned out to be the guilty party. God could not allow an unchristened pagan to live in the village, someone who was, moreover, a werewolf, and as a punishment for this he withdrew his protecting hand from Magdaleena. As for little Toomas, God did not punish him, but indeed blessed him. The little child of a foreign knight was simply so dear to God that he called him to him with all speed and sat him on his knee. The villagers were of course only too happy to believe that hogwash, just as the late Tambet had taken as pure gold everything that spilled from between the slovenly teeth of Ülgas. There was no longer any need to worry about this little child; he was in good hands. In fact they felt a secret pride that such a baby had been born right here, in a simple Estonian village. They spoke of a miracle, and they discussed whether the child's old clothes might be used to keep foxes away from chickens.

Magdaleena was of course mourned, but everybody agreed that one must not stray from God's commands and that my acceptance into the house was a great sin. Since I was conveniently within reach, they all came, together and one by one, to spit on me, and piled up a tall heap of brushwood, on top of which they intended to roast me.

This pyre, however, reminded me of the bonfire at my wedding, which I had built myself from the remains of the grove. On that occasion my mother was cooking venison on it; now there was no more mother, and these dullards were unable to catch deer with their wretched spears—so they had nothing left to roast but me.

I wasn't afraid of death—and why should I be, after all these gruesome events?—but I would have liked to carry on raging. At least I would have liked to do away with Elder Johannes for good, as well as my old friend Pärtel, whom I was now more inclined to call Peetrus. I would have liked to pour out my rage, to harry and plunder, and not to just be burnt to a crisp as a helpless lump on a pyre. But I was very tightly tied up, so that I couldn't even move. Only my mouth was free, but just now Snakish was of no avail. It would have no effect on the obtuse minds of the villagers.

The men grabbed me and hauled me toward the pile of brushwood. I saw that Peetrus was holding one of my legs and I said, "Who could have guessed that one day you would throw Ints on an ants' nest and me on a pyre?"

"What can be done," replied Peetrus. "Everyone chooses their own fate. I invited you to the village long ago, but you came too late and you remained wild."

"Do you really believe I'm a werewolf?" I asked, now in Snakish. "You know that werewolves don't exist!"

For a while Peetrus didn't answer, and I believed that he didn't understand the Snakish words anymore.

"Today in the world they believe that they do exist," he said suddenly, but in human language, not Snakish, as evidently his tongue, gone soft with village food, couldn't pronounce it any longer. "All the new people believe it. Therefore so do I."

"What are you talking about, Peetrus?" asked Jaakop, who was holding my other leg. He hadn't understood my question.

"I'm saying that werewolves are horrible monsters," shouted Peetrus. "Over you go!"

I flew into the heap of brushwood. The sun was shining on my face; I turned my face aside and saw my grandfather flying over the village buildings.

The first one he got hold of was Jaakop, who was just then preparing to light the pyre. Grandfather grabbed him by the head, heaved him into the sky with him, and sank his fangs into the man's neck. Jaakop fell convulsing back to the ground and within a moment he was dead.

Then Grandfather grasped an ax tied to his belt and wielded it up and down several times. The villagers screamed and fled in horror in all directions.

"Are you dead, Leemet?" shouted Grandfather.

"No, Grandfather, I'm alive!" I shouted back. "Just tied up. Set me free!"

Grandfather hovered down to me. His wings were as wide as an eagle's, and the human bones were woven together with miraculous skill. Grandfather stretched out his long nails and cut through the cords with them.

"When I saw you all bloody on the pyre, I thought you were dead and this was your funeral," said Grandfather. "But now I understand that these rascals wanted to burn you alive. Come, boy, let's do a little poisoning!"

He took a long knife from his belt and tossed it to me.

"Something for you to jab with," he explained. "You don't have proper teeth, poor child."

He tilted back his head and howled, and then rushed to attack the villagers. I leapt down from the pile of brushwood, my heart full of joy. This was just what I had been longing for. Grandfather had arrived just at the right time. Merely holding a knife was driving me mad with excitement. I whooped with joy when I got to kill the same bulky peasant who had slapped my mouth earlier, and I rushed on to catch others.

The villagers didn't put up resistance. They didn't even try to fight; the arrival of my flying grandfather had caused such fear in them that they fled as fast as they could. We pursued them and ran them down in the tussocks, but while we were running after one of them, others were scurrying who knows where and it was no longer possible to find them. I searched everywhere for Elder Johannes and Peetrus, but they had vanished like a stick in water. Finally I stood panting, for all the village men had fled, and apart from Grandfather hanging in the air there wasn't a soul to be seen.

"Not bad!" shouted Grandfather when he saw me stopping in bewilderment. "The best view is from up here. Be prepared. There are iron men riding this way!"

A moment later I could see them too. There were six iron men, in the middle of whom rode a fat man on an extremely fine horse and wearing clothes dripping with jewels, on his face a haughty, disdainful expression. This was undoubtedly some important lord, perhaps a bishop. I didn't know. He couldn't be the Pope at any rate, for Johannes had said that the Pope lived in the city of Rome. We weren't very interested in who precisely he was. I went and stood in the middle of the road, knife in my hand, while Grandfather flew in a great arc up behind the iron men. They hadn't noticed him yet, and they hadn't wanted to notice me either; they steered their horses straight in my direction as if I were mere air through which they could calmly ride. Evidently they were hoping that I would humbly step aside, but I didn't, and I met the enraged gaze of the mighty lord. He had noticed me, screwed up his face angrily, and made a movement with his arm as if to wipe me out of the way like rubbish or a fly. One knight drew a sword from his belt.

Then I hissed—and the horses started to break their stride. Two knights fell right out of the saddle. The others managed to remain on their horses' backs, but that was their misfortune, for then it was much simpler for Grandfather to strike them on the head with his ax. He came whirling and howling like that ancient bird whose picture I had seen in the Primates' cave. Twice he struck with the ax, and two iron heads rolled along the ground. He turned right around, and set off again. Meanwhile, I stabbed to death the two knights who had tumbled from the saddle.

The only one left alive was that proud lord in his costly garb. His expression was no longer lofty or scornful at all; now he stared in sheer amazement at the extraordinary winged monster of whose existence he had never heard. This monster looked truly horrifying, with wings made of bones, as well as a long gray beard and two aged, blood-red eyes, sharp crooked claws like a bird's, and unnaturally short legs, actually mere stumps. This must have been a ghastly, unearthly sight in everyone's eyes but mine, for whom this monster was my earthly grandfather.

I stepped up to the proud lord and killed him. Grandfather flew to a nearby tree and perched on a branch of it. Now he looked even more like a bird.

"All of them!" he said with satisfaction. "Pretty good for a start. Oh, my boy, how long I've waited for this day!"

"What kept you so long?" I asked. "I was beginning to think you weren't coming after all."

"I couldn't get those last bones I needed from anywhere!" shouted Grandfather. "It was terrible! After you left, not a single person came to my island. I lay in wait for days on end by the seashore, but not a single ship came. The months passed; a whole year went by. I thought I would go mad. I had these wings nearly ready. You had brought me the windbag, and yet I couldn't get going. There were animals on the island, but their bones weren't right, although I did try for a few weeks with deer and goats. Nothing came of it. You know, boy, I tell you honestly so please don't take offense, but if you and your girl had come upon me at that moment, I would have killed you and put your bones to use. So what if you're my grandson and dear to me. I was completely blind; I was even thinking of ripping a bone of my own from my side and putting it on the wings, but there was nothing to take. In the end I wasn't even eating or drinking; I was just sitting like a rock on the shore, staring at the sea. Ten days ago I finally saw, far out at sea, one ship, but it wasn't sailing toward my island at all, but in the other direction. I jumped into the water, swam like mad, and caught up with the ship. I hauled myself aboard and killed the whole crew, crawling around like a crab, with a long knife in each hand. But then there was a new problem. How to steer the ship to the island? I was alone! Yes, I fumbled around and rowed and tried every trick, but still it took a whole week before I got home. Then I needed another couple of days to clean the bones and finish off the wings. My hands were shaking as I put those little bones in place. You know I had a sort of feeling, like a man who's been starving for a long time, when finally a decent hunk of meat is put in front of him. Tears of joy came into my eyes. Finally the wings were ready. I tied the windbag on to them and took off. I screeched with joy and slaughtered a couple of seagulls just for the hell of it. I flew straight here and found you on the pyre. Why did they want to burn you?"

"They thought I was a werewolf," I replied. "A person who can change into a wolf."

"Why would a being in their right mind change into a wolf?" wondered Grandfather. "That would be stupid. I certainly don't want to be ridden on or milked."

He laughed resoundingly.

"Not that you could squeeze any milk out of me!" he roared. "What isn't there isn't there! I'm not a wolf, but a proper human, and I'll carry on raging so the ground is black!"

He looked at me inquiringly.

"Are you coming with me?" he asked. "Are we going off to fight, as we've been doing? Or are you stuck to your woman and prefer to sit at home?"

"I have no one to be stuck to," I said.

"Ah—that girl who came visiting me with you? Hiie, or what was her name? Didn't you take her after all? She was pretty."

"She was, Grandfather," I replied. "But she's dead."

Grandfather hummed.

"Oh, I see," he said. "Well, now . . . A pity of course, but at least you're free and you can do what you want. Are you coming with me? Of course, first we have to go home and say hello to your mother, my daughter. We can't put that off, because who knows what the future may bring."

"Mother is dead too," I said. "Just about everybody is dead, so let's go right away, Grandfather. There's no point in waiting."

Grandfather stared at me.

"She's dead too . . ." he repeated. "While I've been sitting on my island, you've been living your whole lives through. Well, what's left to me but to get even. Let's go, boy. We're in a real hurry!"

I stuffed the knife back in my belt and set forth, Grandfather floating overhead like a giant bat. The pile of brushwood lay behind us, as did a heap of dead bodies. In this way in the end the brushwood became an ordinary pyre after all; at least I hope it did. By the time the remaining villagers ventured out of their hiding places and started burning the dead, Grandfather and I were already far away.

Thirty-Five

e went to war. It was an odd crusade, because we had not the slightest hope of winning. In the end there were just the two of us against the whole wide world. We were like two aphids who could gobble up individual leaves voraciously, but with no possibility of felling the whole tree. We moved from battle to battle and had no place to turn back to after a successful strike, to rest and to report to those back home: We won! We were warring only for our own pleasure and because we couldn't do anything else in the new world. We didn't need anyone's gratitude or a place to lick our wounds. We kept rushing onward, attacking everyone who stood in our way, killing, stinging, beating, and bashing. We were both burning with a crazed fever, and we knew that when the fever abated, it would mean death.

We were reckless and we didn't retreat in the face of any opponent, for we had no thought of saving ourselves. It made no difference whether we fell now or later. We paid no attention to defense. We were indifferent whether an arrow pierced our chests or whether some iron man could run us through with his lance, and this carelessness was to our advantage. We overcame opponents who were several times our number in strength, and we left their corpses stacked on the road. The arrows they fired in our direction didn't hit us; the sword blows swished past us. We roared with laughter; we howled like wolves and hissed like snakes. We never washed ourselves, and the spattered blood of our enemies covered almost our whole bodies, so that we looked like flayed carrion. We were no longer human, but the living dead, who had risen from death to harass the new world, and that new world could not rid itself of us.

On our travels we passed through villages, and if any villager stood in our way, we would lash out at him. We noticed how, when they saw us, they would abandon their rye fields, toss their scythes over their shoulders, and run for their lives, and we yelled abuse after them. I shouted to them that the Frog of the North had returned, and Grandfather took vigorous turns in the sky, at which the villagers fell to their knees and begged for protection from their new God against the forest-sprites. Nobody helped them and if we had wanted to, we could have bludgeoned them all to death.

I watched as they clustered together, trembling, and I recalled the time when Mõmmi and I went to peep at the beautiful village girls on the edge of the forest, secretly lusting after them, and how I hated the stupid village boys with whom the girls had mischievous conversations, while I, being so wise and understanding the ancient Snakish words, had to suck my thumbs on my own in the woods. I would sit at the edge of the forest, longing and ashamed, and I felt so lonely. And I felt the same now when I saw these same girls—or rather, not actually the same, but very similar—snuggling behind the thickheaded boys, looking to them for protection from Grandfather and me.

Protection from me! Ridiculous! What could be done to me by those miserable creatures whose tongues were too fat and blunt to pronounce Snakish words! How silly these girls were, and how deeply ignorant was their choice! All the same, sometimes I didn't resist, and rushed into a village and killed as many men as I could, and Grandfather, who never shied away from combat, followed, hooting at me. Let these new people once again see the powerful Frog of the North. Never mind that it isn't the real one. This will do! Let them feel one last time the force of his attack! But while the Frog of the North had once fought for them, now he was fighting against them, since they had changed sides and forgotten Snakish. The ancient memories, which in the meantime had degenerated into mere legends, were reawakened and proven to be true. You girls have made the wrong choice! This new world is weak; a bite from the old world will break it like a cobweb. Can all these new tricks save your thickheaded men? No, they are strewn across the ground, and in the evenings Grandfather makes drinking cups out of them by the fire. They wanted a modern life, but they ended it in an ancient way; people will drink water from their skulls, just as they did thousands of years ago.

Do you see how strong and powerful the old world is? Admire it. Love it, girls!

But instead they weep, yell, and flee without looking back. And they're right, because the old world isn't actually strong. Grandfather and I are just like an unexpected snowfall in summer, which in one night can destroy the buds and leaves, but that melts away in the next morning's sun. We would kill and burn, but then we would leave a village. The girls would come from their hiding places and carry on living, finding new men for themselves and bringing forth children, none of whom understood Snakish.

I understood perfectly how useless our fighting was, and every time after destroying yet another village I had the same sick feeling. But I still had battle fever in my blood, and didn't suffer for long.

In the end, who cares? Let the whole new world go to hell!

In the main we concentrated on the iron men. We invented new ways of hunting them. We made use of goats and deer, which we drove into the path of the knights using Snakish words. The iron men could never resist the urge to hunt, and they rushed on horseback after the animals. We would direct the deer and goats into a thicket, where we would lie in wait. And then we would make a quick end to the iron men.

In the evenings Grandfather would polish his skulls while I would roast goats over a fire, because the work of killing all day makes you tired and hungry. We didn't have any use for the skulls, because we couldn't take them with us; otherwise we wouldn't have been warriors anymore, but a walking pile of beakers, our noses just poking out of the heap of beautifully carved skulls. Right at the beginning of our crusade I told Grandfather that there was no point in fussing over skulls, but Grandfather didn't agree.

"It's an old warrior custom that you don't just leave your enemy's skull lying around, but you polish it up nicely and make a cup out of it," he said. "It's polite. If you have enough time to kill a man, then you'll find the time to polish his skull."

"We can't haul all these skulls around with us," I argued.

"That's true," agreed Grandfather. "I didn't say that we have to carry them with us. We simply make the cups ready and leave them on the road. Anyone who wants to can take them and drink from them."

So Grandfather would spend the night making chalices out of all the dead people who passed through our hands, and in the morning we would leave them by the roadside, like a peculiar kind of droppings, which gave the message that two warriors from the old world had passed through.

One evening we came upon a wide clearing on a path winding through a forest, in the middle of which towered a stone stronghold of the iron men. Grandfather alighted on a branch and looked me in the eye.

"Shall we take them on, boy?"

"Of course, Grandfather!" I replied, and we croaked with laughter. It was a completely crazy notion for two men to attack a fortress, within whose walls dozens of mail-coated warriors were moving. Grandfather could of course fly over them, but in order for me to help him I would need at least a ladder, and before I could get over the tops of the walls, more arrows than a bird has feathers would certainly be fired into my body. What could Grandfather do alone up there if the iron men were able to go into hiding in the towers and pepper him with arrows? The decision to attack the fortress was mad, but we didn't care.

"Where do we start, Grandfather?" I asked.

"Let's wait till night," replied the old man. "I smell the scent of bears. They keep them inside the fortress. If the bears come to help us from inside, we'll attack from the outside, and tomorrow I'll have a lot of work polishing all the skulls that will fall our way today."

We hid in the forest until the sun had set; then I crept to the fortress and hissed a few Snakish words. Those words can be heard through walls and simply must be answered, even when one doesn't want to betray oneself, so it was no wonder that I immediately heard a weak and somewhat confused hissing, the sort that bears produce.

I crawled up to where the hissing was coming from and pressed myself against the wall.

"How many of you are there?" I hissed to the bears.

"Ten," came the reply.

"Good!" I said. "We have a plan to capture the fortress and kill all the iron men. If you help us, you'll be released from your prison and you can run back to the forest."

"We're not in prison," came the response through the wall to my great surprise. "We like it here. The chief of the iron men feeds us well."

"Idiots!" I hissed angrily. "Is there so little for you to eat in the forest? What fun can it be to sit in the cellar of a stone fortress behind bars! Don't you long to see the sun?"

"We go for a walk every day," the bears answered. "We all have a strong leather leash. Oh, how beautiful it is! It has silver studs on it, attached by colored ribbons. No bear in the forest has such a beautiful collar. They're made over the seas, in foreign lands. No, we're not going to escape from the fortress."

I hissed a couple of insulting words to them, but the bears didn't seem to care; evidently they were very satisfied to be able to tell someone of their incredible good fortune.

"It's very fine here!" they explained. "All the women have terribly splendid dresses that make them so beautiful it could drive you mad. Sometimes they take us into the banqueting hall, where all the people eat and dance and we're allowed to look on and we're given bones. Not only that, they're teaching us to dance! There's a hunchbacked man here who wears on his head a big forked red cap, with a golden bell on each tip. He's a foreigner, no doubt an important and famous man, who always talks the most at feasts and does somersaults on the floor. Then they all laugh and applaud him. At the feasts he plays on a pipe, and not just with his mouth. Oh no! He can even blow on the pipe with his bottom! Yes, he pulls down his pants, gets down on his back, shoves the pipe into his arsehole, and plays so prettily that all the other lords and ladies roar with laughter and clap their hands together. This same man is our teacher; he blows his pipe and shows us how to move in time to it. He's very kind, and if our dancing goes well, he strokes us and gives us dainty things to eat. Of course we try our very best, because we appreciate that dancing is in fashion these days. All the great lords dance, although not as well as this hunchbacked man with the little golden bells. Oh, how we want to be like him! We want to learn to dance well, because then maybe we'll get a forked red cap and golden bells that tinkle so prettily. We have one great dream. That is we'd like him to teach us to play on the pipe with our mouths and our arseholes, but we're afraid that we're too clumsy and inexperienced for that. We've lived too long in the forest. But who knows!"

"You should kill all those lords and ladies, starting with the hunchback," I declared.

"No!" replied the bears. "We love and admire them, especially our dear teacher. We don't want to kill anyone at all; that's an old-fashioned custom. They only still do that in the dark forest. Now we're dancing bears."

"You should kill all those lords and ladies, starting with the hunchback," I repeated pitilessly.

"Oh no, we won't do that!" came the reply. "Stop it! Who are you anyway, to be demanding such horrible things from us?"

"I'm a man who knows Snakish," I said, sibilating a very long and complex hiss. For once it was silent beyond the wall, and then some crazed roaring was heard. And so there should have been, for that Snakish word took away the bears' free will and awakened their wild desire to kill.

Without being able to see through the wall, I knew what was happening to the bears now. Their eyes were burning, they were foaming at the mouth, they were twisting their bars, biting their collars, and breaking with a roar into the castle. They were striking down every person who stood in their way, smashing up the rooms and flinging down the guards from the walls. The iron men were certainly putting up a resistance, trying to stop the unexpectedly crazed animals, calm them down, and if that failed kill them. They were battling with the bears, and when both parties were running with blood, when the bears had over-turned the whole castle and murdered most of the iron men, Grandfather and I would come in and finish off the job.

I could hear horrid screams from the fortress and I understood that the bears had attacked the humans. Maybe just now they were eating the piper with the red cap who had been teaching them to dance. Now he would be dancing between the paws of the flock of bears driven mad by Snakish words.

I saw one guard flying headfirst down from the wall, and I realized that at least a few bears had got up there. I took a look at him—all was well; he'd broken his neck—and hissed to

Grandfather. He had already realized that the time had come and came flying like a great owl.

"Take hold of me. I'll lift you up!" he shouted, and I clung to Grandfather's hips and felt myself rising into the air. A moment later I was on the walls and a large bear was rushing toward me, its jaws open.

I quickly hissed what was necessary, and the animal turned around to seek another victim, one who didn't understand Snakish and couldn't command it. It found an iron man and leapt onto him, but the iron man ran a spear straight into its heart, and the animal rolled down the stairs into the courtyard.

A moment later it was followed by the victorious iron man, the useless spear still in his hand, for Grandfather had stung him on the cheek straight from the air.

There was actually very little left for us to do, because the bears had ravaged savagely, and although their corpses also lay everywhere, they had killed off nearly all the residents of the fortress. We finished off the last ones.

It only remained to calm the bears down. There were two left, and they were so enraged that they wanted to attack each other. One single Snakish word stopped them, and the bears looked around uncomprehendingly, astonished at the sight of their own bloody paws.

"All right, bears!" said Grandfather. "Finished! The fortress has fallen and all the iron men and their women are dead. You can slip back into the forest."

The bears stared at us dumbly.

"Didn't you understand?" asked Grandfather. "Go back to the forest! You've been good; you did a lot of damage. You can keep the dead bodies if you like. Only the heads belong to me. I won't give you those to gnaw on."

He hovered low over the courtyard of the fortress and fished out from the heap of corpses the body of a slightly built hunchbacked man, from whose head hung a red two-pronged cap. Grandfather ripped the cap off him.

"Remarkable head, this one," he said. "Knobbly like a tree root. This skull will make a splendid chalice."

"That's the piper!" said one of the bears. "He taught us to dance and gave us sugar. What have you done?"

"We haven't broken a single bone in this little man's body," replied Grandfather. "There are a bear's tooth marks on his throat. Maybe you bit him yourself."

He cut the piper's head from the body and stuffed it in his pouch.

"The head for me, the body for you," he said cheerily. "Enjoy it!"

The bears stepped slowly up to the piper's dead body. They nudged it with their snouts. One of the bears took the red cap with the golden bells in its teeth and put it on the corpse's chest. They licked the little man's hands. They wept.

"Eat up quickly, you fools!" shouted Grandfather from up in the air. "We're going to set fire to this heap of lumber now! Boy, come down. I'm putting fire under the eaves!"

A little while later the conquered fortress was blazing and a cloud of sparks rose to the moon. I strode along the road, lit up by the firelight, Grandfather flapping overhead, and I heard him saying, "It's good that they built their house in the middle of a wide clearing, so there's no danger of the forest catching fire."

I was just then wondering whether the bears had left the fortress or stayed to lick their teacher, who was able to play the pipe with his mouth and his arse. But then—what did it matter to me? Let them get scorched and perish if they wanted, together with their hunchback of the golden bells and his pipe.

Who would pity this new world?

"Grandfather, there's another fortress!" I shouted, pointing ahead. "Now it's its turn!"

"Exactly!" replied Grandfather. "Let's attack it now, while we're still warm from the last commotion!"

"Are there any bears here?" I asked.

"Can't smell them," answered Grandfather. "But what the hell, we can do it ourselves."

"Yes we can!" I agreed, feeling the blood rushing to my head. "Let's go, Grandfather! Lift me up over the walls again like last time!"

I grabbed hold of Grandfather and we flew. The fortress, which had seemed in the dark to be a fuzzy dark lump, was right here. I was ready to get into the thick of the iron men's spears and swords, to struggle for my life, and if necessary even to perish. It was all the same to me, but looking at the building from above I suddenly realized that this wasn't a knights' castle but a monastery.

"Grandfather, we're in luck!" I yelled. "There aren't any iron men here, only monks! Grandfather, this will be just like going mushrooming; just cut with your knife!"

One monk was staring at me from down in the monastery yard. He raised his hands and shouted something in his incomprehensible language. The monastery bells started ringing. Not half an hour passed before they were silent again.

Thirty-Six

e took off our clothes and dried them by the fire, because capes wet with blood would get cold at night. Grandfather fiddled with his skulls, and when he'd got one mug ready, he threw it over his shoulder and started to make a new one. Chalices made from skulls were strewn across the forest floor like pinecones.

I went to sleep, and when I awoke to the first rays of the sun, Grandfather was still awake, still occupied with his skulls.

"Grandfather, you haven't slept at all," I said drowsily as I sat up yawning.

"I don't have time for that," replied Grandfather. "I've been squatting too long on the island; if I wasted my time sleeping now, I wouldn't get anything done. Boy, eat your fill and get dressed. I'll soon finish off the last mug and then we'll keep on going and give the iron men another thrashing."

"Yes, Grandfather," I said. "We'll keep on going."

Yet it so happened that as we moved ever onward, so we were also moving backward, for the forest roads were circuitous, and we didn't even try to keep moving in a certain direction, but wandered wherever our feet took us and where there was a chance of meeting iron men or monks. And so I discovered on one such evening that the surroundings were somehow familiar, and having walked a while longer I recognized the place where the wolves had killed the villagers' sheep, the place where I had met Magdaleena, and fallen in love with her for the first time.

"Grandfather, we've come back home," I said. "Our old shack isn't far away."

"Do you want to call in there?" asked Grandfather.

I didn't.

What would be the point. Mother wasn't there anymore. Then it occurred to me that Salme should still be in her own cave with Mõmmi. I hadn't seen my sister for ages. When Grandfather and I last set off from here, I didn't have the time or the desire to say farewell to her. To tell the truth I hadn't even thought of her, for in the terrible avalanche that had buried everyone dear to me in the course of one night, I had quite forgotten that Salme was still alive. "Grandfather, how would it be if we went and visited my sister?" I suggested. "You could get to know your other grandchild."

"The one who married a bear?" asked Grandfather. "Let's go; you have to be close to your relatives. They're your own flesh and blood after all."

We turned off the road into the forest. It wasn't comfortable at all for Grandfather to fly there, for his wings were too wide and tended to get caught on branches. So he rose higher and hovered over the treetops like an eagle.

"Give me a shout when you get there and I'll come down!" he called from above.

"I'll do that," I yelled back. "We don't have much farther to go, that is if Salme's still living in her old cave. Let's hope she hasn't moved out."

Grandfather didn't reply; he was circling over the forest, swooping down and then rising up again with powerful strokes of his wings.

"Boy!" he shouted. "There are iron men in the forest! I can see them! What do you think? Shall we give them a little flogging? Then you'll have a few nice skulls as gifts to take, and a couple of shanks for the bear."

"Why not, Grandfather!" I shouted back. "Where are they?"

"Over there!" he yelled, and in the next instant he was roaring in a terrifying voice, because from "over there" an arrow had come flying from a bow, and pierced his shoulder. Grandfather howled, grabbed the tail of the arrow in his teeth to pull it out, but only bit the arrow in two and fell tumbling out of the sky, catching his wings against the tree branches and ending up lying in the middle of a pile of bones formed from the wings.

"Grandfather, are you alive?" I screamed and rushed over to him, but at the same time the horsemen galloped out from behind the trees, together with their bowmen. They had been hunting in the forest, and their hunt had succeeded, because although they hadn't found a single deer or goat, they had hit my grandfather. It had been a really good shot, and I had to admit that the iron men's weapons were effective. At that moment, of course, I had no time to admire their bows; I had to protect my helpless grandfather lying on the ground, and myself, because the iron men were already attacking. I hissed, and the horses started to bolt as always, and iron men tumbled from the saddle. I rushed at them, and in a few moments my knife was red with blood. But there were too many of them and Grandfather was no help to me. I killed at least half of them, but they were all around me, and at one moment I felt something terribly heavy and sharp falling on my head, my skull crackled, and before I lost consciousness I had time to think that my skull would not make a good chalice, because now it had a hole in it. I fell spread-eagled and didn't remember anything more.

My head hurt terribly. It was the only thing I was aware of. I would have liked to faint again, to be rid of this pain, but I wasn't allowed to. Someone hurled cold water on my face. I opened my eyes with difficulty and saw the grimacing face of an iron man before me. He said something and laughed.

Seeing that I was conscious, he grabbed me by the collar together with another man and forced me upright. I saw that my clothes were covered all over with blood from my head wound. I was very weak and couldn't even stand up, but I didn't need to. The iron men tied me to a tree and the ropes kept me from falling.

Now I could look at my surroundings. We were on the seashore—at about the place where my sea journey with Hiie once began, which took me to Grandfather's island. Back then, the shore had been full of angry wolves, and somewhere in the waves the malevolent Tambet had stood yelling curses at us. Now instead there were iron men. There were many of them and they were all looking toward me conversing among themselves and seemed to be waiting for something.

"Boy, how are you doing?" asked a hoarse voice. I turned my head as far as the cords allowed and saw Grandfather. He was also tied to a tree, standing upright for the first time since he lost his legs. His clothes were bloody. The broken end of the arrow still stuck out of his shoulder and one of his eyes was poked out.

"Now they're going to make an end of us," said Grandfather. "Shitty maggots they are! I got badly bashed when I fell, and when I came around, these badgers had already tied me up. I still managed to bite some of them, so they died on the spot. Then they poked one of my eyes out and bludgeoned me in the mouth to make my fangs fall out—but they have strong roots. Finally they called some fat man with big tongs to pull out my teeth, but I stung him in the hand, and they didn't approach me anymore. Now I'm going to die with my fangs, as I've lived with them. Boy, you and I have had fun. We got properly stuck into these shitbags. A pity that I got this stupid arrow in my shoulder, otherwise we could've given them even more pain."

"Never mind, Grandfather," I consoled him. "It all had to end some time anyway."

"I didn't get to see your sister," he continued. "That's a real pity. There are so few of us left and, well, not even those few can get together."

He was silent for a while, stared at the iron men and hissed loudly. Farther off, some horses tethered to trees started whinnying and trying to tear themselves free.

"No use in Snakish words either," said Grandfather. "The horses might bolt, but these shitbags won't sit in the saddle."

Drums started to roll. Two men came up to us. They had in their hands a leather strap, with which they tied Grandfather's mouth shut, probably so that Grandfather couldn't use his fearful fangs. Grandfather whined bitterly. The men untied him from the tree, and without legs Grandfather collapsed onto his stomach. The iron men laughed and hooted with pleasure.

"Hold out, Grandfather!" I said. "You know I'm very proud of you. If there were more men like you, the Frog of the North would be flying in the sky by now and would gobble up these grinning idiots like a swallow eating a gnat."

Grandfather looked at me and winked his only eye. Then he was dragged away.

On a little mound had been built something like a wooden floor. That was where Grandfather was taken. His clothes were ripped off him and he was shoved onto his stomach. Then his hands were chained to the edge of the floor and one man sat on his stumps, to keep his lower body in place.

Then one of the men took a large knife and cut through Grandfather's back, starting at the neck and ending at his buttocks.

Grandfather snorted with pain and wriggled.

The man with the knife put his hands inside the wound and rummaged there. Grandfather's eyes turned inside out, but he did not lose consciousness. Blood flowed across the wooden floor and dripped down onto the sand.

The man on his back had found his ribs. He took a small ax and started smashing them up.

Then he grabbed hold of them and pressed them outward, so that the ribs bristled out of Grandfather's back like birds' wings.

The iron men on the shore fell to whinnying approvingly and shouted something, flailing their arms as if trying to take flight.

Grandfather was still alive; he hit his head against the floor. Suddenly the strap holding his mouth shut broke. Grandfather roared and sank his teeth into his tormentor's leg, which he had inadvertently left in front of his face.

The man shrieked in a strangely shrill voice and collapsed beside Grandfather. The others rushed to his aid, but after several rapid convulsions the bitten man fell silent. He was dead.

At the same time Grandfather hissed frantically, lashing out with his jaws in all directions and spitting dark blood.

One of the iron men leapt up angrily, grabbed a sword, and chopped Grandfather's head off. It rolled down off the wooden floor and, since it was wet and viscous with blood all over, it was quickly covered with sand, so that it might simply be seen as a large sandy rock.

Grandfather's trunk was lying contorted in a pool of blood. The body lacked legs and bony wings grew out of the ripped back. These were human bones, and therefore quite suitable for flying; they lacked only a windbag.

But of course there was no longer anywhere to get that from.

Then it was my turn. The men came and untied me from the tree. I was still very weak and started reeling, but they wouldn't let me fall and dragged me quickly from the tree to the torture rack. One of the men slipped on the large puddle of blood covering it and my wounded head collided with his shoulder. I could not hold back a scream.

The men laughed and said something in their own language, which I didn't understand, but I assumed they were saying something like: "That was nothing, just a joke. The real pain is still coming!"

I didn't doubt that, because quite clearly it was going to be horrifically unpleasant to have your back cut open and your ribs bent out. But there was nothing to be done; Snakish would not help here.

They bound me up exactly as they had done with Grandfather and one of the men took up a knife. I squeezed my eyes shut and bit my lips, anticipating the first flash of pain on the back of the neck and everything that must follow it.

But the jab didn't come. Nobody touched me, and the strange noises coming from the iron men enticed me to open my eyes again.

They were all still standing just as before—on a wide stretch of the shore, where they could best follow the bloody scene being played out. They were no longer laughing or craning their necks at the murder rack. Their heads were cocked toward the sea, and their necks seemed to have become unexpectedly heavy. There was something uncertain in their stance, giving the impression that their heads threatened to roll off their shoulders, and to prevent that and preserve their balance, they had to take a step toward the sea. And then another. But that didn't help. Their necks would not straighten up; their heads drew them willy-nilly toward the sea, and though the iron men even tried with their hands to point their own heads in a different direction, they did not succeed and they were forced on the path their heads had chosen.

I looked at them from behind. Even those men whose task was to torture me to death no longer stood on the killing floor, but staggered like the other iron men step by step toward the sea, for that was where their imperious heads were tugging them. Their faces reflected extreme alarm and fear; they didn't understand what was going on here with their willful skulls and where they were being drawn to. They squealed and clutched their own throats, but an unknown force that at this moment controlled their heads was stronger than they were.

I was still bound up, and couldn't pull my hands and feet free of my fetters, although I tried with all my might. Here was an excellent opportunity to escape. I could not know how long such a miracle would last, and I struggled for all I was worth.

But the fetters were strong, and there was nothing for me to do but lie and hope that this bizarre event would take the iron men as far as possible from me.

Their heads led them farther and farther toward the sea; the first iron men were already standing with their feet in the water and kept having to step ever farther. Now they were screaming in mortal fear. Ever farther into the sea their heads directed them, and they stumbled on like tethered sheep. They struggled to resist, but kept walking, for they had no strength to resist. One iron man of short build had now got so far into the sea that the water was up to his neck: he screamed like a madman but couldn't stop, and the next moment the water rushed into his mouth. He disappeared into the waves.

Now the iron men all fully understood what kind of end awaited them; they howled and yelped, and one man took a knife from his belt and slit his own throat with it, to rid himself of his own murderous head. Thus he was saved from drowning, but not from death, and his body collapsed into the sea and colored the water red.

The other iron men were not so resolute. They screamed and yelled, waved their arms to heaven, and begged for help from their God, whom they obviously imagined to be lounging up there beyond the clouds, wondering at this peculiar scene. Nothing helped them. One by one they vanished into the sea, and when the waves had taken the last iron man's head, an unexpected silence fell on the shore.

I took a deep breath. I was alive. I had been saved, though I didn't understand how. What force had driven these men into the water, to voluntarily drown themselves? I didn't know, and for the moment that wasn't my greatest problem. I had to get free of my fetters and get out of this pool of blood into which the iron men had forced me, facedown. I wriggled like a snake, but the fetters would not give way.

"Wait, we'll help you!" came a voice. I turned my head and saw two snow-white forms lumbering ahead with difficulty. It was Pirre and Rääk! For the first moment it was even difficult to recognize them, so old had they become. Their long white fur fluttered in the sea breeze and turned the Primates into great downy chicks. They were walking heavily, swaying and stumbling, but finally they reached me and with their long yellow paws unpicked the knots.

I sat up straight and groaned, for my wounded head was again hurting and my now-free limbs were throbbing. But that was nothing compared to the happiness that my back was still intact and my ribs still hidden within my body. I embraced the Primates and declared, "I thank you. How did you know to come here just at the right moment?"

"Everything can be seen from our tree," said Pirre. "It's only that we haven't been walking for ages; that's why it took a lot of time. If we'd been a little quicker, we would have had time to save your grandfather too."

"Yes, it's our fault that he had to die," said Rääk. "We're too old and terribly slow."

"What happened to those iron men?" I asked. "What drove them to drown in the sea?"

"Lice," replied the Primates proudly. "Our dear lice, which we've been studying and training all our lives. We sent them into the iron men's hair and gave the command to move toward the sea. The lice started moving, and drew the men with them. It isn't possible to stay in one place when a thousand lice want to go somewhere in your hair, not if they are given the power by the right Snakish words, the kind that humans no longer remember, not even you, my boy. Special old Primates' Snakish words, which have power even over insects. They saved you and led the iron men into the water, sadly together with the poor lice, who sacrificed themselves for you, Leemet."

"I'm very grateful to them," I said. "But who will you study and teach now that all the lice perished in the sea?"

"Oh, there'll be new ones born," opined Pirre. "But we're hardly likely to train them any longer. We really are too old. Besides, there would be no point, because after us no one will be able to talk to the lice anyway. Those lice that led the great throng into the sea today were the last ones that could be directed with Snakish words; the lice of the future will live their own lives and won't obey anyone any longer."

"So it is," I replied. "All things come to an end. Today the last human with fangs died, the last human who could fly. In the future they'll think that such things were possible only in fairy tales."

I lit a big bonfire by the seashore, on which I burned my grandfather's corpse. Then I said good-bye to the Primates, promising to come and see them soon, and went into the forest, to look for my sister and think about how to go on living.

Thirty-Seven

ccording to Pirre and Rääk, Salme should still be living in her old cave, and that is where I bent my steps. Although some trees had grown taller and others been broken by autumn storms, it was easy for me to find my sister's dwelling. I pushed aside the deerskin hung in front of the cave entrance and stepped inside.

"Hello!" I said in a loud voice. "Still recognize me, sister?"

"You, Leemet!"

Salme got up in astonishment. The cave was dim, but still you could clearly see that in the meanwhile my sister had grown very old. Her hair hung untidily, faded and tangled like last year's grass stalks under melted snow. Her leather cape was torn in places and sooty, as was her face. I must have looked quite taken aback at my sister. At any rate she seemed to feel a slight embarrassment at her appearance; she pushed away the wisps of hair in front of her face.

"I wasn't expecting you," she mumbled in confusion. "Such a long time . . . Where have you been? I really didn't know . . . Nobody ever visits us anymore. Mõmmi, look who's come!"

Mõmmi looked at me and I looked at him, and I saw the fattest bear I had ever chanced to meet. He took up half of the cave. Fat had swallowed up his snout, so that his face was flat and round, as if he were no longer a bear but an eagle owl. Thick folds of flab hung everywhere on him. It seemed that the old fur couldn't manage to cover the gigantically expanded body, and so there were yawning hairless gaps on his skin in several places, like stains or large scabs. Mõmmi's feet weren't visible at all; a rampant paunch covered them like soft brown moss.

"Hello, Leemet," mumbled this mountain of lard, peering at me with his tiny eyes, which hardly peeped out over the fat cheeks. "Haven't seen you in a long time. Nice that you dropped by! Salme, offer your brother something to eat."

"No, thanks!" I said rapidly. In the presence of such a fat animal I couldn't force a mouthful down my throat. Besides, I could smell a strong stink, which filled the whole cave and nauseated me. I presumed that Mõmmi had grown so obese that he couldn't go outside the cave to do his business, and therefore would shit right there. I imagined what might be hidden in that fat furry belly, which covered the bear's feet like flayed skin, and it made me feel bilious. What's more, I saw gnawed bones lying everywhere along with rotting bits of meat; for some reason Salme had not bothered to throw them out, and they stank as well. Great black flies were strutting all over and rubbing their front legs together, as if expressing pleasure at such a grand feast. Mother would never have tolerated such slovenliness and filth in her own shack. Apart from being disgusting, it was shameful. What would the neighbors say about such squalor!

But at the same time I understood that neighbors were what Salme and Mõmmi no longer had. They lived all alone in the forest. Nobody stepped over their threshold; nobody had anything to do with them. They were the only people left in the forest—and actually Mõmmi was a bear. No wonder, then, that their residence had gone wild and was now more like an animal's lair than a human dwelling.

"You really don't want to eat?" asked Salme. "We've got venison. But it's not cooked right through like Mother's roasts. You see, Mõmmi likes it a bit less well done, and so nowadays I don't cook the meat so long. It's juicier that way. Want to try?"

From somewhere behind the inglenook she brought out an enormous dish of cold venison, which to my mind was practically raw. No force on earth could have made me taste it.

"No, Salme, I've just eaten," I lied. "Let's just chat. Mõmmi's grown quite a bit, I see."

"Yes, he has; he can't get outside. You don't know what a calamity he had. The iron men wanted to kill him! They hunted after him, and one of them got him with a spear, which wounded his hip. He was able to escape from them into a thicket and limp back to me, but the wound was horrible. I doctored him as best I could, but Mõmmi's leg started festering and he couldn't move at all anymore. He still can't. He just sits. I'm so sorry for him, but I can't help him at all, because I've tried all the medicinal herbs and the other tricks. I feed him well and take care that he wants for nothing. Yes, he's got a bit fatter, but so what. At least he has a full belly. Haven't you, darling?"

"Yes, I have a full belly," concurred Mõmmi, who, to pass the time, had started devouring the venison she had brought to the table. "You're a dear and good woman."

"That's how we live, the two of us," said Salme. "Quite happily, although Mõmmi would of course like to go out in the forest sometimes. We're not bored. We eat several times a day, and when our bellies are full, we sleep in each other's arms. I hope the iron men won't find us in this cave; they don't usually come so deep into the forest. They are so horrible! How could they hunt a bear? A bear is such a good animal. Oh, Mõmmi, have you eaten all that venison already? Want some more?"

"Give me some more," mumbled the bear, flinging the gnawed bones carelessly on the floor, so that a cloud of flies took to flight in excitement, delighted with a new greasy bone to scurry along.

I felt bad, and it was now that a feeling of great dejection descended on me. Now, not when Grandfather's ribs were ripped out of his backbone, and not even when I had placed his remains on the pyre. Grandfather had got what he wanted: he had fought proudly, killed many iron men, and now been killed himself. He had known he would die beforehand. Sooner or later he would be worn out by his own age; one day even his fangs would become blunt. That a bowman's arrow had struck Grandfather at just that time was chance, but there was nothing shameful in it. A warrior had been doing battle; now, bested in combat, he had to take his punishment. Nobody was to blame; Grandfather's life had ended just as he wished for himself, and in our lousy times his fate was beautiful and uplifting.

What had happened to my sister was quite different. It was terrible; it was shameful. It sometimes happened, even in our home, that Mother forgot a little bit of haunch of hare or some other food in some corner, which when fresh would have been tasty and juicy, but when left to oblivion rotted and became covered in mold. Now my sister was like that haunch of hare fallen into oblivion, as sad as it was for me to acknowledge it. The forest was empty. Only she was left—a forgotten piece of carrion that had not been noticed at the right time, and was now inedible. She had gone bad! Her time had passed; she was no longer human. She wasn't a bear either, but was moving in that direction. She was now happy to eat raw meat, and her hair now resembled shaggy fur. And I couldn't help her at all, because I myself was just the same, a piece of moldy meat, trying spasmodically to preserve its freshness and imagine that it was still good for something. For what? My sister had understood this correctly; she could now just eat and sleep in her bear's embrace. Nothing else. I didn't even have a bear: I had to sleep alone.

So this is my future in the forest, I thought with horror. Wouldn't it have been better if the Primates had been delayed even more, so that bold wings had grown out of my bloodied back and I had flown away with Grandfather—to where all my dear ones had gone, all my predecessors, all my people. "Why don't you eat?" asked Salme again, gnawing hungrily on some half-raw venison so that some reddish substance trickled out of the corner of her mouth. "Are you afraid it isn't cooked enough? If you like I can cook a piece right through for you!"

"No, Salme, don't go to the trouble," I replied. "I'm really not hungry."

I didn't stay with my sister long. I got used to the stink, but we had nothing to talk about. Since our last meeting a lot had happened, but I didn't have the strength or the wish to talk about it.

Therefore I didn't say a word about Grandfather; I didn't talk about my own life in the village, or the battles that followed. I felt that Salme wouldn't understand those things anyway. What for me were precious or painful memories would be for her just some incomprehensible news of an unknown, distant world—an alien, strange smell that would just disturb her dozing in the warm old domestic stench. For them to understand, I suspected that I would have to explain every detail, and even that would be no help.

Therefore I only said that in the interval I had been wandering around. That was enough for Salme. She didn't inquire any further, and Mõmmi nodded his chubby head with satisfaction. Then Salme recalled the death of our mother, the reason for which was quite unclear to her: that is she thought that the snakes' nest where Mother was living had simply caught fire for some reason—and I didn't bother to tell her that it was not so simple. I let her go on complaining and grumbling for a while, and I noticed that meanwhile Mõmmi was falling asleep, a half-chewed bone hanging out of his mouth, as if he were vomiting his own skeleton.

Salme ended her tale with a long sigh and then yawned. I understood that she wanted to go to sleep right then, in the embrace of her gigantically bloated bear, and I said I would get going.

"Where will you live?" asked Salme. "In Mother's old shack?"

"We'll see," I replied. "I haven't thought about it yet. Maybe I will, or maybe I'll build myself a new house."

"In the meantime you can come and sleep at our place. We've got room."

"No, I want a place to myself," I explained. Salme nodded sleepily.

"Keep on coming, then; you can always come for a meal with us. Sadly we can't come visiting; poor Mõmmi is completely crippled."

She looked pityingly at her mountainous bear and added in a whisper: "Of course it's good in a way that he can't go fornicating in the forest anymore. Well, peeping at those village girls. Now he's only my bear and I don't have to worry about where he is and what he's doing. I have my eye nicely on him all the time."

"Yes, that's good," I agreed and started setting off. Fresh air blew in my face as if I'd been sprayed with cold water. It felt downright delicious after the stuffy cave, so that I wanted to bite down into it. I walked for a while, simply feeling the pleasure of breathing. Then I sat down, ate some lingonberries, for my stomach was quite empty, and gave some thought to what to do next.

I didn't want to go back to war without Grandfather. I must have been worn out with rampaging. Instead of the crazed anger and desire for revenge that had foamed in my veins so recently, I was overcome with a complete indifference. Really I couldn't be bothered doing anything anymore. What I wanted most to do was to stay right there among the bushes basking in the sunshine like an adder curled up. The lingonberries were within reach and there were plenty of them. What more could I need? I fell into a pleasant torpor, and recovered from it only when the sun had sunk beyond the treetops and I started to feel chilly.

I got up, stretched, and moved my arms to get warm. I had to seek some shelter, since the autumnal forest was not warm enough for me to lie under the open sky. I didn't want to go to my sister's; it would be silly in the darkness of the night to start building a new dwelling, so all that was left was my old home. For a long time I had been reluctant to visit it, but now suddenly I felt its absence. Why not go there and sleep a little? In the end it was only a shack; so what if for me it was full of sad memories? I thought of my mother and Hiie, but I could find no emotion in myself. The past seemed just like a distant legend, which might be sadder or happier but had no connection with the present moment. Mother and Hiie were just figures in a story that had been told to the end; now there was just the dark, cool forest, which aroused repugnance in me, and an empty shack somewhere on the other side of the forest, where it would be so pleasant to lie down and stretch out. Nothing else was important.

I started heading for my old home, and the road took me along the edge of the forest. I couldn't resist the temptation to take a look at Magdaleena's village; from here it should be quite visible. I turned aside from the path and in a few moments I got to where the trees ended and the fields and meadows began.

From here I should have seen the roofs of the village houses, but there weren't any. The village had vanished, and in the dim light my eyes could not make out exactly whether it had been wiped off the face of the earth or whether there were still at least traces of buildings, ruins, or something similar. I was dismayed, because I hadn't realized how an entire village could suddenly disappear. Grandfather and I hadn't burned it down, and yet there was no village. Had they moved away and taken their houses with them?

Then I saw a human figure off in the distance. I went closer to him out of curiosity, hoping to meet someone I knew. This man certainly was familiar. Elder Johannes was tottering along the narrow road, a stick in his hand and a tattered cloak on his back.

"Hello, Elder," I said, stepping out of the darkness. "Isn't it nice to meet again after such a long while?"

Johannes gazed at me and clutched his stick with both hands, to protect himself from me with it. But I had no thought of

attacking him. My hatred had abated and at that moment I felt
only pleasure that I had met a person whom I could ask about
the mysterious disappearance of the village.

"Don't wave your stick about," I said. "I haven't come to kill
you. Tell me what's happened to the village! Were you struck by
a fire? Where are all the houses?"

"Damned spawn of hell!" growled Elder Johannes. "Now you
come and ask where the houses are! Yes, our village burned to
the ground, and it's your fault!"

"I didn't put your eaves to the torch," I protested.

"Our village burned to the ground because of unprecedented
wickedness, and that wickedness was committed by you," replied
Johannes. "With your flying accomplice you killed the holy bishop
himself, and for that evil murder we had to pay. The noble knights
came and set our village on fire, because the murder of a holy man
is a horrible sin. You'll burn in hell for this! I tried to explain to
the esteemed knights that we had not raised our hand against
the holy father, that it would never occur to us to commit such a
terrible murder. I explained that the bishop had been attacked by
a savage, a werewolf whose dwelling place is the thick forest and
who had previously bitten to death my unhappy daughter and the
son in the flesh of a noble knightly lord. But the gentlemen said
that it was all the same to them which boor had committed the
crime. They said that we were all only brutes and savages, with no
culture and no respect. They said they didn't have time to make
the distinction which of us was Christian and which wasn't, so in
any case we could all bear responsibility for the brutality of our
countrymen. Then they set fire to our village and rode away on
the backs of their thoroughbreds."

"Why didn't you resist and kill them?" I asked.

"Because we are Christians!" declared Johannes, and raised his hand to heaven, as was always his habit when he was in full spate and starting to shout. "We are not wild animals like you, and we know how to behave in the new world. In the end the noble knightly gentlemen were right; the killing of the bishop is the most terrible murder and someone had to be punished for it. If we started to rebel and attack the knightly lords, we would only be confirming their opinion that we do not belong in the ranks of civilized peoples. Therefore we took the just punishment with Christian humility, and we will build a new village. Just today I went to the castle to request permission for one, and the noble knight was good enough to give us a new chance to prove ourselves. We will rise from the ashes and one day we will stand proudly beside the other modern nations and will be precisely as good."

I had been hearing this talk all the time I was living with Magdaleena; they all talked this kind of rubbish.

"Very nice. Carry on building a new village and become a cultured people," I said. "Be modern and pray to your new God. I sincerely wish you success. Farewell!"

I wanted to go, but Johannes was just getting into his stride and didn't want to stop talking so soon.

"Don't mock, you Satan!" he screeched. "Where are you going now? Into the dark forest, to bow down before your abominable sprites and pray for the forces of hell to torment us!"

"My dear man," I said, exasperated. "I promise you I won't bow down in the dark forest before any sprite or pray for anything."

"Faithless!" screamed Johannes.

"That's true," I replied. "I'm not ashamed of that name."

"Murderer!"

"That's not a lie either. But the same could be said of you, old man. Do you remember how you set fire to all the adders? By the way, what's become of Peetrus, who put my friend onto an ants' nest? I hope he was burned up when the iron men punished you."

"Peetrus is the pride of our village!" declared Johannes. "It was he who discovered the dead bodies of the holy bishop and his companions and quickly called the knightly lords to strike at the house and visit punishment. As a mark of thanks he was made a servant of a knight. Just a few days ago he left these parts with his master, on a trip to the holy land, to do battle with the heathens. This is a great honor for our whole people; Peetrus is the first one of us to go so far. Along with the great and powerful peoples, our boy is now making his contribution to creating a new world."

"I hope those heathens flay his skin," I said. "Good night now, old man. I hope you will get chain mail before you die too; you've earned it in every way."

"I'm hardly likely to get such an honor," replied Johannes, yet from his tone I felt that he was pleased by my words. His voice became solemn. "Go on then, boy, and carry on living in your dark past like some primeval animal, a tail still growing out of your backside. I'm going the other way, and as long as I breathe, I shall strive toward the light and a new, better world!"

"Go then," I responded. "And so that the way is easier for you . . ."

I pulled out my knife and stabbed the village elder in the backside.

"There!" I said, laughing, for honestly, there wasn't an ounce of hate in that blow. I had done it simply from a sudden whim.

"Now you needn't fear that you've got a tail on you. Now march away in peace; now you're really a modern person!"

"Werewolf!" screamed Johannes, holding his hand over his bleeding backside. "Murderer! Hell is your place. That is where you'll burn! You killed me! I'll bleed to death!"

"Does cutting off your tail really seem so bad?" I exclaimed. "A modern person doesn't need one. Don't scream horribly now, like some savage! What must the noble knights think of you if you can't behave like a civilized person? Now don't look back at all; keep looking forward! You still have your nose to sniff the wind. What more do you need? Farewell, village elder, and good luck!"

I ran off, suppressing my laughter, but I could hear Johannes's dreadful screaming for a long time afterward.

Thirty-Eight

he prank with Johannes's arse put me in a good mood. I strolled along homeward, humming an old Primate song, but the events of that night had not ended yet.

Somebody was calling me in Snakish. At first I thought it was some adder that had escaped incineration. I hissed back, looking for snakes, but instead I saw Meeme, who, as always, loomed out from among the tussocks.

His existence had completely slipped my mind. So, my sister and I were not the last humans! There was also Meeme, although calling him human seemed a bit of an exaggeration. He had lost his last outlines, and when I stepped closer, I couldn't tell exactly where his body ended and the moss began. The darkness that prevailed in the forest was partly to blame for this, but Meeme really did appear to have dissolved into nature. He was like a melted snowdrift. The same moss that grew under and alongside him also grew on him. Besides, he seemed not to have moved from the spot for a long time, because he was covered by a thick layer of autumn leaves. His face was as dark as the soil and cracked in places, and his eyes glistened at me from that carapace like dewdrops.

"You're still alive," said Meeme, and his voice sounded muffled, as if from underground, and it was hard to understand his words; they seemed to have collapsed in his mouth. "I didn't dare to hope that I'd see you again."

"So you wanted to see me?" I asked, anticipating when Meeme would raise his inseparable wineskin to his lips, take a sip, and choke a cough. I thought that might clear his throat a little, so it would be easier for me to understand what he said. But Meeme didn't drink, and to tell the truth I couldn't have said whether he even had hands or whether they'd rotted away so he'd have nothing to hold his wine vessel with.

"I don't care," he said. "I thought you should still be alive after all, and you'd turn up before I finally disintegrate, so I want to tell you something. Not that it's important; no, it's all senseless. But that's the way."

"What did you want to tell me?" I asked.

"About the Frog of the North," said Meeme.

This was unexpected. I crouched down by Meeme and immediately sensed traces of that rotting stench that emanated from his decomposing body. I shrank away in disgust and Meeme grinned, noticing this, with his moldy mouth.

"Stinks, eh?" he asked. "Stinks! I myself don't notice anything anymore, but I know I don't actually exist. I have rotted away. For a few months I haven't moved from here; I haven't eaten or drunk. I don't even remember the taste of wine anymore, and if anyone poured it into my mouth, it would soak into the ground like rain, because I don't have a back any longer. I can feel plants sprouting inside me; in the spring they'll grow right through me like shrubs, and the goats will eat them without noticing a dead human lying under their hooves. I can't feel my arms or legs anymore. My head has still held out, because it's as hard as rock, but if you'd come a few days later, I wouldn't have been able to speak. I wouldn't have been sad, because what I have to say isn't that important. You see I was a watchman. And before dying the watchmen have to choose a successor. As you understand, that isn't hard for me to do; apart from you, there's no one. You don't have to go to the trouble if you don't want to. The Frog of the North can get by without you. I haven't been to see him for years. But still I thought that if I should happen to meet you again, I'd tell you, and see what you're doing. It's all the same to me."

"How will I find the Frog of the North?" I asked, excited.

"You remember that ring I once gave you?" asked Meeme. "Yes, of course you remember. You came to ask me about it, but then I didn't have a reason to give you an answer. The watchman is only allowed to reveal his secret before his death. Actually I shouldn't have given you that key either, because you were still a child and you might have lost it, but that didn't concern me. All this was senseless anyway. Everything had come to an end long ago and it made no difference whether I was the last watchman or if anyone else came after me. This is only the death rattle and after that comes silence anyway, and the Frog of the North will sleep his own eternal sleep in complete isolation. Maybe I even hoped that you would lose the key; then this foolishness would end sooner. Tell me, have you lost your key?"

"I don't think so. I haven't seen that ring for a long time, but it must still be in Mother's shack. I'm sure I'll find it. How is it used?"

"It's not to do with the ring. That is only a useless trinket, pulled off the finger of some foreigner who was killed. But around the ring was a pouch—thin and so light that the slightest wind could carry it away. The ring was put in that bag as a weight, to keep the bag in place. Do you still have that pouch?"

"Yes, definitely," I assured him. "What is it about the pouch?"

"It was made from the skin of the Frog of the North," replied Meeme. "Once every ten thousand years the Frog of the North sheds his skin; he has already done it countless times and will go on doing it. From that skin the watchman must cut out a tiny piece, which he presents to his successor. That is the key. It will lead you to the Frog of the North."

"How?"

"You have to eat that skin. After that everything happens by itself."

"I'll search for that pouch this very night," I promised. "More than anything in this world I've wanted to see the Frog of the North and now it will be possible."

"Don't forget that he will never see you. He's asleep and there's nothing that would wake him. It's a useless, silly task that you're taking on, and I'd recommend you rather to throw that bit of skin in the fire and give up the whole thing. I had to tell you, but you don't have to obey me."

"But I want to see him!"

"Then off you go. Be happy, and give my greetings to that being. You'll have the happiness of dying with his help."

He closed his eyes. That was the last time I saw him alive, because I rushed straight to my mother's hovel to look for the ring and the pouch, and when several days later I happened upon that place again, Meeme was no longer speaking. His face had crumbled away, and there was nothing left of him but a soggy substance, a puddle among the bushes that you could hop over if you didn't want to get your feet wet.

I hurried homeward and found my own dwelling, silent and cool. It was long since anyone had lit a fire in the inglenook, and the smell of roast meat, which had never left the walls of our home, and that always made your mouth water as soon as you stepped over the threshold, had now vanished. Although I had thought that seeing my home again could not move me, I felt something catching in my throat as I looked at that dark and empty room. But for the moment I was still too occupied by my wish to find the Frog of the North, so there was no time for giving in to sad memories. I started rummaging in chests and drawers, and after a few moments the ring and its pouch were in my hands.

Impatiently I shook the ring out of its precious skin and it rolled with a clink onto the floor like useless rubbish. I studied the pouch, stroked it with my fingers, and came to the threshold to inspect the skin of the Frog of the North better in the moonlight. The little strip of skin was really thin; if you raised it to your eyes, the moon shone clearly through it. I was so excited that it was hard to breathe. I folded the piece of skin into a tiny square and put it in my mouth. I didn't even have to swallow it; the skin of the Frog of the North seemed to dissolve on my tongue. I held my breath and waited to see what would happen to me next. I wouldn't have been surprised if my body had suddenly caught fire, or if I had grown all at once to the height of the highest trees in the forest. But nothing happened to me.

I was still standing on the threshold of my old home with the moon shining on me, but I knew where the Frog of the North was sleeping.

That knowledge did not come to me as an unexpected blow and did not invade my brain as a flash of lightning. It simply seemed to occur to me—like something you have long ago forgotten and quite by chance comes back to your mind. It was roughly: Oh yes, how could I have forgotten such a simple thing in the meantime? I had been seeking the Frog of the North throughout the forest, but his hiding place was so easy to discover! It almost wasn't a hiding place at all; after eating the piece of skin it appeared to me that anyone could easily stumble on the Frog of the North; he was right here. Throughout my life I had been walking past the mouth of the cave beyond which he was sleeping his eternal sleep, and I had never thought to step inside.

I closed the door of my own home behind me and stepped in from the opening that yawned right opposite my old shack—which I had nevertheless never paid heed to before. A wide passage led me straight ahead, slowly descending into the depths of the earth. A light glimmered ahead of me. It was warm and gentle and didn't become too bright or dazzling even as I approached it. The Frog of the North was glowing like a smoldering fire.

Now I saw him. He really did exist, this famous Frog of the North of whom I'd heard so much and whom I'd longed to meet ever since I was a child. He was even bigger and more splendid than I had ever been able to imagine, majestic and awe-inspiring. I made a circuit around him, excited and happy. I was finally here! I hadn't dared to hope that I would after all one day see the Frog of the North: even Uncle Vootele had said he had disappeared forever and would never rise again. No human being was supposed to ever get to see him again, yet I had seen him all the same.

The Frog of the North was lying on his stomach, the great wings on his back neatly folded together, his eyes closed. His enormous claws had sunk into the soft sand. The Frog of the North was asleep, and his sleep was peaceful and deep. This was not an aged creature, dozing through its last days toward death, too feeble and tired to move its heavy eyelids. No, the Frog of the North was large and strong; he still had plenty of life force in him, and one could only imagine what he might still be capable of, if any power could wake him up.

But there was no such power. Thousands of Snakish words uttered in unison might have driven him to mysterious dreams, but only I, his last watchman, his last guardian, still existed. Everyone else had found some more interesting activity; they were already living in a new world, where the Frog of the North was only a figure of ancient legends that grandmothers told in the evenings by their spinning wheels.

I crouched beside the Frog of the North and stroked him, patted his strong yet so smooth skin. He was very warm, and when I pressed my back against him, I felt pleasure. I had a good and certain feeling when I leaned against this sleeping giant. I knew that I could even climb up on his back; it wouldn't disturb the sleep of the Frog of the North. Nothing in this world could disturb or kill him. He was eternal—he was and he remained— yet at the same time he was separated from final dissolution by an extremely fragile thread, and that thread was myself. The world had turned away from him, betrayed and forgotten him, left the powerful Frog of the North in a vacuum. I was his only companion. After me he would have to disappear, because that of which no one knows anything, and which no one has ever seen, actually no longer exists. He was the living dead.

Yet how differently everything could have gone! I didn't feel anger but helpless sadness when I thought of how simple it would have been for us to fight and win, if we had not in a wave of madness abandoned Snakish. For centuries that power had served us, hovering as a menacing yet protective storm cloud over our heads. This had been our secret weapon, which no one else was able to use or knew how to. Now we too were among the others, and the Frog of the North simply slept and slept and no one called on him.

But the world changes, some things fall into oblivion, some rise to the surface. The time for Snakish has passed; one day this new world with its gods and iron men will be forgotten, and something new will be invented.

I leaned against the Frog of the North and closed my eyes. I felt good here; I didn't intend to ever leave here again.

Of course I did go outside the cave from time to time, if only to take care of the Frog of the North. I got the habit of washing him, so that his skin would glisten more beautifully. I wanted him to be as beautiful as possible, even though no one else apart from me was going to see him. I went to fetch food for myself, and sometimes I just went walking in the forest, to see the sun after a long time in the cave and breathe some fresh air. Incidentally, the cave of the Frog of the North had a strange quality: on leaving the cave you could emerge in any place in the forest, just where you wanted to go. Now I understood how Meeme had moved so unobtrusively. He was coming from the Frog of the North; he would leave the cave that no one apart from him noticed, and then crawl back there afterward. So now I finally had the key to that mystery as well.

Occasionally I went to visit my sister and her Mõmmi, but not too often, for the atmosphere in their cave was too depressing and the stink almost intolerable. Mõmmi was now so obese that the fat had gone to his brain and he no longer remembered Snakish, so he and Salme communicated only in mumbles. The last time I saw them they were lying in each other's embrace; the cave was very dim, but I still remember their sad eyes peering at me out of the darkness. I don't know whether they're still alive or not, but I'm inclined to think that Mõmmi choked on his own fat and Salme faded away quietly beside his carcass. At any rate Mõmmi was the last bear who spoke Snakish; those creatures that nowadays come my way do carry out my orders with a growl of dismay, but are unable to reply. They have become ordinary wild animals. Everything is degenerating.

A few days after I found the Frog of the North, I went to visit Pirre and Rääk. I saw the Primates' gaunt old forms resting in the highest branches and I called to them, but nobody replied, and I understood that they had either died or become too tired and feeble to open their mouths, which was the same thing. In the end they had held out well; their world, their story, had come to an end long ago. There they stayed, in the highest branches of their tree, all winter, like two little white furry snowdrifts. In the spring the tree went into leaf, and I didn't see them again. And when winter came anew, the branches were once again empty and bare, as if no Primate had ever lived in the world.

So I was left alone—with the Frog of the North. I have been his guardian for forty years now, and I've grown quite old. Lately I've been going out more and more rarely. I sleep a lot and I dream. Most often that I am a child again, sitting in Uncle Vootele's cellar, and Uncle Vootele is teaching me Snakish. Then suddenly his face turns white, he falls spread-eagled, and dies, but I'm not dismayed. I crawl in under his flanks and I'm nice and warm. I don't care about the rotting stench emanating from my uncle. It doesn't upset me; it actually feels so familiar and secure. Then I wake up and I find myself beside the Frog of the North, but that same stink is still in my nostrils. I know that smell doesn't come from the Frog of the North, for he is eternal; it comes from me, an old man.

I hiss a few Snakish words into the void, the same ones once taught to me by Uncle Vootele, and those words clear the air. Everything else in me may decay, but the Snakish words always remain fresh. The Snakish words and the peacefully dozing Frog of the North.

And I am not concerned about anything; I too can quite peacefully close my eyes on it all again. No one disturbs my sleep. We can rest undisturbed—the Frog of the North and the last man who spoke Snakish.